Mother's War

A Woman's Journey through
the American Civil War

by

Susan and Nancy Brace

To Mary
from Nancy +
Susan Brace

Best wishes

To order:
https://www.createspace.com/34
31251

ISBN: 1450576389
ISBN-13: 9781450576383

Library of Congress Controll Number: 2010901847

Dedicated to

Marge Brace, Jo Ruth, Irene Matthews,
and all nurses who serve our armed forces so generously.

CONTENTS

Preface

This is the story of a woman who nursed Union soldiers during the Civil War. Most of the adventures and some of the dialogue are based on historical records.

Prologue

"What the devil...?"

He lowered the telescope, squinted into the night, and then brought the telescope back to his eye and refocused. His black eyebrows joined in a frown.

"Corporal! Who's that on the field at this time of night? I gave orders hours ago that the field was to be cleared. Who dares defy me? Ride out there, arrest the culprit, and bring him here!" Colonel Logan lowered the telescope again and glared at Corporal Jessup, who was already running toward his horse. The colonel wrapped his greatcoat more tightly around him and watched the activity of the men in camp.

The past few days had been hard on them, fighting against a well-equipped Confederate force twice their size in less-than-friendly terrain. And then the "mopping up" that followed a battle—repairing weapons, sewing torn uniforms, routing the Rebels who strayed behind Union lines, and dealing with the mountain of paperwork the war department required from the officers; all were burdens to the men. *Yes, the colonel thought, the men are righteously tired.* Most had already turned in for the night, but some sat huddled by the fires in small groups, cleaning weapons, whittling, or drinking coffee while warming their hands against their tin cups and talking in soft voices. The colonel looked back at the hill, where a tiny flickering light was intermittently visible. He scowled, turned and entered his tent.

On the hilltop three people moved slowly through the aftermath of a terrible battle. The field was littered with mounds of men and horses frozen in their death agonies. Shapes were jagged. Ice crystals glistened on splintered trees, overturned wagons, broken cannon limber, swords, and guns. Men's faces, shattered and lifeless, were frozen in the muck of the battlefield. The ice captured some in the act of reaching out, as if beseeching god for a few more moments of life. Mud, blood, and the body parts of animals were blue and stiff in the icy night.

A middle-aged woman, wrapped tightly in a gray shawl, held a lantern and moved it slowly over the carnage. Accompanying her were two Union soldiers, both heavily armed and carrying axes. One held a rolled-up stretcher. They shivered and stamped their feet, trying to stay warm while they waited impatiently for the woman. She held the lantern over the bodies on the ground and peered carefully at them. She thought she saw movement, though it could have been her imagination. She knelt down next to a grim pile of bodies encrusted with ice and brought the lantern closer to the face of a soldier, partially frozen in the pile. She put her ear to his mouth and listened. She stood and gestured to the two men, pointing at the man in the pile. They dropped the stretcher and began to swing their axes into the ice.

Corporal Jessup galloped into camp and pulled his horse to a stop near Colonel Logan's tent. Both he and the horse were breathing hard. Long plumes of vapor formed with each exhalation. Colonel Logan heard them, pulled back the flap of his tent, and greeted the corporal.

"Well, Corporal, where is he? What did you find up there?"

"Sir," the corporal said breathlessly, "it's a woman, sir."

"A woman?" repeated the colonel incredulously as his scowl deepened.

Corporal Jessup knew that look all too well. Trouble was a-coming, and he knew he needed to stay as far from it as he could.

"Yes, sir! Said she came in on the hospital boat with General Grant's troops. A matron, I believe, sir, from the post hospital in Cairo."

"Well, where is she?" the colonel asked impatiently. "Didn't I tell you I wanted to see whoever was up there lighting the field?"

"Yes, sir! I told her, sir. She refused to leave. Said she'd be along directly as she was done."

"Refused? Directly as she was done? Who the...?" The colonel paused, disbelief and indignation in his voice. "This is the army! There is no place for a woman! A woman on the field! Corporal, I expect you to obey me. Fetch her now."

"Sir, she's up there with Private Stockwell and Frank Jenkins. She said she was looking for the wounded among the dead."

"It's been over twelve hours since the battle ended. This is nonsense. Escort her to my tent immediately. Is that clear? And, Corporal..."

"Yes, sir?"

"Find out her name." The colonel returned to his tent, snapping the flap shut behind him, while the corporal remounted his horse and disappeared into the darkness.

◌◌

An hour later, the corporal and the woman stood at the entrance to Colonel Logan's tent. The colonel, fury distorting his face, stood at the tent opening. It had been a bad day and he had several hours of paperwork still ahead of him. Now this interruption—a woman, of all things!

The corporal stood at attention and saluted. "Sir. I have brought the lady—I mean, Mrs. Bickerdyke, from the field, sir. Ma'am, this is Colonel Logan."

Colonel Logan nodded and tried to smile but failed. His voice was as cold and hard as the ice. "Mrs. Bickerdyke," he said. "Come in, please. That will be all, Corporal."

Colonel Logan stepped aside for Mrs. Bickerdyke to enter the tent and then he lowered the flap. He motioned to the only chair, which was by a camp desk that was stacked with paper. A small fire burned in the camp stove and light from a lantern flickered against the Spartan furnishings. Both the colonel's and Mrs. Bickerdyke's breath were visible. "Please sit down, madam."

Mrs. Bickerdyke sat primly on the edge of the chair, her back rigid and her eyes downcast. She waited. The colonel remained standing, his left hand supporting his right upper arm. He scrutinized her. Graying hair, once in a bun, was now in wild disarray. Under other circumstances he might have seen her as a handsome woman in her forties, but her current appearance disgusted him. Dirt streaked her face, and her plain gray woolen dress was frozen stiff at the hem with mud, blood, and ice. As she waited, her skirt began to steam from the heat inside the tent. Her hands were folded tightly in her lap. They were rough, cracked, and caked with blood and grime.

Colonel Logan clenched his jaw as he thought about what to say. "Madam, under whose authority are you here? Did General Prentiss assign you?"

"No," she replied quietly, looking up at him with surprise. "No one did. I came here on the hospital boat."

"Well...Mrs. Bickerdyke, is it?"

"Yes, Mary Ann Bickerdyke," she replied.

"This is no place for a woman. It is completely against army regulations for you to be here. You are *not* allowed here, madam. War is man's business. Go back home where you belong. We don't need you here."

As Colonel Logan spoke, Mrs. Bickerdyke's face remained still, but her blue eyes were watching him and began to light with anger. Colonel Logan started to pace the small tent, warming to his topic. He was unaware that her face had suddenly tightened and her jaw muscles flexed as she gritted her teeth. Colonel Logan was a big man and he dominated the area, making the tent seem even smaller.

"This is simply unacceptable. It is not good for the morale of the men. And what of your reputation? What must your family think? An unescorted woman with all these men?

No, this is no place for a decent woman. I will arrange for you to be taken back to the hospital boat and returned to Cairo. If you—"

Mrs. Bickerdyke interrupted the colonel with a quiet voice. "May I have a bowl of water and a clean cloth, please? I see you have a wound there." She nodded in the direction of the colonel's upper arm, where there was a tear and a red stain on his coat.

The colonel halted his pacing abruptly at her voice, glared at her in astonishment at her audacity, and then continued, "Mrs. Bickerdyke, you do not understand—"

"A bowl of water, please. And a cloth," she said firmly. She waited a moment as Colonel Logan stood staring at her, stunned by her brashness. If any of his men had acted in this way they'd be hauled off to the stockade to ride the rail until they could ride no more.

When the colonel made no move toward the entrance, she stood, forcing him to step back. She went to the tent opening, lifted the flap, and addressed the guard outside in a gentle tone. "Young man, bring me a bowl of warm water and a clean cloth. Now, please. Thank you." She dropped the flap and waited by the opening. She looked at the colonel, whose jaw had dropped with surprise. He was not used to being interrupted or disobeyed by anyone, and especially not by a woman.

Mrs. Bickerdyke sighed. She knew she was going to have to spar with this angry man. "Colonel," she said in a soft but firm voice, "you need me here. These boys are fighting and getting wounded and killed in terrible ways. Who do you think will nurse them back to health so they can fight in your army and win this war? Your generals aren't even aware that you need nurses. Oh, no! You make wounded boys care for those worse off, as if—"

A soldier's voice from outside the tent interrupted her. "Sir. Excuse me, sir."

The soldier entered the tent, looking tentatively at the colonel, and handed Mary Ann a tin bowl of steaming water and a cloth. He nodded meekly and left, eager to escape the tension in the tent. Mrs. Bickerdyke walked to the table, moved aside the stacks of paper neatly arranged on it, and put the bowl and cloth down. She wiped her hands on her dress, turned, and fixed the colonel with her blue eyes.

"Take your coat off, Colonel, and let me look at that wound."

The colonel took a step back and said angrily, "Madam, I have no intention of—"

With an edge of steel to her voice honed from years of motherhood, she moved closer to him, making him back up again. "Colonel, it is late, and I'm tired and getting cranky. I have a boatload of wounded men to tend to, and you're delaying me. Now, let me do my job." She began unbuttoning his uniform jacket as if he were a stubborn child, and helped him take it off. She tossed the jacket on the cot; then she turned to the colonel and placed her hands on his shoulders, pressing down to make him sit in the chair. She rolled up his sleeve and moved the lantern closer to examine the gash. "There's no metal or wood in it that I can see," she said. She dipped the cloth in the water and squeezed out the excess.

As she washed and bound his wound, she continued, "Colonel, you may not like it, but I am here, and I mean to stay. I will be where the wounded are. That means on the battlefield, if that's where they're to be found. I wouldn't have been able to fall asleep tonight, thinking there might be some boy dying out there, all alone on that frozen field. No. I do not have that in me. I will go back to the boat, but I will not leave this war. And we can either work together on this or we can be furious enemies. But I'm not going away. These boys need me. I'll stay 'til the end."

She looked at the bandage on his arm. "There. That should hold you for a day or two. You already have the laudable pus. That's a good sign. Now, your hospitality has been grand, but I can't stay here talking to you all night. I've got work to do. Come by the hospital boat in two days and I'll change your bandage. Now, Colonel, would you please arrange for an escort?"

The horse-drawn wagon pulled up beside the river. A hospital boat was tied to the crude wharf made of corduroyed logs. A sentry, wrapped in an ice-crusted blanket, leaned on his rifle at the bottom of the gangway to the boat and watched the wagon approach. Mrs. Bickerdyke climbed down from her seat with the assistance of the wagon driver. She pulled her shawl closer and walked to the gangway.

The sentry nodded to her. "Careful, Mother. It's icy. Watch you don't fall."

She walked up the gangway, and upon reaching the ship's deck was greeted by a tall elderly man in a blood-stained frock coat holding a lantern. The ship swayed gently on the water, and the lantern threw long shadows with each movement.

The man said wearily, "You're back. Good."

"Hello, Carl. There are two more in the wagon. Have the men bring them aboard. How are the others doing?" Mrs. Bickerdyke looked at him inquiringly.

"One of them already died."

"And the other?"

"In a bad way, ma'am. Come." Carl turned and motioned toward a doorway into the boat.

They entered the grand ballroom of what was once a fancy riverboat. Its luxuries had been stripped to make room for the wounded. Bare wood floors and walls now offered little comfort. Candles in hurricane lamps hung from the supporting columns, revealing hundreds of men, writhing, moaning, pleading, and crying. There were men in pain, coughing, vomiting, gasping for breath, and beseeching god for relief. Some had been driven mad from the horrors of battle. Others were dying as they lay next to their brothers who were already dead.

Carl pointed to the corner. "There they are. Next to the wall."

Mary Ann walked among the men, lifting her skirts to step over and around them, bending frequently to touch a hand, feel a forehead, whisper a soothing word, or check a bandage. She approached a soldier lying in the corner and knelt on the floor next to him. His clothes were still icy, his skin blue, and he shivered uncontrollably even though he was unconscious. A blanket had been pulled up to his chest. Slowly Mary Ann began to unbutton his jacket. Ice cracked off as she handled the cloth.

"We'll warm you up, son, and then take a look at that wound," she said softly to the wounded soldier.

She looked over her shoulder and said in a louder voice, "Carl, would you please bring me several bowls of soup— not too hot, now—and coffee? Some dry clothes, too, if you can find 'em. We need to warm these boys up." She paused and looked around the room, seeing mangled men everywhere, piled against each other, moaning in agony. Her face was a mixture of sadness and steely determination.

When the Civil War began on April 12, 1861, neither the Union nor the Confederacy was prepared to care for its wounded soldiers.

At the outbreak of the rebellion there were only 106 doctors in the whole Union army, and many were either physically unfit for active duty or had let their medical skills lapse.

There were no nurses, no ambulance corps, and no means of transporting wounded from the battlefield to the hospitals.

Sanitary practices and public health mea-
sures were still in their infancy and utterly
deplorable.

One million Americans went off to war
between 1861 and 1865. Over 600,000 of
them died. In the Union army, wounded
and ill men were housed by the thousands in
temporary hospitals, without beds, blankets,
running water, sanitation, kitchens, or laundry facilities. Army musicians and the walking wounded served as caregivers until the
women of the North began to volunteer as
nurses.

This is the story of one of those volunteers.

CHAPTER 1

The War Begins

When the war of the rebellion began, Mary Ann Bickerdyke was a recent widow who made her living as a housekeeper and a nurse in the little town of Galesburg, Illinois.

Her household included two young sons—James, who was eleven, and Hiram, who was seven—and her nineteen-year-old stepdaughter, Mary Elizabeth. Mary Ann was also looking after two motherless nephews and had taken in several orphans from the Pease Five Points Mission in New York City.

Trained in the use of botanicals for healing, Mary Ann followed the homeopathic movement that was then sweeping the country. In 1849, she had been one of twelve women recruited as nurses to meet the acute needs of a cholera epidemic in Cincinnati, where she lived just after her marriage.

Mary Ann, who was in her mid-forties, had known upheaval as a child; raised on a succession of farms, she was cast out over and over again by different sets of foster parents. She had lost her mother, her grandparents, her sister, her husband, and her infant daughter.

When Fort Sumter was captured by the Confederates, Galesburg, like many of its counterparts in other Union states, mobilized to provide men and materials for war. The men of Galesburg quickly began military drills in the town square and were immediately sworn in to Company E, Seventeenth Illinois Volunteers. The town's women gathered together in private homes, the schoolhouse, and churches, and sewed uniforms, flags, sheets, and blankets.

Galesburg's responsible citizens between the ages of twenty and fifty years old knew little of war, apart from listening to their grandparents' stories about the Revolutionary War. Seasoned army officers had been in only two military engagements in their lives—the War of 1812 and the Mexican War.

The country as a whole was ill prepared for the political, economic, physical, emotional, and psychological demands of a long and brutal conflict. America was just on the brink of territorial and technological expansion. Land west of the Mississippi, still populated mostly by Native Americans, was viewed by adventurous individuals struggling in the East as a second chance that was ripe for homesteading. Trains replaced stagecoaches, decreased the amount of time it took to travel from place to place, and were beginning to be viewed as convenient and affordable public transportation. The telegraph increased the speed of communication across great distances. The North fully embraced industrialization, promoting increased quantity and quality of supplies and equipment. Industrialization also sparked a wave of mechanized innovations. The South remained primarily a society based on agriculture, dependent on cotton and tobacco plantations for its main commerce, and on human labor for its production.

The history of slavery in America preceded the Founding Fathers. Slavery had been a hotly contested but unresolved issue for generations. The South did not have a monopoly in the use of slaves. At the beginning of the Civil War some families in the North also owned slaves. However, the North's passion for industrialization freed it from sole dependence on manpower. For the people and politicians in the North, the main purpose of the conflict was to preserve the Union and limit slavery to the existing states. For the South, the war was about states' rights to comply with state constitutions rather than submitting to federal control, and about defending their way of life.

Most army officers at that time had been trained at West Point. When the Civil War began, classmates had to choose a side to support, which resulted in friends fighting against friends; it also meant that both sides were armed with military strategy and tactics learned in the same classrooms, from the same teachers. Uniforms were initially similar in cut and color, causing confusion on the battlefield. In the early days of the conflict, the bugle calls that informed soldiers to charge or retreat or wake up in the morning were the same for the North and the South, and could frequently be heard by both sides, creating more confusion on the field. Armies of both sides sang the same songs, though the wording evolved differently with success or defeat. This conflict literally tore the fabric of the nation apart.

In 1861, President Abraham Lincoln called for seventy-five thousand volunteers for the Union army. When the head of a household enlisted, he left his wife and family to tend to the farm or family business. Often there was no way for his family to succeed in getting the crops in or conducting business efficiently without him. At the beginning of the war, men left for induction into the military, taking with them their own homemade uniforms and blankets. Their food was handed out uncooked in the mess tent. On or near payday, soldiers might be paid a portion of their army wages, but they had no safe way to send the money home to their families. The army had a quartermaster corps but frequently few or no supplies.

When a town doctor enlisted, the town was left without medical help. At the outset of the war there were not enough military doctors. As a stopgap measure, the army offered contract work to local civilian physicians. Dr. Benjamin Woodward, one of two physicians practicing in Galesburg, contracted to work for the army from early October 1861 until June 1862.

The majority of the nation's population was rural, and it was common for someone born on the farm to stay within a ten-mile radius of his or her birthplace for his or her entire life. In a medical sense, people and their diseases were isolated. Even though the lessons of sanitation and disease prevention that Florence Nightingale had learned in 1855 at Scutari had crossed the sea, no one in Washington considered the medical risks of mobilizing large numbers of immunologically naive men, until troops became ill by the thousands with typhoid, smallpox, measles, tuberculosis, and camp dysentery.

CHAPTER 2

Recruitment

Galesburg, Illinois, early October 1861

Inside a church, mostly women, old men, and children stood wrapped in heavy coats and homespun woolens. Many held hymnals in gloved hands. It was cold. There was no fireplace to heat the church. Colorful light filtered through the stained-glass windows and slanted across the congregation as it sang the last verse of a hymn. When the hymn was finished, they sat in the pews and looked up at the preacher. As he walked to the podium, his steps were loud on the wooden floor. He looked out at his congregants and cleared his throat.

"Welcome, brothers and sisters in the Lord. We give thanks for this beautiful hymn and our fellowship today. I had a sermon prepared for you this morning on the importance of faith and virtue, but I have had to set it aside. This morning we have a special mission. Brother Benjamin Woodward, our town doctor, has, as you know, given his services up to the Union army at Cairo. He has sent a letter which he asked that I share with you. Let me warn you, this is a direct and disturbing letter, and we must reply as soon as possible to this test of our charity."

The preacher, a portly man of middle age, took the letter from his coat pocket, unfolded it and began to read.

> Dear Reverend Beecher and members of
> my beloved Brick Congregational Church,

When I left Galesburg to assist the Union I was placed in charge of the general hospital at Cairo, situated next to six regimental hospitals at Fort Defiance...

The preacher's words melted into pictures.

Fort Defiance, several weeks earlier

Dr. Woodward, a tall, thin man with graying sandy blond hair and a neatly trimmed beard, stood before Major Simons's desk in his small, bare office. "Please sit down, Doctor," said Major Simons. "We are very glad to have you here. Our brigade surgeon is indisposed, and you will cover his hospitals until he returns. Sergeant MacDonald will see that you are made comfortable in the officers' quarters and will stow your gear. If you'll follow him, he'll help you settle in, and I'll meet you in an hour to escort you through your hospitals."

The two men stood, shook hands, and Dr. Woodward followed the sergeant out of the office.

An hour later, Dr. Woodward and Major Simons walked through a poorly lit area about the size of a ballroom, jammed with ill soldiers suffering from chicken pox, cholera, typhoid, measles, diarrhea, and tuberculosis. Men were lying on straw that had been strewn across the floor. The straw was matted with vomit, feces, and urine. The dead were among the living, and the living were filthy. There was only one window and it was closed. The air was stifling and the stench nauseating.

Visibly shocked, Dr. Woodward said, "These men, they're—"

"Yes, Doctor. The war caught us all unawares. Your pre-decessor barely got started before he became ill. For that reason, these hospitals are a bit behind the others. We've been without a doctor for some weeks now. Work fast, sir. We have not yet had to deal with battle wounds. None of these soldiers have seen Rebel fire. They brought their illness-es with them, or they grew from the foul airs of the swamp this camp was built on. When the wounded start coming in we will be sorely put to the test."

∞

A few days later, a tired and haggard-looking Dr. Woodward sat with Major Simons in front of Colonel Grant's desk. Colonel Grant, in shirtsleeves, paced behind his desk, hands folded at his back.

"So, gentlemen, you think we need a nurse!" said Grant. He shook his head and frowned. He stopped pacing and looked up in thought, frowned once more, and continued pacing. He shook his head again. Woodward and Simons looked worried-ly at each other, and then back at Colonel Grant.

"This could be a matter of some...ah...delicacy—put-ting a woman on an army post. Officers' wives are barely accepted. An unattached woman, however..." Colonel Grant paused in thought. "You say we're losing nine men to disease every..." He paused again. "Have you some-one in mind who could cope with the hardships of an army hospital?"

Dr. Woodward nodded eagerly. "Yes, sir. I know just the person—a woman from my hometown who is an expert nurse, dedicated and strong. She would be able to take on the job if I could find someone to look after her children."

"A married lady?"

"A widow, sir."

Grant stopped pacing and looked at Dr. Woodward. "It would not do to have the men, ah, aroused by a member of the fairer sex. Would that be a problem?"

Dr. Woodward shifted in his chair uncomfortably. "No, sir. She is quite moral—a churchgoing lady, and older—so that shouldn't be a problem."

"Very well, Doctor. You may contact this woman and ask her to come for a brief period to help at the post hospital. But...," Colonel Grant said, with a raised brow as he looked at the major, "if there is trouble, Major Simons, and there will be, I want you to handle it. I don't want this coming back to me. Understood?"

Major Simons straightened in his chair. "Yes, sir. Understood, sir. And thank you, sir."

Major Simons and Dr. Woodward stood. Major Simons saluted the colonel, and they left the office with relief on their faces.

Grant sat at his desk, biting off the tip of a cigar. He smiled to himself. "Oh, Uly, what have you done?"

👀

As the Reverend Beecher folded the letter his congregation was brought back to the present. "And so, Brother Benjamin is asking for a very great sacrifice, indeed. He asks that we find a way to send our own Mary Ann Bickerdyke to him to care for the ill and dying, and he asks us, his spiritual family, to look after her children. What shall we say to our brother? What shall we say?"

The congregants began to whisper and talk; then a hush fell over them and they looked around the group until they saw Mary Ann. She was sitting with her two older children on her left and her youngest son on her right. The daughter and older son looked at each other and at her with worry. The youngest sensed that something was wrong and tugged on his mother's hand, making a pleading sound.

"Mama? Mama?"

"Shush, child. Be still," she whispered a bit sharply, as she gently smoothed his blond hair. She kissed his forehead and slowly stood, facing the preacher. The congregation looked at her expectantly.

Mary Ann cleared her throat and said, "I cannot go to assist Dr. Woodward. I have my family to care for, and I have no experience of the army. No. It is not possible."

But even as she spoke these words, Mary Ann began to feel the spark of a growing conflict ignite inside her.

"My children are important to me. Those of you who know me well know that I grew up being handed from relative to relative, without ever really having a sense of my own family. It is now just a few years since my dear husband and baby died, and I have finally been able to give my own children a family again without mourning or poverty. I cannot see how I can rightly leave all that for an army whose care I know nothing about."

She paused, trying to convince the congregation and herself of the logic of her position.

"You all know my feeling about the Union and this war. Some of you know I helped slaves in the Underground Railroad and that I want to do what I can. You also know that I have a firm religious conviction against slavery."

The Reverend Beecher cleared his throat and interjected, "Yes, Mrs. Bickerdyke. We do appreciate the pain and sorrow you went through as a child, and how difficult your life here in Galesburg has been. And we also know of your strong faith in God and that you are the only nurse here. Dr. Woodward is desperate. Not just any volunteer will do. If your son were out there fighting for the Union, would you not want someone as skilled as yourself to provide for his care if he were wounded?"

"Yes," Mary Ann began, "but my children—"

Before she could finish, a murmur rolled through the congregation.

A woman, holding the hand of a little girl, stood. "Mrs. Bickerdyke, I would be pleased to help look after your children, if you would go to assist the doctor."

An older woman rose, leaning on her cane. "I'll help out a bit as well. My boy's in the army. He could be one of those sick in that hospital."

Another voice from the back of the church, a woman's, said loudly, "I think this is terrible! How could you possibly leave your children? What kind of a mother are you?"

The congregation responded with a wave of uneasy whispering.

A farmer in the back stood and gruffly said, "You know what kind of womens follow the army, Mrs. Bickerdyke? Are you meanin' to be one of 'em? We can't have that in our community or in our church."

The congregants grew louder. The Reverend Beecher stretched out his arms to quiet them and said, "The price of charity may mean that this generous act will be misunderstood by some. I am sure the need is great, or Brother Woodward would not have written."

Another woman stood hesitantly, looking around at the congregation before she spoke. She tugged on her older husband's hand until he stood. "Taking care of the sick has always been the work of us women. Howard and I will help, too. You shouldn't have to worry about your own young'uns when you're helping the doctor. Wouldn't be fair no how, you takin' care of our boys, and we not lookin' toward yours. This is the work of the Lord, truly."

Mary Ann looked down, avoiding the faces of the congregants and of her children. She felt angry, sad, and yet somehow proud. She spoke without looking at anyone, and too softly to be heard by the whole congregation. "Well, maybe I could go for a little while just to help Dr. Woodward settle in. I don't know. I would feel bad refusing to do the Lord's work and just as bad to leave my children."

The Reverend Beecher repeated Mary Ann's almost private thought, but loud enough for the whole congregation to hear and turned it a bit.

"So, Mrs. Bickerdyke, you would not refuse the Lord's work? You would go to fulfill Dr. Woodward's request if we could look after your children?"

Mary Ann looked down at her children. She was deeply sad and quite torn by the decision before her.

Her older two understood the implications of the conversation. They stared down at their shoes, unwilling to meet their mother's eyes. Her youngest child looked up at her, bewildered. She placed her hands on his shoulders.

The Reverend Beecher said, "It's settled, then. You'll leave for Cairo as soon as possible." The congregants gave an audible sigh. "I'll write Brother Benjamin tonight. Let us take up a collection to purchase food, bandages, and blankets, whatever you can spare to ease the lives of our sons, fathers, husbands, and brothers in this war. We'll send what goods we can with Mrs. Bickerdyke. This is the Lord's work we do. Now, let us pray."

CHAPTER 3

Fort Defiance—October 1861

A riverboat blew its horn and, with great splashing, reversed its paddles, slowing so it could pull in to the wharf at the edge of Cairo, Illinois. For the first time in its history this small river town was booming with activity. The dock of roughly hewn timber was crowded. Soldiers, sailors, and civilians were loading and unloading the many boats tied to the wooden moorings. Others carried crates to and from the heaps of supplies on the dock, loading and unloading nearby wagons. Riders on horseback and an occasional carriage passed by on the muddy road. Dodging soldiers and boxes, some barefoot and filthy children chased a dog with a stick in its mouth down the pier. The brown river water slapped at the sides of the dock and gave off a foul, sour smell.

Wooden shops lined the waterfront, offering multiple services to the port. The shops were separated from the wharf by a muddy lane. There was a livery, where one could hire a horse and wagon to transport goods. A sail maker shared a small shop with a maker of hemp rope, conveniently located next to the White Swan Tavern, a favorite for sailors on leave. The town itself, with hotel, dry goods store, and eatery, was several blocks away, discreetly distinct from the riffraff that frequented the docks.

Cairo, a major port at the confluence of the Ohio and Mississippi Rivers, was a strategic site for storing Union supplies and assembling troops. It was still early in the war, and anticipation for a short, easy, victorious end was high. Uniforms of variable colors were new and mostly clean. Each unit had its own style of dress and colors. They had not yet discovered the safety inherent in all looking alike.

Soldiers on the dock were cheerful and full of camaraderie. They worked as a human chain, loading and unloading cargo from wagons and boats. The sun shined and a chilly breeze blew brightly colored leaves from the trees that lined the road.

Mary Ann Bickerdyke, clad in a gray dress, bonnet, and dark woolen shawl, stood on the deck of the docking riverboat. Her carpetbag, handmade of fabric scraps, was on the deck by her feet. She was uncomfortable, and scanned the crowded dock looking for a familiar face.

A small black carriage pulled up as near to the pier as the other wagons would allow. Dr. Woodward, the driver, tied the reins to the cab and waved to Mary Ann from the carriage.

"Mrs. Bickerdyke!" he called. "Over here."

Mary Ann saw him and waved. But the sight of him did not change her sense of feeling very out of place. Without being aware, she straightened her shoulders and began to smile. She grabbed her carpetbag and asked a crewman to help her across the swaying gangplank. She met Dr. Woodward on the platform. He briefly took her hand in his.

"Mrs. Bickerdyke! How good of you to come! I hope your journey was uneventful?"

"Good morning, Dr. Woodward. Yes, a routine trip." She tried hard to conceal her anxiety about leaving her children, and changed the subject. "And how are you?"

"Overwhelmed, quite overwhelmed. I can use your help here most desperately. I cannot tell you how relieved I am that you have come. But forgive me! What may I carry for you? Let me take your bag."

"Nonsense, Doctor, I can take it. But before we go, the community gathered quite a few provisions for you. There are nine crates on board. I believe the crew is beginning to carry them to the dock now." She looked at several piles of crates on the wharf. "Yes, there they are," she said, pointing to a stack of wooden boxes with the name *Brick Congregational Church* stenciled on their sides. She rummaged in her carpetbag and pulled out a list. "Here. I already spoke to the captain, and he assured me they would all be unloaded."

"Excellent. If I may, I'll take that paper and go arrange for a wagon and driver to take the crates to the fort. But first, let me escort you to the carriage. It's right over...or perhaps you need to rest after your journey? I could escort you to the hotel and you could—"

Trying to dispel Dr. Woodward's concern, Mary Ann spoke with more courage than she actually had. "Doctor, I'm fine. I saw the carriage. You go do what you need to do and I'll wait for you there."

Dr. Woodward smiled and nodded, and then tipped his hat to her. He took the bill of lading from her and walked over to a nearby officer, who was directing the unloading of goods from the riverboat. Mary Ann looked around at the port of Cairo with interest; then, bag in hand, she walked to the end of the pier. The carriage was behind two wagons that were being filled with supplies. She looked at the sodden street, hiked up her skirt a bit and stepped off the dock. The mud rose above her ankles and oozed into her high-top shoes. She looked at her feet with dismay. With a determined expression, she walked around wagons and horses making her way to the carriage. Mud sucked at her shoes all the way. Somehow, her dismay fueled her determination.

Mary Ann sat in the carriage next to Dr. Woodward, who handled the reins. A chill breeze ruffled her hair, and she wrapped her shawl more tightly around herself. They left the town behind them. The road was deeply rutted, and the ride jolting, but as they traveled farther from town, the road became firmer.

"I knew I could not do the job without you," said Dr. Woodward. "Colonel Grant gave me permission to solicit your assistance, but I was only able to obtain a one-day pass for you. Women, other than officers' wives, are not usually allowed at all, so this is highly irregular. Unfortunately, I have been called away to another hospital, so I must leave you alone at the Stables, as the men call it. The surgeon in charge there was temporarily relieved of duty for medical reasons, so I've taken it over. There are several other regimental hospitals at Fort Defiance, and they're all about the same as far as conditions go. I feel bad having to leave you on your own like this, but it can't be helped. If I am unable to make it back before dark, then I will try to meet you in town this evening to discuss what you have accomplished. I booked a room for you at the hotel, so I'll meet you there."

Buildings became visible up ahead in the distance. As Mary Ann and the doctor approached, a foul stench enveloped the carriage.

"Good heavens," said Mary Ann. She raised her handkerchief to cover her nose, wrinkled in disgust at the bad odor.

"That, Mrs. Bickerdyke, is Fort Defiance. It's a problem I hope you can resolve," said Dr. Woodward. "Now, tell me, what is happening in Galesburg? Mrs. Bruckner should have had her baby by now, and Tommy Thornton's leg should be just about healed. And who is caring for your children? I am so glad you could find it in your heart to come to my aid."

A short time later the carriage stopped in front of an unpainted, ramshackle wooden building surrounded on three sides by large, neatly aligned army tents. Over the door of the building a hand-painted sign read *Hospital*. Just below that, someone had hung a crudely written sign, *The Stables*. Dr. Woodward stepped out of the carriage and walked around to assist Mary Ann. He reached in back and pulled out her carpetbag.

"Welcome to the Stables, Mrs. Bickerdyke. Again, I apologize for leaving you here unassisted, but I will catch up with you this evening. Oh, the supplies you brought from our community were taken to the quartermaster in charge of hospital goods. I should be able to access them tomorrow. Good luck, Mrs. Bickerdyke. This won't be easy. I am so relieved that you have come, and so terribly grateful to you for leaving your family."

Dr. Woodward gently touched her forearm in a gesture of support and then climbed back into the carriage. He snapped the reins and the carriage moved off. Mary Ann, bag in hand and feeling quite terrified, stepped onto the building's wooden porch and went through the front door, which was propped open with a rock. She stopped abruptly just inside the door.

As she looked into the room, her face registered surprise, then shock, and finally horror. She grabbed the door frame to steady herself and thought, *It can't really be this bad. I must be tired from the journey and seeing things. What needs to be done is overwhelming.*

The huge building's interior was chaotic, filthy, and nauseating. About a hundred soldiers in varying stages of dress were on the floor, some with blankets but most without. Some men sat up; others leaned against the walls or pillars. All the men were ill or had been wounded in training accidents, some very seriously. Many had sores on their skin that ran with pus. Most of the wounded were without bandages. The few bandages that Mary Ann could see appeared old, and were crusted with dried blood and dirt. Some of the men—boys, really—seemed feverish. They ranted and called out. A few of the boys were in the fetal position, rocking themselves. One or two were vomiting on the floor where they lay. Old dressings, rotten food, torn clothing, human waste, gouts of blood, and other debris littered the floor. The men themselves were filthy, coated with campfire smoke and gunpowder. They wore the same clothes they had been wearing when they were brought here, days or weeks before. The room, though cold, reeked of male sweat mingled with the sweet smell of decay. The dead festered among them.

Mary Ann remained in the doorway, steadying herself as she took in the disgusting scene before her. She was certain now that she had made a grievous error in agreeing to come to Dr. Woodward's aid. She felt overwhelmed, scared, helpless, and very much alone.

Toward the back of the room she saw a stone fireplace, in which a weak little blaze burned, and a door. Near that door two soldiers stood talking. One soldier leaned on crudely made crutches; the other was thin and had sickly yellow skin. He was holding a slop jar.

The soldier on crutches nodded at Mary Ann. "Hey, Joe," he said, "who do you think that is?"

"Don' know. Bound to be trouble, though." Joe turned back to his comrade to continue his conversation.

Mary Ann was still standing in the doorway, slowly scanning the room while she accustomed herself to the disgusting smell. Then she raised one eyebrow and set her jaw. She stepped in, put her carpetbag down on the cleanest spot on the floor that she could find by the door, and lifted her skirts to step over and around the sick men. There was no clear pathway through the room. The only men she could see who seemed to be functional were the two standing in the back.

She walked toward them, saying, "Excuse me, please," to the men on the floor. The men who were able stared at her as she passed over them. Some rubbed their eyes, sure that they were dreaming or hallucinating. The room grew quiet.

Mary Ann approached the two soldiers in the back, who by now were looking decidedly nervous. "Who's in charge here, soldier?" she asked the yellow man.

The soldier's eyes widened and he stuttered with surprise. "Ah...ah..." Then he pointed to the soldier next to him on crutches. "He is," he said with relief.

Mary Ann looked at the soldier on crutches. He flinched uncomfortably and swallowed hard.

"Uh, no, ma'am. That'd be Surgeon Banks, but he's not here. I'm jus' helping out, ma'am. Private Absalom Epley, ma'am, Twenty-first Ohio Infantry. Me and Joe, uh...Private White, uh...since me and him be the least sick, we got put to work here."

Mary Ann nodded at both men, not sure what being the "least sick" had to do with nursing. She put her hands on her hips and looked around the room, trying to collect herself and form a plan—any plan that would help her sort out all the problems she saw. Then, to her amazement, she began speaking in an authoritative voice to the two soldiers.

"Well, Private Epley, Private White, my name is Mrs. Bickerdyke. Dr. Woodward brought me here to get this mess cleaned up, and I don't have a great deal of time in which to do it. I'm going to need your help. First, I want you," she said, pointing to Private Epley, "to get a detail of men—healthy men—to find some barrels and cut them in half. Then make several fires out front and start heating water. These men need to be bathed. And while that's getting done, this place needs to be cleaned from top to bottom. Then we'll need clean clothes, fresh dressings, bedding, blankets, and food. And we'll need strong men to remove and bury the dead. Now, where can I put my bag and shawl?"

Private Epley looked nervous and confused, like a cornered animal who'd give anything not to be where he was at the moment. He stuttered, "Uh...uh...ma'am? Cleaning, ma'am? But Surgeon Banks won't...your bag, ma'am? Uh...why...there, ma'am." He pointed to nail on a supporting column. "But, ma'am, women aren't allowed here."

Mary Ann felt hostility in the room, and it strengthened her.

"Good. My bag is by the door. Get it for me, please, Private White, and then see about those barrels and that hot water." She moved toward the supporting column, and behind her back the two soldiers looked at each other worriedly and rolled their eyes. Without speaking, they angrily mouthed words at each other, pointing and laying blame for this predicament on each other. Mary Ann placed her shawl and bonnet on the nail and began to roll up her sleeves.

Horrified by the situation they were in, Private Epley spoke. "No, ma'am. This is not a good idea, ma'am. Surgeon Banks will not like this, and we don't have the authority to help you. We don't even know who you are. You shouldn't be here, ma'am."

Mary Ann ignored this. "Well, gentlemen, shall we get started? Where can I find a broom and a mop?" Doing what she knew how to do gave Mary Ann a feeling of comfort. Using her organizational skills allowed her to begin her work without showing her terror.

The afternoon sun threw shadows across the front of the hospital. Outside, men recruited from the ranks of the healthy put wood on six large fires and refilled cauldrons with water. Other men took buckets of steaming water from the pots and poured it into barrel halves. Thirty or so soldiers were already bathing or being bathed in the chilly air. Private Epley was hesitantly directing several other soldiers gathering stones.

"Pile some more stones up next to the fire, lads. The lady wants the stones put close to the sickest, to keep them warm tonight."

Mary Ann stood near a fire, stirring a large kettle suspended on poles. She took the wooden spoon out of the liquid, tasted it, and looked toward a soldier standing near her. "More salt," she said. "And see if you can round up any more potatoes. It's still a little too thin. Here, young man. Take over the duty of stirring." She handed the spoon to another soldier, who backed up as if she were handing him her corset.

He reluctantly grabbed the spoon and dipped it into the soup.

Then she walked over to Private Epley.

"Absalom, what about the straw? When will it be here?"

"The boys who went to the quartermaster said it shoulda been here by now. I'll go check on it." He turned to look at the doorway of the hospital, where soldiers were picking up heaps of dirty bandages to take to the fire.

❧

At the same time, in the outer room of a small, rough, two-room building near the center of the fort, several soldiers sat at desks writing amid stacks of paper. The room was poorly lit by two lanterns and one window, through which the late afternoon light shone, dust motes dancing in its beam. At the back of the room, the door to the inner office was slightly ajar. The voice of Brigadier General Benjamin Prentiss, commander of Fort Defiance, was heard coming from this room. "Who is she, Major?" The soldiers at the desks stopped writing in order to listen. They grimaced at each other, thankful they were not in the major's shoes at the moment.

General Prentiss, a large, balding man with dark brown pork chop sideburns, sat in shirtsleeves at his desk in the inner office, writing a report on the day's activities. A major stood at attention before him.

"A Mrs. Bickerdyke, sir. Said she was sent here to help Dr. Woodward at the hospitals. From a church somewhere in Illinois. Arrived today, by riverboat. Somehow Woodward arranged for a one-day pass."

"And...?" the general muttered without looking up, stabbing the pen in the inkwell.

"Some of the boys, sir. They're complaining. Said she'd feed them supper if they worked for her, helping to get the sick bathed and the hospital cleaned up."

"I assume there's a bigger problem besides the fact that there's a woman who doesn't belong in the fort?"

"Yes, sir. It's the boys who weren't asked to help. They're the ones complaining. Say they can smell her cooking and it reminds 'em of home."

The general put down his pen and finally looked at the major. "Women. Always trouble. Arrange transport for her back to Cairo, and then escort her off the grounds. If she only has a one-day pass, then this problem will resolve itself in less than an hour."

The major saluted smartly. "Yes, sir. Right away."

The sun had just set, and the interior of the hospital was lit by lanterns. Mary Ann and several soldiers swept out the last of the debris that had collected on the floor. Behind them, several other soldiers were on their knees scrubbing the wooden floor with rags and a brush someone had scrounged. Mary Ann's dress was filthy. Her hair straggled out from its bun. Her sleeves were rolled up and dirty. Every sweep of the broom made a large dust cloud. Dirt streaked her face. The major stood at the doorway. He had been there for a few moments, quietly looking around. Then he and the four soldiers who had accompanied him stepped into the room and approached Mary Ann. Sensing trouble and anticipating some entertainment, the soldiers who had been working outside crowded in the doorway for the show.

The major took off his hat and said, "Mrs. Bickerdyke? Ma'am?"

"Yes?" She continued to focus her attention on her sweeping, but internally she felt a flush of fear, as if she had been caught doing something wrong. All others in the room stopped working and watched the major and Mary Ann. Once again the room became very quiet. The major hesitated, looked around again at all the eager faces, and then continued.

"Ma'am. I'm Major Mackenzie, aide to General Prentiss, commander of Fort Defiance. He has ordered me to escort you off the fort. No women are allowed on the premises after dark."

Mary Ann stopped sweeping and thought about her situation. She had promised Dr. Woodward to take care of this hospital. Now she was being stopped by an authority she did not know how to approach. With a bravery she didn't feel, she looked at the major incredulously. "But, Major, I have only just started the work that needs to be done. Dr. Woodward asked me to come here to care for this hospital. I cannot leave now."

"Sorry, ma'am. Orders from higher up, ma'am."

"No, Major. This won't do. This just won't do. Where is this General Prentiss? Take me to him, so that I may speak with him."

"Sorry, Mrs. Bickerdyke, but he's in conference and left orders not to be disturbed. Now, if you would come with me, I have arranged transport to Cairo for you."

Mary Ann paused. Dismay was written on her face. "Very well, sir. But first, let me speak with the men here." In a louder tone, she said, "Gentlemen, if you please, your attention. Gather round."

The major and his men stepped away from her and watched as the soldiers in the room and from the doorway crowded around her.

She spoke in a voice steadier than she felt. "Men, I'm told I must leave you for the night. But there is still much to do. If you continue to work, I promise you two meals tomorrow—good, home-cooked meals."

At this statement Major Mackenzie raised his eyebrows in surprise.

"Now," she continued, "Absalom here will be in charge until I return. Finish sweeping and scrubbing the floor. Be generous with the lye soap. The good Lord knows this place needs it. After it's dry, there's fresh straw outside to be put down as bedding. Then bring the men back in. Keep the fireplace wooded all night so they stay warm, and keep warm stones lined up around the weakest. I'll see about getting fresh bandages to change all the dressings tomorrow. I'm a good cook, gentlemen, so work hard." She handed her broom to the closest soldier, and the men looked from the major to Mary Ann before they went back to their work. Mary Ann slowly unrolled her sleeves. She put her hands to her head and tried to smooth back her hair until she realized it was hopeless. She retrieved her shawl, bonnet, and carpetbag, and then approached the major.

"Well, Major, shall we go?"

"Yes, ma'am," he said, and nodded solemnly.

Escorted by the four soldiers, Mary Ann and Major Mackenzie walked toward the entrance. She laughed to cover her anxiety. "I am impressed, Major, that you brought so many soldiers with you to see me safely off the grounds."

The major blushed. "I, ah, had expected a bit of trouble, ma'am. I had heard you were a formidable woman."

"And now that you've met me, Major?"

He stopped walking and faced her, smiling. "I see what you're doing here, ma'am, and I know the men will be better off for it. And, yes, ma'am, I think this escort is just the right size." He put on his hat and gestured for her to lead the way.

She smiled, more at ease with him, and they left the building.

∞

Later that night Mary Ann and Dr. Woodward sat in the dining room of the Cairo Hotel. The candles throughout the room had burned low and shadows darkened its corners. Mary Ann and Dr. Woodward were the only two left in the room. They sat at a small round table covered by a stained cloth that at one time had been quite elegant. They kept their voices low, as if conspiring together. Mary Ann, still in disarray from the day's work, shook her head wearily and picked at a drop of wax that had fallen on the tablecloth from the candle. As the night deepened, her mind turned to her children and all the worry of leaving them burdened her. She was also astounded by the size of the task before her.

"Absolutely not, Doctor. It will take more than one day. If I had twenty trained nurses here it would take more than one day. I must have a pass that does not restrain me, and I am going to need helpers, access to supplies, bandages, blankets, nutritious food, and the like. These soldiers can't make do with what they have."

"I do not have the power to provide you with assistance, nor do I even know of twenty trained nurses who might help. If I can arrange a pass that permits you to stay as long as you need to do your work and speak with the quartermaster about supplies, will you stay and help?"

"Of course. I can see that I am needed here, and I will stay as long as I can, but not a minute longer. I feel horribly guilty about leaving my children, yet I am overwhelmed by the amount of need I see here."

Dr. Woodward had been folding and refolding a corner of the tablecloth, a habit he had when anxious. "You understand you will meet with some…ah…resistance? The army is not used to dealing with women."

Mary Ann smiled. "You know, Doctor, I am up to the challenge, but I've never been really good with authority figures—generals are just men, after all."

They sat quietly for a moment, each lost in thought.

Mary Ann looked up. "Now, on to more important matters. I spoke with the owner of this establishment, and he referred me to a Mrs. Safford, whom I intend to seek out in the morning. She is president of the Women's Auxiliary for Cairo. I am going to solicit her assistance in asking the community for supplies. Mr. Canby, the hotel owner, agreed to let me borrow several kettles to start a diet kitchen for the men. I promised the soldiers helping me at the Stables two meals tomorrow."

Dr. Woodward looked relieved and nodded. "I need to warn you, Mrs. Bickerdyke, that even though we do our best, there will be hell to pay. We are fighting a huge and powerful institution which has not yet become aware that it needs us. With that warning, let me bid you good evening and thank you again for coming to my assistance. You must be very tired after your journey and all the work you've done."

⊙⊙

Up in her room, Mary Ann walked to the bed and ran her hand over the coverlet, thinking how much finer it was than the quilt she'd made from homespun hand-me-downs shortly after getting married so many years ago. She traced her finger along a seam and remembered the seam of her wedding dress, the prettiest dress she'd ever had. It was material from that dress she had used to sew her boys' baptismal clothes. She was lost in a feeling of sadness, missing them. Realizing that these memories would paralyze her, she scolded herself. "This won't help, Mary Ann. Attend to the task at hand."

She refocused her attention on the room. It was sparsely furnished, but more elegant than her bedroom at home. On a small table placed against the wall was a porcelain basin and ewer. On the wall next to it was a wavy mirror in a frame with peeling gold paint. A clean towel hung on a rack beside it. Pegs poked out from the wall in lieu of a closet. A small round parlor table and a chair were positioned by the one window, which overlooked the main street. A beautiful crystal lamp, a remnant of better times, sat on a tiny bedside table and sent a warm golden glow across the room. The warmth was imaginary, however. It was cold, and Mary Ann blew on her hands to warm them.

I am so tired, she thought, and looked longingly at the bed.

With a sigh, she pulled a piece of paper and a pencil from her carpetbag and sat at the small parlor table. Slowly she started to write. An old scratch in the wood of the table reshaped her words.

> My dearest children,
> I pray that you are well and taking care to be good visitors at Mrs. Smithfield's. I have arrived safely and spent part of the day with the good doctor. There seems to be much to do here.

She paused, trying to find a guiltless turn of phrase, but there was none.

> I believe I will need to stay a bit longer than anticipated. I will try to send you some money and Reverend Beecher can help you obtain necessities.
> In the meantime, be good little Christians. Say your prayers, and obey Mrs. Smithfield. Now, it is late, the day has been long, and your mother is very tired. I am not good at writing, but I will send you letters as often as possible. You can write to me care of Dr. Woodward at Fort Defiance. I miss you. All my love,
> M. A. Bickerdyke

The next morning, a clean and refreshed Mary Ann walked purposefully up the porch steps of a small yellow house and knocked on the front door. A moment later, an elderly woman with steel gray hair and an apron over her dress opened the door. The elderly woman said, "Yes? May I help you?"

"Good morning," said Mary Ann. "I am so sorry to trouble you. May I request the pleasure of speaking with Mrs. Safford? It is rather urgent, I'm afraid."

The elderly woman looked surprised. "Why, I'm Mrs. Safford." She paused a moment and then smiled gently. "Forgive my manners. I'm not used to callers at this time of day. Won't you please come in?" She opened the door wider and stepped aside to reveal a polished wood floor entryway. Mary Ann stepped inside, and Mrs. Safford closed the door.

"May I take your shawl and hat, Mrs...?" said Mrs. Safford.

"Bickerdyke. Mary Ann Bickerdyke. Thank you." Mary Ann removed her bonnet, shawl, and gloves and handed them to Mrs. Safford, who hung the shawl and bonnet on the cloak rack and laid the gloves on the entry table.

Mrs. Safford then turned to Mary Ann. "Come this way, Mrs. Bickerdyke," she said, and led Mary Ann down the hall to a large sitting room, elegantly furnished and warmly lit by the morning sun.

"Please make yourself comfortable, Mrs. Bickerdyke. I shall see about making a fresh pot of tea. I shan't be but a moment." Mrs. Safford bowed slightly to Mary Ann and left the room. Mary Ann walked over to the davenport and sat, all the while looking around the tastefully decorated room.

A couple of minutes later a young girl of twelve ran into the room, out of breath and laughing. She saw Mary Ann and abruptly stopped, and stood with surprise on her face. "Hello. I'm sorry for being rude. I didn't know anyone was in here. Does my mother know you're here?" asked the girl. Her striking red hair was dressed in two long braids.

Mary Ann smiled at her. "Mrs. Safford will be back momentarily. My name is Mrs. Bickerdyke, child."

"And I am Mary Safford," the girl said as she curtsied. "A pleasure to meet you, Mrs. Bickerdyke."

The rattle of china and the sound of footsteps in the hall made both Mary Ann and little Mary look toward the doorway. Mrs. Safford entered the room, holding a tray with a steaming pot of tea, two china cups and saucers, and a plate of home-made bread and butter. She looked at the two of them and smiled. "Ah, I see you've met my Mary." Mrs. Safford put the tray on the low table by the davenport. "Run along and play now, Mary. I believe we have serious matters to discuss."

"Oh, Mother. May I please stay? I promise I won't be in the way. I shall be as quiet as a butterfly."

Mrs. Safford laughed and looked at Mary Ann inquiringly; Mary Ann nodded her assent. Mary sat on the other end of the davenport, eyes wide with excitement. Mrs. Safford sat in a chair across from Mary Ann and poured the steaming tea into the delicate cups. She handed one to Mary Ann. "Sugar? Cream? Ah, there's nothing like a good hot cup of tea. Now, Mrs. Bickerdyke, how may I help you?"

"Mr. Canby, from the hotel, said you might be able to assist me. I was appointed as a nurse to care for the boys in one of the hospitals at the fort. I visited there yesterday and found that the task will take more resources than I have available to me—far more. Since you chair the Women's Auxiliary of Cairo, I thought you might be able to assist me."

"How interesting, Mrs. Bickerdyke. The Auxiliary has been looking for a means of helping the war effort. Tell me what you're thinking about."

᎒᎒

As noon approached the next day, Mary Ann was in the Stables, leaning over and stirring a huge iron kettle of stew. The fire crackled loudly. Mary Ann tasted the stew with a thoughtful look and then placed the spoon on the stone mantle over the fireplace. She picked up the poker and rearranged the coals to cover several Dutch ovens, half buried in glowing embers. The homey smell of soup and biscuits filled the room. Then she straightened and looked around. Conditions at the Stables were improving. The floor was clean and spread with fresh straw, and the men were lying in orderly rows. They had all been bathed. They still wore the same clothes, but their wounds had been cleaned and dressed. The room was crowded with men, eagerly waiting for their portion of the food.

Mary Ann heard the sound of horses and wagons approaching. She walked to the entrance and opened the door. Three open-bed wagons pulled up in front of the hospital. In the first wagon, Mrs. Safford held her hat on her head and clutched the wooden seat. She smiled at Mary Ann and spoke to the driver sitting next to her. Little Mary was on a crate in the back of the wagon, waving excitedly.

"Hello, Mrs. Bickerdyke! We're here! We've brought clean clothes, blankets, food, and cloth for dressings," said Mrs. Safford.

"Yes. The whole town is helping!" yelled Mary, over the racket of the horses and wagons.

"Mrs. Safford! Mary! How kind of you. Come in. Please, come in."

The driver of the first wagon stepped down, walked around the wagon, and helped Mrs. Safford down, and then lifted little Mary to the ground. Holding hands, they walked up to the porch. Mary Ann greeted Mrs. Safford with a hug. "Bless you, Mrs. Safford. You've performed miracles. And such a help it will be! Now come, I've stew and biscuits almost ready. Perhaps both of you can join us for a simple meal."

The three of them walked into the hospital and stopped in the entryway. Mrs. Safford and Mary looked around the room, taking in their first view of an army hospital.

"You, too, have been very busy it seems, Mrs. Bickerdyke. Conditions are much improved from what you had told me." Mrs. Safford looked at her daughter, whose grip on her hand tightened uncertainly as she viewed a room full of ill men for the first time. "You say there are five more hospitals here at the fort?"

"Yes. And I've yet to begin on the tents. There are ten tents out front there, each holding around fifty men. There's much to do. But this is a grand start, Mrs. Safford. When the supplies are off the wagon, I would like to set up two or three kettles to wash these boys' clothes as soon as possible. Did you happen to bring any soap along?"

"Yes, soap and a wringer, donated by the Women's Auxiliary."

Mary Safford looked up eagerly. "I'm here to help, too. Where do you want the supplies—the porch? I'll show the drivers where to put them. I'm a hard worker, and I can help you. You'll see!" She disengaged her hand from her mother's and ran back outside. Both ladies smiled at her exuberance.

"Ah," said Mary Ann wistfully, swallowing the beginning of tears. "She reminds me of my own daughter. What a joy she must be to you."

"That she is. I could not do what you are doing and leave my darling daughter behind. You are a brave woman to take on the misery you see here. Now, how have you arranged to stay longer than your one-day pass, Mrs. Bickerdyke?" asked Mrs. Safford.

"Dr. Woodward arranged for a month's pass—over the objections of an officer or two. Now, Mrs. Safford, how would you feel about helping a few of these boys eat? Some of them are so weak they can't even hold a spoon. Your caring hand will be much appreciated. Come."

CHAPTER 4

Surgeon Banks

Days later, conditions in the hospital were vastly improved. The dead had been removed and given Christian burials. Each of the wounded or sick had a blanket, rested on a bed of clean straw, had been bathed, wore clean clothes, and had fresh dressings. Some soldiers played checkers while some drank from tin cups. Two soldiers helped a third to a privy that had been set up in the corner, complete with blankets hung for privacy. Covered chamber pots were placed throughout the room. A small table held a pitcher of water and tin cups. Several soldiers dressed the wounds of the more seriously ill. Mary Ann sat on the floor by a soldier, propping his head up and spoon-feeding him soup. She wiped his chin with the edge of her apron and murmured encouragement to him. She looked tired.

Suddenly, the back door banged open. An unkempt man in a dirty uniform, with his shirt unbuttoned over his long johns and his shirttail hanging out, staggered into the room. His suspender straps were falling off his shoulders. He reeled back toward the door, paused, lurched forward, and then tripped, grabbing the nearest pillar for support. He looked bewildered and confused; he was obviously drunk.

In a booming voice, he said, "What in damnation is going on here?"

Everyone in the room stopped and looked at him. Mary Ann put down the spoon and looked at the soldier she had been feeding. She said tenderly, "This will take just a moment, young man." She rose and brushed the straw off her skirt.

The drunken man squinted at her and looked around the room; he seemed unsure he was in the right place.

"Who in the hell are you?" he screeched.

Feeling very unsafe and not knowing what to do, Mary Ann walked slowly toward him. "You, sir, should not swear, especially in the presence of a lady. And lower your voice! You are disturbing these men. They need their rest."

"A...a...lady!" He peered at her, shook his head as if to clear it, and then peered again. Then he yelled, "Private! Private! What's going on here? Who is this banshee? Where did my hospital go?"

Private White, who was tending a soldier in the far corner, stood slowly and nervously approached. "Ah...sir... ah...this is...ah...Mrs. Bickerdyke. Here to help us."

The man swung his head from the private to the woman and loudly stuttered, "Mrs. Blick...Blicker..."

Feeling both put on the spot and the beginning of a fine anger, Mary Ann stepped forward and said with some firmness, "Mrs. Bickerdyke, from Galesburg, Illinois. I have come here to help, and a good thing it is, too. People are kinder to rabid animals than what I found here. And who are you, and how dare you come in here causing this ruckus?" She squared her shoulders and took a step closer to him.

The man squinted again, shook his head, and slurred, "Who am...ruckus...woman, I'll hab...have you know I'm Slurgeon Banks and this is my surglery you're standing in!"

The first whiff of whiskey from the man's breath made Mary Ann grimace and back up a pace. Then she moved even closer, almost nose to nose with the man. Her closeness made him step back. She remembered her husband, Robert, and how unreasonable and incapable he had been when he was drunk. She remembered the only solution was to overpower the drunkard. With steel in her voice and an odd smile on her face, Mary Ann said, "Well, Surgeon Banks. You're just the man I've been looking for. But you're quite drunk! You're not fit to discuss anything at the present time," she said, waving her hand to dissipate the alcohol fumes coming from his mouth.

The surgeon hiccupped a reply, "Woman, I'll have you—"

Mary Ann interrupted him. Looking behind him, she said, "Private White, please escort the surgeon to his quarters, where he can recover from his indiscretion." She looked at Surgeon Banks. "After you've recovered we shall meet to discuss the deplorable conditions I found here."

Surgeon Banks staggered backward and began to rage. "Madam, you are a—"

Private White hastily grabbed the surgeon's arm. Interrupting, he said, "She's right, sir. You can't tackle this one until you're sober." Private White turned Surgeon Banks around and started walking with him toward the back door. The surgeon began howling, "I'll have you court-martialed for this, Private! You'll be wishing you were nebber born! I want her out of my surglery, NOW! HOW DARE A WOMAN...A WOMAN!"

Private White stopped and looked worriedly over his shoulder at Mary Ann. The surgeon leaned heavily on him, still rambling. Mary Ann said quietly, "Go along with him now, Private White. I'll see to it that you're not court-martialed." She smiled at Private White, who nodded uneasily and escorted the surgeon out of the room. Mary Ann knew that she was in some kind of trouble, but had no idea of the conflagration to come.

The sound of the surgeon yelling diminished as he was led away from the building. Mary Ann returned to the soldier she had been feeding and picked up the spoon. She was noticeably trembling from the incident with the surgeon. She forced herself to mentally refocus on her task. Then, noticing how quiet the room was, she said to the stunned soldiers, "Be on about your work. We have no time to waste."

The episode with Surgeon Banks was so distasteful, so abusive, and so full of memories of Robert when he was drunk that Mary Ann set a piece of iron down inside her heart. Care would be provided to these men no matter what the cost.

❦

Outside the hospital, around noon the next day, Mary Ann directed soldiers in cleaning up a tent. Sick soldiers were being carried to a makeshift area beside a tarp hung to cut the chill breeze.

In the midst of this activity, wagons pulled up in front of the hospital building. Little Mary Safford, who sat by the driver of the first wagon, saw Mary Ann. "Oh, Mrs. Bickerdyke! We're back! And wait 'til you see what we've brought! A stove with a cook oven, Mrs. Bickerdyke! A real stove!" Mary jumped off the wagon and ran toward Mary Ann. She continued, breathlessly, "And Mother has contacted a friend who knows someone who can arrange for supplies from something called the Sanitary Commission. She's writing the letter now. And the whole town is rallying. People have been bringing food and clothing all morning to our house. Oh! And Mother apologizes, but she was very tired and thought she had better rest today. But she sent me to help! And—"

Mary Ann interrupted her with a laugh. "Breathe, child, or you'll be no use to anyone. And help you shall! We've much to do. With a cookstove we can set up a diet kitchen right in the hospital. These boys are too ill to cook or eat the beans and salt pork they're given. They need custards and softer foods that will sit better in their stomachs. Come, Mary Safford. Let us see what you've brought." Smiling, Mary Ann put her arm around Mary's shoulders, and they walked together toward the wagons. Little Mary talked excitedly all the way, her red braids bouncing with every step.

❦

Later that same afternoon, a now sober and spotlessly clean Surgeon Banks approached the headquarters of Fort

Defiance. As he reached the building, he straightened his uniform and squared his shoulders. He walked up the steps to the porch, and in an authoritative voice said to the guard at the door, "Colonel Banks to see General Prentiss."

Major Mackenzie, the general's aide-de-camp, walked from inside the headquarters to the entrance and saluted. "Sir, Colonel Banks. Yes. The general has been expecting you. Come in, sir." The guard stepped aside and Surgeon Banks entered.

The general sat at his desk, one hand holding up several directives and the other delicately holding a pen. He had been speaking with Colonel Grant, who lounged in the chair facing the desk. Major Mackenzie stood in the entryway to the office and said, "Excuse me, sir. Colonel Banks is here to see you."

Colonel Grant stood hastily. "Well, General, I must get back to my duties. This has been enlightening, sir. Thank you." He saluted and left the office. Colonel Grant chuckled to himself and nodded to Surgeon Banks as they passed each other in the doorway.

General Prentiss said wearily, "Take a seat, Colonel Banks." Then, looking at the major, he said, "That will be all, Major." The major nodded and closed the door. With an audible sigh, General Prentiss looked up from the papers on his desk. "What can I do for you, Colonel Banks?"

"Sir. There is an unauthorized woman in my hospital. She has destroyed the order there. She has gone through it like a cyclone. She has caused a complete disruption of the routine and—"

General Prentiss interrupted. "I know, Colonel. Mrs. Bickerdyke has already been here to see me. She complained to me about you."

"About me?" Colonel Banks responded with surprise. "But, sir—"

General Prentiss interrupted again, this time with a commanding tone. "One moment, Colonel Banks. We are at war, and that means we must all do things beyond the ordinary—things we'd probably rather not do. I agree with you that a hospital, an *army* hospital at that, is no place for a woman. But Mrs. Bickerdyke has the backing of the entire town of Cairo, and we *need* Cairo's support. We need its dock, and we need the cooperation of its citizenry. If we run her off now, we will anger many of the good people of this town, and that could make our lives—especially mine—very uncomfortable."

Colonel Banks listened, stunned. Then, with a note of rising hysteria in his voice, he said, "But, sir, I cannot tolerate this woman in my hospital. She doesn't belong there, and she is a bad influence on the men. She ordered me out of my own hospital, sir, she—"

General Prentiss interrupted again. "I understand you were drunk, Colonel. If I were you, to handle this woman, I'd stay sober."

"Sir, you cannot mean that she's to stay! That would—"

General Prentiss rose, put both fists on the desk, and loomed over Surgeon Banks. "Enough. Now stop talking and breathe!"

The surgeon looked up at the general with meekness and confusion. "Breathe, sir?"

"Yes, breathe. What do you smell? Nothing! That's sweet air you smell. I thought this fort was a hellhole. Why, a wagon full of skunks dead nigh on a week smell better! You couldn't even wash the stink out of your clothes. Well, Colonel, that smell is gone! She did that! It was your hospital that reeked, and she cleaned it up. Anybody who can do that can have the run of the place, as far as I am concerned, even if she is a woman. So you stay out of her way, Colonel."

Surgeon Banks tried to protest, "But...but, sir...I believe... this is most irregular—"

"That will be all, Colonel. Good day." General Prentiss nodded dismissively, sat down, and then looked at the papers on his desk. Surgeon Banks saluted, turned on his heel, and stalked out. As the flustered surgeon passed through the staff room, Major Mackenzie looked up from a report he was reading and smiled, his blue eyes crinkling with amusement.

※※

At the same time, inside the hospital, Mary Ann was speaking to Private White. "Well, that takes care of that, but now we need more bowls and spoons for this evening's meal. What do you suggest?"

The private cleared his throat and looked around. He leaned close to Mary Ann and said, "Excuse me, ma'am, but how did you keep me from getting hanged? I thought by now I was a goner."

Mary Ann smiled. "Why, Private White, I spoke to the general, of course. He's a very wise man. I talked sense to him!"

※※

A few days later, in November 1861, in an effort to keep morale high, Grant struck the first blow against the Confederates. A Rebel force had been massing in and fortifying Columbus with heavy cannon. Near the Kentucky-Missouri border, Columbus is strategically situated on the Mississippi River across from Belmont, Missouri. To avoid the guns at Columbus, Grant led three thousand Union troops and two wooden gunboats against an encampment the Rebel General Polk had established at Belmont, Missouri, twelve miles downriver from Cairo. The skirmish was brief, and Grant took Belmont, but his victory was temporary. Discipline in Grant's forces disintegrated, and his soldiers looted the Confederate camp. Confederate reinforcements moved in. Outnumbered, Grant was forced to retreat to Cairo. The battle for Belmont was a small military engagement that resulted in only 485 Union soldiers wounded, missing, or dead. Boats steamed back upriver to Cairo, carrying the war wounded to the fort's hospitals.

The hospital area was a flurry of activity and chaos. An amputating table had been set up inside the main hospital building. Two blood-splattered surgeons were sawing off shattered limbs. Wounded men coated black with gunpowder seemed to be everywhere—standing, sitting, and lying down. Their screams mingled with curses, cries, and prayers. Off to the side, the blue and stiff dead were laid out next to each other and stacked like cordwood.

Mary Ann walked among the wounded as if in a trance; her apron and the hem of her dress were smeared with blood. Her hands were bloody, and there was blood on her face and in her hair. The horror she saw around her paralyzed her for a moment. A part of her was detached, watching the suffering as if from afar. Then she visibly shook the mantle of fear off her shoulders so she could attend to her duties.

She waved to some men who were coming out of the main hospital building. "Sergeant, please tell them we need more dressings, more bandages. And have the men build fires to heat bricks and stones. It's going to be a cold night for these boys."

The sergeant nodded, stepped away from the other men, and returned to the building. Mary Ann turned and knelt next to a young soldier whose left eye and jaw were gone. He was having difficulty breathing. She used her apron to wipe his face a bit, and then propped his head up on a coat offered by another soldier. She covered him with a blanket and murmured softly to him.

Mary Safford walked up behind her. She was also bloodied and crying. Mary whispered, "Mrs. Bickerdyke, the barley gruel is almost ready. And the..." She paused and looked down at the soldier Mary Ann was tending; she raised her eyes to the sky, hoping to keep more tears from falling. She swallowed with difficulty and tears rolled down her cheeks. She continued in a shakier whisper, "And the corn bread is done. We have two cases of apple butter, jarred mutton, potatoes, and beans that just arrived from the Sanitary Commission. There's also a case of dried beef and two of clean shirts and shoes. We've made room in the hospital for forty more. The rest will have to stay in tents or out here." She paused and looked around her. "There will probably be enough blankets for everybody, unless more wounded keep coming."

Without looking up from the soldier she was tending, Mary Ann replied, "Bless you, Mary. You're an angel. Have the men start to move the more seriously wounded into the hospital. Tell them to be careful, now. These men are already hurting. I'll be along directly."

Mary Safford walked away, stepping around and over wounded soldiers. Some raised their hands to her as she passed. She touched them tentatively at first; then ignored them and began to run.

Mary Ann leaned closer to the wounded boy and murmured, "Son, make your peace. It won't be long." She gently caressed his forehead, sighed, and then stood. She moved from wounded man to wounded man amid the cries of agony. She offered water here and a hand grasp there. She knelt to hold the head of a soldier while he vomited. Then she stood, put her hands on the back of her hips, and stretched her back with a slight grimace. She looked to her left and frowned. She saw several scrawny dogs pulling amputated limbs out from the refuse of the hospital. She looked around until she saw a young soldier leaning against the water wagon, drinking from a ladle.

"Private! The dogs are back! We must keep them away. It's most upsetting for these boys to see that!"

The private looked over at the pile of surgical debris and saw what was happening. He dropped the ladle, sprinted over, and chased the dogs away. Mary Ann stared at him caustically before she turned to tend more of the wounded. An overwhelming anger began to rise in her. She felt rage that this private had not done his job, but the rage was really steeped in the feeling of complete helplessness to do anything about what she saw around her. She carefully folded up these feelings and put them in a place where they would not get in her way.

One soldier was crumpled on the ground, his head thrown back, struggling for breath. His shirt was torn and saturated with blood. A sucking sound accompanied each breath, and blood bubbled up through his shirt. He reached for Mary Ann as she passed by.

In a weak voice, the soldier gasped, "Mother? Mother? Is that you?"

Mary Ann knelt, took his hand, and bent low over him. Gently she whispered into his ear, "Yes, my son. Mother is here. Close your eyes and rest now. That's a good boy."

He closed his eyes, and his hand fell back on the ground. Bubbles of blood seeped from his mouth. Mary Ann straightened. She roughly wiped away her tears with the back of her hand, leaving a red smear across her cheek. Other soldiers around her reached for her. They raised a dreadful chorus, "Mother, Mother, help me!" It was a sound that followed Mary Ann into her sleep and filled her with dread. Most of all, she feared she would not be able to do what was required of her. Night after night she awoke abruptly, remembering the sight of a shattered face or broken chest covering her with blood. The war was now being fought in her dreams, and it had captured her with its horror.

It took several days for the hospitals at Fort Defiance to triage and treat the first battle casualties from Belmont. Finally, a sense of order was restored to the Stables, and Mary Ann was able to institute a daily routine for the care and well-being of her patients. She feared the nights, however, as disturbing images of the day invaded her sleep. She tried to escape the images by working throughout the night, but that exhausted and depleted her.

Dr. Woodward was successful in obtaining an unlimited pass which enabled Mary Ann to stay on fort grounds by the hospital. Several soldiers rigged a small space in one of the storage tents for her, with a cot, a table, and a lantern.

One of the soldiers she was nursing asked her about her own family. This simple question sat heavily on her mind and demanded her attention at the oddest moments. She was helping a soldier put on his shirt when memories of doing the same for her little boys overwhelmed her. She gave a bowl of soup to a soldier, and some familiar movement he made reminded her of her son James. She had been too busy to write her children, because she felt pulled into the war in a new way. The sting of guilt for ignoring her motherly role penetrated her heart. One evening, she forced herself to make time to write her sons. She sat in candlelight at a table with paper and pen, but the words would not come. The wreckage of the war crowded out all other thoughts. She knew now that some internal tide was turning her life's focus to the war and orphaning her children. She felt her only response was to be where she was as completely as possible, so that she could survive the war and return to mothering James and Hiram.

Her daily routine began with making and serving breakfast for the wounded; this was followed by visiting each soldier to change bandages and inspect wounds. Many of the soldiers with old wounds were getting sicker as infection and dehydration occurred. One morning, Mary Ann was wrapping a bandage around a soldier's thigh while Private Knight held the soldier's foot in the air. As she turned the cotton bandage, Mary Ann casually asked, "Tell me, Private Knight, have you seen any surgeons today?"

Private Knight hesitated and uncomfortably shifted his weight. "No, ma'am. They won't be makin' much of a fuss today. They was havin' a good ol' time las' night."

Mary Ann, who had heard the ruckus during the night, nodded. "A little higher, please, Private. It's a wonder to me that anyone could be so jolly, when there's such serious medical work to do. Well, we need a surgeon to look at the wound in this man's leg. It's starting to turn black and has the sweet smell. I don't think it can wait too long."

Private Knight wrinkled his nose at the smell. "Ah'll go raise one after we're done here, ma'am. Maybe I kin wake one."

Mary Ann nodded her thanks and continued wrapping the cotton cloth around the soldier's leg, but internally, she was smoldering that innocent young boys would die from their wounds because surgeons chose to sleep off a night of drinking.

A few hours passed, and still no surgeon had appeared. Private Knight was helping a soldier sit up against the wall when Mary Ann walked in through the back door, scowling. She stepped into the room, looked around and saw the private. "Private Knight? May I have a word with you?"

"Ma'am?"

"Do you know what might have happened to the raisin wine we received from the commission? There were two cases of it in the supply tent just yesterday. Now those cases are empty as can be."

Private Knight looked down at his feet. "Well, ma'am. Ah...ah think ah seen a surgeon goin' in the supply tent yesterday after dark. Ah do believe it was Surgeon Cranston. Going in ta look for bandages. But I might be mistaken. It was dark an' all."

Before Private Knight could finish, Mary Ann turned on her heel and, with a swirl of calico, left the Stables. She walked directly toward the surgeons' tent. In her wake, Private Knight mumbled to himself, "Somebody's in fer hell now."

Marching like a general, her blue eyes fiery with anger, Mary Ann made her way purposefully through a maze of white tents. Soldiers saw her coming and jumped out of her path, turning to watch as she passed. A few of them followed at a distance, anticipating a little break in the monotony of camp life. She approached the chief surgeon's tent and stopped outside. "Surgeon Banks! I need to speak with you," she said, in a tone both commanding and threatening.

A groan was heard from inside the tent. Surgeon Banks was on his cot, with his arm thrown over his rheumy eyes. He rolled painfully to a sitting position and held his head between his hands, moaning. He wore wrinkled uniform pants and a dirty, rumpled shirt. He grimaced as her voice cut through his tent.

"Surgeon Banks! Are you there?"

Surgeon Banks could not believe his misfortune. He rubbed his eyes, wishing it were a dream. "What does that banshee want now?" he mumbled. And then, louder, in an impatient tone, "All right, all right. I'm coming. Give me a minute." He stumbled out of bed and leaned over bowl and ewer. Shakily, he poured water into the bowl and splashed it on his face. Grabbing a towel, he left the tent as he wiped his dripping face. Squinting in the sunlight, he winced when he saw his visitor. "Why, if it isn't our wonderful Mrs. Bickerdyke," he said sarcastically. "And what might I do for you on this fine day?"

Mary Ann replied, "Sir—"

Surgeon Banks took a step back and closed his eyes. "Madam, please don't yell."

Mary Ann stepped forward to intimidate him. "Sir, someone took U.S. Sanitary Commission supplies out of the hospital supply tent last night. They were meant for the wounded. I will not tolerate such an abuse. Do you know who the culprit might be?"

Surgeon Banks looked at her incredulously. "Me, madam? Why would I know that?"

"Surgeon Banks!" she said angrily, stepping back to avoid his foul breath. "It is well-known that you and your colleagues had another alcoholic carousal last night. Where did you come by the liquor that caused such drunkenness? Is it mere coincidence that the wine is missing from the hospital supplies?"

"You accuse me of thievery?" he roared. "Be damned, madam. I have had enough of you! We had peace before you came, and we shall have peace once you have left. We would all be better off if you would go back to where you belong. I for one don't want you here, Mrs. Bickerdyke."

Righteous anger overcame any respect for protocol that Mary Ann might have had. "Listen well, Surgeon Banks. You will be gone long before I leave this place. If you force me out the front door, I shall come back in through another. And if you bar all the doors, I shall come in through the window—my patients will help me in. If anybody leaves, it will be you, sir, as I am certain you were involved in the thievery last night. I caution you, do not do it again, sir, or you will live to regret it."

When she finished speaking, she hesitated, and then looked him squarely in the eye for a moment too long. Then she turned and walked away to find a surgeon who could deal with her patient's infected leg. Surgeon Banks stood at the entrance to his tent, holding the towel. He squinted after her and grumbled to himself. A few of the soldiers who witnessed this drama started wandering back to their duties, chuckling.

CHAPTER 5

The Ward Master

For the next several days, in an uneasy truce, Mary Ann and Surgeon Banks stayed out of each other's way. Meanwhile, Mary Ann tackled a new problem; mounds of dirty uniforms and bedding that had accumulated on the ground outside the Stables were attracting rats and other vermin. Mary Ann, a firm believer in the benefits of soap and water, enlisted Mary Safford as a co-worker in her laundry. Every Tuesday and Thursday morning, the two of them moved between large fires where three huge pots of clothing boiled in lye soap. They lifted the steaming clothing out of the wash water with long wooden poles and dropped it onto pallets. When the laundry had cooled, they piled it into a wagon and drove down to the river for rinsing and wringing. There, they draped the clean linens and clothes on nearby bushes to dry. The work was hard and extremely time-consuming. As soon as possible, Mary Ann appointed little Mary Safford as the head of the laundry and began to recruit volunteer soldiers to do the heavy lifting.

In the previous weeks, Mrs. Safford's health began to fail and she elected to stay at home while little Mary took over the task of helping Mary Ann. Mrs. Safford continued to support the effort by writing letters to the head of the Northwest Branch of the U.S. Sanitary Commission. The head of the commission delegated Mrs. Mary Livermore as the primary correspondent. Through these letters Mrs. Livermore learned about Mary Ann Bickerdyke's work, and she did everything in her power to respond to Mrs. Safford's requests for materials and supplies.

One afternoon, as her patients finished their midday meal, Mary Ann entered the ward, carrying a stack of clean sheets and humming a tune. Most of the soldiers were wearing new shirts or were wrapped in new blankets stamped with the U.S. Sanitary Commission insignia. Mary Ann placed the sheets on the floor by a rocking chair. Next to the chair were two baskets, one filled with torn cloth strips and the other full of neatly rolled bandages.

Before sitting down, Mary Ann nodded to the ward clerk leaning a broom against the wall.

"Joshua, it's chilly in here. Wood the fire, please."

"Yes'm." Joshua moved toward the fireplace.

Mary Ann sat in the chair, and with a gentle rocking took up a strip of material and rolled it into a bandage. She placed it in the basket and grabbed another strip. As she did this, the ward master entered the room through the back door. He took off his coat and hung it on a nail on the wall, and started to walk toward her. She froze. The stamp of the U.S. Sanitary Commission adorned his clothing.

Mary Ann growled, leapt from her rocker and rushed toward him. Everyone in the room, except the ward master, stopped to watch.

The ward master, oblivious to the impending attack, said, "Afternoon, Matron Bickerdy—"

Mary Ann tackled him to the floor. He was shocked and surprised. She was on top of him and began wrestling off his shirt.

"These shirts, these supplies...were meant for patients... not for the...likes of you! You should...know better than..."

The ward master struggled to rise against Mary Ann's weight. His face was in full blush, and he grabbed at his clothes as she tried to pull them off him. Everyone in the room was watching, and the soldiers began to hoot and whistle, laugh and holler.

There was a rising chorus of "Git 'em, Mother!" "Whooee!" "Watch out, Mother, he's gaining on ya!"

Mary Ann continued to wrestle the clothing away from the ward master. First his shirt, and then his pants, slippers, and socks. He now wore only his long johns. Breathlessly, she stood up and leaned over him, shaking the clothes in his face. He tried to cover his privates and scooted away from her on the ground.

"Now," she shouted at him, "you rascal! Let's see what you try to steal next!"

The humiliated ward master got up, still covering himself with his hands, and bolted for the back door, looking over his shoulder to see if she was following. There was loud laughter from the soldiers, both inside and outside the hospital.

One of her patients looked up admiringly and said, "Ma'am, we sure coulda used you in our skirmish line. No Johnny Reb's a-goin' ta tangle with you!"

CHAPTER 6

The Poisoned Peaches

Food was an ongoing problem in the hospitals. All soldiers received a ration of raw food from their quartermaster every three or four days; soldiers were expected to cook and store it themselves. Sick soldiers frequently couldn't stand in the line long enough to collect their rations and lacked the energy or resources to cook. A typical three-day ration for a healthy man was a pound of meat, a few green coffee beans, two pounds of white army beans, and some corn-meal or wheat flour. Soldiers were expected to supplement their diet with game or birds they shot and fruit or vegetables scavenged from the countryside. Sutlers and peddlers often sold edibles to the soldiers who could afford them, but the ill couldn't take advantage of these options.

In the hospital setting, the sick frequently went hungry. Soldier-nurses often did the cooking, but lacked knowledge of how to cook for the ill or wounded. Mary Ann used every skill known to a country housewife to prepare nutritious and tasty food for her soldier-patients. But supplies from the quartermaster were often short. She became more and more dependent upon the foodstuffs that the U.S. Sanitary Commission collected as donations from Northern households.

It was a bleak, gray morning with an irritating, cold drizzle. Mary Ann stooped over a hissing fire outside the hospital, stirring a huge pot of gruel. Nearby, several soldiers gathered near steaming pots suspended over fires and learned how to cook soup.

51

"And now add the potatoes," she said in a loud voice. Soldiers slit the necks of the potato sacks and dumped the contents into their pots.

"Jamie," she said, nodding to a young soldier sitting by the fire, "could you please bring a ham from the—oh, don't bother yourself. I'll do it." She turned from her cooking fire, wiped her hands on her apron, and walked to the tent used as a storeroom. She entered. A moment passed. She came out looking very angry and approached Jamie.

"Jamie, you told the others where to put the supplies from the shipment yesterday, didn't you?"

Jamie nodded, "Yes, ma'am."

"I thought we received four large hams in that commission delivery?"

"Yes, ma'am, we sure did. Nice ones, too—looked real good."

"Well, Jamie, they are presently absent from the supply tent. By any chance, would you know where they went or who escorted them away?"

Looking surprised and disappointed, Jamie replied, "No, ma'am. Dang it all! Begging your pardon, ma'am. I was sure looking forward to a sliver of that ham." By the time he finished speaking, Mary Ann had turned away and was back to her task at the fire, mumbling to herself, "This has got to stop! I'll see to it."

A man rubbing sleep out of his eyes and scratching his crotch walked over to the fires. He was unshaven and dirty, and wore a filthy apron over greasy, grimy clothes. With an irritable grunt he ripped the spoon out of one soldier's hands.

"Here. Lemme do that," he said roughly.

Mary Ann turned to him and said, "Ah, Tom. Good morning. I don't suppose you know who might have taken the hams from the supply tent? They seem to be missing this morning."

Tom scowled at her. "Why should I know anything? I's jus one of the cooks at this damned camp." He turned his shoulder to her and leaned over the pot. He coughed up a gob of phlegm and spat it into the fire, barely missing the pot of soup he was stirring. "Bugger the old woman any-way!" he cursed to himself. "Too dang early to be taking orders from the likes of her!"

◯◯

Later that day, Mary Ann and little Mary returned to the supply tent. Little Mary sat on a box and used another for a desk. She had paper and pen. Mary Ann paced the few steps inside the tent, dictating a letter to Mrs. Safford.

"This is an unusual request, and I understand if it cannot be fulfilled, but these are dire circumstances. Our sick soldiers are suffering because of theft. Please do what you can. It will be much appreciated."

◯◯

A few days later, while both Mary Ann and little Mary were sweeping out old soiled straw inside a hospital tent, they heard a loud commotion outside. Heavily loaded wagons from the Sanitary Commission were arriving.

"Why, that sounds like a delivery, doesn't it, Mother?" said little Mary.

"Go and see, child. I'll be along directly."

Little Mary tightened her shawl around her shoulders and ran out of the tent with an expectant look on her face. Mary Ann bent down to one soldier.

"Here, son. Lean on me, and let's get you onto some soft, clean straw."

A few minutes later, outside the hospital tent, Mary directed six soldiers who struggled to off-load a large wooden box from the wagon. It slipped in their collective grip and settled to the ground with a thud and a puff of dust. The men sighed. Mary Ann stood by the tent opening, smiled, and walked toward them.

Mary Safford ran up to Mary Ann. "Goodness, Mother. Is this the refrigerator you ordered? It came so fast!"

"I believe it is, child, and not a moment too soon to stop the thievery around here."

Mary Ann walked around the box. The soldiers stepped back and out of her way.

"Ma'am, this thing is heavy," said one of the soldiers.

"It's a refrigerator that has come all the way from Chicago. It will keep the meat from going rancid so fast."

Mary Ann approached the wagon and spoke to the driver. "Thank you, sir, for making this trip. There was supposed to be a lock with it. Is it in the box?"

"No, ma'am. It's in the wagon. Biggest lock I ever seen—it'd take a fourteen- pounder to get through that!" he replied.

Mary Ann stepped closer to the driver and lowered her voice. He nodded his head and handed her a small cloth bundle that she slipped into her dress pocket. She turned and addressed the six soldiers.

"Thank you, boys. When you get your wind back, uncrate it and move it into the supply tent. And bring that lock with you. There should be ice coming on the train. We'll need a few good-sized blocks of it to place in this refrigerator."

Mary Ann turned and walked toward the supply tent, with a visibly thinner Mary chatting by her side. Tom, in the same filthy clothes as before, appeared from around the corner of the hospital building, blowing his nose into his apron. He saw the box and stopped in his tracks.

"What in tarnation has she gone and done now?" he wondered aloud.

A nearby soldier replied, "She's on to you, Tommy, ol' boy." All the soldiers who stood close by started laughing.

Tom grimaced, spat, and walked on. "To hell with ya all!"

A few hours later, Mary Ann and Mary finished putting the last of the perishable food inside the refrigerator. Mary Ann then nodded to the soldier who stood holding the lock and chain. He wrapped the big chain around the box, pulled to make sure it was snug, and then locked it with the padlock. Mary Ann tried to open the refrigerator door, but could not.

"Good. I'll take that key," she said.

The soldier handed her the key, and she put it in her pocket with a smile, just as Tom entered the tent.

"Thomas, you scoundrel, you have stolen the last bit of food from me that you will ever steal," she snarled at him.

The three walked out of the tent, leaving an irritated Tom staring at the chained refrigerator.

Several evenings later, inside the hospital cook tent, Mary Ann ladled hot spiced peaches into large flat pans. Tom entered the tent, casting a shadow across the pans.

"Ah, Tom. Good!" Mary Ann said, looking up at him. "These peaches are for the boys' breakfast tomorrow, but they're too hot and need to cool. I'll leave them on the table under your guard. When they have cooled, please cover them for the morning."

Tom gave her a distressed look but agreed to the task.

With her back to Tom, Mary Ann took from her pocket the cloth bundle she had received from the wagon driver earlier in the week. She undid the knot and removed a glass vial labeled *Tartar Emetic*. She opened the vial and dumped some of the white powder into each of the pans, stirring it in. She smiled, put the vial back in her pocket, and set the spoon aside. The peaches glistened in the lantern light.

"There!" she said. "That should be a treat for the boys in the morning. Now, Tom, make sure that nobody gets into these peaches tonight." Squinting at her pocket watch, she continued, "My goodness! I didn't realize it was getting on so. I must make my rounds. I'll leave this pot for you to wash."

Picking up one of the lanterns, she tied on her fascinator and left the tent, smiling to herself. The scent of cinnamon, sugar, and cloves drifted out of the tent behind her.

In the early morning hours, long before the dawn, Mary Ann was awakened from sleep by the sound of men retching. She lay on her cot wrapped in her blankets against the cold. Usually she would have rushed to assist anyone who was suffering so, but this time she stayed in bed, taking a small delight in justice. After a few moments, she slowly rose and dressed.

By the time she left the tent, lantern in hand against the starry night, the chorus of retching was worse. She made her way through the tents toward the sound. As she approached one tent, the flap was suddenly jerked back and a partially dressed man bolted from the inside, doubled over in pain, whimpering as he ran into the night. Mary Ann quickly stepped back and out of his way. Without announcing herself, she then entered the tent and held her lamp high.

Shadows flickered on the faces of ward clerks, ward masters, surgeons, and cooks, including Tom. They were vomiting into their hats, hands, or pots. Some were doubled over; others were holding their bellies and moaning. On the ground were several of the large pans in which the peaches had been left to cool earlier in the evening. There was not a peach to be seen. Mary Ann took in the scene coldly and smiled.

"Gentlemen, I see you've sampled my peaches. Tasty, were they? But they don't seem to be agreeing with you. What a shame. I would expect that you'll feel a bit sickly for a few days to come. That's if I calculated my dosage right."

"She poisoned us! I told you she poisoned us!" said one man.

Another, disgorging an orange chunky stew, moaned, "I'm dying."

A third man pushed the second man and hissed, "Don't puke on me, you bastard!"

"Gentlemen, gentlemen, such language. And over peaches! You all ought to be ashamed of yourselves," she admonished. "I thought the lock on the refrigerator would stop your stealing, but it didn't even last a week before some rascal broke it and ransacked my supplies. The peaches should teach you a lesson. And let me warn you that this is nothing compared to what will happen to you if you continue to steal from my kitchen and supply tent. I will poison the lot of you with ratsbane, and when that happens, you won't recover. Take me seriously, gentlemen."

Then she looked at Tom and shook her finger at him. "And you, Tom, will come to no good over this."

Mary Ann turned to go, but hesitated in the tent opening, enjoying the irony. With an acid tone, she said, "I wish a very pleasant morning to you all. I hope you have a good day."

A golden dawn began to paint the encampment as a furious Mary Ann made her way to the office of the provost marshal. A tired sentry outside straightened to attention as she approached.

"Mrs. Bickerdyke to see the provost marshal, immediately, if you please," she said.

The flustered sentry said, "One moment, ma'am," and ducked inside the door.

Twenty minutes later, Mary Ann hurried back toward the hospital, two armed soldiers following her, as the provost marshal rushed to catch up while putting on his hat and shrugging into his coat. They approached the back of the hospital. Two wounded soldiers were just leaving the building, and Tom the cook was about to enter.

"Oh, no, you don't, you thieving rogue! Not one foot into my hospital!" Her words whipsawed across the cook's sallow face.

Before he could reply, the provost marshal quietly arrested him for the theft of U.S. Sanitary Commission goods. Flanked by the two soldiers, a surprised Tom was dragged to the guardhouse. Mary Ann thanked the provost marshal and turned to the small group of soldiers who had collected to watch the drama.

"Boys, you must keep what you've seen and heard to yourselves. No talking about this, please. You wait and see. You'll be glad Tom isn't making mischief anymore. You'll be getting the supplies the commission is sending for you. The treachery has been stopped. Go along now. There's work to do."

The men chuckled to themselves and backed up so Mary Ann could enter her hospital.

CHAPTER 7

Mail Call

The days grew colder, and the autumn wind had stripped the trees of their leaves. The fire inside the hospital needed to be fed twenty-four hours a day. The boys in the tents had extra blankets, thanks to the growing friendship between Mrs. Safford and Mrs. Livermore from the U.S. Sanitary Commission. In addition, the food supplies were supplemented with home-cooked meals from the women of Cairo, who also took in some of the mending and darning.

Late one afternoon, Mary Ann kneaded biscuit dough in the hospital cook tent. Her sleeves were rolled up, and she was white to the elbows with flour. Flour smeared her face and was in her hair as well. A couple hundred biscuits cooled in cast-iron pans by the tent flap, and the aroma of freshly baked biscuits had drawn a small band of soldiers who lingered nearby.

Mary Ann heard a wagon approach and the announcement, "Mail call!" It stirred the soldiers to activity, and they moved toward the soldier bearing the mailbag. News from home was always welcome, and the men were excited to hear from their loved ones. The mail carrier started to yell out names, and soldiers who were able walked up to his wagon to receive their parcels and letters. As the men received news from home, they became quiet, drawn inward to the life they left behind.

Mary Ann stepped out of the cook tent and approached a soldier. "Be sure the mail gets to those inside my hospital.

News would cheer them up and help them get their minds off their discomforts."

She turned to go back into the cook tent, but the mail carrier called after her.

"Mother! There are two here for you!"

"For me?" She wiped her hands on her apron and walked over to receive her letters. She looked curiously at the writing on the envelopes.

"Who would be writing to me? Perhaps it's my boys." She opened the first envelope and removed a single piece of paper on which she saw the perfect script of her son James. Her breath caught as she began to read.

> Dearest Mother,
> I am writing for Hiram and me to tell you how much we miss you...

Tears came to her eyes, and she quickly folded the letter, placed it inside the envelope, and put both letters in her pocket. She moved back to the kneading board, and with a newborn sense of urgency, she worked the dough.

◔◔

Later that night, after her chores and night rounds were finished, the camp was quiet. A few soldiers sat and talked or sang softly by their fires, but most were asleep. Inside her tent, Mary Ann sat at a small camp table, the lantern's light making shadows flicker on the canvas. She pulled the letter from James out of her pocket and laid it on the table in front of her. Without opening it, she put her hand on it and felt all her worries for her children well up inside her. All these worries had been tucked away behind her endless duties at the hospital, but now they overwhelmed her. She put her hands to her face and sobbed.

After a few moments, she sighed heavily, roughly wiped the back of her hands across her face, and reopened the letter.

Dearest Mother,

I am writing for Hiram and me to tell you how much we miss you. Reverend Beecher visits us sometimes and we see him at prayer service. We have stayed at Mrs. March's until her husband got bad rumatism. Then the Hunter family took us in. The work is hard here. Hiram likes the chickens, but they make me sneeze. I have a hole in my boot, and it gets wet a lot. We see Mary Elizabeth once in a while. I rode a cow last week. Come home soon. We want it to be like it was.

Very truly yours, your son,
James Bickerdyke

Tears rolled down her face as she held the letter to her chest. She pulled a locket from inside her blouse and opened it. The locket framed two miniatures. One was a crude portrait of James and Mary Elizabeth, and the other of Hiram. She held it close to the lantern and stared at the likenesses. They brought her back home with a feeling of shame for how her decisions had moved her away from those she loved. She slowly shook her head and whispered to herself, "Oh, what have I done? What kind of mother am I? My babies, my babies..."

From her carpetbag she pulled out a tablet of paper and a pencil. Wiping away her tears, she began her response.

My dear, dear children,

I send this by way of Reverend Beecher, for you may have moved to a new household since your last letter. I received your note today, James, and sweet it was to hear from you. I know I haven't been as good about writing you as I should be. It is hard, I know, for all of us to be so far apart. I miss you both very much, and my heart is torn without you.

There are so many tasks to do here—important work that may save a life or two. As difficult as it is for us to be apart, I must stay as I promised. It won't be long though, until my work at Fort Defiance will be finished, and I'll be home. Until then, take good care of little Hiram and mind Mrs. Hunter. I will send you money for new boots as soon as I am able. Please give my love to Mary Elizabeth when you see her next. I remember you every night in my prayers.

Your loving mother,
Mrs. M. A. Bickerdyke

Mary Ann sat for a long moment, stunned, unable to reread what she had written or to seal it in an envelope. She felt torn between two enormous responsibilities and did not know how to resolve this conflict. After a long while, she folded the letter and addressed an envelope to her boys in care of the Reverend Beecher at the Brick Congregational Church in Galesburg. Then she laid it to the side on the table.

Out of her pocket she withdrew the second letter, with an official seal from the U.S. Sanitary Commission in Chicago. It was an introductory letter from Mrs. Mary Livermore, an agent for the Northwest Branch.

Dear Mrs. Bickerdyke:
I have received a wonderful report of your outstanding work at Fort Defiance from our mutual acquaintance Mrs. Safford of Cairo. She speaks most highly of you and your diligent work with the soldiers at the hospital there. I have shared this letter with other members of the commission, and they are equally impressed. The commission wishes to thank you for your willingness to sacrifice your personal life for the war effort. Women

in the North can feel more secure knowing that their boys are being cared for by you.

By now I hope you have received the refrigerator and have put it to good use. I am curious about the lock and the tartar emetic but trust your good judgment. Please write to me directly in the future if you have further needs that we might accommodate. We hope to be able to send an agent in the near future to your part of the country. With the help of God, the two of you will meet and develop a relationship of mutual benefit to you, our soldiers, and the commission.

Mary Ann placed the letter on the table and stared for a long time at the candle flame. Her eyes moved to the letter she had written to her sons and then to the letter from Mrs. Livermore. She held her head in her hands and whispered to herself, "I just don't know what to do."

CHAPTER 8

Meeting General Grant

On a brisk morning late in November, General Grant and General Prentiss rode the perimeter of Fort Defiance. Their staff followed a short distance behind. The two generals were engaged in a discussion about forming lines of defense around Cairo, should such be necessary. General Prentiss looked over his shoulder and motioned for Major Mackenzie to ride forward. As he and Major Mackenzie began to speak, General Grant winced and muttered softly to himself.

"Damn it!"

"What's that, General? I didn't catch it," said General Prentiss.

Grant replied, "Sorry, sir. It's nothing, really. Got stepped on by a horse the other day, and my foot is bothering me. Throbs like a son of a gun."

General Prentiss said, "Why don't you have a surgeon look at it?"

"The cutters? Oh, no. I'm partial to this foot of mine and want it where it is after the war, General."

Major Mackenzie, who now rode alongside the two generals, said, "Excuse me, sirs. If you will allow me, General Grant, I believe I know someone back at one of the fort's hospitals who might be of help."

General Grant hesitated, and then said, "Why, thank you, Major. If it's not a cutter, I may take you up on that. I'm sorry, General, you were saying...?"

An hour and a half later, the tour completed, they arrived at headquarters. General Prentiss dismounted and handed his reins to a waiting soldier. He looked up at General Grant who was still astride.

"Do you have time for a quick drink, Sam? I've whiskey just in from New York. Smooth, very smooth."

Grant replied, "I think I'll take Major Mackenzie up on his offer,"—he looked at the major—"if now is a good time?"

The major said, "Certainly, sir."

Grant looked at General Prentiss. "Thanks for the offer. Another time, then." Grant turned to his staff, still sitting their horses. "Men, get something to eat and see to your horses. I'll see you later. Major Mackenzie, lead the way, please." And together the two men rode through the fort until they reached the Stables.

∽∾

Outside the hospital building, Mary Ann stood stirring a huge pot of boiling clothes. Her apron was soaked and steam and sweat glistened on her face. A soldier, an assistant at the laundry, stood next to her skimming lice and other vermin off the top of the boiling water and throwing them in the fire. As General Grant and Major Mackenzie approached and dismounted, all the able soldiers in the area came to attention. Mary Ann, unaware of the visitors, continued stirring. Major Mackenzie and General Grant walked up to Mary Ann.

Major Mackenzie cleared his throat. "Mrs. Bickerdyke, ma'am, I'd like to introduce General Grant."

Mary Ann dropped her stir pole into the pot, turned toward the two men, and wiped her hands on her apron. She fussed with her hair and said with surprise, "Why, I wasn't expecting company. A general? How do you do, General?"

General Grant tipped his hat to her. There was a hint of a smile at the corners of his mouth. "Ah, Mrs. Bickerdyke. Your reputation precedes you. I'm glad to finally meet you."

Major Mackenzie said, "Ma'am, we were wondering if we could speak with you privately?"

"Of course, gentlemen," Mary Ann replied. "Come this way. I believe there's privacy to be found in the hospital supply tent." She led the two men around the corner of the hospital to the supply tent. Inside the tent were boxes, barrels, and crates stacked five and six high. Stopping in the small clearing in the middle of these supplies, she turned to the two men.

"How may I help you, gentlemen?" she asked quizzically.

Major Mackenzie looked at General Grant. "Sir, I'll leave this to you. I'll wait with the horses. Good day, Mrs. Bickerdyke." Major Mackenzie left, dropping the tent flap as he exited.

Mary Ann looked with a raised brow at General Grant. He blushed slightly and looked down.

"Horse stepped on my foot a few days ago, ma'am. Throbs like the dickens. Major Mackenzie thought you might be able to do something that the cutters wouldn't think of."

She said, "The cutters, General?"

"The surgeons, ma'am. That's about all they seem able to do."

"Well, let's take a look at it, General. Take off that boot and your sock, if you've got one on," she said, suddenly all business.

Grant sat on a crate and winced as he pulled off his boot and sock. His foot was badly bruised, and the great toenail was dark purple and swollen. Mary Ann knelt down and put a small box under his foot. Pointing to his great toe, she said, "This looks very sore, General. Is this where it hurts the most?"

"Yes, ma'am," he replied.

"Well, I think we can fix that, General, if you don't mind a momentary unpleasantness. I'm going to have to make an opening in your nail to let the swelling go down. The rest of the damage just needs time to heal. Now, I need to get a few items. Wait here, please. I won't be long."

General Grant's eyes twinkled as he said, "Before you go, ma'am, I have, ah...heard...some things about you, Mrs. Bickerdyke. Something about...peaches?"

Over her shoulder, on the way out of the tent, Mary Ann said, "Ah, yes, peaches. It is well-known, General, that not everyone finds peaches agreeable."

❧❧

A few minutes later, Mary Ann returned with a tin cup full of coals from the fire, a long metal sewing needle stuck in them, and a clean cloth. Grant's eyes widened, and he retracted his foot from the small box on which it rested. Mary Ann knelt in front of him and put his foot back on the box.

Grant said, "Now, ah...ma'am, maybe I'd better just wait and let the surgeons take care of this."

"Not at all, General. I think you'll find my touch to be more gentle than a surgeon's. This will hurt just for a moment. I'm going to hold your foot tightly. Just relax. I'm told there's great relief to be had afterward. Tell me, General, is your family with you here at Fort Defiance?" As she said this, she quickly stabbed the red-hot needle in his toenail and then pulled it out. It sizzled. Grant jerked his foot back with a look of pain on his face that quickly changed to surprise.

He said, "Why, ma'am, I'm pleased to say your remedy works. It feels better already."

"Now, General, you'll need to keep this clean. It may drain for a few days—pus. Nothing to worry about. Change that sock at least once a week—and stay away from clumsy horses."

CHAPTER 9

The Demise of
Surgeon Banks

After Tom's recent disappearance, other soldiers pitched in to help cook for the men too weak or infirm to cook for themselves. Most of these volunteers had no experience, and the meals were rugged. The boys complained about sticks and rocks in the food and raw, rancid meat. The food itself was becoming a source of illness.

One afternoon the wind howled outside the hospital building. The sound of tent canvas snapping like sails on the high seas could be heard inside the hospital. A fire roared in the hearth and occasional gusts of smoke and embers blew back into the room. A detail of boys, assigned to put out the embers, rushed to hot spots with every gust.

Mary Ann, working among the sickest, helped a boy sit up and bathe. She knelt by his side with a white enamel basin of water, a crude bar of soap, and a drying cloth. As she helped him off with his shirt, the door at the back of the hospital opened. A cloud of dust and grit accompanied Surgeon Banks into the room. He slammed the door shut against the wind and brushed dirt off his greatcoat. He looked around, nodded to a few of the boys, and then walked to Mary Ann.

"A blustery day, Mrs. Bickerdyke," he said.

Looking up, Mary Ann greeted him and returned to her work.

He hesitated near her and then said, "When you have a moment, there's an issue we need to discuss."

"Of course, Surgeon Banks," she said. "But the work will never end. May we discuss this now?"

"Well, if we must. I was hoping to find Tom back in the diet kitchen today. I haven't seen him for several days, and the meals delivered to the surgeons have suffered terribly. Have you seen him, perchance?"

"Why, no. Not in days, sir. Do you think something has happened to him?"

Surgeon Banks sighed. "I fear poor old Tom has gone on another spree. He has been known to do so. Maybe he's fallen off the dock and drowned. If he were under the influence of strong drink, he might not have been able to save himself. Well, now it seems I must get someone to run the hospital kitchen. I was wondering—"

Mary Ann interrupted, "Why, sir, it would be an honor to help out in this time of need. I can run the diet kitchen and continue my work in the ward, if you would like."

With obvious relief, Surgeon Banks replied, "Thank you, madam. I will accept your proposal as the most expedient." He paused and looked down, breaking eye contact. "I know you and I have had our...disagreements, but...well, this is most gracious of you. Most gracious. You'll take on these duties today, then?"

Mary Ann continued to gently wash the soldier, and without looking up she said, "Of course."

"Thank you," Surgeon Banks said, and left the hospital.

Across the room a soldier began to laugh. Another asked, "What's so funny?"

The laughing soldier replied, "Oh, nothing I kin talk about."

❦

Since Mary Ann arrived, she had been cooking and feeding the most grievously ill men in the hospital. By officially assuming the duties of the diet kitchen, she became responsible for all the meals for the men in the Stables. She immediately drafted a group of soldiers to assist her. The quality of the food improved for both the patients and the surgeons. Then one day, while Mary Ann and two soldiers were kneading a huge mound of bread dough on a rough table outside the diet kitchen tent, an angry voice split the air.

"Where is she?"

The two soldiers stopped kneading, looked at each other, and then at her. With a sigh, Mary Ann stopped kneading dough and wiped her hands on her apron.

"It appears someone's looking for me," she said to them. "You boys keep at this, or there'll be no bread for supper. I'll go find out who's looking for me." She had walked a few feet away from the table, when a red-faced Surgeon Banks rounded the corner of the tent and faced her. Mary Ann looked at him inquisitively. There was total calmness in her demeanor. The two soldiers kneading bread stopped and watched, as the tension mounted. Surgeon Banks was overwhelmed with anger. His fists were tight at his side, his jaw clenched, and as he spoke, fine strands of spittle flew from his mouth.

"Mrs. Bickerdyke! What is going on here?"

Mary Ann smiled and said gently, "Why, good day, sir. We're—"

Surgeon Banks interrupted. "You have meddled enough, and I have had it! You have spent your last night here! I was passing the guardhouse this morning, and who do you suppose should hail me from the window? Tom the cook! And he said he was put there by you! You and your innocent act, taking over the diet kitchen! Well! We shall see about this!"

Surgeon Banks turned on his heel and strutted out. Mary Ann walked back to the dough table and said to the two soldiers there, "Come on, now, we can't stop working or the bread won't be ready when we need it."

One of the soldiers said, "Gee, ma'am, he sure seemed mad. You're in for it now."

Mary Ann formed a large ball of dough that she punched down with her fist. She smiled and said, "As he said, we shall see. We shall see."

By this time in their troubled relationship, Mary Ann was used to Surgeon Banks's threats and took them less seriously. She had also built up a reputation as a friend to the common soldier and an accomplished nurse, which the command staff valued highly.

An hour later, inside the provost marshal's tent, Surgeon Banks stood at attention with utter disbelief on his face.

"But," he whined, "you can't really believe—"

The provost marshal sat at his camp table, shuffling through some papers, and without looking up he interrupted Surgeon Banks.

"Oh, but I can, and I have! By order of General Sam Grant, as soon as your replacements arrive, you and your staff will be returning to the field for a little action." The provost marshal glared at Surgeon Banks. "In the meantime, Colonel Banks, do not interfere with Mrs. Bickerdyke in any way. Am I clear?"

"Clear, sir."

CHAPTER 10

Going Home—1861

Mary Ann stood on the dock, snug in her borrowed great-coat. Her carpetbag was by her feet. A winter wind tugged her skirts, and stray hairs flew chaotically around her bonnet. Steely light glinted off the river. With sadness in his face, Dr. Woodward stood by her, holding her hand and thanking her for her hard work at Fort Defiance. She listened to him through great exhaustion and a feeling of urgency to return home.

"Really, we could not have done it without you. You've made an amazing difference, and I am loathe to see you go. Would you please reconsider? Soon it will be Christmas, and these boys will need you more than ever."

"Dr. Woodward, I am very grateful that I could come and help you. But I missed Thanksgiving with my children, and I am worried about them. They have been shuffled from household to household, and their schooling has suffered. I need to find a better circumstance for them before I can consider continuing here." While she spoke softly and clearly to Dr. Woodward, her thoughts were on the hardships of her children and were darkened by the shadows of her own childhood losses. "Even so, the Reverend Beecher has written that he has a barn full of supplies that he'd like me to escort back. I just don't know...I must...I must think about it."

The riverboat's whistle sounded, drowning out the rest of her comment. At its shrill sound, Dr. Woodward picked up her carpetbag and escorted her up the gangway.

He again took her hand in both of his and said, "You will never know how much... If you can find it in your heart, please come back." He turned and walked quickly off the boat.

◑◑

As the riverboat docked in Galesburg, Mary Ann saw the Reverend Beecher in a carriage. He had come to meet her. On the drive back into town they talked about her time away and her children. The Reverend Beecher relayed his gratitude for her return and her willingness to personally escort supplies that the community had collected. There was much talk about supplies being left to rot at docksides or being diverted for nonmilitary uses. He also discussed his concern about her two boys. His daughter, the town's schoolteacher, had noticed some changes in the boys since Mary Ann left. One of the other children had reported that James had "used a bad word." The reverend found this most distressing. He felt a sense of responsibility toward her children, especially because it was through his urging that she had left for Cairo in the first place. He offered to speak with his daughter about watching over her boys.

"Perhaps, Mrs. Bickerdyke, your absence has resulted in undue harm to your boys. It has been difficult to find them a stable home. Their schooling has suffered. I take responsibility for this, and address you now as a dear friend and pastor. My daughter could help make things right here, and once you have settled in, I would like to speak with you about this in a little more detail. But right now, on to other matters. Dr. Woodward has sent wonderful reports of your selfless work at the hospital. Many in our community are grateful because you have cared for their or other mothers' sons. There are numerous stories of the dreadful treatment of the wounded and ill in the Union army. But my dear Mrs. Bickerdyke, I am so glad that you are here. You look very tired. If there is anything I can do to help you and your boys, I hope you will tell me. Ah! We're here. The O'Donovans have been caring for James and Hiram for about three weeks. Collect your little ones, and I'll drive you all to your house on Prairie Street. We've aired it out for your return."

The reverend pulled the carriage to a stop in front of a two-story white house, framed by a patch of dry yellow grass and skeletal trees. From around the corner of the house, drawn by the sound of the carriage, came a little boy. He saw who was in the carriage and stopped running for a moment. Then with a cry of, "Mommy!" he hurled himself toward Mary Ann.

She waited for the carriage to stop, and then jumped out, ran toward the child, and enfolded him in her arms.

"Why, Hiram, look how tall you've grown! You're almost a man. Mother has missed you so much. Ah, now, don't cry. I'm back, and you're too big now to cry. Where's your brother? I want—" She stopped, hearing James calling her from an upstairs window.

"Mother! You're back! Mother!" James said, and then he disappeared from the window and moments later ran out the front door and into her arms. "Oh, Mother, we have missed you so. You're finally back. You're going to stay, aren't you?"

"Now, James, my dear little Jimmy, we'll have time to talk about all of this later. Right now, I need to speak with the O'Donovans. You and Hiram need to go up and pack your things. The Reverend Beecher is going to take us to our house on Prairie Street."

Hiram, still snuggled in her arms, looked up at her and said, "Will Mary Elizabeth be there, too?"

The Reverend Beecher, who had left the carriage to stand close by and watch the reunion, said, "Yes, Hiram, Mary Elizabeth will be spending the night with you. You'll be a family again."

Mary Ann brushed the hair away from Jimmy's eyes, kissed Hi on the forehead, and said, "Now, go along, boys, and get your things. Mrs. O'Donovan and I need to have a word."

The carriage, packed with belongings and children, arrived at the old house on Prairie Street. Mary Elizabeth came out on the porch to greet her mother and brothers. The boys scrambled out of the carriage, dancing with glee to be home, whooping and hollering. Mary Elizabeth convulsed in laughter as she walked down the porch steps to hug them. The Reverend Beecher helped Mary Ann out of the carriage, and mother and daughter hugged each other tenderly.

"My beautiful daughter. You're a grown lady, on your own in the world. I am so glad you've come to greet us and spend the night. How I missed you, my little prairie flower."

The family walked inside the house while the Reverend Beecher unloaded the carriage. As they entered the hallway, they were met with the inviting aroma of a roasting turkey. Mary Ann looked quizzically at Mary Elizabeth.

Mary Elizabeth said, "The reverend kindly filled the larder. I put the turkey in early, so it would be ready for supper tonight. We'll have the Thanksgiving we missed."

Mary Ann's eyes filled with tears. Her heart overflowed with a sweet ache. She looked from Mary Elizabeth to the reverend, just coming in with the bags. "How can I thank you—both of you? This is such an unexpected kindness. Reverend, would you like to stay for dinner? Collect your wife and come back? We would be honored."

"No, Mrs. Bickerdyke. You must have a lot to talk about with your family. Take these first two days and spend them with your children. We'll talk on Wednesday. And now, I must be going. Mrs. Schmidt has been abed for several days with the ague, and I thought I would stop by on my home."

In the dining room the fire crackled in the stone hearth. Both the wood-paneled walls and the floor had been scrubbed to a shine. Jimmy used a poker to roll the blackened potatoes over to one side of the coals, next to corn on the cob, which was wrapped tightly in blackened corn husks. Biscuits baked in a Dutch oven nestled in the midst of the coals. A bowl of raisins and dried apples sat on the polished wooden table. The places were set with plain pottery dishes. Lighted candles on the table and the mantel cast a warm golden glow on the tiny dining room, highlighting patches of cranberry colors in the old woven rug. A bowl of wild raspberry jam glistened like rubies in the light. In the center of the table, next to a pitcher of fresh milk, sat a jar transformed from old into beautiful by a bouquet of dried wildflowers. The dining room opened onto the kitchen, where Mary Ann and Mary Elizabeth carved the turkey and scooped out the corn bread stuffing. Hiram stood waiting to take the bowl of stuffing to the table.

The dinner lasted well into the night, with Hiram and James relating their adventures at each of the households where they had lived. There were hilarious tales of hide-and-seek, cowboys and Indians, squirrel hunting, and riding cows. Mary Elizabeth told her story of life on her own for the first time, finding a roommate and a place to stay, where she could begin a business as a seamstress. All the children's stories reopened the doors to Mary Ann's family life, and then back into her childhood. She recalled her life with her grandparents and her uncle, and how difficult the transitions had been for her. She had always left a place feeling that she had been an unwanted burden and helpless to change that.

Then the three children asked Mary Ann about her work with the soldiers. She told them about meeting Mary Safford and about starting the laundry together. She told them about working alongside Dr. Woodward.

The boys wanted to know about the guns and the cannon. Mary Elizabeth was more curious about little Mary Safford and how she began her career in the army.

Mary Ann felt quite enlivened as she told her children about the work she had been doing at Fort Defiance. This was a puzzlement to her because she had expected to feel terrible telling her children about what had kept her from them.

Little Hiram began to look sleepy and said, "Mommy, you're going to stay home now, aren't you?"

"We'll talk about that tomorrow, Hi. Now, Mary Elizabeth, Jimmy, and I have a lot of work to put the kitchen in order before we can go to sleep. Enough stories for now. I'll tell you more tomorrow. Off to bed with you, Hiram. Who wants to wash and who will dry?"

The next day, the family gathered in the backyard; Hiram and Jimmy played ball while Mary Elizabeth and Mary Ann, wrapped in coats and shawls against the chill breeze, sat on the back porch in rocking chairs.

Mary Elizabeth said, "Are you home to stay, Mother?"

"No, child, I'm not. This is but a brief visit. The Reverend Beecher has gathered much-needed supplies that I'm to take back to Dr. Woodward. There is still much to be done at Fort Defiance."

"I've been reading the newspapers and listening to the talk at the town hall," said Mary Elizabeth. "Conditions sound terrible. This is a horrible war—Mrs. Crowley was notified that her son was killed last week. I fear what will happen if the war does not end soon. But, I am proud that you are there. I know you can help those soldiers."

"Thank you, dear. I am very concerned about all of you. You're strong and understand that I must leave, but the boys...I don't know how to tell them I'll be leaving soon. I don't think they'll understand. I don't want to hurt them again or make them feel angry or bad."

Mary Elizabeth responded, "They've been moved around so much. That's a big part of the problem. The townsfolk have treated them as well as they can, but there's no one stable in their life—no one like you. It's very hard on them without you."

Mary Ann replied, "I know, dear, but I have to trust that the needs of my boys can be met by the good people of Galesburg. The needs I have seen elsewhere are huge, and they cannot be met without great effort. The Reverend Beecher said he would talk to his daughter, Samantha, about having the boys move in with her. But I don't know how long she can take them. He and I will talk tomorrow."

"I'll help you tell the boys. When are you planning on leaving?"

"Friday morning. I have a ticket on the boat, and space has been reserved for the supplies."

"How long will you be gone?" Mary Elizabeth's voice betrayed her concern and fear.

"Honestly, dear, I don't know. I have every intention of coming home to celebrate Christmas with you all, but nothing is certain. If the war ends, I'll be home for good. But if it progresses, how long it might be...I don't know. I feel like I belong there in a way that I've never felt before. And I know it isn't quite right, but you and the boys have all these good people around you, and the supplies required to meet your needs. Your lives are predictable and safe. You are growing up the way I did. It could be happier, but it will do for a while. Those young men are away from home— some for the very first time—and have very little. They need me. Jimmy and Hi are safe, and they can get along without me. They have you, the Reverend Beecher, and some good people of the congregation. Mary Elizabeth, there are no other trained nurses at the hospital, and I feel a terrible responsibility because of that. Those boys have nothing and no one to help them."

After a pause, she continued, "And, there is another concern, dear. I'm not being paid for the work I'm doing with the army, and I'm not sure how long my little savings will last. The congregation has been very generous, as has the

Reverend Beecher, but I don't know how long we can count on that. If the war continues, there may be much sacrifice and poverty across the land. If we can no longer afford this house, we must let it go. I hope to have found a permanent place for the boys long before that time."

"It sounds like you think you'll be gone a very long time, Mother," said Mary Elizabeth, turning away to hide her tears. She desperately wanted to be brave and not disappoint her mother.

CHAPTER 11

The Decision

In early December 1861, Mary Ann returned to Cairo with mixed feelings and several crates of supplies. The soldiers in the Stables arranged for a concert to welcome her back. Members of the band who had been serving as nurses in the hospital took up their instruments and played several lively tunes while the patients who could gave her a standing ovation. Little Mary Safford was there, waiting to greet her friend and mentor.

After putting her things away and arranging for soldiers to store the supplies, Mary Ann took Mary Safford into her tent, where they talked about what had happened since Mary Ann had left. Mary Safford was thin and pale, with large dark circles under her eyes. She seemed fragile and worn. She had aged far beyond her chronological years.

"Dear," Mary Ann said, "you look so tired. Have you been getting enough sleep?" She focused on the practical as she experienced a growing sense of alarm about how she might have injured little Mary by expecting too much from her. It was hard for Mary Ann to remember that Mary was still a child, because she was so capable and was the only person on whom Mary Ann could rely.

"Oh, Mother. I didn't want to be the one to tell you this, but Jeremiah died while you were gone. He went peacefully. His fever was so high that we couldn't get him cool. We even put him in the river, but that didn't help. I know he was a favorite of yours."

Mary Ann nodded, looking down. "Thank you for telling me." There was silence. Then Mary Ann continued, "You look ill, child. Maybe this work is too much to ask of such a young girl."

"Oh, no, Mother! I am of use here—I must stay. Every day I feel that this confirms my intent to become a doctor."

"But, Mary, can't you see what a price you're paying? Your health, dear. It's not—"

A soldier outside the tent interrupted, "Mother? Are you there? Private Santis is yelling and screaming, and seems out of his head. Can you come and take a look at him?"

"Mary, dear, lie down here and rest. I'll see to this," said Mary Ann. "Son, you go on and get the surgeon. I'll go to Private Santis and wait for you."

After Mary Ann left the tent, little Mary threw herself on her cot and cried.

❧

The next afternoon, Mary Ann and Dr. Woodward met in his office at the hospital. He was delighted to see her and asked about her trip home and her family. Her face clouded with sadness as she told him of her recent parting from her children. He reached over and touched her hand.

With great concern in his voice, he said, "What an enormous sacrifice you are making to do this work. I can't tell you how much your presence is appreciated. In fact, that's why I've asked to see you. What I am about to say must be kept in strict confidence. It comes from the highest authority here at Fort Defiance. As you know, the battle at Belmont resulted in several hundred wounded that sorely tried our hospitals, which were already full of sick men. I have been told to prepare for a major campaign that will happen soon, possibly with many thousands of casualties. I am going to need you here. The Union soldiers are going to need you here. I have asked to meet with you today to beg you to continue your work here at the hospitals and not to leave again—at least in the foreseeable future. I know you're very concerned about your children, and if it would help, I'll write the Reverend Beecher myself and tell him how important it is for you to be here."

Mary Ann sat quietly for a few moments with her eyes downcast. Finally, she shifted in her chair and looked directly into Dr. Woodward's eyes. "You ask a great deal of me. And while you have asked me to stay on several times, I will need to think about this."

"Of course, Mrs. Bickerdyke. Of course."

Mary Ann and Dr. Woodward stood. She moved toward the door. He opened it and gave her a slight bow. "Until tomorrow, Mrs. Bickerdyke. Thank you."

She felt caught in a web. If she stayed, she betrayed her children. If she left, she betrayed the soldiers who had come to depend on her. She felt called to this new work of army nursing in an almost religious way. This was the Lord's work. Her own congregation confirmed this.

That evening, Lemuel Santis's condition worsened—his fever raged, and his skin erupted with pustules and a foul drainage oozed from them, soaking his blanket. He screamed for his mother. Mary Ann hastened to his side, where she cradled his head in her lap and wiped his brow with a cold cloth. She spent the entire night at his side, as his fever fluctuated. At one point she had ice brought from the refrigerator to be placed on his chest and groin in an attempt to cool him down. Just before dawn, he began to speak in a raspy voice. Through cracked and bleeding lips he said, "Oh, Mother, thank God you're here. You brought me into this world and now you can see me into the next. It is you, Mother, isn't it? I have longed to see you before I die." He looked up at Mary Ann, but his eyes were glazed and seemed to be looking at something very far in the distance.

Mary Ann tilted the lamp away from her face and said, "Yes, my son. I am here. You are not alone." And she began to pray softly. At first light, he slipped into a coma; she stayed with him until he died. She gently closed his eyes, covered him with his blanket, and then stood up. Several of the patients had been watching her through the night, and a hush fell over the hospital, which should have been noisy with the sounds of morning. Mary Ann walked to one of the soldier-nurses and said, "Take him. I will write to his mother."

The soldier nodded, "Yes, ma'am. Will you be helping with the baths today?"

Shaking her head slowly, she said, "Not today—if you can manage without me." Not waiting for his response, she left the ward, her heart on the very edge of a sadness that scared her.

Exhausted, Mary Ann returned to her tent, but she could not sleep. She sat on her cot with her head in her hands, her thoughts jumbled. She remembered the feverish face of Lemuel Santis, and then she thought of her little Hiram and his excited face when he saw her. Her mind turned to Mary Safford, her face tired and thin, obviously drained by the work she had been doing. Finally, she thought of Dr. Woodward's face, so full of hope and respect. At that moment she had no sense of herself or her future. She had no recognition of what her own face looked like.

◉◉

Hours passed as she struggled with her feelings. Then, slowly, she rose from the cot, sat at the camp table, and began to write a letter to her children.

> Dearest Children:
>
> I was so happy to see you in such good health on my recent visit. I am glad you can take care of each other in these hard times while I am gone. I have arranged with Dr. Woodward to purchase a new pair of boots for you, Jimmy. You should go to the Reverend Beecher because he will know about this and will help you. There is a roll

of silk in the top drawer of the sideboard. Please give it to Mary Elizabeth. Perhaps she can sew something with it and earn a bit of money.

I have made a decision to stay at Fort Defiance until just before Christmas, when I will return home. We will have Christmas together as a family, but then if the war continues, I have agreed to return to the hospital. I am working very hard to find a stable situation for you. As we discussed before I left, Samantha Beecher will look after you until the end of the year.

Keep up your schoolwork and remember to always say your prayers. I love you.

With fond affection,

M. A. Bickerdyke

Later that night, an exhausted Mary Ann lay on her cot, hoping for a few moments of peaceful unconsciousness. She dreamt she was holding the hand of the dying Lemuel, but his face was gray and shadowy. As she looked closer, she saw his face transform into that of her son Hiram. She screamed and dropped his hand, and then suddenly saw herself as a little girl standing at her grandmother's casket. Someone held her up so she could see the wizened face of her grandmother, now a waxy white in death. But her grandmother's hands were bloody and bruised. Mary Ann awoke abruptly to find her pillow wet with tears.

CHAPTER 12

Scavenging the Laundry

In late January 1862, snow flurries swirled around the tents and buildings at Fort Defiance. The fort was chaotic as soldiers in heavy woolen coats readied their equipment for transport down the river, where they expected an imminent battle. Troops drilled on the parade ground with a new urgency. A layer of ice crunched under their boots as they marched, and their breath steamed in the crisp air.

Inside his office, Dr. Woodward and Mary Ann discussed plans to follow the troops downriver. They huddled near the small camp stove that warmed only a tiny area of the office.

"I'm not sure this has ever happened before—a woman accompanying a hospital ship to care for the wounded after a battle. I wasn't sure how you'd take such a suggestion. But, General Grant asked for you, personally. The hospital ship—it's called the *City of Memphis*—will be arriving in Cairo sometime in the next few days. You must stock it quickly with whatever you think you'll need. I don't know how many wounded to expect. Grant plans on taking Fort Henry and Fort Donelson, and both are well defended. It will probably be a river battle, which means that you will not be able to get to the wounded until the river is secured by Union forces. A small number of surgeons will set up a field hospital before the battle. Your responsibility will be to care for the men from the field hospital. They will wait for transport by the dock. This is going to be extremely difficult. I am not going with you, and even though General Grant has requested your presence, most army commanders will not expect or approve of a woman on board a hospital ship. There may be trouble. Do your best and we'll sort it out afterward. You have my full support."

Mary Ann nodded, "I'll do my best. Now, Doctor, I have a request of you. I need a driver—a strong, healthy soldier to help me load and unload supplies, and to help me with the laundry and whatever else I need. I need someone who will take orders only from me, and who will be with me wherever I go. I've been using the strongest of my patients, but it's not enough. They try very hard to do as I ask, but I need someone fit on whom I can rely without question."

Dr. Woodward looked thoughtfully at Mary Ann. "Well, Mrs. Bickerdyke, every able-bodied man is needed for the field of battle now. I will ask for you, but don't get your hopes up."

❦

On February 6, federal gunboats took Fort Henry; this gave the Union control of the Cumberland and Tennessee Rivers. Even the weather seemed to celebrate, with a short unseasonably warm spell that melted the snow and caused soldiers to abandon their heavy coats, tents, and backpacks. Seven days later, as the battle for Fort Donelson began, the weather changed to bitter cold. Fort Donelson was an earthen fort under the command of Confederate Brigadier General Pillow. Shortly before the battle, other troops under the commands of Brigadier Generals Floyd and Buckner joined Pillow's men as reinforcements. Grant marched his army from Fort Henry to Donelson, but found the Confederate defenses too strong to breach. Eventually, Brigadier General Wallace's men from Fort Henry arrived to strengthen Grant's army and to outnumber the Southern troops by ten thousand men. The battle was fought with gunboats on the river and troops on the ground. Generals Pillow and Floyd anticipated defeat and withdrew their men from the fort under cover of darkness, leaving General Simon Bolivar Buckner to negotiate the terms of surrender with Grant. On February 16, Buckner surrendered Fort Donelson to Grant. Twelve thousand Confederate soldiers were made prisoners of war, and because of this success, Grant was later promoted to major general. Grant and Buckner had been West Point classmates. After the surrender, the two men relaxed in conversation with drinks and cigars.

⚭

Mary Ann left the port of Cairo on the riverboat *City of Memphis*, heavily laden with supplies to care for the wounded. By the time the hospital ship was allowed access to the dock below Fort Donelson, a heavy blanket of snow lay on the ground.

For several days, Mary Ann tended both Union and Confederate casualties streaming in from the field hospital. At night, she haunted the battlefield, looking for soldiers who might be dying alone in the freezing mud. After most of the boys had been cared for and safely housed aboard the hospital ship, Mary Ann started to look for ways to keep her boys warm. She returned to the battlefield to scavenge for anything she might be able to use.

That night, Colonel Logan, wrapped in his greatcoat and still shivering, stood in the doorway of Union headquarters at Fort Donelson using a field glass to scan the battlefield. He mumbled to himself, "Now what is she doing?" Raising his voice, he called, "Corporal!"

The corporal responded, "Sir!"

"What is going on up there on that battlefield?"

The corporal answered, "It's that nurse again, sir. You remember the one."

"I remember. But what is she up to now? I told her to go home."

"Sir, something about a laundry. She's gathering up the clothes left on the field. Says she's going to wash them and keep her boys warm with them."

Colonel Logan looked with disbelief at the corporal. "Wash them? What's wrong with her? Doesn't she know that anything left on the field is soaked with blood and crawling with vermin? It's only fit to be burned!"

❦

Up on the battlefield, Mary Ann and a contingent of soldiers picked up discarded clothing, stiff with snow and blood, and piled it on wagons.

"Remember, men," Mary Ann said, "keep the best aside for the wounded. Put the rest into the crates."

One of the soldiers asked, "Ma'am, do you want us to pick up what Johnny Reb left?"

"All of it, please. It will warm one of our boys in a few short days, God be willing."

The soldier leaned over and picked up a butternut-colored homespun shirt. The front was torn and stiff with blood. He mused, "I guess Johnny Reb bleeds, too."

❦

The next morning, Mary Ann shivered on the make-shift dock on the Cumberland River below Fort Donelson. Several wagons were lined up for unloading at the dock, heaped with clothing retrieved from the battlefield. Soldiers took armloads of the clothing and packed them into crates. After the soldiers filled crates, they nailed on wooden tops. The *City of Memphis* crew was busy readying the boat for the trip to Cairo.

When the lid of the last crate was nailed shut, Mary Ann asked, "Is that the last of it? Good. Private, did you bring the paint? Excellent. Paint my name on each box, and next to it paint *Cairo*. Then have the boys load them on the boat. The captain says we can use the top deck, so stack the crates wherever they'll fit."

The private stood in a canyon of crates with a paint-brush and a bucket of whitewash. He said to himself, "Glad I ain't the one who gets to open 'em. By the time they get to Cairo they'll be ripe."

A few days later, on a cold, clear, sunny day, the *City of Memphis* docked at Cairo. After the boat was secured, the ill and wounded soldiers were evacuated to the hospitals at Fort Defiance. Mary Ann stood on the deck with the boat's captain.

"I'm just glad it's not a hot summer's day." The cap-tain nodded toward the crates, and said, "These smell bad enough now, but the smell would be intolerable in the sum-mer. Mrs. Bickerdyke, the next time you ask a favor of me, I'm going to be far more careful in answering."

"Captain, you are most kind. These will someday pro-vide warmth and comfort for our boys. And the good Lord said, 'Waste not, want not.' Perhaps you should be far more careful in responding to this request, but I shall ask one more favor."

The captain smiled. "Is this favor going to smell bad?"

Mary Ann smiled and looked down. "Not at all." She pulled a letter out of her dress pocket and handed it to the captain. "Would you please see that this letter gets posted as soon as possible? If I'm to expand my laundry, I'll need pots and soap. I'm hoping the Sanitary Commission in Chicago will be generous enough to provide them."

The captain smiled and put the letter in his breast pocket. "Of course, madam. Now, if you will allow me, I'll see that the crew unloads these crates."

The major form of treatment in the field hospitals was limb amputation. Soldiers unlucky enough to have wounds to the chest or abdomen received little or no treatment at the field hospitals beyond having these wounds roughly packed to stop the bleeding. The swelling of the brain caused by penetrating head wounds was treated with a hastily performed trephine—drilling a hole in the skull to release pressure. Opening the head usually resulted in high mortality from infection. With their acute wounds tended, soldiers were moved to post hospitals.

Back at Fort Defiance, the hospitals were overwhelmed by the number of wounded from the two battles. At the Stables, soldiers were shoulder to shoulder inside the building and tents, and several hundred men were outside without shelter. There was an unending din of moaning. The surgeons quickly ran out of painkillers, and brandy was substituted. Surgical dressings ran short, and those wounded who were able used any cloth they could find as bandages. Food supplies were inadequate. The mortality rate was dreadful. Those who didn't die from their wounds or blood loss faced a slower death from infection or pneumonia.

Mary Ann spent several frenzied weeks tending to the wounded; with promises of meals, she recruited soldiers to help her tend "her boys." Mary Safford was a constant assistant. The workload slowly eased, as those with mortal injuries succumbed and the others improved. The burden of work shifted from caretakers to burial teams.

Finally, Mary Ann had the time to turn her attention to the stack of crates shipped from the battles of Fort Henry and Fort Donelson. She thought she could salvage cloth from the crates for more bandages and use whatever was left for bedding. One morning, three privates and a sergeant walked over to the forty-two wooden crates stacked against the outer wall of the quartermaster's warehouse. The sun shone on the crates, and a foul smell emanated from them. Some of the lower boxes appeared to be oozing a brown liquid through the wood slats. A stray dog rounded the corner of the warehouse and stopped to sniff the crates with interest. He lifted his leg, pissed on one, and then wandered off. Several flatbed wagons were lined up near the crates. The horses swished their tails to keep the flies off themselves.

One of the privates looked at the sergeant and said, "No, sir! Not those boxes. I ain't a-gonna get near them things. They're a-leakin' and a-stinkin'."

The second private agreed, "Yes, sir. They be full of somethin' dreadful bad."

The sergeant was unmoved. "I don't care if they be full of the black death, soldier! The lady wants them loaded on wagons and moved closer to the river. That order comes from the general himself. Now, get moving, or you'll find yourselves under arrest!"

The first private stretched and dusted off his uniform. "Sooner work in the dead house. Can we wear gloves, Sarge?"

The sergeant grew more irritated. "You can wear ladies' dresses for all I care. Get moving."

The three privates moved reluctantly toward the boxes. The third private grumbled to himself as he looked over his shoulder at the sergeant, "Yeah, yeah. I don't espy you grabbin' up any of them boxes."

The second private muttered, "Now they got us movin' crates of maggots covered in dog piss. 'Tain't enough we get shot at..."

The crates were loaded on the wagons and driven to the river's edge, where Mary Ann and a lieutenant were already supervising the unpacking of three large wooden boxes marked with USSC. The soldiers broke apart the three boxes, exposing huge iron kettles.

"Oh, well, I had hoped for more than just three, but we'll make do with these. Boys, fill them with water from the river and set them to boiling. Wood the fires well. I want these kettles boiling the whole time. Now, that last crate there?"

Mary Ann pointed to a smaller crate. "That should be the lye soap. Put plenty in each kettle." Then she looked at the lieutenant. "Are you sure the contrabands are coming?"

The lieutenant looked around the area and replied, "Yes, ma'am. A half dozen or so said they would be here."

At that moment, a ragged group of several dozen black men and a few black women came into view, walking toward them along the riverbank. The lieutenant said, "Ah. Here they are now."

"Excellent timing!" Mary Ann replied. "Have the men unload the remaining crates from the wagons and leave them by those two pots. Then have them take the lids off."

The lieutenant said, "Of course, ma'am." Addressing the privates, he said, "You heard the lady. Get on with it." Then the lieutenant turned to the contrabands. "Moses, is that you?"

The oldest of the black men walked up to the lieutenant and said, "Yassir! It's me!"

The lieutenant said, "Mrs. Bickerdyke, this here is Moses. He and his friends have volunteered to help you empty the crates and boil up the kettles. They all say they've worked in a laundry before."

Mary Ann looked directly at Moses. "Is that true, Mr. Moses?"

He nodded. "Yas, ma'am. I brung my wife. She kin hep out, too. We's all worked in launderin' before."

Mary Ann said, "Mr. Moses, you understand I cannot pay you?"

"Yas, ma'am. Soldiers say you feed us, though."

"Yes, Mr. Moses. I can feed all of you if you help me with this work. Work first—then eat."

Mr. Moses nodded enthusiastically. "We kin do dat. Oh, yas, work firs and den eat."

"Mr. Moses, inside those boxes over there are the blankets, dressings, and uniforms left on the battlefield at Fort Donelson. I want what's inside those crates boiled in these two pots, until all the vermin and filth are gone. Can you do that? It will not be a pleasant task. Those boxes were packed with dirty clothes some time ago."

Mr. Moses replied, "Oh, missus, we can boil dem clothes up—tha's for certain. No worry they was packed up dirty. We can clean 'em fer ya."

Mary Ann said, "The fires are getting hot. There's soap and water in those two kettles. There's only water in that one. Once the water boils, wash twice, and then rinse in that pot. Pile the clothes over there, and give them a final rinse in the river. Then the women can wring the water out and hang the clothing to dry on those bushes." She pointed to several huge leafless willow bushes along the river's edge. "When you're working with the boiling kettles, Mr. Moses, use the long poles. The water will get very hot, and it won't do for you to get burned."

As she said this, she remembered the night many years ago, when she was a little girl, coming down the stairs to find her father leaning over her mother. Her mother was lying on the floor by the fireplace, her dress soaked and steaming. An empty kettle smoked on its side by her. Her mother's face and hands were scalded a bright red, and huge blisters were forming. Mary Ann was too little to understand why her mother was lying down by the kettle. But she knew it was very bad when neighbors came and carried her upstairs to bed, and the women were crying. Mary Ann never saw her mother again. From that time on, she always believed boiling water was a terrible danger.

She shook off this memory and said to Mr. Moses, "Any questions?"

The lieutenant said, "My men will have the lids off those crates real soon, ma'am."

Mr. Moses said, "No questions, ma'am."

The three privates were busy prying the lids off the crates with crowbars. Inside each crate was a foul mass of cloth, red gelatinous substances, and writhing maggots.

Mr. Moses looked down inside the closest crate. "You sure, ma'am, you's wanting us to boil this?"

Without looking in the crate, Mary Ann said, "Yes. I am absolutely certain."

The pots were steaming. Moses and Mary Ann stood by the first kettle as men used long poles to move the cloth from kettle to kettle. By the time the laundry reached the second kettle, the articles of clothing had begun to disintegrate. When the material was finally pulled out of the last pot, it resembled neither clothing nor blankets but a wad of gummy fiber. The water in the kettles was covered with yellow foam.

Mr. Moses, his face showing something between wonder and disgust, said to Mary Ann, "Ma'am, dis here is powerful strange laundry you got here, to change shirts and blankets into dees lumps."

Mary Ann looked with concern at the mass of fiber the women were draping and stringing onto bushes. She said, "Hmm, Mr. Moses. I wasn't expecting this...however, we shall proceed. From now on, have one of your helpers skim off the yellow foam, the maggots, and the lice, before you transfer the laundry to the next pot."

Mr. Moses replied, "Yas, missus, we kin do dat. We be needin' to dump dat firs water, I 'spect, before it gets to be stew."

Mary Ann paled a bit. "Yes, I'm guessing so, too. But, luckily, we have plenty of soap and water. It's just going to make this an all-day project." She sighed. "I suppose it can't be helped. Pour it out in the river downstream, Mr. Moses." Mary Ann looked at the laundry operation before her. "Do you have this laundry under control, Mr. Moses?"

"Yas, ma'am. An if I hab questions I kin ax da soldier dere."

"Yes, or you can ask him to get me. I'll be back at the hospital, catching up on my chores there. Otherwise, I'll see you at four o'clock, with supper for you and your helpers."

Several hours later, Mary Ann returned to the makeshift laundry in a small wagon driven by a soldier. The wagon was jammed with baskets of bread and a huge pot of soup. The driver helped Mary Ann down, and she walked toward the boiling pots and the contrabands. She looked anxiously at the bushes surrounding the entire laundry area, over which tattered fibers were draped like a huge, chaotic spider web. Moses approached her.

"Afternoon, ma'am. You comin' at de right time. Looky see at dis work we done. All dem boxes git emptied today, fo sure. But we ain't got one shirt outta da lot."

Mary Ann said, "Yes, so I see." She walked to the bushes where the laundry was spread to dry. She picked up a piece of the matted fiber and moved it between her thumb and fingers. A look of disgust crossed her face.

Mr. Moses continued, "Mostly old rags, ma'am. Come clean apart in de kettles."

Mary Ann looked disappointed and said, "Well, Mr. Moses, you've done a good job getting them clean. And we shall not waste what we have. These pieces will make do for lint or padding in the surgery." She turned back to him with renewed energy. "So, Mr. Moses, are you ready for dinner?"

"Yas, missus!" he said eagerly. "We all worked hard and are powerful hungry."

Mary Ann said, "Well then, get your people together and go wash up in the river. I've a hot vegetable soup here, plenty of bread, and some dried apples. I hope you'll be back tomorrow. I want you to meet the supervisor of my hospital laundry, Mary Safford. I'd like to continue the use of your services. The more wounded we get, the more laundry there is. We could use your continued assistance."

Five days later, inside a hospital ward at Fort Defiance, Mary Ann held a large basket of laundered cloth and was arguing with a surgeon.

The surgeon said, "I don't care. I have no use whatsoever for these. Not as bandages or lint or padding or as anything else."

Mary Ann replied, "But, Doctor, you need them. You have nothing to pack your patients' wounds with."

The surgeon became furious that his judgment was questioned. His face reddened and he raised his voice. "Burn them, Mrs. Bickerdyke! I would sooner do without. Now, get out of here. I have doctor's work to attend to and can't afford to waste another moment on your nonsense."

"Very well, Doctor," she replied brusquely. "But when this war grows past our resources, you will sorely need what you so arrogantly turn down today."

The surgeon pointed at the door and bellowed at the top of his lungs, "Out!"

Mary Ann turned to leave with her basket, saying to herself, "Grant me patience, O Lord, or I shall surely—" Before she could finish, a soldier approached her in haste.

"Mrs. Bickerdyke?" he asked.

"Yes?"

"A letter for you, ma'am, from General Grant." The soldier handed her the letter, tipped his hat and left.

Mary Ann put her basket down and opened the letter. She read:

> Mrs. Bickerdyke,
> I understand you requested a driver be assigned to you for the duration of the war. Your request has been a cause of some consternation at headquarters. But, I am still working on this. Do not give up hope.
> Yours,
> U. S. Grant

Mary Ann smiled, folded the letter and put it in her pocket, and then picked up the basket and walked on.

CHAPTER 13

The *Fanny Bullet*

April washed into Cairo with a blinding rain. The camp was sunk in mud and alive with activity. Soldiers packed their gear and struck their tents, in preparation for a major assault on the Rebel stronghold near Savannah, Tennessee. Soldiers, already massed on the shore and dock, waited their turn to board gunboats to take them downriver. Long lines of sodden men walked from the harbor staging area onto several boats. One gunboat had its name written in faded red letters on its bow, the *Fanny Bullet*.

A sergeant stood near the top of the gangplank to the *Fanny Bullet*. In a slicker and with rain pouring down the front of his slouch hat, he looked down at a clipboard and checked off names with a pencil. Each soldier boarding stated his name, rank, and company. The sergeant found the soldier's name and checked it off. Then, without looking up, he bellowed, "Next!"

A feminine voice responded, "Mrs. Mary Ann Bickerdyke, nurse, Twenty-first Illinois Volunteers."

The sergeant looked up, startled. "What the...? Oh! Mother, it's you! What are you doing here? We're on our way to a big battle, ma'am. This is a gunboat, not a hospital ship."

Mary Ann stepped closer to the sergeant. "Well, it's a lucky thing for this army that I don't require a hospital boat to work in, isn't it? This gunboat will do fine, young man. Now let me pass. You have hundreds more men to get on this ship today, and I have work to do."

The sergeant looked bewildered. "But, ma'am, my orders are fighting men only. You can't—"

"Of course I can," she interrupted. "Don't worry. I'll be fine. Your General Grant needs me, and he'll vouch for me. There are no hospital ships heading down there, so this boat will have to do. Now, Sergeant, I'm going to get out of this rain. You get back to work. Can't have these boys standing in the wet and cold all day or they won't be fit to fight. Oh, by the way, I had a few crates loaded this morning. They're in the hold. Things I'll need. They're marked with my name. Thank you, son."

With her carpetbag in hand, Mary Ann moved past the sergeant, who looked after her, shaking his head. As the next soldier approached, Mary Ann found her way inside the boat and sat against some crates filled with guns. She was visibly trembling after her boldness with the sergeant. She had not been sure if she should go headlong into a battle, and if so, how she was to get there. She had hoped her fearless appearance would help her board the boat, but she really had no idea of what was to come. And the stresses that made the soldiers on board either too loud or too quiet quickly infected her—Mary Ann was terrified.

A light rain fell as the *Fanny Bullet* was off-loaded at the Savannah dock. Soldiers massed by the hundreds and marched off to a staging area. Mary Ann stood on the dock, motioning to several soldiers on deck who hoisted a huge crate labeled *M. A. Bickerdyke* and *Laundry*. She yelled over the din of the dockside chaos, "Yes, that's the one! There's one more. Find it and bring them both down here."

Her bonnet, waterlogged with the rain, drooped sadly around her face. Wet strands of gray hair were plastered to the back of her neck. Water ran in rivulets down the folds of her woolen cape, and her shoes sank into the mud of the earthen dock. She turned and scanned the long line of wagons entering the loading area on the corduroy road, until she saw the Sanitary Commission insignia. She raised her hand high and hailed the driver. On the seat of a large flatbed wagon pulled by two draft horses sat a man bundled against the weather. He returned her wave, pulled the wagon closer to the dock, secured the reins, and jumped down.

As he walked toward her, she said, "Are you from the Sanitary Commission? I have crates....," and she gestured toward the *Fanny Bullet*.

"Yes, ma'am. I'm the only wagon they allowed down here. Drivers of other Sanitary Commission wagons are still trying to find a boat to bring them down the river. When they finally arrive they should be full of supplies. But this is all we have right now. Here, let me get you out of this rain. Be careful, the first step is high."

"Thank you, sir, but you mustn't fuss."

He lifted her effortlessly onto the seat and pulled an umbrella from under it. He opened it and handed it to her. "Sorry. It's a little bent, but it'll do. I'll go see to the loading of the crates."

When he returned to the wagon, he asked, "Where to, ma'am?"

Mary Ann was still dabbing her face with her handkerchief in an effort to appear presentable. "Let's go to the army hospital on the outskirts of Savannah. We'll see if they can use a nurse."

A half hour later, the rain had stopped. The driver sat quietly in the wagon outside the military hospital headquarters on the edge of Savannah. The horses patiently shifted their weight from hoof to hoof. The driver winced at the loud voice booming from inside the building.

"Under *no* circumstances whatsoever! We neither want nor need the services of a woman here! It is a failure of good judgment for you to be here at all. I don't care who will vouch for you."

There was a moment of quiet. At the doorway, a red-faced older man appeared, hustling Mary Ann out the door and down the stairs. From the bottom of the stairs, she said with cold anger, "Very well, then. I will take shelter in Savannah and nurse the soldiers of the regular army. You may be able to bar me from your hospital, but you cannot prevent me from doing my work!"

She turned in a whirl of wet calico and wool and stomped over to the wagon. The driver saw her coming and was there to assist her onto the seat.

Mary Ann said, "Doesn't need me, indeed!" Then she paused, and in a modulated tone said, "Thank you, sir. It seems I'll be needing rooms in town for a bit. Are there any Christian Commission agents in Savannah who would help set up a diet kitchen and a laundry?"

The driver snapped the reins, and the wagon moved off toward the heart of Savannah.

Mary Ann continued, "There must be contrabands in town who can help. Maybe you can find them for me. And we'll need to rustle up a few farmers willing to trade eggs and milk for some of the supplies I brought. Then we'll have to make do until the commission can get its supply boat down here—probably in a week, or maybe more. So, anything you can forage will be useful."

The driver replied thoughtfully, "Yes, ma'am. I'll scout around and see what I can do."

❧❧

Over the next few days, Mary Ann established a diet kitchen on the edge of the army encampment, and her laundry began to bloom on the riverbank. She also set up a tent to serve as her clinic headquarters.

One afternoon, a long line of soldiers snaked through the barracks toward the entrance of her clinic. Inside, Mary

Ann sat at a table made from a door balanced on two barrels. Behind her were baskets of hard-boiled eggs, jams, jellies, canned meats, and root vegetables scrounged from the local farmers. Inside the tent, several weary soldiers lay on the ground, covered with blankets.

"Come to the light at the entrance, son. I need to look in your mouth," she said to the soldier at the head of the line. "Sure enough. It's all swollen, and you have bleeding around your teeth. You need some pickles, son, or some vinegar. Fresh greens would do, too. I have a barrel of pickled potatoes back in my room. If you'll go with me when I leave here, I'll get you some." She looked him up and down. "And if you give me that shirt, I'll wash it for you, too." She peered outside the tent at the line. "Looks like it'll be several hours. Come back here around sundown, and we'll get those potatoes." Then she said, "Next."

As the soldier at the front of the line moved into the tent, a nine-year-old boy in uniform ran up and pushed himself to the front. He was breathless from running and wide-eyed as he looked at the supplies in the tent. He said, "Gee willikers! Look at all this stuff!"

Mary Ann's eyes traced downward, until she reached the face of the boy with great surprise. "Well, look at you! How'd you get here? Are you from Savannah?"

The boy puffed up his chest. "No, ma'am. I'm regular army."

"Regular army? What's your name, son?"

"John Clem, ma'am, drummer boy for Twelfth Michigan Volunteers."

"Well, John Clem, what can I do for you?"

John paused. "Why, nothing, ma'am. I just wondered why everybody was in line. This here is some kind of hospital?"

"Yes," she smiled. "It's some kind of hospital."

John's eyes kept moving from Mary Ann to the jams in the basket behind her. "I don't suppose any of that jam there was made for nine-year-olds?"

"Perhaps—but you'll have to trade for it."

"But, ma'am, I've got nothing," he said, with disappointment in his voice.

"Well, you've got a drum, haven't you? You could play a tune for these boys in line."

John Clem looked up at her with childish delight on his face. "Yes, ma'am! I'll be right back," he said, and raced out of the tent.

A moment later he returned to the clinic with his drum. He wiped it off with his shirtsleeve and slipped on the shoulder strap. Then he began to tap out a cadence with his sticks.

Mary Ann stopped him. "No, John, not in here. You'll be appreciated much more out there."

"Oh! All right!" he said enthusiastically, and left the tent. He started to play again and the soldiers in line began to keep time with him, clapping and stamping their feet. One soldier pulled out his harmonica and began the sad tune of "All Quiet on the Potomac Tonight."

Mary Ann's hands continued tending soldiers, but the music pulled her into reverie. She remembered one sunny summer afternoon years ago, at her house in Galesburg. Standing in her back doorway, she watched her young sons play in the tall grass of the backyard. Jimmy played the role of an Indian and beat a homemade drum with a wooden spoon. Hiram, in the role of a soldier, marched with his tree-branch rifle behind a fort fashioned from a broken wagon wheel. Suddenly, the soldier saw the Indian and shot his musket. "Bam! Bam!" The Indian drummer fell over, holding his chest as if he had been shot. The little drum rolled away in the grass.

John Clem had stopped drumming and now stood before her expectantly.

"Oh!" she said with surprise, reorienting herself. "That was nicely done! Your mother would be proud. And you helped these boys get their minds off their troubles."

John grinned. "Do you have chokecherry, ma'am? It's my favorite!"

"Why, let me see," she said, turning to search through the baskets. "Yes, here's a jar just for you!"

John grabbed the jar from her, held it like a treasure to his chest, and bowed. "Thank you, ma'am. Now, I best be off." He tipped his hat to her, turned, and ran out of the clinic.

Mary Ann chuckled to herself and said, "Next?"

The next soldier stepped forward. "Howdy, ma'am. Would you look at my hand, please? I burned it on a log the other day." He stretched his hand toward her.

She said, "It's blistered pretty bad, son. We'll put some butter on it and watch it for a few days."

He replied, "Mother, I don't know if I have a few days."

She said, "What do you mean?"

"It looks like the Rebs are massing in the woods, up by Pittsburg Landing. Hear tell it's General Beauregard's army. Word is we're moving out tonight or tomorrow, to a meeting house in the woods. Maybe you've heard of the place—it's called Shiloh?"

"Can't say as I have, son."

CHAPTER 14

Shiloh—April 1862

In February, General Albert Johnston, in charge of the western Confederate forces, and General P. G. T. Beauregard, second in command, combined armies with four other Confederate divisions at Corinth, Mississippi, twenty miles from Pittsburg Landing. At Pittsburg Landing, Grant had amassed forty-two thousand men with the intention of practicing drills and marches. He assumed, incorrectly, that the Confederates would still be recuperating from their involvement at Fort Donelson. Forty thousand Rebels surprised Grant's forty-two thousand troops in an early morning attack and many thousands of Union soldiers responded by fleeing in terror. Grant regrouped his forces and held a strong defensive line at Pittsburg Landing, an area the Confederates called Shiloh. Ferocious fighting ensued for days, with Grant finally attacking and routing the Confederate forces, causing them to retreat to Corinth. Shiloh was the bloodiest battle of the war to date, with almost eleven thousand Confederates and thirteen thousand Union soldiers killed, wounded, or missing. Strategically, the battle's outcome defended the Union gain at Fort Donelson and boosted Union morale while it demoralized the Confederates.

On the second day of the battle for Shiloh, the weather had turned miserable. A heavy rain fell, churning the ground to deep mud. Sounds of terrible fighting echoed in the distance, and burning powder from artillery shell explosions lit the evening gloom. Thousands of wounded and dying soldiers lay, sat, or stood on the wooden dock of Pittsburg Landing. Campfires hissed in the rain and wounded men huddled around them, trying to keep the flames from being drowned. Wagons carrying more wounded and dead came from the front, jolting and bouncing through the deep black mud with difficulty. Wagon masters unloaded their freight of human misery with unseemly speed and then hastened back to the field hospitals for more.

Two soldiers on picket duty looked anxiously upriver. One said, "See anything yet? Must be a whole boatload right here."

The second picket answered, "Nothing yet. She's a-comin'. Gots to be. These men are hurtin' bad. Hell, we all want to git outta here."

A team of mules pulled a wagon toward the landing, struggling to get through almost wheel-high mud. The wagon bed was open to the rain. In it were ten wounded men lying next to and on top of each other. They were all bleeding, in terrible pain, and screaming with every jolt of the wagon. The mules came to an abrupt halt about twenty yards from the landing. The wagon lurched. The driver yelled, "Hold on, boys, we're stuck in a hole! Mighta broke a wheel." He hopped off the wagon into the mud and slogged his way to the wheel. He leaned over and peered in the dark at it. "Naw," he hollered, "we can pull her out!" He grabbed the reins and whip, and started to yell at the mules. "Come on now, Bessy, Tilly—harawww! Git up, you lazy mules." Two men from the landing struggled through the mud to help him. With great effort, the mules pulled and the men pushed the wagon out of the hole. As the wagon approached the landing, men swarmed over to unload it.

Down at the far end of the landing by a smoky campfire, a drenched Mary Ann, in a cape and slouch hat, knelt in front of a wounded soldier who sat on a wooden crate. She wiped his face and began to dress his head wound with a roll of bandage.

"Thank you, ma'am," the wounded soldier whispered.

"Shush, now," Mary Ann replied. "You need to rest. Let me finish this. There. Now, when did you eat last, son?"

The soldier replied weakly, "Don't know—can't remember, ma'am."

"Let me get you some soup. It'll warm you through, and then you can try to sleep some." She stood up and walked over to the fire. A big iron kettle hung on a tripod over the fire that was hissing and spluttering in the rain. She picked up an old tin cup, knocked the rainwater out of it, and dipped it into the kettle. She wiped the edge of it with her sodden skirt and then took it back to the soldier she had just left, saying, "Here you are, son. Not too fast, or you'll burn yourself."

Behind her, a man dressed in the slicker of a Union surgeon stood watching her. He had just escorted several wounded from the front and noticed her. Curious, he watched as she knelt by another soldier who was clearly delirious. The stump of this young soldier's newly amputated arm bled into the rainwater and mud that was collecting at his side.

Mary Ann said, "Hello, son. Let me see what I can do for you." She automatically felt his forehead for fever. "Why, you're burning up, and you're bleeding clean out of your arm." She looked around, saw the man in the slicker and nodded to him. "Sir, please bring me some dry cloth to bind this man's wound. You'll find some in those boxes at the end of the landing." The man nodded, making rain pour in a stream off his hat. He walked over to the boxes and returned with several rolled bandages he'd kept dry under his slicker. He handed the bandages to her, one at a time. Then he knelt down beside her.

"Maybe I can help you with that," he said. He gently lifted the man's arm above the stump and held it out so that Mary Ann could wrap the bandage. As she worked, he said, "I have been watching you, madam. You have the hands of a skilled nurse. You are knowledgeable about wounds, and yet you also cook, feed, and comfort the men. How did you find food to cook here? Where did you come by boxes of bandages?"

Mary Ann wasn't listening to him. She leaned close to the wounded soldier and whispered in his ear, "Now, you rest, son. In the morning, you'll feel a bit better." Then she looked over at the man in the slicker kneeling next to her. "Is there any way to get this boy out of the rain? Maybe by the boxes over there?"

The man looked back at the boxes, and then stood and called two soldiers over. "Restack those boxes, soldiers, to form a little shelter. Then get this man here out of the rain."

Mary Ann stood and said, "Maybe you'd be kind enough to help me over here, sir?"

"Yes, of course, madam."

They walked to a small group of soldiers and together began to tend their wounds.

Without pausing in his work, the man said, "You seem to be part nurse, part physician, and part mother. May I ask, who sent you here and appointed you to this work?"

Mary Ann did not look at him as she continued her work. She said, "The Lord, sir, gave me this work." Feeling like he might tell her to leave, she added, "Have you some authority that ranks higher?"

He replied humbly, "No, madam, I do not. I am grateful you are here. My name is Colonel Richard Walker, and I am a surgeon at the army hospital in Savannah. We very much need your services there. Our patient load has increased by two thousand in the last day, and we are in sore need of skilled nurses and doctors. Please consider coming to the hospital after these men have been evacuated."

Just then, a boat whistle sounded over the din of battle, and the picket peered into a wall of rain.

"Hospital ship a-comin'!" he hollered.

CHAPTER 15

Mrs. Eliza Chappell Porter of the U.S. Sanitary Commission

Within a week of the Union victory at Shiloh, the city of Savannah, Tennessee, was transformed into a giant hospital. After the battle, the wounded poured into the city by the thousands, overwhelming its medical personnel and its resources. Both Rebel and federal wounded were quartered in every available building and in fifteen hundred tents.

The rain had finally stopped and the sun shone. Dr. Walker made rounds in a ward tent packed with patients. Mary Ann was in the same ward, handing out freshly laundered clothes. A soldier entered the tent, holding his hat under his arm. He approached Dr. Walker, saluted, handed him a folded paper and waited.

Dr. Walker read the message and said, "Thank you, Private. That will be all."

He placed the message in his pocket and approached Mary Ann. "Mrs. Bickerdyke, the Sanitary Commission agents have arrived. They have boats full of supplies and request assistance distributing and storing them. One of the agents has specifically requested an introduction to you. Let's meet with the agent now, and we'll finish up here later."

Dr. Walker and Mary Ann left the ward. They walked through the maze of tents to Dr. Walker's office. In the hallway of his office, they met a man and a woman. The man was tall, with graying hair and spectacles. He wore a clean black coat and a black beaver hat. A gold watch chain hung from his vest. His hands were clean and his nails neatly manicured. He wore a simple gold ring on his left hand. This dignified man removed his hat, smiled, and extended his hand to the doctor.

"Dr. Walker? Good day, sir. I'm the Reverend Porter, here from Chicago, with three boats full of Sanitary Commission supplies. Or should I say, I've accompanied a Sanitary Commission agent from Chicago?" He turned to his female companion, a petite, impeccably dressed, auburn-haired lady. "Dr. Walker, may I present my wife, Mrs. Eliza Chappell Porter."

Dr. Walker bowed to Mrs. Porter.

"It's a pleasure to meet you," said Mrs. Porter as she looked at Mary Ann, who stood next to him. Mary Ann's dress was dirty and in tatters. Her apron was filthy and her hair was in wild disarray. "And this is…?"

Dr. Walker blushed. "Oh, please forgive me. Without this woman, we would have lost many hundreds more of our casualties," he said gesturing to Mary Ann. "Allow me to introduce Mrs. Bickerdyke, the only trained nurse we have here."

Mrs. Porter walked up to her and took both of Mary Ann's rough, cracked hands in her own silk-gloved ones. "Oh, Mrs. Bickerdyke, I have heard of your wonderful work from Mrs. Mary Livermore, and that is why I have come. I have been looking for you since I left Chicago. It is such good fortune to meet you here."

Mary Ann curtsied, but kept her face down in embarrassment. With some discomfort, she said, "I wasn't expecting visitors, especially an agent from the Sanitary Commission. I'm afraid I'm not at all presentable!"

Mrs. Porter patted Mary Ann's hands. "Oh, my dear, there's no need to be concerned. It's not your clothes we came to see. It is the remarkable woman responsible for so many good deeds!"

Mrs. Porter looked at her husband. "I found her! Jeremiah, dear, would you and Dr. Walker please deal with the bills of lading and secure the supplies with the quarter-master? Mrs. Bickerdyke and I have so much to talk about, and I'd like to start right now."

The Reverend Porter smiled at his wife's enthusiasm. "Of course, my dear. We'll meet up later?"

Dr. Walker suggested, "How about meeting for dinner in the surgeon's dining tent, say, about seven?"

Mary Ann said, "Mrs. Porter, I am honored, but I have many chores to do before then."

Mrs. Porter smiled. "No, dear, I am honored to be able to assist you with your chores." She took Mary Ann by the arm. As they left the doctor's office, Mrs. Porter said, "Now, take me to your ward and show me everything."

Mary Ann was curious about this well-dressed woman who wanted to help her with the daily chores—curious and a little afraid of being judged. But Mary Ann knew she needed the help, and if this woman was trained at all in car-egiving, she would be an unexpected blessing.

Mary Ann gave Mrs. Porter a brief tour of part of the hos-pital on the way back to the ward in which she had been working. By the time the two ladies entered the ward Mrs. Porter was noticeably pale. She said, "Mrs. Bickerdyke, there is so much to do! Put me to work. How may I help you? I am not a trained nurse, but I've birthed over seven children, and I can cook and clean and wash clothes."

Mary Ann said, "I didn't expect that you would want to help me. I...I thought you were merely shepherding the supplies."

"Not at all, dear lady. In these times, one must help in any way one can. While I'm here, use me." She untied her bonnet and took off her gloves. As she started to roll up her sleeves, Mrs. Porter looked at Mary Ann and said, "Now, call me Eliza, and where can I find something to serve as an apron?"

Mary Ann replied, "Please call me Mary Ann. I...I feel overwhelmed with gratitude. The difficulties here have been so great, and I have felt very alone. It will be a comfort to work with you."

For hours they worked together—a formidable force against the suffering confronting them. Mary Ann's suspicions were put to rest by Eliza Porter's capacity for the work. Only then did Mary Ann realize the extent of the work to be done, and how lonely she'd felt since leaving Fort Defiance. Her spirits were lifted considerably by having the company of a female colleague. For the first time, Mary Ann recognized the true enormity of the task she had undertaken.

Eliza Chappell Porter had not felt this surge of commitment since her last child was born. Eliza had always wanted children and felt that all seven of them were gifts from God. As they grew toward independence, Eliza felt a new stirring in her heart to make a contribution. First, she had tried working in her husband's church, but there were already many ladies of the congregation who gave generously. Church work did not satisfy her.

When the war began, Eliza signed on with the Sanitary Commission. There, she met other ladies of stamina who made it their business to care for the Union soldiers. Working with these ladies, she felt a lightheartedness open in her, and the good feeling of being useful. But it was not enough. She felt she had something more to give, but didn't know what it was. At the Sanitary Commission, she met Mrs. Mary Livermore, who was highly placed in the Western Branch. Eliza was very impressed with Mary Livermore. Her organizational skills and focus made things happen.

At Mrs. Livermore's request, Eliza traveled to Savannah specifically to meet Mrs. Bickerdyke, whose reputation was growing among the women of the North. Mrs. Livermore wanted Mary Ann Bickerdyke to work for the commission, and Eliza was the ideal person to accomplish this.

As she worked with Mary Ann that first day, Eliza realized that the nursing care they were providing was very important and she could shape her life around it.

The table in the surgeon's dining hall was so small that both Dr. Walker and the Reverend Porter kept their plates on their laps. Several candles sat on the table and lanterns hung on the tent poles helped light the room. The other diners had already finished their meals and left for their evening rounds. Over tin cups of steaming coffee, Dr. Walker and his guests discussed politics, the war, the Sanitary Commission, the battle of Shiloh, and the hospital.

"It must have been a huge battle. From what I've seen here, it must have been dreadful," said the Reverend Porter.

"Yes," Dr. Walker admitted. "We have thousands of wounded because of it. We weren't prepared for this, and didn't even have enough hospital ships available until a few days after the battle. The kind of medicine required to treat wounded men is something very few of us know anything about," he said, his voice heavy with concern. "We're even having trouble getting the wounded off the field—most lie there for days. It's one of the reasons I am so glad to see you. We lack every kind of supply and have had to make do with poor substitutes." Dr. Walker turned to Mrs. Porter. "I understand you toured a portion of the hospital. Did Mrs. Bickerdyke show you her laundry and bakery? They are wonderful additions for the comfort of the men."

Mrs. Porter looked with surprise at Mary Ann. "You have a bakery as well as a laundry?"

"Yes, I started a little bakery with some bricks from chimneys that came down in the shelling. With the help of contrabands, we make about five hundred loaves of bread a day—enough to feed many of the wounded. As I'm sure you're aware, the hardtack they're issued is fine for a healthy soldier, but the wounded boys need something softer. I'll show you the bakery tomorrow, as well as the laundry. The contrabands also staff the laundry, which has grown so that I can't handle it myself."

Mrs. Porter asked, "Contrabands? What are contrabands?"

Mary Ann said, "Former slaves freed by the Union army or souls who took flight in the war's chaos. They are folks committed to freedom. Why, Mrs. Porter, they're heroes. The army expects even a wounded or sick soldier to cook his own rations. You've seen these boys. They can't do that. They need help and the contrabands provide it."

"Well, I heard about your laundry from Mary Livermore. The commission sent you two kettles some time ago."

"We started with those two, but it has certainly grown since then. Now we probably wash about four thousand articles of clothing from the hospital a day. It's a mammoth undertaking, but clean clothes and bedding restore health."

"After we see the bakery, I would very much like to see your laundry."

The Reverend Porter interjected, "And the army supports your efforts?"

Mary Ann's face flushed in the candlelight. "The good Lord grants me strength several times a day, Reverend, to deal with army nonsense. The army is not used to dealing with women, but I usually get my way, and General Grant and Dr. Walker have both been generous and supportive."

"Ah, I just remembered a question I was instructed to ask you, Mrs. Bickerdyke," said the Reverend Porter. "The commission gave me a receipt for one hundred pounds of Rebel beef. Apparently you signed this receipt and said that the commission would pay. Do you know anything about this?"

"Of course, Reverend Porter. I bought that beef on credit several weeks ago off a Rebel butcher, who cut it up and delivered it to the hospital. It made a fine stew and fed hundreds of men. I was fairly certain the army wouldn't pay for it, so I charged it to the commission."

116

"And why is that, Mrs. Bickerdyke?"

"Well, the quartermaster gives the men salted something or other that's crawling with maggots and so tough it won't even soften at a boil. Men can't get healthy eating that. The Sanitary Commission wants what's best for the men. I did what was best."

Both the Reverend Porter and Dr. Walker laughed. The Reverend Porter said, "Eminently sensible, Mrs. Bickerdyke. Since you're spending our funds anyway, would you consider working under the auspices of the Sanitary Commission? We thought that you might have readier access to supplies and more authority with the army medical establishment as a new agent."

"And," said Mrs. Porter, "there's a small salary that comes with the position. You could send it back to your family in Galesburg."

Mary Ann was silent for a moment while she considered this. "Back in Galesburg, I always worked for Dr. Woodward, one patient at a time. Here, even though I'm overwhelmed, I've been able to do things my way. I'm concerned that if I worked for the commission, I would not be as free as I am now. I would have to answer to people who would be making rules about all this"—she gestured to indicate the hospital—"without ever visiting."

The Reverend Porter said, "There's another way to think about it. You could do so much more with the power of the U.S. Sanitary Commission backing you. No surgeon would ever refuse you entry to a hospital."

"Well," said Mary Ann slowly, "what would I need to do? I don't have much time for fiddling and fussing to get things done. If I did, it would take time away from caring for these boys here."

"Leave it to me, Mrs. Bickerdyke. I shall write a letter and send it immediately." The Reverend Porter was visibly excited that Mary Ann had agreed.

Mrs. Porter added, "Good! In a month's time you shall have your commission, if I know Mary Livermore! Have you met Mary? She heads the Western Division of the Sanitary Commission. An absolutely delightful woman, and she knows most of the community leaders in Chicago."

Mary Ann shook her head. "Alas, no. We haven't met, but have communicated through letters. I have found her efficient, and a woman of her word." Mary Ann looked to Dr. Walker. "This was an excellent dinner, Doctor, and I thank you, but I have my night rounds to do before it gets any later."

"Mrs. Bickerdyke, it's already half past ten," the worried doctor said gently. "And I know you will work for hours more. We have ward masters and soldiers to assist the men. Can you not stay?"

Mary Ann pushed her chair back from the table and stood. "No, Doctor. The ward masters and soldiers sleep at night. I do not." Mary Ann nodded to the Porters. "Good evening, Reverend and Mrs. Porter. This has been a pleasure. Eliza, if you will meet me in the ward about eleven tomorrow morning, we can tour the bakery and the laundry. Until then, sleep well."

∽∾

The next morning Mary Ann and Eliza walked over to the bakery. In a large clearing were five huge, square brick ovens that emitted heat and steam. Beside them sat big wooden kneading tables. Contrabands were in the process of scraping these tables clean so another batch of bread could be kneaded and shaped. Hundreds of loaves sat cooling on boards on the ground, and the air was redolent with the homey fragrance of freshly baked bread. A large wagon with a V-shaped bed held hundreds of pounds of dough rising for the next baking. Nearby were enormous wooden vats in which the contrabands mixed flour and water. Several hundred barrels of flour were stacked behind the ovens.

"Eliza, this is the bakery. About twenty-five contrabands work here. We have no money, so we give them bread and

118

do their laundry. When the weather is good and we have the flour, we bake three times a day. The ovens come clean apart, so we can move them if we have to. They're just bricks set one on the other. Let me introduce you to the woman who makes this miracle happen. She was a former slave who had managed a household in the South. Her organizational skills have really made this possible. I couldn't get on without her."

Mary Ann led Eliza over to an old, wiry black woman with a bandana wrapped around her head. A huge white apron covered a tattered but clean dress. She was barefoot.

"Nettie? I'd like you to meet Eliza Porter. Eliza, this is Nettie."

Nettie looked flustered and wiped her hands on her apron. She curtsied and said softly, "Ma'am. I wasn't expectin' no visitors!"

Eliza said, "Nettie, I am so impressed with what you're doing here. This is remarkable, and the U.S. Sanitary Commission shall hear of it."

"Nettie, it looks like we'll have two more bakings today," said Mary Ann. "Mrs. Porter brought plenty of flour. The quartermaster should be delivering it shortly. Now, we won't take any more of your time. Thank you, Nettie." Mary Ann then looked at Eliza. "Let's go see the laundry."

The two ladies sat in a covered carriage driven by a soldier. He took them down a rough, dusty dirt road by the sandy river's edge. As they rounded a bend, they saw a scene of energetic activity. Twelve huge iron pots balanced on pieces of old railing over several fire pits. Some contrabands fed the fires with wood while others stirred the garments boiling in the pots with long wooden poles. They moved the clothing from kettle to kettle, until the clothes were piled high on a wagon for a final rinse in the river. Shirts, trousers, underwear, blankets, and dressings were spread out on every bush and shrub. Drying lines stretched between the trees and bushes, and bowed down under the weight of their burden of clothing.

"Mary Ann, this is so big and so...so organized!" Eliza exclaimed. "How did you manage this? We had no idea of the scale of your efforts!"

"This is not the result of my efforts alone. It truly could not be accomplished without the work of many hands. The boys scrounged up a number of the kettles by trading whatever they could with the local community. They found the railings along the railroad. They also organized wood-cutting details, in which both soldiers and contrabands contribute their time and energy to supply fuel. We pay the soldiers with bread and laundry services, just as we do the contrabands. After we organized the laundry, the contrabands took up the management and now run this laundry by themselves. Of course, the commission supplies the soap, and I hope that won't change."

Eliza, still astonished, said, "Rest assured that my report to the commission will be so positive that you will never run out of soap—no matter how much you need!"

"Now that you have seen the laundry, Eliza, I would like to return to the hospital and draft a list of critical supplies necessary for the medical care of the soldiers here in Savannah. Would you be amenable to delivering the list to the commission and explaining its importance when you and the Reverend Porter return to Chicago?"

"My dear Mary Ann, I will not only deliver it and argue its importance, I will help you draft it. The reverend and I are planning on leaving for Chicago in the next day or two. I'll see to it that the commission fills your request, and if at all possible, I will escort the supplies here myself. It would be an honor for me to stay on here as a nurse under your authority."

Mary Ann was speechless at Eliza's generous offer. Grateful tears welled up in her eyes. She had not expected this outpouring of support. Eliza put her arm around Mary Ann's shoulders and held her. Mary Ann felt a torrent of relief in Eliza's tender hug. Every thought was momentarily blacked out by their warm embrace.

CHAPTER 16

Little Mary Safford's Breakdown

The Reverend and Mrs. Porter returned to Savannah on May 6, 1862. They arrived accompanied by six female nurses, a steamboat loaded with supplies, and a U.S. Sanitary Commission field agent's appointment for Mary Ann. In addition, Eliza brought along a surprise visitor.

Mary Ann was busily at work in the main ward of the hospital. Eliza entered the ward, saw Mary Ann bent low over a patient, and said loudly, "Excuse me, ma'am, could you use a nurse?"

As Mary Ann recognized Eliza's voice, she stopped her work in surprise and smiled. She stood, turned, and said with pleasure, "Eliza! My little brown bird! What joy it brings me to have you in my hospital again! Welcome back. I have missed you."

The two women embraced each other. Mary Ann held Eliza at arm's length looking at her for a moment. Then, with great pride in her voice, she addressed the soldiers in the ward. "Boys, this is Mrs. Porter from the Chicago Sanitary Commission. She has brought us the supplies we need to take care of you."

Those soldiers who could gave Eliza the typical Union cheer, "Huzzah! Huzzah! Huzzah!" Eliza blushed and clapped as she turned to thank all the soldiers in the ward.

"Oh, Mary Ann! It is so good to see you. I've come to stay a while and have brought the reverend with me. I'm going to help you out here. But before I roll up my sleeves and get to work, I have a surprise for you. I brought some-one I think you know. She's waiting outside. Come."

Mary Ann was filled with curiosity as she and Eliza left the ward. Mary Safford, all of thirteen but looking much older, stood on the steps outside. Mary Ann's face lit with happi-ness, and she took Mary Safford into her arms and held her tightly. Mary Ann said, "Oh, my little angel of Cairo, you have come to visit me." She held little Mary by the shoul-ders. "Let me look at you. Why, child, you've become a woman!" she said as she hugged her again. Mary Safford, safely enfolded in Mother's arms, started to cry.

Little Mary sobbed through her tears, her words muffled against Mary Ann's shoulder. "Mrs. Porter was...was kind enough to...to bring me with her. I...I have come to say... good-bye."

"Good-bye, dear?" said Mary Ann, holding little Mary by the shoulders again so she could see the girl's face.

Mary Safford's crying intensified, and Eliza placed her hand on Mary Ann's arm.

"Let me take her to your tent. She has had quite a long and tiring journey, but was adamant that she wanted to see you before she rested. We can all get together and talk after you've finished in the ward, Mary Ann. Now, my child, come with me." Eliza tenderly pulled a pliable little Mary away from Mary Ann and escorted her down the steps. Eliza, worry etched on her face, looked over her shoulder at Mary Ann as they walked away from the ward.

Mary Ann stood on the steps for a moment, collecting herself. She felt a sudden jumble of emotions—joy at seeing her little angel again, shock at how old and distressed she looked, and worry, concern, and bafflement by little Mary's tears and the finality of her statement. Mary Ann watched the two women walk away and felt engulfed with the sad-ness of yet another loss. She recalled how she felt when she first parted from her children. For an instant she was paralyzed by a feeling of loneliness. Memories of her family flooded through her.

Though it was only months ago, it seemed like a lifetime. Mary Elizabeth, James, and Hiram, along with several "adopted" orphans and nephews, had gathered around her in the bedroom of the Prairie Street house. All the children were crying as Mary Ann folded clothes and tucked them into her carpetbag.

"I'm scared, Mother. Don't leave."

"How long will you be gone?"

"Who'll look after us?"

"Why do you have to go?"

"Now, this isn't going to be forever, children. Mary Elizabeth, you're nigh on nineteen and old enough to have a family of your own. You'll only be watching over Hiram and Jamie, and they're both good boys. They'll help you with the chores. Your cousins are off to Ohio, and you boys from the Five Points Mission will go to the Hightower and the McDaniel households. Mary Elizabeth, the Reverend Beecher will make sure you also have the support of a fine family. Hush now, dry your tears, children."

"But, Mother, we need you here. How are we going to grow up without you?"

Mary Ann sighed heavily, knowing her sternness was not the right response for her children, but not knowing how else to deal with this. She couldn't face her children's feelings of abandonment and continue to do what she needed to do. But, no matter how hard she tried, she could not find consoling words to express this. She gently caressed Mary Elizabeth's cheek and then turned her back on the children to continue packing her bag. There were only a few more items left on the bed waiting to be packed. As she folded her nightclothes Mary Ann recalled how sad she had felt when her grandparents died, and she was forced to go live with her Uncle Henry. She'd been with them for eight years, ever since her father had remarried after her mother's death. There, she had been comforted by the presence of her older sister, Eliza. But Eliza had left to start her life in the world shortly after the two of them arrived at Uncle Henry's farm. Mary Ann remembered how horrible it had felt, on the threshold of adolescence, to lose the only family she had known and to be forced on willing but almost perfect strangers.

"Mother!" cried Jamie, as tears rolled down his face. He clutched and enfolded himself in her skirts.

Her memories melted into the military hospital of her present and the two sorrows flooded her. She sighed again in an attempt to shake off this heaviness of heart. Then, Mary Ann turned and crossed the threshold into the hospital. She scanned the room, completely disoriented, and said, "Now, where was I?"

A soldier by the door who had watched her enter said with concern, "Mrs. Bickerdyke, ma'am? Are you all right?"

"Yes, son," she said. Then she said under her breath, to no one in particular, "This is just so hard."

"Yes, ma'am," said the soldier. "I fear before it's over this war will break all our hearts."

She leaned down and picked up an empty tin cup. As she rose, she said, "Well then, we shall just have to mend them back together, as we have no choice. This thing must be played out—no matter what it costs us."

That afternoon Mary Ann returned to her tent to check on Mary Safford, who had been sleeping fitfully. As she entered her tent, Mary Safford sat up; with a cry, she opened her arms wide and enveloped Mary Ann in an embrace.

"I can't do it anymore, Mother, I just can't do it. I feel as if I've failed you. I see their faces in my dreams. They follow me everywhere."

"Oh, Mary, my child. My poor, dear child," Mary Ann said, as she caressed Mary Safford's hair. "What have I done to you? This has been too much for such a little one. It is I who failed you. I should have realized that youth needs to be protected from the dreadful realities of war, and in my great need I have not done that. I am so very sorry. You have been an angel, little one, and I have given you more than even angels can bear. I have needed you and used you. Can you forgive me?"

Mary Safford continued to sob, and with tears rolling down her own face, Mary Ann knelt down and held her. The two stayed that way for a long time. Little Mary finally calmed in Mary Ann's embrace. Mary Ann, though, felt a new wound opening deep inside herself that was filled with guilt and something like shame.

A few days later, Mrs. Porter escorted little Mary Safford home to the loving arms of her family.

In the spring of 1862, Union troops successfully attacked the Rebels holding Corinth, Mississippi, and took control of a strategic railway crossing. Once Corinth had become the center of Union activity, the Savannah hospitals needed to be evacuated to a large post hospital that was to be established at a town named Farmington, which was five miles away from Corinth. Meanwhile, General Grant was reappointed to take control of the Union troops in that area. When Mary Ann heard of Grant's return, she asked to see him.

In his office, Mary Ann sat across from General Grant and asked him about the progress he had made on securing her a driver.

"And, I could certainly use more wagons and men to drive them."

"Well, Mrs. Bickerdyke, I believe I may have good news for you on both fronts. I have assigned Private Andrew Somerville from the Seventh Iowa Infantry to assist you for the duration of the war. He will be your driver and see to whatever else you need. He'll be reporting to you later today. There is one condition, however—please do *not* get this man court-martialed. Now, as far as the wagons go, have you heard of a surgeon by the name of Letterman?"

She paused, and then said, "No, I don't think I have."

"Well, he's been making noises about an ambulance corps. Surgeon General Hammond thinks men are dying needlessly because the wounded stay on the field for days after a battle has ended. He wants a way to remove casualties from the battlefield and get them to field hospitals. Letterman thinks that using men and wagons dedicated to removing the wounded from the field as quickly as possible will decrease the mortality rate, and he has been charged with solving this problem."

"This is good news. It is a huge problem, removing the wounded from the battlefield. By the time I reach them, most of my boys have been lying on the field a good three days or more, dying of thirst and with wounds packed with maggots and filth. There must be some way to get to them quicker. I also need a way to follow you and your army with hospital supplies."

Grant furrowed his brow, thought for a moment, and then looked at Mary Ann. "I agree, madam. To that end, Mrs. Bickerdyke, I will lend you—*lend*—do you hear me, Mrs. Bickerdyke? I will lend you a few ambulances and drivers to help you remove the wounded from the field. One day, you will have to give these back. Do you understand?"

Mary Ann smiled. "Of course, sir. How many ambulances and men?"

"Hmm...I can spare twenty wagons and forty men."

"Is that all, sir?" she said, with a sad face and disappointment in her voice.

"That should be adequate."

Mary Ann sat up straighter on the edge of her chair. She leaned toward Grant. "Over ten thousand of *your* Union boys passed through the hospitals in Savannah after the battle. Twenty wagons? Twenty is not enough!"

Grant settled back in his chair and thoughtfully stroked his beard. His eyes twinkled. "Well, Mrs. Bickerdyke, what if I could lend you thirty wagons and sixty men?"

"I need at least forty wagons, I should think."

"Forty! Where do you think I can find forty wagons and eighty men not already in use? You ask too much, madam."

"It's for a good cause, General. You know I will put them to good use."

"You drive a hard bargain, Mrs. Bickerdyke. Forty it is, but no more."

"But I will need an ambulance as well. One specific for my—"

He interrupted her with a chuckle. "I've already assigned you Private Somerville. Leave me some men and equipment with which to fight this war, madam."

"Of course, General. Now what about—"

With a wave of his hand, Grant interrupted her again. "That's all I can do for you for now, Mrs. Bickerdyke. But be assured, you do have the upper hand. I hope to see you in Farmington."

Mrs. Bickerdyke smiled and stood. "Forty it is, then, sir. This is a great help. Thank you." She curtsied to Grant and left the room.

Staff at the army hospitals in Savannah prepared for deployment to Corinth. Many of the wounded had already been transported by rail from the Savannah hospitals to others in the North. The Sanitary Commission's boats had finally made it downriver with a small contingent of nurses and many crates of much-needed hospital supplies.

With Andy's assistance, Mary Ann directed the removal of the last of her patients who could withstand travel. They were carried on stretchers from the hospitals to the rail station. She had made arrangements with the local medical authorities for the continued care of those boys who could not leave yet. Then she directed the packing of Sanitary Commission supplies into the forty wagons that would be used later as ambulances.

Outside the hospital, Andy sat in the driver's seat of the first ambulance, its mules snorting and chewing their bits. With amusement, Andy turned and watched Mrs. Bickerdyke as she walked down the single-file line of the wagons, inspecting each and directing the two men assigned to each wagon to reposition the crates and barrels. By the time she reached the fifth or sixth wagon, Andy could see the men looking at him and furtively gesturing with frustration. Andy decided he'd better go help her.

"Look, young man, you could make room up there for two more barrels," Mary Ann said to a wagon driver. "There's no reason to waste space. Don't know if flour will be hard to come by in Farmington. The bread it makes might fill your own belly, as well."

The driver of the wagon walked around and pulled himself up into the wagon bed, looking at the pallet of boxes, crates, and barrels. "No, ma'am, I don't believe there is any more room up here."

"Nonsense. Why, look. Right there," she said, pointing to a small space between several crates. As he hesitated, she said, "Give me a hand up, son," and stepped up onto the back of the wagon. She started to push things this way and that, making the driver hastily jump off the wagon and stare at her. Andy walked up and joined her in the back of the wagon.

"Mother Bickerdyke," he said, "you really shouldn't be up here moving things around. Let me help you."

"Thank you, Andy. That needs to go there," she said, and pointed to a spot. "And if you move that next to it, another barrel will fit nicely."

"Yes, ma'am, I'll see to it. Now, let me help you down. I'll go check on the other wagons to be sure all the supplies will fit. Don't you worry yourself."

After Andy had cajoled the soldiers into adding a few more supplies to each wagon, he returned to Mary Ann. All the supplies had been loaded. She stood on the ground with her hands on her hips, looking with satisfaction at the long line of ambulances filled with goods. "I believe this is going to work, Andrew. Are the six new commission nurses on board?"

"Yes, ma'am. They're in the tenth wagon," he said, and pointed. "Still pretty tired from their work, but ready to go."

"They'll have time to rest on the way to Farmington," she replied. "Now, I'm just going to say good-bye to Mrs. Porter, and I'll return directly. You've done a good job, young man." Then Mary Ann walked over to the hospital office.

Inside, Mary Ann and Eliza embraced each other with tears in their eyes.

"Eliza, thank you," Mary Ann said. "I hope we shall meet in Farmington. I shall miss you, my little brown bird. When do you and the Reverend Porter go north?"

"Next week," replied Eliza. "The commission is sending a hospital boat to transport the remaining wounded. The reverend and I will accompany them, and I'll tend them on the journey. God keep you, Mary Ann. I'll write to you after I've had a chance to rest and see my children. I'll inform Mrs. Livermore at the Sanitary Commission about all that's happened down here."

The two women embraced again. Mary Ann turned to leave, but then stopped in the doorway and turned to face Eliza. "I'm worried about you. Promise me that you'll put some meat on your bones and get as much rest as you can."

Eliza smiled through her tears and nodded. "You too, dear," she whispered after Mary Ann had left.

Outside, Andy helped Mrs. Bickerdyke board the ambulance. Then he yelled down the line of wagons, "Ready, boys?" He climbed into the driver's seat next to her and snapped the reins. Mary Ann's ambulance corps was on its way.

CHAPTER 17

Farmington and the Furbelows

The tent hospital at Farmington was located on a ridge, five miles outside of Corinth. It accommodated fourteen hundred sick and wounded soldiers. The hospital tents covered many acres of ground. Here, Mary Ann, with the help of her contrabands, established a diet kitchen, a bakery, and a laundry. But for Mary Ann, cooking so many meals over open fires had become too great a chore that took too much of her time away from her patients. Besides, her skirts often caught fire as she stirred or added ingredients. She paid such little attention to herself that she rarely noticed this danger, but her soldier helpers often were quite alarmed by her burning skirts. They began to keep pots of water available whenever she was cooking to "put her out."

Mary Ann eventually wrote about the hardships of outdoor cooking to Mary Livermore in Chicago. Mrs. Livermore, fresh from meeting with Eliza Chappell Porter and hearing about Mary Ann's remarkable accomplishments, immediately negotiated with a Chicago hotel to purchase its giant stove. The Sanitary Commission transported this stove to Farmington.

The stove arrived as Mrs. Bickerdyke and Dr. McDougal, the chief surgeon of the hospital, were discussing an outbreak of scurvy. They sat at a camp table cluttered with papers. The tent flap was open, and outside the hustle and bustle attested to a well-run hospital.

"There are four hundred new cases, and I've been reading that some doctors are successfully treating this with antiscorbutics," said Dr. McDougal.

"Well, I've used pickled potatoes and fresh vegetables when I can get them. They seem to work just as well," said Mary Ann. "If I had more supplies, Doctor, I could stop this outbreak."

"Ah. I meant to tell you earlier, Mrs. Bickerdyke, that a shipment of goods from the Sanitary Commission arrived this morning. The quartermaster hasn't had time to move them to the hospital supply tent, but since you're a commission agent, perhaps you would deal with this?"

"Of course. I will see to it."

"Oh, and one more thing, Mrs. Bickerdyke," said Dr. McDougal slowly. "In all my years as an army surgeon, I have never worked with women nurses and was adamantly opposed to women working in any army hospital. When you were assigned here, I complained bitterly to my commanding officer and threatened to resign my commission. But, my experience with you has made me change my mind. I have found myself feeling grateful that you are here, that you sit all night with a dying soldier or cook some special treat when the patients' morale is low. They call you Mother, and I understand why."

Mary Ann blushed with embarrassment, looked down at her hands folded in her lap, and said, "Thank you, Doctor." She felt flustered, not knowing how to handle such a direct compliment. She stood up abruptly and, still looking down, rushed out, mumbling, "Now, I must see to those supplies."

Over at the hospital supply tent, Mary Ann directed soldiers in storing the crates and barrels, and unpacking the new stove. Soldiers crowded around the stove, marveling at its size.

"Whooee!" said one soldier. "You could cook a horse on that thing, it's so big!"

"Looks like somebody's gonna get pie tonight, boys," said another.

"Young man, if you and your friends set that stove up properly in the diet kitchen, there just might be a piece of pie for each of you tonight. That depends, of course, on how well you do your job," said Mary Ann with a smile.

Suddenly, the soldiers who had lifted and were moving the stove became filled with enthusiasm and energy, and other soldiers rushed to help. *Pie* was the magic word.

Later that afternoon, Mary Ann and several soldiers reviewed the bills of lading and matched the appropriate bill to each crate in the supply tent. Suddenly, Mary Ann noticed one box with her name on it. She bent down and peered at it.

"Well, what could this be?" she wondered out loud. She carefully pulled off a battered envelope that had been nailed to the box. On the envelope, written in a rough hand, was: "To Missus Bikerdike, Nurs, personly." She turned it over and then slowly opened it. She read aloud, forgetting the soldiers in the tent with her.

Deer Mrs. Bikerdike,
Yu nursd my boy n savd his lif. I sends this
here shert in hope you kin use it. I sewd it fer
ma husband, but hes ded now. Thank yu.
Ruhanna Watson from Fallsburg, Ohio

"There's more like that, ma'am," said a soldier. He pointed to the back of the tent. "Most of the rest of these boxes here have some note or other on them addressed to you."

Mary Ann looked at the stacked goods and began to notice the many letters affixed to the boxes. She looked puzzled and then thumbed through the bills of lading. In among the list of supplies she saw a letter, with the official seal of the Western Sanitary Commission. She opened it and walked to the tent's entrance, leaning into the fading light of the afternoon. She began to read.

Dear Mrs. Bickerdyke.

Ladies from all over the North have heard about your kind deeds and are deluging the Sanitary Commission offices in Chicago with gifts addressed to you. We are happy to forward these on to you, as it must be difficult for you to obtain items for your personal use when you are with the army and so close to the front. The North is buzzing with stories about you, and many are very curious to know more. If you could ever manage a trip to Chicago, could we arrange a lecture for you with the proceeds to benefit the commission and the soldiers? The ladies of the community would be honored. Take good care of yourself. I shall write more later.

With shared devotion to the cause, I am your humble servant,

M. A. Livermore

"Well, I'll be. I had no idea," Mary Ann mumbled to herself. Then, to the soldiers she said, "Boys, could you open all these for me, please?"

As the soldiers pried off the wooden lids, Mary Ann stepped outside the tent to get a lantern.

An hour later, Mary Ann was alone in the hospital supply tent; she sat on a low wooden crate, surrounded by a jumble of open crates and letters. She had already rummaged through some of them, leaving their contents in disarray on top of the packing material. Mary Ann leaned to her right and removed the packing from the box by her elbow, to reveal a woman's embroidered nightdress. She unfolded it and held it up in front of her. It was delicately sewn and made of the finest batiste and lace. She returned it to the box, and from another removed a silver-handled mirror and matching hairbrush. Other boxes contained a hand-knit blanket, a pink crocheted shawl, black woolen stockings, a crinoline petticoat, and a parasol. So many things, from so many women. Slowly, she brought the shawl to her face and inhaled its faint lavender scent. For just a moment, there was no war; the sounds of music, the turn of a blue cotton skirt, and the feeling of her husband's hand at her waist flashed through her mind, only to vanish in the darkness.

"Silly you are, Mary Ann," she said.

Later that night, the warm, homey smell of currant pie drifted throughout the tents of the hospital.

The next morning after breakfast, Mary Ann asked a soldier to fetch Andy. "He can find me in that tent, over there," she said, pointing.

When Andy arrived, he stood for a moment at the entrance to the tent. Mary Ann was tending one of the soldiers at the far end and was unaware of his presence. His gaze slowly took in the room, and he smiled and chuckled to himself. Then he walked through the tent, greeting the wounded men as he went. One man's arm was wrapped in a pink sling made from something that looked like a piece of lady's shawl. Another man was sitting up having his hair cut by the soldier next to him, while he held up a silver mirror to observe the progress. Throughout the tent, bits and pieces of lady's refinements had been used for the comfort of the men.

"You sent for me, ma'am?" said Andy, smiling as he approached Mary Ann.

"Yes, Andy. Thank you for coming. I would like to speak with you about something important, but not here—perhaps behind the cooking tent. I'll be there momentarily."

Behind the cooking tent, Mary Ann gestured Andy over to the cookstove that was still warm and smelled of the morning's porridge. With a stern look at him, she said, "Do you see this stove, Andrew? It was supposed to be used in a grand hotel in Chicago before the war. Many people worked miracles to get this stove to me, and our boys are already benefiting from the food cooked on it. I can't afford to leave behind another stove. Why, Andrew, this good Northern stove is a hero. And under no circumstances would we leave a hero behind if we needed to evacuate camp in a hurry, would we?"

Andy looked bemused for a moment, and then smiled and nodded. "I understand, ma'am. It wouldn't be right to leave a hero."

"Now, Andrew, that goes for my bakery, and my laundry, too. Whatever equipment can be saved must be saved. We may be able to obtain bricks from broken chimneys again, but finding a stove like this, or the bread wagon or the kettles, would not be likely. I leave this in your hands, Andrew, and I know you will not fail me."

◑◐

A day or two later, as Mary Ann was rewrapping a dressing on a soldier's foot, a young soldier ran into the tent. He looked over his shoulder at someone outside and said, "Mother will know what to do." The young soldier came to a sudden stop inside the entrance, took off his kepi, and then sheepishly approached Mrs. Bickerdyke. He stood there huffing and puffing for a long moment, wanting but not wanting to interrupt her.

"Yes?" said Mary Ann, not looking up from her task.

"Ma'am," he said, still out of breath from running. "We got a life-and-death situation going on out here and need your help mighty bad—if'n you could spare a few moments...ah...please, ma'am!"

"Oh? Did someone get hurt?" she said.

"You gots to come with us a little ways, over by that old shed. Zeke—that's my friend—well, he's found somethin' mighty important, but they'll die if'n you don't help."

"All right, son. Let me just finish this, and then I'll follow you," she said.

"Thank you, ma'am!" He quickly turned to leave, and then slowly turned back. He looked chagrined that he had dispensed with the usual convention. He straightened his shoulders and stood at attention. "Private Daniel Preston at your service, ma'am. Sorry, ma'am. I forgot—that part shoulda come first."

"Quite all right, Private Preston. Now, shall we go?"

He turned a bright shade of red and stood aside for her to precede him from the tent.

Outside, Private Preston took the lead, weaving them through the tent city. He tried without success to contain his excitement, and frequently looked back over his shoulder to make sure she still followed.

As they left the hospital tents behind them, Mary Ann saw a gently sloped hillside covered with wild grasses and weeds. About halfway up the hill stood a ramshackle wooden shed, abandoned long ago.

"See, Zeke! I told ya she'd help!" Private Preston yelled toward the shed. Then, looking back at Mary Ann, he said, "You can call me Danny, ma'am."

As they approached the shed, a huge man with a red beard backed out of it on his knees, and then stood waiting for them.

"Ma'am, this is Private Ezekiel Mariah, my best friend, and near as you can get to a brother. We been together since we joined up. Ain't we, Zeke? Zeke here, he's kinda shy, so don't 'spect much talking out of him. He found 'em, ya see. Heard 'em moaning. Well, here, you can see for yourself," he said, gesturing for her to enter the shed.

The shed's door was missing, one wall of rotted boards and part of the roof had caved in, and the back wall was splintered and disintegrating. Mary Ann looked at the two men, wondering if this was a joke, but they urged her on with frantic hand motions. She leaned forward and ducked her head under the lintel. Inside, in the dusty half-light she saw a litter of kittens in a small pile of rags. No longer concerned about the stability of the shed, she entered, knelt, and took one furry creature in her hands. The kitten, its eyes not yet open, mewed softly.

"Why, for land's sake, in the middle of a war," she murmured, as she cradled it over her heart. "You poor little ball of fur. So tiny. You must be cold and hungry and terribly frightened." Looking over her shoulder at the two soldiers, she asked, "Where is the mother?"

Private Preston replied, "We think she up and left. Maybe she got lost in the war. Zeke found 'em this morning, and we ain't seen any cat come near here since. Figure they're getting mighty hungry, but we ain't got nothin' for 'em."

"Well, I'm sure we can find something for them in the diet kitchen. You boys will have to feed them and be diligent about it for several weeks. These are fresh born and can't do anything on their own." She gently gathered them in her apron and walked toward the diet kitchen. Both soldiers followed her, huge grins of relief on their faces.

Danny playfully smacked Zeke on the arm and said, "I told ya the boys were right, that she would help!"

∽∾

Several days later, Mary Ann and Andy were out in the countryside foraging for fresh fruits and vegetables, honey, eggs, chickens, fresh milk, and cream. They drove their wagon from one secessionist farmer to another, and traded the remaining gifts sent to her by the women of the North for goods her boys could use. Most of the farmers, especially their wives, were eager to trade, as the ravages of war had thoroughly scoured luxuries from the land.

Andy drove the wagon, following a rail line for several miles. Around a bend they saw a number of boxcars on a deserted siding.

"Andy, let's stop here and see if there's anything useful inside these cars," Mary Ann said.

He pulled the mule team to a stop and helped her out of the wagon.

"How does one get into a boxcar, Andrew?"

"No worry. I'll use a crate as a step. But you'd best stay here and let me explore first."

He took a crate from the back of the wagon and used it as a step to the first boxcar. He climbed up with a grunt. There were only a few empty and broken boxes inside. He turned around to leave the car and saw Mary Ann, who stood expectantly on the ground by the entrance.

"There's not much here we can use, Mother. Let's go check the others."

He set the crate by the door of the second boxcar and got in. Mary Ann followed him and said, "Help me up, Andy."

As he pulled her up, a gruff male voice threatened from a dark corner of the car. "Who the hell are you? We got guns here, you secesh dirt."

"I don't know who you are, but how dare you use that language with a lady!" said Mary Ann indignantly.

Andy discreetly drew his pistol and said, "Hold on there, boys, we're Union." As their eyes adjusted to the darkness of the car, they saw two soldiers huddled in the corner on a thin pile of rancid straw. Their clothes were filthy and torn. They looked haggard and scared.

Andy growled, "Who are you boys? We're from the Union Medical Corps."

"We're federal soldiers. We was riding the train to Chicago 'til you came along."

Mary Ann and Andy exchanged quizzical looks.

Andy replied with a chuckle in his voice, "Soldier, you're going nowhere. There's no engine hooked to this car."

The other soldier swore, "Dang it! I told ya something was wrong. We'll never get home now."

Mary Ann walked closer to the corner and peered at the men in the darkness. "You are lost, and you look hurt. Andy, put that gun away, for goodness' sake. Open the door all the way to let in some more light. I think I'm going to need some supplies, but first, bring me a lantern. I can't work if I can't see."

Andrew replied cautiously, "You'll be all right while I'm gone? I don't want to leave you here alone with them."

"I'll be fine, Andy. I think I could whup both of these boys at once. Now, I'm Mrs. Bickerdyke from the hospital at Farmington. You show me your injuries, and I'll take care of you."

The first soldier said to his compatriot, "Well, Jeb, by golly, she's a lady. What's a lady doing here in the middle of a war?"

Jeb addressed Mary Ann directly. "You sure you're not secesh? We don't want nothing to do with secesh."

"I'm sure," she replied. "Now quit fussing with me and let me get to work. Phew, you boys stink! How long have you been here?"

"Don't rightly know, ma'am," replied Jeb. "Maybe a week or maybe a couple of days. Nathaniel here had a bottle of whiskey, and we kinda lost track of time. My name is Jeb Whitlaw, ma'am, and this here is Nathaniel Stoner. We both got wounded skedaddling out of Mississippi. Our commanding officer ordered us to go to a Chicago hospital. Only, you're telling us this train ain't a-going to Chicago."

Andy returned with a lantern and a bundle of things that he placed on the floor beside Mary Ann. "I brought a canteen of water, in case you need it," he said.

"Thank you, Andy," said Mary Ann. She knelt down by the two men and asked Jeb, "Where were you injured, son?"

Jeb said, "My leg, ma'am. I think it's broke."

Mary Ann felt Jeb's leg through his tattered trousers. "Are you hurt any place besides that leg? I think you're right, it's broken."

"No, ma'am, just my leg. But Nathaniel's hurt worse 'n me."

"Well, Nathaniel, from the looks of it you have a pretty bad shoulder wound there," she said.

"Yes, ma'am," he said, and then blushed.

Jeb nudged him with his elbow. "Go on. Tell her."

"Naw. I don't think so."

"Go on," Jeb said again.

"Tell me what?" asked Mary Ann.

Nathaniel looked down at his lap and wouldn't meet Mary Ann's eyes. There was a long pause.

Then Jeb said, "Well, if you won't tell her, I will. He's got him a minié in his behind, ma'am. Shot straight through, begging your pardon, ma'am."

She looked at Nathaniel inquiringly.

With a horrified look on his face, he poked Jeb hard in the ribs, and then meekly said to Mary Ann, "Everything works, ma'am, if...ah...you know what I mean, ma'am, but it sure does hurt like the devil. But, no reason for you to bother yourself, ma'am. I'm sure it's doing fine."

"Well, Nathaniel," said Mary Ann, "let's get a look at you. I'll help you off with your shirt and then you drop your drawers."

"Why, ma'am, why...I ain't gonna do no such thing, you being a lady an' all, ma'am. Wouldn't be decent," said Nathaniel quietly. He wished he had crawled into a hole and this whole unfortunate incident had never happened.

In a commanding voice, Mary Ann said, "Andy, help this boy here to get rid of his clothes and then wash his...um... nether regions. I'll take care of his shoulder."

Nathaniel scooted back against the wall, shaking his head.

Andy pulled his pistol again, and suddenly Nathaniel's head moved quickly up and down. He said, "Yes'm, right away, ma'am."

"Thank you, Andrew, for being so convincing. After we dress these wounds, we'll bring a change of clothes. Surely we have something these boys can use in the ambulance."

An hour later, both men were clean and their wounds dressed. Two sturdy tree branches splinted Jeb's leg, to support it and keep it straight. A sling of calico supported Nathaniel's arm and shoulder.

"There," said Mary Ann. "Now, for some clean clothes. Andrew, I see you've found two pairs of britches. No shirts?"

"No, Mother. We're clean out of shirts."

Mary Ann frowned, crossed her arms on her chest, held her chin, and thought for a moment. "Andy, are those two furbelows still in the wagon?"

"Yes, ma'am, they're there. But what do you want with furbelows?"

"Andrew, I've had an inspiration! Would you go get those furbelows for me? The good Lord gave them to me for a reason, so I'll put them to good use."

Andy soon returned from the wagon. "Here they are, Mother," he said, holding out the nightgowns.

She took them from him, put one over her arm and shook the other one out. It was a beautiful cotton nightgown with a soft ruffle all around the hem. "Perfect!" she exclaimed.

Jeb looked at Nathaniel with concern and said hesitantly, "Ah...ma'am? What...um...are you intending, ma'am?"

Mary Ann ignored him and continued to exclaim, "Perfect! These are perfect for you boys to wear as shirts. These will do nicely."

Jeb said to Nathaniel with a laugh, "I do believe you'd look lovely in that gown. Why, right purty. You can sashay into Chicago and tell 'em that minié ball made you a changed man."

Nathaniel replied adamantly, "No, sir, er...no, ma'am. No way am I gonna wear a lady's furbelow. But you go on ahead, Jeb, if'n that's where your tastes lie. I never woulda guessed it, though." The two of them started poking each other.

Mary Ann scolded them both. "You two boys stop that. Wait and see. These will be softer on your wounds than those filthy rags you've been wearing, and they'll smell a sight better, too." She tore the nightgowns in half and handed the lower ruffled parts to Andy. "Put these back in the ambulance. We'll use them for something else later."

She looked sternly at Jeb and Nathaniel. "Boys, don't be foolish. Nightgowns or nightshirts—what's the difference? Put them on and wear them home. If anybody says anything, tell them you took them from a secesh. Folks will think a sight more of you. Come now, put them on. Then we'll get you back to the hospital so a doctor can look you over, and you'll soon be on your way to Chicago."

CHAPTER 18

Old Whitey

By early September 1862, Union troops in Corinth were preparing to move southeast against Iuka Springs, in northeastern Mississippi, in an attempt to wrest the rail lines from the Rebels. General Grant commanded the local Union forces and requested Mary Ann's presence to establish a field hospital to serve the wounded from the impending battle.

The town of Iuka Springs, a forlorn hot springs resort, had been deserted for days by its citizens, who feared that the meeting of two great armies at their little settlement would bring massive destruction. Two railways converged in Iuka Springs, so it was strategically valuable to both sides. Confederate General Price had driven a small Union force out and occupied the town; he planned on using Iuka Springs as a supply depot from which to deploy his Rebel troops to retake Corinth. His plans went awry when General Grant engaged the Rebels in a bloody two-hour skirmish at the outskirts of Iuka Springs. The Confederates retreated and Union troops moved into the town. But Grant knew that Corinth was their primary objective. With great urgency, he ordered all soldiers capable of fighting to return to Corinth, leaving only a small contingency to guard the railhead.

Upon Mary Ann's arrival in Iuka Springs, she assisted the surgeons at the field hospital in the town's hotel. Grant had ordered all medical personnel to identify those men still able to bear arms, and to return them to Corinth as soon as possible.

After the battle, the railway station at Iuka Springs was a sight of tumultuous activity. First the able-bodied men and then the walking wounded were evacuated to Corinth by rail. Mary Ann was in charge of getting the wounded to the staging area and loaded onto the boxcars. She realized immediately that crowding wounded men into empty boxcars for any length of time would only lead to further injuries. There wasn't even straw available in this forsaken outpost to cushion the boys from being battered by the motion of the cars. She pondered this problem for some time, and then realized the solution was in the hotel that had been used as a field hospital. She asked Andy to gather together her ambulance drivers, strip the furnishings from the hotel, and bring them to the rail depot as quickly as possible. Within an hour, a series of wagons full of mattresses, chairs, cushions, pillows, and draperies arrived at the station. Mary Ann directed the men to load these luxuries into the boxcars. At the same time, stretcher bearers brought the wounded to wait on the landing. As each car was furnished, Mary Ann identified the wounded to be lifted inside.

"There, young man, put that boy on the bed. He has a broken leg and has to lie down," she directed. "Yes, that's right. No, he can't sit on the chair. Lay him on that pile of draperies. Good. That should be fine." The wounded were surprised and marveled at the hotel's fineries, positioned just so in the boxcars for their comfort.

As she continued to direct the placement of the wounded within the cars, a soldier left a small group of men by the stables across the road and walked toward her. He looked uncomfortable and crushed his hat in his hands. He walked haltingly, looking back over his shoulder at the small group he'd left. They urged him on each time he looked at them. He stood to Mary Ann's side and slightly behind her, so she did not notice him. After several moments, he cleared his throat and said, too softly to be heard over the din, "Mother?" When she did not respond, he cleared his throat again and said in a louder voice, "Mother Bickerdyke? Ma'am?"

Without taking her eyes off her task, she said with a hint of irritation in her voice, "What is it, son?"

He took a step back and looked at his shoes. "We...uh... we have...um, something—"

She interrupted him, "Do you need attention? Have you been wounded? Do you need transport out?"

"Um...no, ma'am. No, I'm not," he replied nervously.

"Then it will have to wait a few minutes," she said impatiently. "I'm busy. Stand back now, son." She returned her attention to the loading, "Yes, put that boy on the armchair. He might need to be tied in."

Feeling intimidated and spurned, the soldier backed away, mumbling, "I'm so sorry, ma'am, I didn't mean to disturb you." He hung his head, turned, and walked slowly back to the group. They conferred, and after a moment, the group walked a little farther away. They led a starving and lame white horse on a halter. Its ribs stuck out, and there were large running sores where a harness had rubbed through its hide.

Fifteen minutes later, the train whistle blew a warning. The last of the wounded were hurried aboard, and the boxcar doors were pulled closed and secured.

Andy walked up to Mary Ann on the station platform as the train whistled its shrill farewell. "That's it, Mother. I didn't think we could do it in that short a time. I'm going back, to pack us up and hunt around for whatever supplies the secesh left."

"Thank you, Andrew. It was a good day's work. But before you go, do you happen to know who the soldier was who approached me a few minutes ago?" she asked.

"I think, Mother, that'd be him over there, by the corral. There are a few other boys with him."

A hundred yards behind the station platform was a crude corral, where a couple of paint horses were stretching their necks to get at the sparse grass just outside the fence. Several soldiers stood by the corral. One held the lead to a scrawny, dirty horse. As Mary Ann approached them, the men walked slowly toward her. They pushed the soldier with the crushed hat out ahead, and one of them said to him, "Go on. You tell her."

"Tell me what?" asked Mary Ann, smiling. "I'm sorry to have been so short with you, young man. Now, what is it you have to tell me?"

He gestured with his rumpled hat toward the filthy white horse and, not daring to meet her gaze, said, "Ma'am, we got this horse for you. It's a Johnny Reb horse that's been used hard pulling artillery. They left it behind when we routed them—probably thinking it was so bad off it would die. He seems gentle enough, and we think he might do you right, even if he is secesh. We heard you was wanting to ride a horse rather than sit in that ambulance all day. He's also kinda hurt and could use some of your healing, ma'am."

Mary Ann looked with surprise from the man to the horse to the men. She wiped her hands on her apron and smiled. "How thoughtful of you, gentlemen. Let's have a look," she said.

The little group of soldiers parted for her. Their gift to her was an older Arabian gelding with a gray blaze on his face. He hung his head, as if he'd been worked half to death. Mary Ann walked up to the horse, murmuring reassurances. She ran her hands over his nose and jaw. He softly nickered and twitched his tangled mane. She walked around him and ran her hands along his sides. Then, she looked closely at his many wounds. "Why, he's a beauty!" she exclaimed with pleasure. "With a little grain and some kindness, I reckon he'll do just fine." She looked at the men and beamed. "Boys, this is a wonderful surprise! He reminds me of a horse I had at home for years—Old Whitey. In fact, that's what I'll call him. Thank you. I...I don't know what to say. You've made me very happy."

Mary Ann took Old Whitey by the lead and walked him away, patting and talking to him the whole time. The men burst into excited chatter, congratulating themselves and feeling good about their gift.

Mary Ann and Old Whitey approached the outside of the now ransacked hotel. A light ambulance was waiting out front, packed and ready to go. Andy was checking the harnesses. Mary Ann handed the lead rope for Old Whitey to Andy. "Andy, this is Old Whitey. Hitch him to the back of the wagon. He's a gift from the boys. We need to take good care of this old fellow. When we stop for the night, he'll need extra attention."

CHAPTER 19

The Tin Cup Brigade

Later that week, Mary Ann returned to Corinth to resume her nursing duties. The Women's Seminary, a grand old stone building on a beautiful estate, had been turned into a temporary hospital. The building sat on a gentle grassy hill bordered below by a dirt road. Huge old oak trees spread their branches over the grounds and made the scene at once peaceful and bucolic. *Corinth Women's Seminary* was chiseled in Gothic letters into the gray stone over the entryway. A hand-painted sign on a rough-hewn wooden board read *Hospital*. A green and yellow flag, signifying the medical corps, waved below the Stars and Stripes on a flagpole in front of the building. The building was several stories high and the upper floors, previously a dormitory, now housed recovering soldiers. The lower floor had become a surgery, while the grassy area in front of the seminary was used by the wounded as a place for rest and relaxation. Several of the men with wounds that permitted them to walk paced the grassy knoll for solace.

The windows and doors of the hospital had been left open to the breeze. It was an unusually warm day for the first of October, and heat shimmered off the dirt road. Recovering soldiers relaxed under the shade of the oak trees, and a few braved the sun on the hot stone steps of the building. Some leaned casually on the wrought-iron fence that edged the seminary grounds.

A large number of Union soldiers marched along the road and past the seminary, wool uniforms soaked with sweat and covered with dust. Occasionally officers on horses galloped past, creating an even larger dust cloud. All the recuperating soldiers outside on the seminary's lawn watched the formations pass by. Patients frequently leaned out the seminary windows or came out on the porch to view this sight. The wounded soldiers by the fence hollered out encouragement to the marching men, who often shouted back in easy camaraderie above the din of the marching.

"Hey, mister! Here's your mule!" yelled a soldier standing inside the fence.

"Soldier boy, where're you from?" shouted another of the wounded at the marchers.

"Forty-Seventh Illinois, laddie!" yelled a soldier passing by.

"How'd ya get wounded?" yelled another soldier in the formation.

"Johnny Reb was just lucky. Where ya off to?" replied one of the patients.

Several soldiers hollered back, "We're off to see the elephant!"

One of the patients cried out, "Second Minnesota, is that you? Keep your head low. It gets mean out there!"

"How long you been marching?"

"Three thousand miles."

"My whole life."

A soldier-patient lifted the stump of his leg and said, "Well, be glad you can!"

As this banter continued, Mary Ann came out and stood on the porch of the seminary, watching. She asked a nearby attendant to quickly bring a tray of water and bread for the soldiers. Then she walked over to the fence, and soldier-patients moved aside to make room for her. She leaned on the gate and looked down the road toward a huge dust cloud. Riding in front of the dust cloud a short way down was an officer and his aides. Their men had lagged behind them a bit and were still enveloped in dust.

Mary Ann opened the gate and stood on the edge of the road, waiting for the officer. She ineffectively smoothed her disordered hair and rolled her sleeves down in an attempt to look presentable, before waving to him.

At her greeting, the colonel and his aides reined their horses over to the side. The tired, footsore color guard emerged ghostlike from the dust cloud and continued to march past, looking absolutely miserable.

The colonel raised his riding crop to his hat and said, "Good day, ma'am."

"Good day, Colonel. Have you come far?"

"We've been on the move since dawn, with a ways yet to go, ma'am."

"May I offer you and your men some refreshment, or at least some bread and water?"

The colonel smiled, "Why, thank you, ma'am. I would be obliged for some bread if it's not too much trouble, but my men don't have time."

When she saw the attendant with the tray she motioned him over. "Give some of the bread to this colonel, please, and his aides," she said.

The attendant held the tray up to the colonel and asked, "Water, sir?"

The colonel responded, "No. Just the bread will do, thank you kindly. I have enough to drink." Patting the four canteens tied to his saddle, he nodded to Mary Ann. "Much obliged, ma'am," he said, and then spurred his horse to take the lead in front of his aides and the color guard. As he rode away, Mary Ann watched him reach in a pocket and pull out a flask. He uncorked it and took a long swig. Then the dust cloud swallowed the colonel, his aides, and his color guard.

Mary Ann muttered to herself, mimicking the colonel, "The men don't have time." Then, with anger in her voice, she said, "What good will these boys be on the battlefield if they are exhausted from marching? What is wrong with these officers? I'm surprised there's anyone left to fight for them!" She looked in the direction from which the men were coming and saw another bedraggled company wearily dragging itself toward her, every man choking on dust and suffering in the stifling heat. Suddenly, Mary Ann turned to the attendant and said, "Fill every cup you can find with water. Get every piece of bread and hard cracker in the hospital. Bring it all out here. Use every able-bodied man to help you. Quickly, now! Let's give these men some sustenance before they fall over and die from the heat."

The attendant nodded, and as he ran to the hospital, Mary Ann addressed the men around her. "Boys, if you're able, bring some water and bread out to these men. They look like they could use it."

She and several of the men hurried to the seminary and ran up the front steps. Moments later, a winded Mary Ann appeared in the second-floor window. She took a deep breath, leaned out, and looked down the road after the colonel. He was nowhere in sight. *Good*, she thought. She cleared her throat, and in a low tone bellowed, "Company, halt! Fall out!"

The company of exhausted men marching past immediately came to a grateful halt. They crowded to the side of the road, dropped their haversacks and equipment, and sought shade from the trees. They sat on the ground, groaning. Many took off their shoes and rubbed their sore and blistered feet, while a contingent of nurses and wounded soldiers rushed from the seminary to offer them trays of food and drink.

One of the soldiers looked up as a hand offered him a cup of water. "What is this, the tin cup brigade?" he asked. "No matter. We Wisconsin boys are mighty thankful. We were almost done in from this heat and dust."

Meanwhile, a mile farther down the road, the Wisconsin colonel and his aides rode up a small hill to confer with the colonel from Hamilton's division, whose column was ahead of them. Their two companies had been leapfrogging each other all day, and the colonels had a bet to see whose men could withstand the most forced marching. The Wisconsin colonel said, "Well, I thought for sure you were behind us eating our dust. Give it up, now. Your men don't have a chance. My men are seasoned soldiers. They've marched all day and could keep going all night. They'll do anything for me."

The other colonel laughed. He turned in his saddle and looked down the road. "And just where are your men, Colonel?"

The Wisconsin colonel turned to look back toward the seminary. The road was empty, except for a small cloud of dust in the distance. Embarrassed and aggravated, he swore, "What the hell?" He glared at his closest aide and snarled, "You. Go find out where those men are. Have them come here, double time." The aide saluted, turned his horse around, and galloped back toward the seminary.

The colonel from Hamilton's division chuckled. "Well, John, it's easy to lose a few hundred men out here in the dust and all. If you're lucky, maybe they'll turn up before the battle and do you proud."

At the seminary, Mary Ann continued to lean out the second-floor window, looking down the road. She saw a lone rider approaching rapidly from the direction the colonel took. She yelled again in a low tone, "'Tention! Fall in! Forward, march!"

At her command, the Wisconsin soldiers hurriedly took their last gulps of water and shoved bread into pockets and knapsacks. Then they scrambled back into their column and marched away.

CHAPTER 20

Writing Last Words before Battle

The night turned cold as healthy soldiers lined up in the dark hallway outside Mary Ann's small room that she used as both office and sleeping quarters. The queue was long, going from her door, down the hall, and out of the building. The soldiers waiting outside stamped their feet and blew on their hands to keep warm. Even inside the seminary, their breath formed clouds of vapor. As one soldier left Mary Ann's office, another entered. Each visit seemed to last about five to ten minutes.

Inside her office, Mary Ann sat in the only chair by the small table. On the table was a stack of small pieces of paper, a pen, an inkwell, needles and thread, and a lantern that cast a soft golden light. A fire in the small camp stove barely warmed the room. Mary Ann's hands were rough and red from her daily duties, and this night her fingertips were stained with ink.

A soldier had just left as the next soldier, a young private, walked in. He took off his kepi and held it nervously in his hands. He nodded at her awkwardly. "Uh…evening, ma'am. This is right nice of you."

Mary Ann replied, "Come, stand over by the camp stove, soldier. Get yourself warm while you tell me what you want me to write."

The private moved closer to the stove and stretched his hands out to warm them.

Mary Ann pulled a sheet of paper from the stack and dipped her pen in the inkwell. "What's your name, son?" she asked.

"Howard, ma'am. Private Robert Howard, Fourth Ohio Infantry. They call me Robbie, though, ma'am."

Mary Ann had started to write, and without looking up she questioned the private. "Who are your folks? Where are you from, Robbie?"

Private Howard responded, "My pa is Elijah Howard from Orrville, Ohio. My ma is Sarah."

There was silence for a moment while Mary Ann wrote this down. Then she looked up. "Mmm...here," Mary Ann said, as she put a threaded needle between her lips. "Let me sew this on to the back of your shirt. I'll read it to you as I sew it. Turn around, son." Mary Ann stood and sewed the small piece of paper on to Private Howard's uniform.

> My name is Private Robert Howard, Fourth Ohio Infantry. They call me Robbie. My folks are Elijah and Sarah Howard of Orrville, Ohio. If something happens to me, take what you can out of my pockets, and send this note and whatever else you find to my folks. Tell them I love them, and that I died bravely.

Mary Ann knotted the thread and cut it with a small scissors. "There. Now, I want you to promise me something, Robbie. If you make it out of this war alive and well, I want you to learn your letters. There's nothing more important than reading the Good Book, and you can't read it if you don't know your letters."

"Yes, ma'am," replied Private Howard, nodding eagerly. "Thank you, ma'am." He turned, opened the door, and left the room. In walked another soldier.

"Come in, son. Warm yourself by the stove while..."

CHAPTER 21

Corinth, Mississippi

The battle for Corinth occurred on October 3 and 4. The heat and humidity on both days were oppressive. By the second day, wounded filled the seminary hospital building and overflowed onto the grounds. Those wounded who could walk from the front limped or crawled toward the hospital, while others were brought in by Mary Ann's ambulance drivers, who assumed the role of stretcher bearers during battle. There were so many wounded, the stretcher bearers only had time to tip the stretcher and dump the wounded on the ground, before running back for another. On the road beside the seminary, soldiers tried to control scared teams of horses that galloped past, pulling wagons of equipment and ammunition. The battle had moved close to the seminary grounds. The sounds of shell and shot were deafening to those inside the hospital. The ground and building shook with each artillery impact. The air was thick with black powder smoke and dust.

Surgeons worked both in and outside the makeshift hospital. There were not enough rooms on the first floor to accommodate the wounded and the surgeons, so several amputation stations had been set up outside the front door. Any flat surface was used as an operating table. Flies swarmed on all the wounds and took up residence on bloody clothing and bandages. Men cried and screamed, beseeching anyone for water or begging that someone save their shattered limb from the cutters. Some pleaded for relief from pain and sometimes, even for death.

One of General Grant's aides approached the seminary building at breakneck speed, dismounted in the midst of the wounded, and ran inside. A few minutes later, General Grant and his aides de camp rode to the hospital and dismounted by the front steps. The aide who had been sent ahead met Grant on the steps and said, "This way, General. She's in here."

Before walking inside, Grant gave orders to his aides. One nodded, turned his horse, and galloped away. To another, Grant said, "Get a message to General Rosecrans. He must move his troops to Battery Robinett and go after those fleeing Rebels."

"Yes, sir!" said the aide, as he spurred his horse and headed off.

Inside the building, the aide guided Grant and his staff over and around the wounded lying on the floor toward the back of the room. There, Mary Ann was bent over a soldier, wrapping a bandage around his hand while giving orders to her soldier-nurses. Next to her was a table stacked with bandages and bowls of bloody water. With every artillery shell that fell nearby, cement dust from the ceiling clouded the air. Wounded were everywhere. Their cries and moans competed with the sound of artillery. It was chaos.

Without looking up from her task, Mary Ann yelled to a nearby orderly, "We need more water! Dump those bowls—they're too bloody. Where's Andy? We're running out of lint. Bring in some more. We'll need lanterns if it gets much darker in here. Move that boy out, he's dead."

Grant walked over to the where she was working. "Ma'am," he said loudly, and nodded to her before he turned his attention back to his aides. Without breaking stride in his stream of orders, Grant removed his hat and took off his coat, and handed them to an aide. The aide helped Grant roll up his bloody sleeve to expose a four-inch splinter deeply embedded in his upper arm. Mary Ann looked up at Grant, and after a brief moment of eye contact, he shrugged.

Mary Ann shifted her attention from the soldier she had been tending to General Grant. She started working the splinter out of his arm while she continued giving orders to her own staff. "Somebody put some pressure on that man's groin! Todd, that's his tongue. I think it's still attached. Just wrap his jaw together for now, but make sure he's not choking on his own blood."

Grant winced as she removed the frayed splinter, pushing part of it through his flesh to avoid the greater damage that would have occurred from pulling it out.

Andy ran up to her, yelling, "The surgeons say there's no more lint for the dressings! They have used it all."

"Nonsense, Andy. There are twenty boxes of lint out back. I brought them myself, from Shiloh!" she shouted, as she poured water from a pitcher on Grant's wound to wash out the dirt. Andy didn't wait to respond and ran out of the room. She then began bandaging the general's arm.

Another of Grant's aides came up for orders. Grant yelled, "Tell Harmon to come hard at their right—just past the salient!"

"Yes, sir!" shouted the aide, and ran for the door.

Grant rolled his sleeve down and put on his coat, and nodded to Mary Ann as he and his staff left. Mary Ann resumed caring for the wounded men around her.

An hour later, a messenger riding a frothing horse pulled to a sudden stop at the entrance of the hospital. He yelled, "The Rebs have broken our flank and they're moving this way—fast! You need to evacuate!" Then he spurred his horse and rode away. Chaos turned to terrified frenzy as the wounded outside tried to save themselves. Several of the walking wounded ran into the building to alert the staff there. Moments later, an artillery shell exploded near the front of the hospital, killing those unlucky enough to be caught in the entryway. The impact of the shell blew shards of glass from windows and body parts into the hospital. Everyone inside who was conscious looked horrified. Some of the men started to scream. Mary Ann picked up her skirts and ran out of the building to one of the amputation stations.

"Doctor, the shells are too close, and the wounded are in mortal danger."

"I can't stop right now!" the surgeon roared. "Find a suitable place for the wounded and evacuate them. I'll be responsible for these men here. Leave the supplies. There's no time."

She grabbed her skirts and ran back into the hospital, yelling for Sergeant Johnson. "Get these boys out of here!" She ran to the front door, hesitated, looked around the hospital grounds, and then pointed to a grove of trees down a small incline, about a mile away. "Take them there!" she yelled, pointing. "It might not be far enough, but it's the best we can do for now. Don't worry about supplies—just get the boys out of here. Every man who can walk, grab the closest person to you and help that person evacuate. If he can't walk, put him on a blanket and drag him out. We are not safe here!" As she finished, another shell struck the side wall of the hospital with a shattering boom, filling the hospital with shrapnel of cement and thick masonry dust.

The word to evacuate spread rapidly, and men started hobbling away from the hospital and nearby tents. Mary Ann helped three blind soldiers to stand, and with their hands on each others' shoulders led them to the hospital entrance. She looked at one of the men who was moving rubble from the entrance and said, "Jubal, put this man's hands on your shoulders and walk him and these other fellows to the grove. Quickly, now!"

Mary Ann saw Andy helping a wounded man out of the seminary. "Andrew, make sure every room is empty. Check upstairs. We've been ordered to leave everything and flee. We might not return."

"The stove, ma'am?" Andy yelled.

"Yes, the stove! Remember!" replied Mary Ann.

Andy yelled to her, "When the last man is gone, I'll wait behind with a few of the boys. We can't let the secesh have that wonderful cooker!"

"It will be very dangerous, Andy!" yelled Mary Ann.

Andy nodded.

"See if you can't save a few boxes of lint, too. Be careful, Andy!" said Mary Ann.

The sounds of battle raged nearby, the smell of powder was thick in the air, signal bugles blasted competing commands, and fighting soldiers appeared and disappeared at the edge of a huge cloud of dust and smoke. The hospital was shelled but remained standing.

Several hours later, frenzy and chaos still reigned. Soldiers ran with the newly wounded on litters, occasionally dropping them in their haste to reach the grove. Mary Ann knelt, pressing one knee on a man's wounded thigh to stop his artery from spurting. Looking around, she called to Stuart, one of her ambulance drivers who was helping the wounded, "Get some bandages over here. This man is bleeding to death!"

Stuart answered, "There aren't any bandages!"

"Andy brought some from the hospital. Those boxes, over there," she said, and pointed. "Break them open—they're full of lint."

Stuart ran to several filthy crates and used a bayonet to pry one open. He grabbed armfuls of lint and bandages, ran to Mary Ann, and dropped them near her.

"Stuart, stop this man's bleeding with a tourniquet. Pack his wound with lint, and tie it as tight as you can. Then go back and take lint to all the surgeons' tables." Stuart nodded and took her place on the soldier's wounded thigh.

Mary Ann took a brief moment to assess her newly established field hospital. Some of the men were sweltering in full sun. The flies had followed them.

"Zeb!" she yelled to a young drummer boy nearby. "Go and drag those tent pieces here. Build a lean-to for those men over there. They need to get out of the sun. Then start ladling water into whatever you can find. We need to cool these boys down."

The battle for Corinth raged for three days, and then suddenly the cannonade from both sides stopped as if orchestrated. An eerie quiet enveloped the field. Somewhere in the distance birdsong tentatively threaded its way to the field hospital. A half hour later, a weary battle-torn soldier rode up to the edge of hospital.

"Where's the surgeon in charge?" he asked a wounded soldier nearby. This man pointed to the far side of the grove, and the rider turned his horse and headed in that direction.

Shortly afterward, the surgeon approached Mary Ann. His butcher's apron was now stiff and caked with blood. The flies swarmed on the apron and the surgeon's sleeves, arms, and face. The flies no longer left when shaken off, but had to be crushed into an ever thicker layer of gore. Mary Ann sat on the ground in partial shade, with an unconscious soldier's head in her blood-soaked lap, wiping the man's forehead with a wet rag. The man was gut shot—a hopeless wound. Knowing he would die, Mary Ann spoke soft, gentle, mothering words to him, offering what comfort she could, in case he could still hear.

"Mrs. Bickerdyke," said the surgeon, approaching her. "The general sent a messenger to tell us it is safe to return to the seminary building—whatever is left of it. The Confederates have been routed, and we have taken the day. The men might be cooler and more comfortable within the seminary walls. I leave you to tend to this. By the way, where's that fellow who was assigned to you? Um...I've forgotten his name."

"Andy? Andrew Somerville," said Mary Ann.

"Yes. I've not seen him around. He's usually helping us at the cutting tables," said the surgeon.

"Why," replied Mary Ann, looking around, "I haven't seen him either. Maybe he got lost in all the confusion."

The surgeon nodded and walked away with the weary step of an exhausted man.

An hour later, inside the hospital building, all the wounded who were able helped sweep the floors, clear out debris, and rebuild the fireplace from the bricks scattered on the floor. Some of the wounded had already been returned to the hospital and rested on straw bedding. Two soldiers started to ready pots and pans for cooking. Mary Ann directed all this activity. She walked to the entrance, where only half the porch remained. She looked out to see several hundred men limping, walking, or being carried from the grove in a more orderly manner than that with which they had left the hospital. In their midst was a wagon driven by Andy, with three other men in the wagon bed holding on to the stove. The wagon was jammed with kettles, bricks, and tins of laundry soap, and towed the bread wagon. The horses strained to pull all this weight, and some of the men limping toward the building passed the wagon by. As Andy pulled up to the front of the seminary, an officer approached him.

"You're Private Somerville, aren't you?" asked the officer.

"Yes, sir," Andy replied.

"Soldier, where have you been? We could have used your help when we evac'd the hospital."

"Sir, artillery spooked the horses and we got lost in the woods. Same thing happened to these other fellers. It was just luck we happened to meet up."

Mary Ann overheard the conversation and rushed down the steps to stand next to the officer.

"Oh, Andy! How wonderful! You thought to bring the stove! Now we can give the surgeons and wounded a hot supper tonight!" She turned to the officer. "Thank you for your help, sir. I can oversee the setting up of the diet kitchen. I'm sure you have much more important things to do." Then Mary Ann redirected her attention to Andy. "Pull that wagon over there. That's a fine place to set up the kitchen. We'll have these boys eating a hearty supper in no time." With her back to the officer, she gave Andy a broad smile.

That afternoon, while Mary Ann was tending to a soldier whose wounds had broken open, she saw out of the corner of her eye a soldier standing next to her. He was shaking, filthy from the battle, and tears made pale streaks in the gunpowder and smoke on his face. She looked up at him.

"Ma'am," said the young soldier, his voice cracking with emotion. "Do you, ah, remember me?"

Mary Ann looked at his face a moment, and then slowly nodded. "Yes, I think I do. You're Danny, aren't you? Wait just a moment." Mary Ann called to a soldier-nurse by the door. "Come help with this boy here."

As the soldier-nurse took over, Mary Ann rose and grasped Danny by the arm. "Now, Danny. Are you injured, son? What's wrong?"

Danny started to openly sob, and Mary Ann put her arms around him and held him for a moment. Tentatively, she asked, "Is it Zeke, your friend? Is he dead?"

Danny nodded his head and sobbed, "It...it's worse... I...I...you have to help me, Mother. I can't do it alone. I just can't."

"Danny, there are men newly wounded here, other boys just like Zeke, wounded and dying. If Zeke is dead, whatever we need to do for him can wait a while, can't it? We need to help these men first. I'll help you, but first you must help me. Can you do that, Danny?" asked Mary Ann.

Danny nodded, trying to stifle his sobs.

"Now, you're sure you're not hurt?" Mary Ann asked. Danny nodded again. "Good. Help me move this boy into a more comfortable position."

An hour later, Mary Ann followed Danny through the makeshift hospital. He was still crying and saying between sobs, "Dirty Rebs. They had no call to do that. We was doing all right and then...aw...jeez..."

They reached the edge of the hospital where the dead were being laid out. *There are so many*, thought Mary Ann with great sadness. *Mothers' sons—all of them.* Then she looked at Danny and said, "Where is he? Do you know?"

"There," Danny pointed, "I think. By that one with the green sash."

They carefully stepped through the debris of bodies, trying not to slip on the pools of blood. As they passed, they disturbed thousands of flies that rose in great clouds. They approached Zeke's body. His face was black and his teeth were bared in a final grimace of pain. The body of a boy was slumped over Zeke, but from what they could see, most of Zeke's chest and abdomen had been blown away, leaving a red gaping wound.

"Danny," said Mary Ann, "help me move this boy off Zeke and clear a space so I can get close to him." They moved the body of a boy who couldn't have been more than fourteen years old off Zeke, and together moved three bodies away from Zeke's side. Mary Ann knelt down next to Zeke and started pulling remnants of his shirt away from and out of his wound. She looked at the wound and hesitated, stifling a moment of profound nausea. Then she slowly put her hand into the hole in Zeke's chest. She felt around with a studious grimace on her face and then paused.

"Ah!" said Mary Ann, pulling a bloody clump of meat from the wound. She dropped it in her apron and started to dry it off. She muttered to herself, "Taking cats into battle. That's the strangest thing I've heard yet."

Danny stood beside her, sobbing. He gasped out through his sobs, "He had nowhere to put 'em. Nowhere but his shirt. He loved those little critters, always was talking about 'em, and named 'em even. Ah, Zeke. Ya had to go and get yourself shot!"

Mary Ann handed the blood-covered kitten to Danny and said, "Well, this one's alive at least. I don't think he's too hurt, but it's hard to tell until that blood gets washed off. How many more, do you think?"

"Three, I think," replied Danny.

Mary Ann grimaced again and put her hand back into Zeke's gaping chest wound.

The day passed quickly with the transfer of the wounded back to the seminary. In the evening, Mary Ann made her rounds in the hospital. She paused by one particular soldier. *Something's familiar about him*, she thought, but couldn't quite place him. Could he be the son of someone in Galesburg? The young man's wounds were obviously mortal. Something had torn off his right arm and the side of his chest wall from shoulder to mid-abdomen. His right lung and the damage to it were clearly visible. A steady seepage of blood drained from his chest onto the ground. Part of his bowel hung out of the wound. He struggled for air, most of which bubbled out the right lung in a bloody froth. She knelt down next to him and with her apron wiped the dirt away from his face. He was conscious, in agony, and terrified.

"Why, I know you. I know those green eyes. I have cared for you before, haven't I? Cecil, wasn't it?" she asked.

Between gasps for air the young man mumbled, "Mother." With his left hand he grabbed her skirt in a tight fist.

Mary Ann tenderly stroked his forehead and pushed the hair away from his eyes. "Cecil...Cecil Acton. From Shiloh. You were brought in on the second day with a bad wound in your thigh. You'd lost a lot of blood and were nearly dead. But you pulled through. I hadn't realized you had returned to duty so quickly. And now..." Mary Ann could not finish the sentence. She knew he would die. For his sake she hoped it would be soon.

"Son," she said gently, "make your peace with the Lord. Your wound is grievous, and it won't be long now. I wish I could help you. I wish I could take the pain away, take that look of utter fear from your eyes. Oh, my poor boy," she said, as tears rolled down her face to land on the remnants of his uniform shirt. "I should have sent you home," she said very quietly. "You shouldn't have come back. Oh, son, I'm so sorry. This is partly my fault." After a long pause, she whispered, "Don't fight so hard to breathe, my son. Let go. Let the good Lord take you and free you from all this suffering. I'll wait with you, so you do not die alone. I remember, you're from somewhere near Springfield, Ohio, and I will let your family know. I'll tell your mother about your courage and bravery. I'll take care of everything for you. Just let go, my son. Let go."

Mary Ann knelt there for about a half an hour. Her tears continued to flow, and she stroked his forehead and cheek, occasionally moistening his cracked dry lips with a wet cloth. She prayed to God to lessen his burden and take him quickly. She pleaded for an end to his suffering.

His fist, which had a tight hold on her skirt, began to slowly relax as his breathing became shallower and less tortuous. She stayed by his side as his breath came softer and slower. Unconsciously she breathed with him, matching his rhythm of gasps. They became slower and slower, until his chest was still. Mary Ann held her breath, waiting. Then his chest expanded in one last agonal intake of air, his body twitched in reflex, and he was gone. A mother's son. A mother's pride. Gone.

After he died, the look of pain on his face disappeared, until his countenance was that of a handsome young man in his prime. Worry free and relieved of all suffering. She closed his eyes and whispered, "God have mercy on you." Mary Ann waited a few more moments. His hand still gripped her skirt, as if even in death he didn't want to leave her or had wanted her to go with him. She gently opened his fist and her skirt fell free.

"May God have mercy on us all," said a soldier sitting nearby, his leg in a splint and his hand a ball of bloody bandages. "Especially on both of us. Soldiers create hell and kill our kin and friends and neighbors, and you bind our wounds and heal us, so we can go out there again to extend this hell. There is something crazy in all this. No wonder some of the boys' minds break to pieces in this stupid, meaningless war."

A heavy sense of guilt and shame for not understanding earlier her role in these men's deaths flooded Mary Ann, and she paled, visibly shaken by the realization that her work fed this war machine that mercilessly chewed up boys and men, and spat them out to die in horrible ways. She covered her face with her hands.

"Are you all right, Mother?" asked Sergeant Johnson, a soldier-patient who walked up to her.

She pulled her hands away and looked up at him, for a moment not comprehending. Then she sighed and said, "Yes. I'm all right," and wiped the tears from her eyes with her filthy apron.

"Mother," he said, "we have confirmed that all the wounded are now in the hospital building and surrounding tents. Tomorrow morning I'll send men out to retrieve whatever useable items remain in the grove."

Mary Ann nodded and thanked him. Slowly, she rose and returned to walking through the rooms, checking on the wounded. This had become a routine duty, but tonight there was an added weight of sadness.

Several hours into the night, she began to worry that there might be someone left behind at the grove, someone too wounded to call for help. This thought haunted her until she gathered her shawl around her and took a lantern out to see for herself.

In the grove, she walked slowly, stepping over equipment, items of clothing, bloody bandages, dirty dishes, and other remnants of war. She held the lantern up and peered into the shadows, reassuring herself that no wounded had been overlooked. She proceeded methodically into each lean-to, noting what items she might need up at the seminary. She looked under soiled blankets and piles of rags— the smell was foul, even though there was a night breeze.

She scrutinized a pile of tree boughs and moved it with her foot. Satisfied that nothing was there, she turned to leave, but heard a slight rustling noise from the corner. She stopped and listened; then she turned and held the lantern high and waited. The rustling noise came again. She walked toward it and stopped abruptly when a large brown rat scurried out of the pile and along the side of the lean-to. She watched it with a furrowed brow and said to herself, "Rats. Wretched creatures. What are you feeding on?" She quickly knelt down and placed the lantern on the ground. She pulled at the tree boughs and rags and trash with an increasing sense of foreboding. More rats scurried out and away. She continued to clear the pile and suddenly saw a filthy face appear. She stopped, startled. "My Lord!" she gasped, and moved the lantern closer to examine the face for signs of life. For a long moment everything was still. Then, without warning, the eyes opened and caught the light of her lantern. She jumped back in fear, but then realized that she had found someone who was alive. Terror and agony filled the man's face. She quickly cleared away the rest of the rubbish piled on top of the soldier. She saw that he had been shot through both cheeks and his tongue was half gone, the remaining part swollen black to bursting out of his mouth. She began to murmur, "There, there, now, we'll have you out of here in no time, you poor fellow." She noticed he had a badly shattered arm and a leg that would need to be amputated. Insects had infested his wounds. The lantern light revealed hundreds of maggots. And the rats or other animals had been eating the flesh of his leg.

"Young man, I must leave you for a moment, to bring help. I will return. I promise. I will leave the lantern here. The light might keep the rats away." She rushed out of the lean-to and yelled angrily for Sergeant Johnson as she hurried toward the seminary in the pitch-black. With each step her fury grew.

"Sergeant Johnson!" she bellowed into the night. "There is a wounded man in the grove. Bring soldiers and a litter now, and see that they carry some water." She turned and hurried back to the lean-to.

Sergeant Johnson came running to the front of the hospital, swearing to himself, "Oh, shit and snockered pigs!" Then, to several attendants, he said, "Boys, I need help. Three of you grab a litter and some water, and come with me. Run!"

Mary Ann met Sergeant Johnson halfway down the hill. She was fury itself.

"How could you! You told me you had confirmed that all of the wounded were removed. How dare you leave this man behind? Someday, I hope you will be in his position, and you will learn what it means to be abandoned. This man has suffered much longer than he had to because of your negligence. Bring him up to the hospital now. I will deal with you, later. Be gentle with him."

The men carried the forgotten soldier up to the seminary while Sergeant Johnson made one last sweep of the grove area to check for anyone else who might have been overlooked. Then slowly, and with great dread, Sergeant Johnson walked toward the seminary building.

The wounded man had been placed on a table, and the surgeon and Mary Ann hovered over him.

"It must come off, and we must do it now if we wish to save this man's life. You three, hold him down," said the surgeon. "While I'm doing this, I want you, Mother, to clean his wounds and get rid of those maggots."

174

By lantern light Mary Ann picked out maggots and bits of bone and dirt from his facial wound. Some other soldiers were watching, but many were asleep or blissfully unconscious. Once the man's wounds were cleaned, his arm set, and his leg amputated, he was settled, unconscious, on a straw pallet. Mary Ann sat by his side and murmured softly to him. "I will be here with you when you wake. Rest now, my son."

Then Mary Ann rose and walked toward Sergeant Johnson, who was huddled in a shadowy corner with several other men. She hissed at him, "Follow me to the back room. Now."

Once in the room with the door closed, Mary Ann whirled around and stepped close to the sergeant. With her index finger almost jabbing his eyes, she raged, "Never in all my years of experience as a nurse have I ever seen such gross neglect. How dare you! This man was totally dependent on you for his welfare, and look at what you have done. You have shamed yourself before the Union army and before me. You should be court-martialed, or sent to the front to take this man's place to see how you like it." While saying this, she moved toward Sergeant Johnson and he backed up. "I am going to go to the general and have you removed from this hospital. I cannot tolerate someone being abandoned in his time of need. Believe me—I know what I'm talking about. There is no more frightening experience than to be left helpless and alone. This man was giving everything for his country. He deserves better than you gave him!"

At this point, Mary Ann stopped speaking and slapped him across the face as hard as she could. Sergeant Johnson was stunned. Then without another word, she turned and left. Johnson sheepishly rejoined his comrades, knowing they had heard it all in spite of the closed door.

Mary Ann returned to the room with the forgotten soldier and walked over to the surgeon who was changing a dressing on another man. "What about him?" she whispered to the surgeon, nodding toward the forgotten soldier.

The surgeon looked at Mary Ann and slowly shook his head. Mary Ann looked down at the soldier, still unconscious and barely breathing. Then she turned and left the seminary. She stood by a broken pillar outside in the darkness and began to cry. She could not—would not—think about the soldier in that room behind her. But memories of loss consumed her: first her mother and grandparents, and then her uncle and sister. The pain and fear that accompanied such loss broke through her strong façade, and a palpable helplessness surged past her defenses. She crumpled to the ground with her face in her hands and sobbed, "I cannot bear this."

CHAPTER 22

Old Whitey and the Geese

For days, the ambulance drivers were busy bringing wounded from the battlefield to the seminary. Mary Ann walked through the wards, checked on her boys, and made her rounds. She passed a young man lying on his back with his eyes closed. She paused, turned back to him, and noticed a large festering wound in his gut. "George?" she said softly, and moved her lantern up close to see his face. "George Matthews, is that you?"

"Yes, ma'am," George responded weakly. "It's dark... it's cold...I'm...I'm scared. Water...I need water..."

She knelt down next to him and said, "Little George, I didn't know that you had joined up. Let me see your wound, boy. Let me see if I can help." She gently unbuttoned his blood-encrusted jacket and peeled away the remnants of his bloody, torn shirt. Most of his intestines were exposed. She looked for just a moment, and then quietly replaced his shirt and covered him with his jacket. She stood and scanned the room for a blanket not in use. She found one on a dead soldier. With the blanket and a cup of water, she returned to George and knelt beside him. Taking the hem of her dress, she dipped it in the cup and pressed it to his lips. She leaned close to hear him whisper. "Tell...tell my mother...that I always wished..." And George's breath slowly left his body. Tears rolled down Mary Ann's face, and she roughly wiped them away with the back of her hand. "Dear, dear boy. May God have mercy on us."

The medical and nursing needs of the wounded from the battles of Iuka Springs and Corinth exhausted the U.S. Sanitary Commission stores, but by this time in her career, Mary Ann was an excellent forager. Whenever possible, she asked soldiers to accompany her to the quartermaster storehouse to see if there were any supplies she could use.

On this day, the quartermaster met her at the door and said, "We have no hospital supplies. They have all been given out."

Undaunted, Mary Ann smiled and said, "Well, we'll take whatever you've got. It doesn't have to be hospital supplies. We'll make do." The quartermaster protested, but she ignored him and ordered her soldiers to take bales of hay and cotton, saying, "These will make softer beds for the wounded."

The quartermaster raised his voice and said, "But you must bring me an order before I can release these stores to you."

"An order? Do you think I have time to go hunting up officers for an order? Do you know how busy my hospital is?"

The quartermaster continued to protest. "I need an order for these. I cannot simply give them to you just because you need them."

Mary Ann said to her soldiers, "Keep loading the wagons, boys. I'll make sure everything will be all right."

The quartermaster, needing to balance his books of supplies in and supplies out, filed a complaint against Mrs. Bickerdyke, and she was summoned to meet the charge. The summons, like other unimportant pieces of paper, went into her dress pocket until she found the time to respond. Paperwork always came after caregiving. When her chores neared completion, she sent a soldier-patient to the provost marshal indicating the time she expected she would be able to meet with him.

When she arrived at the provost marshal's office, he gave her a cold reception. He did not offer her a chair, but made her stand in front of his desk.

"Mrs. Bickerdyke, you are charged with stealing supplies from the quartermaster without orders. What have you to say?" said the provost marshal.

"Well, who do you think ordered the tents put up on the college grounds?" she countered.

Not expecting this response, the provost marshal hesitated before answering, "Why, I did."

"Well, why did you put them up?"

With growing exasperation, he answered, "To provide shelter for the wounded, of course."

"Did you expect wounded soldiers to lie on the ground in those tents?"

"You should have obtained orders for the supplies you took. That's the way it's done in the army," he said angrily.

Meeting his anger, Mary Ann said, "I have no time to obtain orders, sir. Why didn't you order the hay and the cotton, so I didn't have to bother the quartermaster?"

"I did not think of it," he replied.

"But I did, and I was pressured by the needs of wounded men. If you need an order, why don't you sit down and write one and give it to the quartermaster?" With that, Mary Ann turned around and walked out.

The provost marshal sat muttering, "That damned pugnacious woman!"

The next night during her rounds Mary Ann knelt by a soldier who had been crying out. He had a shattered and open pelvis. He said to her, "I don't want to die—I don't want to. I want to go home. I'm not ready." He grabbed her shoulders and began to pull. Surprisingly strong, he pulled her down until her face was just inches from his own.

"Don't you understand?" he said. "I can't die now. I have a wife and three babies who need me. They can't make it on their own. They'll starve. You *must* save me." He glared up at her for a moment; then suddenly, a look of surprise came over his face, his grip loosened, and he exhaled his last breath.

Mary Ann rose slowly and walked to an orderly. She pointed to the man who had just died. "Please find out where that boy came from and his name. I need to write to his family."

"Yes, ma'am." He hesitated. "Ma'am, are you all right? You're as white as a ghost. Do you need to sit down?"

"No," Mary Ann replied. "Thank you, son. I just need some fresh air, is all. I'll be back shortly."

Mary Ann left the hospital and walked to the nearby barn. She walked slowly past the stalls, noting the comfort she received from the warm animal and earthy smells. It was familiar and somehow safe. She walked to Old Whitey's stall. He was munching the last of the hay, but looked up and nickered when he saw her. She opened the gate of his stall and stepped close to him. Shadows in the stall were deep and dark. Moonlight penetrated the barn entrance but went no farther, leaving Mary Ann and Old Whitey in darkness, seemingly cut off from the world. She put her arms around the horse's reassuring neck, pressed her face to him and sobbed. "Old Whitey. Dear Old Whitey. I just can't do this anymore."

Glorious purple and apricot clouds painted the sky over the hospital the next evening. A breeze with a hint of fall rustled the trees. Since the stove from Chicago was not large enough to feed all the wounded, cooking fires were also situated outside. Mary Ann, haggard and tired, bent to stir a huge kettle of soup suspended over an open fire.

Soldiers sat all around her. Some wore bandages, some drank out of their canteens, some cleaned their weapons, and others talked in low tones. Somewhere a soldier was playing a sad tune on a fiddle. The seminary building in the background had just been lit by lanterns. Mary Ann straightened up, spoon in hand, put her hands behind her hips, and stretched. Then she was still. She had heard something, far off in the distance. She looked up and saw against that magnificent sunset a flock of geese in formation, high up, honking as they headed south. She was transfixed by the sight.

A soldier sitting across the fire from her lifted his rifle to sight on the birds. A nearby officer pushed the soldier's rifle down. The soldier looked up quizzically and somewhat angrily at the officer, who shook his head no and nodded toward Mary Ann. The soldier looked from the officer to Mary Ann and saw tears streaming down her face.

She said quietly to herself, "I forgot how normal everything else is. How can everything go on as usual, when all this pain and suffering is happening?"

☜☞

Later that same night, an exhausted Mary Ann sat hunched over the small table in her quarters at the seminary building. Somewhere a sleepless soldier played a harmonica. The sad melody entered her room and gently mingled with the memories of the day. A candle flickered and splashed wax on the table. Mary Ann had pen in hand and was writing a letter, speaking the words as she wrote:

> Dear General Grant,
> My work here at Corinth is almost over. Everything is in good order, and the local staff manage the work smoothly. I have not seen my children for almost a year and am hoping

to spend Christmas with them. I plan to return at the start of the new year. Where will you need me? You can reach me care of Mary Livermore at the U.S. Sanitary Commission in Chicago. I will await word from you.

May the Lord protect you and
your men.
M. A. Bickerdyke

CHAPTER 23

Christmas in Galesburg—1862

Worn and weary, Mary Ann returned to Galesburg by train and boat. Her last letter from her children, months ago, indicated there was some sort of problem with their situation, and she was worried about how she could care for them as well as the soldiers. She also knew how eager the relatives of soldiers were for word of their loved ones. Whenever she traveled she always filled her satchel with buttons, locks of hair, or notes from her wounded soldiers, so she could give their anxious relatives some small bit of comfort.

On her arrival she was met by the Reverend Beecher, who asked her to help raise funds for the Sanitary Commission while she was in Galesburg. She felt very torn by this simple request. She had missed her children terribly and was quite worried about them. She was also uncertain of the length of her stay here. She felt drained of energy and emotionally depleted; she had nothing left to give. She was afraid if just one more person asked her to do one more thing, she might lose her sanity. She did not want the few precious moments she might have with her children shortened by more war duties, but did not see how she could refuse him.

"Let me find a better situation for my children, and we shall see how much I can accomplish while I'm here," she replied.

Mary Ann spent a week in Galesburg, but the opportunities for placing her children with other families were few. The war, now more than a year old, had begun to consume resources from civilians at an alarming rate. Accommodations with even her closest friends were not possible; they had no way to feed another two mouths.

Dejected, Mary Ann traveled to Chicago and met with Mrs. Livermore at the U.S. Sanitary Commission offices. Mary Ann wasted no time discussing the problem of a placement for her children with Mrs. Livermore. As head of the Western Branch of the Sanitary Commission, Mrs. Livermore was well connected. She knew of a preacher and his wife who were taking in orphans from the war and thought this might be a possibility. Mrs. Livermore contacted them and an agreement was made. Mary Ann's boys would travel by rail to Chicago shortly after Christmas.

While in Chicago, she accompanied Mrs. Livermore to a wedding. Mary Ann was so tired that at the onset of the service, she fell asleep sitting up in the church pew. Mrs. Livermore awakened her afterward for the customary greeting of the bride and groom. As Mary Ann approached the couple, the young groom recognized Mrs. Bickerdyke, and with great excitement announced to those present that she had nursed him after the battle of Fort Donelson. She had stood between him and a surgeon and prevented the amputation of his leg. He was now completely recovered and standing on his own two feet, all because of her kind care. He and his new wife expressed their gratitude to an embarrassed and surprised Mary Ann, while others in the wedding party whispered, "So that's the famous Mrs. Bickerdyke!" Then the women in the room clustered around her, asking if she had any news of their husbands, fathers, brothers, and sons who fought against the rebellion.

Mary Ann returned to Galesburg and spent Christmas at home with Hiram and James. Both boys were upset that she would be leaving them once again, and that they must go to the home of a stranger in a strange city. They cried, feeling abandoned and hopeless. She reassured them that Mrs. Livermore would periodically check on them and send reports to her, but there was little comfort in this for small children. Their sadness stifled any seasonal cheer, and it was a tense and gloomy time for all. Mary Ann promised to write them as often as she could, but she left unspoken her fear that when she returned to Grant's army, there would be little time to spare for letters to her sons.

She said a tearful good-bye to Hiram and James at the train station as they left on their journey to a new home. It was a heart-wrenching parting for all. The boys clung tightly to Mary Ann and shrieked, "No, no, don't make us go!" Two porters eventually had to carry them into the car just as the train was beginning to pull away from the station. As soon as Mary Ann could no longer see their little hands waving from the windows, she returned to pack her belongings and await word from General Grant.

The newspapers kept the North informed about Grant's travels and confrontations in the western campaign. In the fall of 1862, Grant had massed his Army of the Tennessee, forty-five thousand men, at Memphis, intending to take Vicksburg, Mississippi, by land. A previous riverboat assault had been unsuccessful. Vicksburg was considered a critical stronghold and supply line for the Deep South. The Union hoped that in taking Vicksburg it could break the back of the South. Grant's first attempt to take the city failed when the Rebels repulsed General Sherman's forces at Chickasaw Bluffs.

Mary Ann did not have to wait long for word from Grant. He sent her a letter.

Mrs. Bickerdyke,

I need you in Memphis. To assist you in your work I am issuing you a permit good for the duration of the war.

General U. S. Grant

The permit read:

All pickets let Mrs. Bickerdyke pass. All quartermasters allow this woman to draw from your stores. This permit is valid for the duration of the war. By order of General U. S. Grant

The trip to Memphis was a tiring one. Mary Ann did not feel rested from her brief but busy time in Galesburg and Chicago. She had begun to feel weary of never having time to spend with her children, chasing after armies, and always making do with skimpy supplies. She never felt she accomplished enough or worked fast enough to save the life of that next, dying soldier. Gore and death crushed her, and she was haunted by the faces of her sons, knowing that she was a failure as a mother. As she stepped off the train at the Memphis station, she felt a thousand years old.

CHAPTER 24

Adams Block Hospital, Memphis, Tennessee— January 1863

In Memphis there were a number of hospitals divided between the regular army and those wounded in battle. Hospitals treating the regular army were full of men with contagious diseases. War wounded were confined to other army facilities. Memphis was a fortified city that the Union used as a main supply depot for another planned attack on Vicksburg. Memphis had also turned into one huge hospital, caring for Union and Confederate alike.

When Mary Ann arrived, Dr. Irwin, the head surgeon for the army hospitals, refused to let her tend the wounded. Instead, he assigned her to a hospital for soldiers ill from diseases that plagued the regular army. For several weeks she worked at her tasks with growing discontent. Her patients had dysentery, cholera, influenza, scarlet fever, and measles. She had dealt with these diseases many times in the past and found them to be less than challenging.

Her experience at Corinth in the field hospital, as harsh as it was, had opened something up in her and given her feelings she had never had before. She knew what she offered was very important to the desperately wounded and different from what the surgeons and soldier-nurses had to offer. At Corinth, for the first time, Mary Ann felt she had found the way to make a genuine contribution to the war effort. However, deep in her heart, she wondered if her contribution would mean more suffering for the wounded rather than of less. She carried this doubt like a weight of stones. Instead of the doubt softening, it began to grow a hard edge in her that she had not had before.

She worried that "her boys" weren't receiving the care they needed. Wounded continued to flow to the hospitals. Many needed her care, but each time she approached Dr. Irwin for a transfer to work with wounded soldiers, he dismissed her as a histrionic woman. He hoped she'd leave Memphis and return to her civilian life. With each approach, his temper raged more intensely.

Dr. Irwin was a tall, lean man with pale skin. He was dark-haired, with jet-black eyes and a full mustache. He carried himself like an officer and did not believe that women belonged in a hospital, let alone a military facility.

One morning inside the hospital, she approached him again. He snapped at her, "Woman, you must stop hounding me with your requests and go away! If you don't, I will have you escorted out of the city."

Mary Ann's face reddened. "I am not going away," she replied. "It has been a month, and you are not allowing me to do anything useful for the wounded. It is a shameful waste. The wounded men need me more than the regular army men I am tending. You are depriving them—"

Before she finished, Dr. Irwin turned to face her. Trying to contain his anger, he said through gritted teeth, "Woman, I deprive them of nothing." He punctuated this with a sweeping gesture toward the Sisters of Charity who nursed in the ward. "These sisters provide us with all the nursing we need, and they don't talk back!"

Feeling anger boil up inside her, she said, "Well, you may have enough sisters to give care in this hospital, but the city of Memphis has many hospitals and upward of nine thousand beds of sick and wounded soldiers. This hospital cares for only a few hundred. What of the others?"

Dr. Irwin closed his eyes and said, "You are exasperating! Will you never let well enough alone?" He paused and put a hand to his forehead. "Very well, I have been informed that I *must* place you as matron of one of our hospitals. So your first duty will be Adams Block. I do not wish to lay eyes on you or to hear from you until that hospital is running like a clock. And don't ask *me* for any help." Without looking at her, he shook his head and made a gesture of dismissal. "Now, be gone." He turned and stomped off down the hallway.

Mary Ann smiled and watched Dr. Irwin depart. When he was just far enough away to be out of hearing, she began to mimic him. She put her hands on her hips, shook her shoulders and said, "And don't ask *me* for help!" For a moment she considered making an unladylike gesture, but instead raised her eyes to heaven and murmured, "The Lord be praised. It's not what I wanted, but it's something. I'll wear him down yet."

Mary Ann spent three weeks organizing Adams Block. One afternoon, during dressing-change rounds on the ward, a number of ladies dressed finely in black satin and lace walked in through the main door and stopped in the entry-way, whispering to each other. Then one woman broke from the group and walked up to the closest soldier-nurse. "Excuse me, but can you tell me who's in charge here? I'm looking for my brother, a Confederate captain by the name of Brent Beauregard."

The soldier-nurse responded, "Dr. Irwin is in charge of this hospital, but there is no way for you to reach him. If you had a mind to, you could go over to that room there"—he pointed—"and see Mother Bickerdyke. She knows almost everyone here at Adams Block."

"Thank you, sir," said the lady. She turned toward the entryway and motioned with a gloved hand for her friends to follow her. As a group they walked into the next room. As they passed wounded soldiers lying on the floor, one fellow tugged at the skirts of one of the ladies and said, "Water. May I have some water?"

The Southern belle said, "Why, certainly. Let me find a cup and water, and I'll bring it to you."

One of the other ladies whispered, "Rebecca! We did not come here to care for the Yankee wounded!"

Rebecca hushed her, and looked around the room for water and a cup. She saw what she was looking for on a table in the center and walked quickly to it. As her gloved hand was about to touch the cup, a dirty, blood-streaked hand grabbed her wrist.

Mary Ann, holding the woman's wrist, asked, "May I help you?"

Startled, Rebecca pulled back and looked at Mary Ann. "I was just trying to get a cup of water for that gentleman over there."

"Have you come to help me nurse these boys?" asked Mary Ann.

"No. I'm looking for my brother, a captain in the Confederate army named Brent Beauregard. Can you tell me if he's here?"

"I'm sorry, I haven't heard that name. But there's a roomful of Confederate soldiers over there," Mary Ann said, nodding in the direction of an open doorway. "They have recently arrived, and I've not yet had time to care for them. You are welcome to look there. And if you are so inclined, I could really use your help in nursing these men—Union and Confederate alike." It was a small beginning, but several ladies of the South began working beside Mary Ann to care for the wounded.

As the work at Adams Block hospital became more routine, Mary Ann sought out Dr. Irwin.

He sat at his desk in his office, working on a pile of paperwork. He did not look up when footsteps stopped in front of his desk. He growled, "I thought I gave orders that I was not to be disturbed until this damn paperwork was finished!"

"People come before paperwork," said Mary Ann.

Dr. Irwin dropped his pen, held his forehead in his hands and groaned, "Oh, no. Not you again." He looked up at Mary Ann, and with great irritation said rudely, "What are you doing here? What do you want now? I thought I told you to put Adams Block Hospital in order and not to disturb me until you succeeded."

"The hospital is in order. I invite you to come and see."

"Do you mean to tell me that Adams Block would pass inspection?"

"Yes, indeed."

"That cannot be. You have not been there a month—it isn't possible."

Mary Ann leaned over and put her hands on his desk. He backed up his chair to keep his distance and met her eyes. She said, "There are five hundred men there. They are all bathed and their wounds are freshly dressed. Their fevers and scurvy are being treated with poultices and fresh fruit. They rest on clean bedding. The bakery makes over six hundred loaves a day. The laundry washes one thousand articles every morning. The floors are swept and the grounds well policed. Every wall has been whitewashed. The dead have been buried and their kin notified. The hospital can run itself. It won't need someone like me until you have a major battle. What more would you have for me to do?"

"I don't believe you, madam!" replied Dr. Irwin. He threw down his pen, stood, grabbed his coat, and brushed past Mary Ann, leaving her to follow him out of his office.

An hour later, they stood on the front porch of Adams Block Hospital. "Well, Mrs. Bickerdyke, this is a good start, but obviously you have hardly been challenged. I want you now to go to Fort Pickering, to the smallpox pest house. You will not find that as easy as your work in Adams Block."

He stroked his chin and looked at her malevolently, hoping she would flee at the dreaded word *smallpox*. "Smallpox doesn't frighten you, does it?" he asked.

"Not in the least, Doctor. And I assure you, I will not ask you for any assistance—"

Dr. Irwin interrupted her, saying, "That is correct, madam—you will receive no assistance. Only the worst cases of smallpox are sent there. The mortality rate is so high that no one wants to volunteer to work there. And doubtless your contrabands won't follow you there either." Dr. Irwin smiled, tipped his hat to her, and left her standing on the porch of Adams Block. On his way back to his office, Dr. Irwin's anger at Mrs. Bickerdyke intensified. He couldn't believe that this woman could accomplish so much and worried that in comparison, his reputation would fade. He was convinced action was required to maintain his stature.

CHAPTER 25

Fort Pickering—1863

At Fort Pickering, Mary Ann found the conditions deplorable. Many of the staff, terrified of the pox, had fled, leaving the patients on their own. The dead patients outnumbered the living. No caution had been taken to keep the pustular cases from the recovering ones, and medicine was unavailable. Smallpox cases arrived at this pest house from all over the North, burdening the small staff that remained and their minimal resources. There were no supplies of fresh food, disinfected bedding or clothes. Infected soldiers had to assume the role of nurses. Regular army rations were the only food offered to the patients, who were often so ill that they could not tolerate such a diet. Bedding had not been changed in months, and in addition to the pox, men were plagued by lice, bedbugs, and the foulest of odors.

Mary Ann set to work as usual. She organized the Pickering smallpox hospital as she had Adams Block. In addition, she raised such a complaint about the poor quality of medical care there that a number of medical officers were eventually replaced.

One evening, she stood at a small table washing out a pus-stained cloth in a basin of water. A pockmarked soldier sat in the chair next to her, writing a letter by lamplight. She dictated as she worked:

> I need you here as soon as possible. If you can, bring supplies of all kinds but especially disinfectants. The soldiers are in dire need

of spiritual comfort as well. If the Reverend Porter could accompany you, it would be a blessing for the men. And see if you could bring more washing equipment from the Sanitary Commission. The bed capacity at Memphis will soon exceed 10,000, sorely taxing my laundry here.

Yours, with fond affection,
M. A. Bickerdyke

She waited for the soldier to stop writing. "See that this goes out with the next mail," she said.

Several weeks later, Mary Ann stood at the entryway of Fort Pickering smallpox hospital and embraced Mrs. Porter. She took Mrs. Porter's cloak and folded it over her arm as she escorted her inside. "You must be exhausted from your travels," said Mary Ann. "May I offer you some tea? We can talk in a room back here. I've been using it as my office." She turned toward the soldier minding the fire. "Samuel, please bring some tea. We'll be in the office." The two ladies entered the office and Mary Ann closed the door.

Light from a small window brightened the room. Mary Ann hung Eliza's cloak up and then sat down next to her in front of the desk. Eliza read the papers that had been spread out across the desktop. She had a worried expression as she looked at Mary Ann.

"But what about Colonel Stoutner? Wasn't he just assigned here a few months ago?"

Mary Ann shook her head and said, "A miserable man. Didn't care at all for the patients and wouldn't go near anyone with the pox. I went to the provost marshal with complaints, and Stoutner was replaced."

Samuel knocked and entered the room with two metal cups of steaming tea that he set before them. Eliza did not seem to notice. She was still looking at the papers. "And assistant surgeon McGrath?"

"Gone."

"Oh," said Eliza, raising her eyebrows and reaching for her tea. "What about Dr. Williams?"

Mary Ann shrugged her shoulders.

Eliza said, "Well. I see you've had some personnel difficulties here. How are things now?"

"Splendid, since you have agreed to be the matron here. I know these boys will receive the very best care from you. But you must be tired from your travels. I'll help settle you in here tomorrow, and then I'll return to Memphis as quickly as I can."

Eliza responded, "Oh, Mary Ann, I was hoping that you and I could spend some time together here. You are looking so tired and thin. I'm worried you're not taking good care of yourself."

"My dear little brown bird, I wish we could have time, but I have already received notice that I'm needed back in Memphis at Gayoso Hospital, where there are outbreaks of scurvy and the black diphtheria."

☺☺

During that same month, Dr. Irwin hosted a meeting of the U.S. Sanitary Commission officials and the assistant surgeon general of the Union army. They had just finished a tour of Adams Block hospital and were crowded inside his office as Dr. Irwin pontificated on his accomplishments. "To date, twelve thousand men have passed through the hospitals in Memphis. As I was saying, many have been ill from cholera, dysentery, and measles. I think you'll find that we in Memphis have the best application of field sanitation in the army."

The official from the U.S. Sanitary Commission responded, "Dr. Irwin, we are so impressed with your organization and the care you've provided at Adams Block. If it is representative of the other hospitals here in Memphis, we owe you a debt of gratitude. Your gift for administration and organization is outstanding. Involving the community to supplement your manpower was sheer genius. And adding a laundry and a bakery—you've set a new standard for medical care! The Union army is fortunate to have you."

The assistant surgeon general added, "Yes, indeed, Doctor. We knew that transferring you here from Florida was the right move. After my report about what I've found here, you can probably expect to add a stripe to those shoulder straps. We could also use you to review and advise other hospital sites, when you can be spared from Memphis. Impressive—very impressive."

Dr. Irwin glowed under these compliments. "Well, thank you, gentlemen. I have been very busy here, and I am glad to hear that my hard work will be officially recognized. The health and well-being of our soldiers come first."

CHAPTER 26

"She Ranks Me"—March 1863

Several weeks later, the smallpox hospital had been reorganized and was running smoothly under the reliable hands of Eliza Porter. Mary Ann returned to Memphis, where Dr. Irwin assigned her as matron to Gayoso Hospital.

One day around midmorning, after she'd been working there several weeks, she was greeted by a worried-looking ward master standing near her office door, wringing his hands nervously. "Arthur, why do you look so concerned? Is there a problem? You look like you expect a shell to hit this hospital any minute. What's wrong?"

"It's Davey, ma'am. He's not doing so good...started bleeding again. I couldn't get it to stop until a little while ago, but he's lost too much blood, I think."

Mary Ann dropped her cape and bonnet on her desk and walked swiftly down the ward. Arthur followed, looking down at his shoes. Mary Ann approached Davey's cot. He was very pale, unconscious, and barely alive. He was missing both legs from an earlier amputation, and from the stain on the linen she could tell that it was one of these surgical wounds that had been bleeding profusely. Mary Ann knelt down, took a cloth, and gently wiped it across his brow. She looked up and whispered to Arthur, "How long ago?"

Arthur shrugged somewhat guiltily. "Middle of the night," he whispered back.

Mary Ann said, "Why didn't you call the doctor?"

"We did, ma'am. Sent a runner and everything, but he was...ah...unavailable, ma'am."

Mary Ann, now louder and angry, said, "You mean he was out on the town again, avoiding his duties? Enjoying himself instead of helping these suffering souls? Well, I will deal with this. For now, put pressure on this to stop the bleeding. He's lost so much blood that I'm sure he hasn't much left." She stood and left the ward as the ward master and soldier-nurses looked at each other apprehensively.

Moments later she was at the entryway of the surgeon's tent. She entered without an announcement and proceeded to the cot of the Gayoso surgeon on call. He was lying there in a rumpled uniform and had not even bothered to take off his boots. Looming over him, she began to yell, "You wretched, unfeeling, hard-hearted, wicked man! You call yourself a doctor? What do you mean by leaving your patients alone all night while you go out to your...your... ladies of the night! How dare you!"

The doctor, awakened and surprised, attempted an explanation, "But I—"

Mary Ann interrupted, continuing her diatribe as her anger built. She glared at him. "Not a word, sir. I will hear none of your nonsense. Pull off your shoulder straps right now and get out of *my* hospital! This is the fourth time this month that you have shirked your duties, and it will be the last time you abandon my boys for your evil ways! You'll be out of here in less than three days, I promise you that."

The surgeon attempted to push Mary Ann away from his cot, and yelled, "Get away from me, you stupid old woman! How dare you threaten me! You have no idea of the stress that—"

He tried to push her away again, but she had attached herself to the straps on the shoulders of his jacket and began pulling hard. After an energetic tussle a ripping sound was heard, and Mary Ann walked out of the tent grasping the captain straps she had torn from his coat. Without cape or bonnet, she made her way directly to the general army headquarters in Memphis and to General William T. Sherman's office.

☙❧

Two days later, the same surgeon stood at attention before General Sherman. The general held a piece of paper and continued to look down at his work. He said, "So, you've been dismissed by the surgeon general. What do you want me to do about it? I have no authority over the surgeon general."

"But, General, surely you can intervene in a matter of perjury," the surgeon whined. "I have been attacked, slandered, and undermined by a mere civilian who knows nothing of army protocol or medical practice. I can prove to you that all the statements against me are false!"

"Oh?" General Sherman looked up, finally interested in the surgeon. "Who is your accuser?"

The doctor felt a little more secure in the situation and said, "Well, you've probably heard of her. It's that…ah… miserable old woman—the venomous Mrs. Bickerdyke. She has had a grudge against me since she came to Gayoso. She is a rancorous, meddlesome woman—she even tells me how to care for my patients!"

General Sherman's face seemed to soften at the sound of her name. He questioned the surgeon further. "Mother Bickerdyke, you say?"

As the surgeon began to respond, Sherman stood and walked to the window, where he looked out with a small smile on his face. With his back to the surgeon, Sherman interrupted him, saying, "Well, if it's Mother Bickerdyke, Doctor, then I can't help you. She has more power than I do. She ranks me." General Sherman turned from the window and looked at the open-mouthed surgeon, who seemed to be having a hard time understanding what he had heard. General Sherman said simply, "Dismissed."

CHAPTER 27

The Closing of the Laundry—March 1863

A few days later on a rainy afternoon, Mary Livermore sat with Mary Ann and Eliza Porter in Eliza's office at Fort Pickering. Steam rose from the spout of the metal teapot on the desk and from the ladies' tin cups. Mrs. Livermore was a refined woman of delicate stature, elegantly dressed. Mrs. Porter, as always, was in her brown dress with lace collar and cuffs. Mary Ann was dressed in her rough blue woolen dress with a soiled and threadbare apron over it. The three of them were visiting for the first time in weeks.

Eliza said to Mrs. Livermore, "What a pleasure it is to see you again. I am so pleased that you could come to Memphis to visit the hospitals here."

Mary Livermore replied, "I promised the Chicago Sanitary Commission that I would visit every patient in Memphis—little did I know how large an undertaking that would be. Did you know that, with the exception of your hospital here, Eliza, every soldier with whom I spoke knew Mary Ann Bickerdyke's name but could not tell me the name of the surgeon in charge? And Eliza, you have done such remarkable work here. In the past, I have heard such horror stories about this pest house. I am delighted to find a clean, orderly, and well-managed facility, and the patients competently cared for. I am quite secure that this is a result of your presence and skill, Eliza."

Mrs. Livermore shifted in her chair to face Mary Ann. "I assume you have received the mangles, washboards, and other laundry supplies you've asked for? Word of your laundry has spread—all the ladies' groups in Chicago are talking about it. Women feel so much safer, knowing that their loved ones will have gentle care and clean bandages if they are wounded."

Sitting back to face both women, Mrs. Livermore continued, "Our Sanitary Commission has thus far been the main supplier of hospital goods for the entire Union army—at enormous expense, I might add. Who would have dreamed this brutal war would continue so long? Towns and villages are generating funds through charity events, but the need remains ever so great. The commission prints a newsletter on a regular basis that's sent to donors, so they may see how their donations are being used. Many of these newsletters have included your name, Mary Ann. The most recent was about your outstanding work at Adams Block Hospital. Oh, and I should tell you that Mrs. Jane Hoge and I are planning to have a Sanitary Commission fair in Chicago this fall. It will be a major effort to collect a large amount of money—all of it, of course, going to our wounded and ill in the army."

"Mary, what a splendid idea!" Eliza replied excitedly.

"How can we help you with this?" asked an enthused Mary Ann.

"Rest assured, ladies, that I will call upon your expertise in the future."

Eliza poured more tea for the three of them and said, "This is to fortify us. We have a few more buildings to visit."

It took the rest of the day for a thorough inspection of the smallpox hospital at Fort Pickering. Afterward, Mrs. Livermore and Mary Ann left in a carriage for Gayoso Hospital. A steady rain pounded into their carriage as Andy skillfully maneuvered it to avoid the large and seemingly bottomless mud puddles. The three of them were soaked.

They reached Gayoso, grateful to be out of the rain. Mary Ann proceeded to show Mrs. Livermore her room for the evening. "Sleep well, Mary. I will see you in the morning. I am just going to check on the kitchen and the laundry before retiring." Both took a candle from the box in the entryway and lit them from the lantern hanging there.

Mrs. Livermore said, "Good night, Mary Ann, pleasant dreams," as she entered her room. Mary Ann continued down the hallway, her candle throwing light into the darkness of the doorways.

She entered the kitchen and was surprised to find it empty. Long shadows fell across the tables. Bowls of batter sat with spoons still in them, as if abandoned quickly. A lone lantern, turned low, sat forlornly on the counter. The stove fires burned low and needed stoking. No food had been prepared for the morning's breakfast. She paused, blew out her candle, grabbed the lantern, and moved quickly through the kitchen to the back door. Moments later she was outside, walking in the rain toward the laundry house, which was oddly dark. She walked to the door and saw an official order posted there. "This laundry is shut by order of Surgeon J. D. Irwin. Contrabands are ordered to their camp. March 30, 1863."

Mary Ann angrily ripped the notice off the door. She said to herself, "Oh, no, he won't!" She turned and rushed back to the hospital, through the kitchen, and down the hallway to Mrs. Livermore's door. She knocked and said loudly, "Mary, dear, get up and get dressed. We're going out."

Mrs. Livermore, in her nightclothes, opened her door and asked, "Going out—now? At this time of night? In this weather? What is wrong?"

Mary Ann replied through gritted teeth, "There is some trouble that must be dealt with tonight, and the post commander is the only one with enough authority. I'm going to go wake Andy and will meet you at the carriage."

Hard rain poured down and angled its way into the covered ambulance, the only conveyance Andy could find quickly. He handled the team, Mary Ann sat up front next to him, and Mrs. Livermore, swathed in a black wool coat, was in the back. Everyone was soaked. Lanterns swung on both sides of the wagon, lighting the way through the dark, war-torn city.

Memphis was in Union hands but was still considered a hostile city, so sentries were posted every few hundred yards. A sentry stopped them, musket drawn, and asked, "Who goes there and what is the password?"

Mary Ann answered, "It's Mother Bickerdyke, son, from Gayoso Hospital. I have urgent business with the post commander. You must let us through."

The sentry said, "What is the countersign, ma'am?"

Mary Ann replied, "Now, I don't have time for countersigns and the like. Let us through. Your wounded brothers depend on this errand. Don't you be responsible for adding to their suffering. A countersign, for goodness sakes."

The next morning, the inside of the kitchen at Gayoso Hospital was ablaze with light. At the window, the beginnings of a sunrise could be seen through the drizzle. Mary Ann leaned over a huge pot on the stove, stirring grits with a wooden spoon. She took a taste from the spoon, added more seasoning, and stirred. The room was filled with contrabands who tended other pots, washed dishes, poured batter into bread tins, and roasted and ground coffee beans in preparation for the morning meal.

Suddenly, a door slammed and determined footsteps were heard. Dr. Irwin entered the room and angrily addressed Mary Ann. "Did you not receive the order I posted on the laundry room door?"

Mary Ann ignored him and continued to stir the pot, adding a pinch more salt. She then replied, "I did, sir."

The kitchen became quiet, and all but Mary Ann were looking up from their tasks and watching apprehensively.

Dr. Irwin raised his voice a little louder. "It was an order, was it not, to close the laundry and kitchen and to dismiss the contrabands?"

Mary Ann looked up and said, "Why, it was precisely, sir."

With increasing indignation, Dr. Irwin said, "When I issue a direct order I expect to be obeyed!"

"I suppose you do, sir."

Dr. Irwin's face was red, the tendons in his neck stood out, and his hands were balled into fists. He stepped closer to Mary Ann and said menacingly, "And why has my order not been obeyed, Mrs. Bickerdyke?"

She reached into her pocket and brought out a piece of paper, which she handed to him. She said in a casual tone, "Why, General Hurlbut gave me this order last night to keep the laundry open and to keep the contrabands here until he dismisses them. I reckon that the general outranks you, Doctor."

Dr. Irwin's anger overflowed, and he yelled, "That does it, God damn it! I won't have my orders subverted by a meddling, power-hungry civilian—and a woman, to boot! I'll have you thrown out of here on your fat ass, Mrs. Bickerdyke. Put that spoon down and get out of here! You are no longer welcome. I will win this one, Mrs. Bickerdyke, you mark my words."

In counterpoint to his yelling, she said quite softly, "Dr. Irwin, I'm not going anywhere. I've come here to help these boys, and I will stay until this war is won. You're going to have to get along with me. We can work together peacefully, or you can fight with me." She swept her arm toward the hospital. "Surely the wounded and dying will benefit more from the presence of two caretakers? We need to stop wasting our time and energy in pitched battles against each other. Please reconsider."

Dr. Irwin, silent and stone-faced, turned on his heel and left. The kitchen crew resumed their work very quietly.

Mrs. Livermore wrote to the Sanitary Commission in Chicago and described what she had seen in Memphis, and of her meetings with Mary Ann and Eliza Chappell Porter.

I have visited every ward in every hospital of this enormous medical effort. Gayoso Hospital stands above the rest. Mother Bickerdyke is the matron there and everyone in Memphis calls it Mother Bickerdyke's hospital. Mary Ann and Andy, the soldier who is assigned to help her, work as one, carrying out an organizational plan that is as vast as it is detailed. Mary Ann also has scores of contrabands, which allow her to expand her services to meet the demanding and fluctuating needs in Memphis. I can't really recall any of the names of the surgeons or stewards in Gayoso because Mary Ann overshadows them all.

CHAPTER 28

Supplies for Vicksburg—May 1863

On his way to Vicksburg, Grant marched his men from Tennessee across three-fourths of Mississippi and fought and won several battles—Port Gibson, Raymond, Jackson, Champion's Hill, and Big Black River.

In April 1863, after several unsuccessful assaults on Vicksburg, Grant had his forces dig in, surrounding and trapping thirty-one thousand Confederates in the city, completely cutting them off from their supply lines. They resisted fiercely and protected their defensive lines with tenacity. This siege lasted weeks and severely stressed the food supplies of those soldiers and civilians trapped in Vicksburg.

Sick and wounded Union soldiers by the hundreds streamed back to the hospitals at Memphis. As the fighting raged on, there were a number of outbreaks of scurvy. Fresh fruit and vegetables were in short supply in the battle-torn countryside. The army had used Memphis as its headquarters for so long that the surrounding areas had been scoured of edibles. The army requisitioned antiscorbutics from the Sanitary Commission, which publicized the need. The women of the Midwest responded by sending hundreds of gallons of sauerkraut, pickled potatoes, onions, and cucumbers to Memphis. These went directly to the soldiers in the field, since the needs of fighting men took priority over the sick and wounded.

Mary Ann also noticed a terrible shortage of fresh eggs and milk. She was provoked by the inflated prices that Southern farmers asked for their watered-down milk and spoiled eggs. She wrote to Mrs. Livermore in Chicago and requested a thirty-day furlough, during which she would travel to Chicago to obtain fresh beef, eggs, fruits, and vegetables. She asked Mrs. Livermore to arrange donations from the local farmers in Illinois. She also wrote that on her way to Chicago she was planning to escort a large number of amputees to the hospitals around St. Louis.

Within a week of Mary Ann's arrival in Chicago, the Sanitary Commission's offices had been turned into a huge barn. There were hundreds of cages of hens and roosters. Goats, sheep, and cattle were penned up in and around the offices and in the hallways. Crates of fresh vegetables and barrels of pickled potatoes lined the walkway in front of the building.

The weather was unseasonably warm and the commission offices could be smelled from blocks away. Mary Ann shortened her stay in order to remove the supplies quickly. She thought about trying to visit her sons, but realized that the perishable supplies she had asked for limited her time. In a way she was relieved. Too busy and too rushed to put herself back in the face of what she knew was a terrible conflict, guilt welled up, but she forced herself to focus on her work, building the strange wagon train of supplies she would lead back to the hospital.

Several days later, on a hot and sunny late May morning, the townsfolk at the outskirts of Memphis saw a huge dust cloud moving down the road toward them. Loud cackling and lowing was heard. Many of the townspeople and soldiers rushed to their windows and porches to see what was happening. Down the main street came a long parade of wagons with dust and feathers flying. Mary Ann, shading herself under a blue and white parasol, sat in the lead wagon that Andy was driving. Behind them, stacked and tied ten high, were chicken crates emitting a din of cackling and crowing. Twenty wagons followed, each stacked with more chicken crates, barrels of pickles, mounds of vegetables, and sacks of grain. Following the wagons was a herd of a hundred head of cattle, under the attention of wranglers.

Mary Ann said to Andrew, "Let's stop at the quartermaster's. He'll know what to do with these livestock."

A half hour later, Mary Ann walked up the steps of the quartermaster's office. He greeted her at the door, astonishment on his face. "Well, Mrs. Bickerdyke, I see you've been to market."

"Something like that. These supplies are for the patients in the hospitals. I've gone to a lot of trouble to get all of this here, and I want you to be sure that it gets to the right people. I'll suffer no theft. Do you understand?"

The quartermaster nodded and said, "Yes, Mother. I have just the place for them. We can off-load the barrels and grain here, but we'll ferry the livestock out to President's Island, in the middle of the Mississippi. You trust your contrabands, don't you? We'll have them tend the animals. No one will be able to steal them from the island, and there's plenty of forage for them there."

Mary Ann turned back to Andrew, who was standing behind her. "I want you to supervise the transport of these animals to President's Island. You make sure it's done right. Then have the contrabands milk some of the cows and get the hens to laying. There will be pudding tonight!"

CHAPTER 29

The Laundered Lint, Jackson, Mississippi— July 1863

The siege of Vicksburg had been horrific for soldiers and civilians trapped in the city. The blasts of cannon and shot had not stopped for weeks. Day had turned as dark as night from cannon smoke. The air smelled of fire and the ground rumbled with a continuous earthquake of explosions. As the soldiers and inhabitants began to starve, they were eventually reduced to trapping and eating rodents, dogs, and every sparrow they could catch. Disease was rampant, and without adequate medical supplies simple wounds festered. The mortality rate of the Confederate soldiers soared.

To avoid the shelling, the Confederates had dug caves along the outskirts of the city and surrounded the entrances with breastworks of sharpened logs. The Union army responded by digging tunnels below the city and setting off explosives below the caves. After months of the terrible siege, Confederate General Pemberton surrendered the city to General Grant on July 4. After the surrender, the two former West Point classmates shared a bottle of whiskey and discussed old times and military strategy, unaware that another great battle was occurring that very moment in Gettysburg, Pennsylvania.

After Vicksburg was secured, General Sherman pressed on to attack and take Jackson, Mississippi, capturing its large store of supplies and the forty locomotives at the railhead.

Mary Ann traveled between Memphis and Jackson, working in the hospitals there until all the wounded from the Vicksburg battle were rehabilitated and returned to the army or transported north for long-term recovery.

Inside a Jackson hotel converted into a hospital, every available space was being utilized for the wounded. Two stretcher bearers lifted a dead soldier from the floor onto their stretcher. The first bearer said, "So, Shorty, you really think this was worth it? Look what happened to these men here."

Shorty replied, "We didn't pick this fight, Mathias. The Rebels did, remember? And the Army of the Tennessee seems to just get stronger. The Rebs oughta know better than to fight Grant and Sherman."

Off to the side of the main salon, Mary Ann cleaned the wound of a young soldier resting on a cot. As she worked, she had tears in her eyes and fought to keep them under control. Across the room, Dr. Irwin worked on a soldier with a wound that was bleeding profusely. He addressed the soldier-nurse assisting him. "What do you mean, we have no more lint? How can I pack this wound? Go and look again. Look everywhere. I will use anything you can find for packing."

After the soldier-nurse left, Mary Ann carried a basket quietly up behind Dr. Irwin. "Maybe these will help?" She offered him a handful of her newly laundered wound padding and the washed remnants of battlefield detritus from Shiloh.

Dr. Irwin looked down at her hand and then up at her in surprise. He noted the tears in her eyes. His face mirrored her concern. "Why, yes, I believe they will," he said. "I thought all our lint went to the front."

"Yes, but I've been washing out old bandages and boiling blankets. They come as close to lint as you can get."

He took a handful of lint and packed the wound. "Thank you, Mrs. Bickerdyke. I will use all of this that you can supply."

He paused, and then said, "Mrs. Bickerdyke, we have...ah... had our differences, but perhaps I have judged you too harshly. I am...ah...well...sorry if I have doubted your usefulness or your skill. I still don't like women working in military hospitals, but I think—"

With a gentle smile, Mary Ann interrupted him and replied, "Apology accepted, Dr. Irwin, and I'll admit to sometimes being a bit of an old biddy. But it is for a good cause. I am pleased we have worked together here in Jackson."

As she finished speaking, Mary Ann turned around to complete her other duties. She felt a pair of eyes riveted on her and her line of sight followed them. In the corner, propped up against a wall sat a soldier with his left arm bandaged in a sling. His face seemed oddly familiar. He was pale and thin. His long, greasy brown hair hung down to his shoulders, where it mingled with his beard. He was smoking a clay pipe. The silvery smoke escaped his mouth and danced slowly upward, tumbling in the light of the window. Below it, his gaze was steady and penetrating.

Mary Ann looked at him as she mentally shuffled through the hospitals and the wounded of the past two years. She knew she'd seen him before, but couldn't recall the details. She wondered what his long gaze at her could mean. She began to walk over to him, hoping something he said would remind her, but he didn't speak. Finally, she knelt down before him so she could be level with his face.

"Young man, you have been looking at me very intently. Do you need something? Are you in pain?"

The soldier took his time in answering her. "We have met before, Mrs. Bickerdyke. You don't remember? I am the one you called 'philosopher.' It was after the battle of Pittsburg Landing."

Mary Ann unfastened her gaze from his and looked down while she reconstructed a picture of the hospital at Shiloh. Then she remembered. This was the soldier who had sat, badly wounded, as she tended another who was dying. After he died, this man, the philosopher, had spoken to her.

"How can you stand this? Don't you see that all the nursing in the world can come only to this? You can only send us to our deaths or back into battle, which is its own kind of death."

At the time, Mary Ann had felt a sharp criticism in his words, and a truth that she refused to examine, and had said, "You are a philosopher as well as a soldier, and you are wounded. Let me see to your wounds." He had not spoken again, except to whisper his thanks when she finished his dressing. Since then his words had floated uncomfortably in her dreams, but she refused to address them.

Now she felt speechless. She felt that somehow all she had done for all these men was wrong and hurtful. She felt stained and dirty. His eyes looked at her accusingly. She tilted her head toward his bandaged arm and managed only to say, "Yes, I remember. And I see you have a clean bandage for your arm." She lowered her eyes and turned away, working hard to compose herself so she could return to her duties.

CHAPTER 30

The New Attaché—August 1863

Staff at the hospitals in Jackson prepared the wounded and ill for transport north to hospitals there. Wounds were washed and dressed. Men were helped into clothes. Meals were packed. Crutches and canes were whittled for the wounded who had difficulty walking.

The ward master walked over to Mary Ann, who was wrapping a bandage around a boy's head. "We have five hundred ready to move north. Another three hundred can't be moved yet. If we move them now, most of them will die. Given the small number of transport wagons we have ready at the door, some who can go will have to wait a day, maybe two," he said.

A colonel entered the hospital, looked around, and saw Mary Ann. He walked up to her, saying, "General Sherman sends his regards, ma'am, and requests your presence as soon as possible."

Mary Ann left the hospital with the colonel and approached the tent that General Sherman used as his headquarters. He saw her coming and stood, and then offered her a chair opposite his camp desk. "Good day, Mrs. Bickerdyke. Come in, please. That will be all, Colonel."

She sat down and looked expectantly at him. He sat at his desk, leaning forward on his elbows and resting his chin on his clasped hands.

"So, Mrs. Bickerdyke, how is the transport north going?"

"The transport is going well, General. Is that why you wanted to speak with me?"

"No, Mrs. Bickerdyke," he smiled. "May I offer you some coffee perhaps?"

"No, thank you, but...if you have extra, I'll take it back to the hospital for the boys."

General Sherman smiled again. "I'll see what I can do. The reason I asked you here is because the U.S. Sanitary Commission has replied to my request to have you assigned to my corps permanently. They are enthusiastic about the idea and will support it if you agree. It means you would be joining me near Lookout Mountain, in Tennessee, in the autumn. General Grant will be there, and we're expecting fierce fighting and many wounded. From there, I can't say. Much depends on the outcome of that battle. But if you would agree to do this, there would be enough time for you to spend a week or two with your family in the North. It will take me at least that long to move my troops into position. Then I would want you to come by rail to Chattanooga. It's the fastest way, but it could be very dangerous. The rails are always an easy target for Rebel explosives. My army needs you, Mrs. Bickerdyke, and the Fifteenth, my special corps, has asked for you." He paused, and then said, "Would you like time to think about this?"

Mary Ann shook her head and said, "None whatsoever. I'll be at Chattanooga when you request it. Things are fairly well set here, so I'll leave immediately with the first transport of wounded. You can contact me at the commission headquarters in Chicago when you need me. Now, General, about that coffee..."

CHAPTER 31

Chicago—Autumn 1863

By the autumn of 1863, Mary Ann was a celebrity to the press in all the major cities of the Union, but she loathed the spectacle of being in the public eye. She spent only a brief time with her children at the Reverend Nichols's farm outside Chicago. Her sons were thinner and paler, but they wore warm clothes and boots without holes. Their excitement at seeing her was dampened as she explained that they would only have a day or two to visit. Hiram started to cry, and said how much he missed her and wanted her to stay to be his mama.

Mary Ann replied, "Oh, Hiram. I am your mama and will always be your mama, but for right now, you and James must stay with the Reverend Nichols. You have a good life here, with a God-fearing family. So many other boys have given up their families and their lives, just so that you could have yours. Please, please, my little ones, try to understand this." But even as she spoke, Mary Ann was filled with longing and guilt. Having absolutely no idea how to resolve these feelings, she changed the subject.

"Show me around the farm. Who rides the horse? Where is the reverend?"

And the boys complied, feeling utterly helpless as children to alter their mother's course.

Mary Ann occupied most of her visit up North meeting families of the soldiers she tended at the front. Early one morning, she made a call to the Eaton family. She had cared for Mrs. Eaton's husband at Gayoso. Mrs. Eaton sat on the

217

davenport in her parlor. Her little girl sucked her thumb and hid bashfully behind her mother's skirt. Mary Ann sipped her tea, politely giving Mrs. Eaton a moment to collect herself. Tears rolled down the woman's face. Her little girl sensed something was terribly wrong with her mother and gently pulled on her skirts. Quietly, Mary Ann put her teacup down on the saucer and put her hand in her dress pocket. She pulled out a small packet of dirty cotton cloth. She gently gave this to Mrs. Eaton, who opened it to find a button from her husband's uniform. She clasped it in her hand and then raised it to her breast. Tears streamed down her face.

Mary Ann said, "He was very brave, Mrs. Eaton. In his last moments, he prayed for God to protect you and your little one. I am certain the good Lord took him into his loving bosom. He loved you very much. He died peacefully in my arms, and we buried him outside Gayoso Hospital in Memphis. It was a good Christian burial, and we marked his grave."

Mrs. Eaton sobbed quietly, and then leaned over to clutch Mary Ann's hand. "Thank you, Mrs. Bickerdyke. I would always have wondered and worried about him. I think it is better to know than to have that emptiness of not knowing for the rest of my days. Oh, my Bobby. My dear, dear Bobby. It is so hard to believe..." Mrs. Eaton hid her face in her hands and tears slipped through her fingers. Mary Ann moved closer and held her, mourning with her. As Mrs. Eaton's sobs subsided, she said, "I have a brother in the Army of the Potomac. The last relative I have. I only hope if he is wounded, he has someone like you to care for him."

Mary Ann placed her other hand on top of Mrs. Eaton's, and with tears in her eyes and voice said, "The Sanitary Commission provides many nurses for the comfort and care of the men in the Union army. Should your brother be wounded, he will be cared for. But let us pray to God that he will make it through this conflict without injury. Mrs. Eaton, this is a terrible war and families have been torn apart and suffered greatly because of it. We can only put our trust in the Lord and pray that it will end soon." She paused a moment, and then said gently, "I must go now. I am so very sorry to have met you under such sad circumstances." They both rose from the davenport and walked together to the front door. The little girl still clung anxiously to her mother's skirts. In the entryway, Mary Ann leaned down and took the child's face in her hands. "Now, child," she said gently, "you must be brave and strong. Your mother needs you."

Mrs. Eaton opened the door, but then hesitated. "Wait. Wait, please, Mrs. Bickerdyke. Can the Sanitary Commission help when a family can't pay rent? The father, uncle, and two sons have all gone off to war. For the past few months the father hasn't been sending his pay. We don't know if he's been killed or if he's just out of reach of the paymaster, or perhaps the money was stolen on the way home. This family is in dire need—their rent is six months in arrears." Mrs. Eaton clasped Mary Ann's hands in both of hers and pleaded, "They are in danger of losing their home. You have been so kind to me. Do you know how I might obtain help for them?"

Mary Ann considered this a moment and said, "Tell me the family's name and where they live. I'll see what I can do. Perhaps the commission can help. Give me the name and address of their landlord, too, if you have it."

Mary Ann's first stop after leaving Mrs. Eaton was not the Sanitary Commission, but the business of the landlord of this destitute family. In his well-appointed office, she tried to reason with him and begged his mercy for this family, but he heartlessly refused to put off the planned eviction. He refused to take the war into consideration and cared only that this family hadn't paid its rent. He became so irritated with Mary Ann that he ordered her rudely from the premises. Anger flushed her face as she approached the door to leave. Then she noticed a Bible on the bookshelf by the door. She grabbed it and whirled around to face the landlord, who in his surprise stepped back.

"Now, my good woman, you can't—" he said, to which she replied aggressively, "Aha!" She opened the book to chapter 16 of Luke and read aloud, "And so, it happened that the beggar died and was carried by the angels into Abraham's bosom. Now the rich man also died and he was buried and cast into Hades, into Hades—*into Hades*," she repeated, her voice raised in anger, spitting out the words. "He was tormented. And the rich man lifted up his eyes from his own torment and saw Abraham a little ways off, holding Lazarus in his bosom." She snapped the book shut and handed it to him. "You selfish, dreadful, greedy man—do you see how you're behaving? The time of your own death may not be so far off. You should pay attention to this parable. May God have mercy on your heartless soul! You'd do well to read this, sir!" With that, she placed the Bible in the astonished man's hands and left in a flurry of skirts.

Later that same day, Mary Ann stood inside a ramshackle home. It was almost completely bare, most of the family's belongings having been sold long ago. The fire was out and there was no wood. A mother and three small children were wrapped in blankets, shivering. They sat on the floor around one small lantern that lit the room. "We must hurry," said Mary Ann. "A new home awaits you, and the Sanitary Commission will pay your rent until it determines your husband's status." The mother looked up fearfully at Mary Ann, who replied tenderly, "Don't worry, now. It's all taken care of."

A few days later Mary Ann prepared to return to the front. She was in Mary Livermore's guest bedroom, packing her few belongings.

Mary Livermore stood by the four-poster bed and protested, "Won't you please reconsider and stay a week or two longer? You haven't really had a chance to visit with your children for very long, and you must be exhausted. And the newspapers indicate that travel to Chattanooga is quite dangerous. You could spend more time resting with your children while the army makes it a little safer. A few more days will not make much of a difference, will it?" Mary Livermore looked at Mary Ann, and continued before she could respond. "I know! I could arrange a speaking engagement for you. I know it would earn a great deal of money for the cause. Your fame has spread throughout the North. Every woman with a husband, son, or brother in the army would come from miles around to hear you speak."

Mary Ann continued to pack, but looked over her shoulder and said, "No, Mary, not this time, I'm afraid. I have to be in Chattanooga in October—it's a promise I made. And I have imposed on your generous hospitality long enough. I promise you, I will return when time permits. In the meantime, though, use my fame to get the women of the North to provide more foodstuffs, pickles, bandages, and blankets for the boys. If for some reason they hesitate to donate to the commission, have them send the goods directly to me. I'll put anything that comes my way to good use." As Mary Ann said this she already had a faraway look in her eyes. She paused a moment, but then resumed, "Dear Mary, you have been so kind, I hate to impose on you further, but would you help me by keeping an eye on Hiram and James? I am so worried about them. They seem to be settled in, but they were so sad. I know it is not like having their own home with me, and I have agonized over my loyalty to them and to the soldiers. But for now, at least, they have a home to keep them safe. Let me know if there's anything they need." Mrs. Livermore and Mary Ann embraced.

CHAPTER 32

Chattanooga—Autumn 1863

On a blustery day in October, Mary Ann stepped off the train station platform and wrapped her shawl tighter around her. The train, one of the last to make it to Chattanooga intact, had been a troop transport, and Mary Ann had been one of the few civilians allowed on it. The smell of burning coal filled the air. Flakes of snow had just begun to materialize in the wind, colored a sickly gray by the ash from the train's stack.

Andy Somerville was waiting at the station to meet her. He walked up smiling and said, "Mother, it is a pleasure to see you again, ma'am. I hope your time in Chicago was a comfortable one and that you are well rested?" He took her carpetbag from her and escorted her to the carriage.

"It's good to see you, too, Andy. My journey was long, but I am so glad to be back. In an odd way, I think that life with the army is simpler than life back home."

"Well, Mother, you are sorely needed here. We have an outbreak of typhus in the regular army, and the Rebs routed us at Chickamauga, so there are thousands of wounded. But our biggest problem is the weather. It's been below freezing every night. We don't have enough room inside for everyone. Many sleep outside and freeze to death during the night."

"We'll see what we can do about that. I've brought many supplies with me. The porter has made arrangements to have the crates stacked at the side of the platform. You will need to arrange to transport these to the hospital. But first, will you take me there so that I can tend to those poor freezing boys?"

"Yes, ma'am," he said, but hesitated before helping her up into the carriage. "Ma'am, even though Chattanooga is in federal hands, it is not yet a safe city. Do you see that mountain?" he asked, and pointed to Lookout Mountain, which was shrouded in swirling snow clouds. "There are still Rebel cannon up there and all throughout the forests. They pretty much surround most of the city. Be careful in this place, Mother."

Chattanooga was a major port on the south side of the Tennessee River. River traffic and a large railroad crossing made it strategically critical to both the North and the South. The rails accessed the heart of the Deep South. The northwest line ran to Nashville and Louisville, the northeast to Knoxville and Richmond, and the southeast to Atlanta. General Rosecrans, under Grant's command, fought against Confederate Generals Braxton Bragg and James Longstreet at the Chickamauga River for control of the territory around Chattanooga. Chickamauga, a Confederate victory and one of the bloodiest battles of the war, resulted in eighteen thousand Union and sixteen thousand Confederate dead and wounded. The Union retreated to the city of Chattanooga, which they had recently wrested from Confederate forces. There, the Union army was trapped by geography because the Rebels held Missionary Ridge, Chattanooga Valley, Lookout Mountain, and Lookout Valley. From these vantage points the Rebels harassed traffic into and out of Chattanooga, effectively cutting off the Union's supply line.

Mary Ann's field hospital was about five miles from Chattanooga, situated at the edge of a forest. The winds howled down from Missionary Ridge, and the temperatures at night dropped to well below zero. Officers ordered that surrounding trees be cut down and huge fires built in the middle of the tent and log cabin hospital. Besides heat and light, these fires also provided a place to cook. The sound of axes felling trees, along with an occasional curse from the cold workers, rode in faintly on the wind. The smell of pine sap filled the air.

Near the fire, a soldier with a bandage around his neck sat wrapped in a blanket, warming himself and smoking a clay pipe. Mary Ann stood nearby, stirring a huge pot of soup hung from a tripod over the edge of the fire. She said to the soldier, "Well, it sounds like it will at least be warm tonight, doesn't it, Ambrose?"

"Yes, ma'am, it does. I heard that officer tell his men to take the entire forest down. We'll be warm for a spell, that's fer sure. But them Rebs have the high ground and the whole city is surrounded, I hear. There won't be no supplies coming in, with this bad weather. It could get mighty rough here as the winter deepens."

"Well, we're warm, and there's soup for today—it'll do for now," Mary Ann said philosophically. "Let's be grateful for that."

As she leaned over to stir the pot, her calico dress brushed a burning log and the hem caught fire. Ambrose saw what happened and yelled, "Mother! You're on fire!"

Without looking up from her task, she said, "Well, put me out, son! This soup requires my full attention!" Ambrose frantically beat at her dress with his blanket, putting out the flames.

"Thank you, Ambrose. Whoever thought that women should wear these long skirts to be proper never had to cook over an open fire. When it happens again, don't get all excited. Just do me the kindness of putting the fire out. My, how I do miss my stove. I hope it's being well taken care of in Memphis."

From then on, the soldiers saw to it that one of them was always nearby when Mary Ann was cooking—they called it fire detail.

Union supplies dwindled as Confederate forces tightened their control of the countryside surrounding Chattanooga. What supplies did make it through the blockade went directly to the soldiers defending the city. There was nothing left to give to the wounded and ill.

December 25, 1863, was bitterly cold and windy. The water in soldiers' tin cups quickly turned to ice whenever they left the warm perimeter of the campfires. Keeping the fires lit was a challenge, and a half circle of men stood or sat close together as a windbreak around each fire pit, in the hope of staying warm and maintaining their source of heat. The wind lifted burning embers that flew and danced in the air to land on the sick and injured lying downwind. Small fires quickly started up in their blankets, clothes, or hair, only to be smothered by the next gale. The sounds of slapping tent canvas, crackling fires, and the howling wind made it difficult to hear what comrades were saying to each other.

Mary Ann stood in a tent in the field hospital with her shawl wrapped tightly around her head and shoulders. It did nothing to keep her warm. She addressed several of the less severely wounded soldiers who stood near her. Occasionally, she had to yell to be heard.

"Have you checked their haversacks? What did you find, Jeremy?"

Jeremy, teeth chattering, replied, "Just a little bit of coffee and a few hard crackers. The boys are about out of everything, too."

"Well, we'll just have to make do. Put what you've got next to Theodore's pile there. Any word about supplies?"

Another soldier responded, "No, ma'am. Bragg still has us surrounded. Nothin's gettin' through, and engineers can't work on the rails 'til the weather breaks."

"It's a sorry Christmas for these boys," said Mary Ann with a sigh. "Well, we have wood, so let's do what we can to keep them warm. Let's give them some coffee—there's not much there, but it'll taste better than water and will warm them some. Use two kettles—just one handful of beans for each kettle. It won't be like the coffee they're used to, but it's better than nothing. See that everyone has some, and help the boys who can't raise up on their own to drink. The smell of coffee alone might cheer some of them."

Mary Ann pointed to a soldier and told him, "Gather up all those crackers and fill two kettles with water for me. I'll make a bread soup. It will be more warm than nourishing, but...," she shrugged. "Ashley, move some of the men out of the tents farthest from the fires and double them up with boys in another. Fit them in as close as you can. Then take the empty tent and put it over the other. Tie it tight to keep out some of this wind. Keep warm rocks around the sickest, and make sure you remember to change the rocks for warm ones when they cool. Anything we can do for these boys will help. And be cheerful, gentlemen—it's Christmas. Now," she said, looking at the men standing in front of her, "who can sing?"

The soldiers looked at each other, befuddled by the question. They mumbled among themselves, sure that she couldn't have asked what they thought she had asked.

"Ah...sing, ma'am?" said Jeremy warily.

"Yes, sing. None of you?" said Mary Ann, looking quizzically at them. "Good. Neither can I. Let's give the boys some caroling after their meal. It'll remind them it's Christmas and get their minds off their aches and pains. Might even encourage a few to say a prayer or two."

The strains of an off-key "O Little Town of Bethlehem" were lost in the blustery wind, but somehow, Christmas night felt a little more special.

That night Mary Ann dreamed of the philosopher. He was looking at her and on either side of him were her children. She woke with a feeling of anxiety, but the film of the dream quickly melted away, and she fell back asleep, huddled against the cold.

On New Year's Day, the sky was icy blue and the wind still howled. Many of the more seriously wounded had already died from a combination of blood loss, the cold, and starvation. The dead had been removed to the edge of the encampment and stacked in gruesome piles covered with ice. The ground was too cold for burying, and the men too tired to dig.

Great fires still burned in camp, but there were no cooking kettles warming over them, save for one or two heating water. Mary Ann sat on the ground, softly cradling an unconscious, shivering soldier as she tucked warm rocks and bricks under his blanket, using her shawl to keep her hands from burning. Suddenly, she stopped and listened. A few of the soldiers were standing and pointing to the northeast. Then she stood and looked around. Above the wind could be heard the faint sound of wagons approaching. She shaded her eyes and squinted into the wind. There in the distance, she saw two wagons. More of the soldiers were standing, and a man cried out, "Boys, we're saved!" A weak cheer flowed through the camp.

"Build up the fires, men, and put the kettles on. Those folks must have some food with them!" cried Mary Ann.

A sense of excitement flowed through the camp, and soldiers rushed to get the kettles. As the wagons drew nearer, Mary Ann said to herself, "Well, I'll be!" Then louder, "There'll be supper tonight boys—that's a Sanitary Commission wagon!"

Mary Ann began to walk quickly toward the approaching wagons. At the edge of the tent hospital she broke into a smile and started to wave. The lead wagon drew up to her. A woman, bundled in blankets except for her eyes, sat next to the driver. She placed a hand on the driver's arm and indicated he should stop the horses. She leaned down and put a gloved hand out to Mary Ann, who clutched it and then helped her down off the wagon.

The two women embraced, and then Mary Ann held the other woman a bit away from her and laughed.

"Why, Mrs. Porter! What a sight for sore eyes! You are heaven sent, surely! How did you get through the Rebs? Nothing's been able to get through for weeks!" Mary Ann hesitated and then told Mrs. Porter and the driver, "But come, you and your drivers must be frozen. Come close to the fires and warm yourselves.

Mrs. Porter said with relief, "Mary Ann, thank God you are all right! We heard you were in a terrible situation. Tons of commission supplies rotted on railroad cars outside of Nashville because no one could get through to you. I was so worried! Then I thought, well, what would you do? I just knew you'd take a wagon or two and try to get past the blockade. A woman would have a better chance of making it through Rebel lines than the army. So here we are!" Mrs. Porter raised a hand to Mary Ann's face and said, "Oh, my dear, your face is gaunt. You look so thin."

Mary Ann began to cry, but then rubbed the tears off her face roughly with her shawl. "I'm a silly fool. Forgive me. We've been out of food for some time. I've been so worried. I didn't know how we were going to get by. I thought perhaps this was it, and we all were going to die."

Mary Ann closed her eyes and Eliza held her tenderly. Eliza touched Mary Ann's hair and said, "Come, let's get warm and we can talk."

Mary Ann recovered and said, "Oh, I just can't thank you enough. You're saving the lives of these boys!"

The two women turned and walked toward the field hospital headquarters tent. The wagon drivers moved their teams forward so the supplies could be unloaded.

"The locals tell me this is the coldest it's ever been here. And you sat in that wagon for a good many hours, I think. There is so much to do here, and I have much to tell you. But first, let us warm a bit by the fire and then cook something for these men. Later you must tell me what is happening in the world."

"Mary Ann!" said Mrs. Porter, turning around to take in the full spectacle of the field hospital. "There must be thousands of wounded here! How have you managed? I would have brought more wagons but was afraid the greater number would mean we'd be stopped by the Rebels."

"Many have died, too weak from their wounds to keep warm. It has been...difficult...for all of us."

"Mary Ann," said Mrs. Porter, "I will stay the night, but I must return these wagons and horses to the Sanitary Commission tomorrow. Other hospitals need to be resupplied as well."

CHAPTER 33

Chattanooga Breastworks

By January 1864, thousands of wounded and ill swelled the field hospital into a sprawling tent camp. It had expanded up a slight rise and encircled a small log cabin in sad disrepair. The cabin's roof had huge holes in it from cannon shot, and the log walls had gaps through which the wind blew. The cabin's only useful feature was the stone fireplace, burning brightly, which made the one-room shelter slightly warmer than the outside. The fire cast dark shadows into the corners. The cabin used to house the men who were the most grievously wounded, but they were moved out so the doctor, who had arrived from Chattanooga just a few days ago, could have a place to work. A small, rickety, three-legged table leaned against the wall for balance. Papers lay scattered on the table, with rocks as paperweights so the wind could not take them. The doctor stood before the fireplace, leaning toward it with one hand on the mantel.

It was cold outside. When the wind subsided, huge snowflakes fell like downy feathers and covered the already white ground. Mary Ann, in her ragged gray homespun, tended a huge kettle of soup at one of the fires. Soldier-nurses walked among the tents, distributing bread to the men inside, changing dressings, and lighting lanterns as evening approached. The snow made the night bright, as if the moon were shining. Some men tended the fires, but the wood piles, so high in the days before, were becoming smaller and smaller.

The doctor came to the door of the cabin and stood there looking at the camp. He saw Mary Ann, pulled on his greatcoat, and buttoned it as he moved toward her.

"Mrs. Bickerdyke, may I have a word with you?"

"Of course," Mary Ann said, and turned to the young soldier on fire detail. "Jeffrey, take over for me, please. Make sure the porridge doesn't stick to the bottom and burn. And have the boys add a few more bricks to the fire. It will be even colder tonight." She then turned to the doctor.

"In my office," the doctor said. "We must get out of this blasted...ah...I beg your pardon, madam, for my vulgarity. The cold has got the better of me. This way, if you please."

They walked together to the cabin and the doctor took time to shake the snow off his coat before he closed the door, which screeched loudly.

The doctor turned his back to her and began gathering his belongings and stuffing them into his saddlebag. "Mrs. Bickerdyke, I have orders to leave for Chattanooga, but I will try to return in the morning. I leave you in charge here for the night."

"Doctor," said Mary Ann, "my boys are freezing to death. I'd like to send some men out to look for wood. We are running short—"

"Absolutely not," interrupted the doctor. "It is too late, and the forest is too distant. I won't send men out in a snowstorm to cut trees this late. There's no telling where the Rebs are or what kind of injuries might result from leaving the safety of the camp. No. I know the situation is serious, but you must make do until morning."

"But, Doctor," Mary Ann protested, "you must see—"

"I'm sorry, Mrs. Bickerdyke. Truly, I am. I understand your concern, but...well, just do the best you can. I'll bring what wood I can find in Chattanooga with me in the morning. Now I must leave," he said, as he grabbed his saddlebag.

Mary Ann stood there for a moment and then followed him out to his horse, where he tied his bags behind the saddle. "Are you sure, Doctor?"

"Just do the best you can," he said, irritated. He mounted and turned his horse, which slowly picked its way through the wounded toward the snowy road to Chattanooga.

Mary Ann stood in the falling snow. Her jaw was set, her facial muscles clenched, and her eyes blazed with anger. She turned and looked at her hospital. No trees were to be seen anywhere. Nearby, two wounded soldiers added wood to the fire from a rapidly dwindling pile of boards. Over the wind she heard the anguish of those shivering and in pain. Several stretcher-bearer teams walked past her, heads tucked down against their coat collars. They carried away the newly dead, already stiff with a covering of snow.

"How quickly they lose their warmth," she said to herself as they passed.

A soldier approached her, panting from the walk up the slight rise. "Mother, we're running out of soup."

She was pulled from her reverie and said, "I'll be along directly, Joseph." Just then, a fierce gust of wind barreled through the camp, blowing sparks everywhere and toppling tents. Men writhed under the fallen canvas, making the tents look like strange, otherworldly creatures. Mary Ann and several soldiers rushed to right the tents and comfort those inside.

"You three men!" yelled Mary Ann, looking at the hardiest soldiers close to her. "Bring those men into the cabin and lay them on the floor."

⚭

About an hour later, the fires in camp had burned to coals. There were few sparks flying now and most of the wood piles were gone. Men huddled around each fire. They reached their hands out greedily toward the warmth. When it felt like their hands were just about to burn, they quickly stuffed them inside their coats to nestle in their armpits.

It continued to snow. The wounded were quieter. Mary Ann tended a cooking kettle hung over glowing coals. She knew many would die tonight from the cold. They always seemed to die at night, especially just before dawn. The wind blew down more tents and putting them back up quickly became a fruitless labor. Canvas flapped in the wind against tent poles but no one rushed to right them.

"Mother," said a soldier walking toward her, "the fire over by the Iowa boys is almost out. We ain't got no more to burn."

"How are the other fires? Can those boys spare any?" she said.

"From what I saw coming here, the others are pretty low too, ma'am."

He had started to walk off, when Mary said, "Wait a moment, please. There's a little wood in the major's office. Use that."

"Yes, ma'am." He walked toward the cabin and she turned back to her cooking pot. A few minutes later he returned. He cleared his throat awkwardly and then said, "Ah...ma'am?"

"Yes?" she said, not turning from her task.

"Ma'am, I looked. There ain't no wood in there. It's been stripped bare."

"That little table and the chair. Burn them."

"The doctor's desk and...ah...chair, ma'am? You want me to burn those? He's gonna be awful mad, ma'am."

"I expect he will be. Don't worry. I shall see to the doctor in the morning."

Another hour passed, and the fires were almost out and no longer even hissed when the snow fell on them. Mary Ann, and those soldiers still able, helped tend the wounded. They rushed from man to man, laying warm rocks and bricks against them, returning the cold ones to the heaps of coals.

At about this same time, a column of soldiers on mules approached the edge of the hospital. The man on the lead mule spoke to the first awake patient he saw.

"Soldier, who's in charge here?"

The wounded boy, no older than sixteen, was lying on the ground, shivering. His teeth were chattering so much he could not talk, so he merely pointed toward the tiny cabin in the distance.

"Wait here for me, boys. I'll be back directly," said the lead rider. He left the column and rode off in the direction of headquarters. His mule stepped lightly around the wounded. Men on the ground stirred and looked up from their blankets as he passed, a dreamlike figure in the snow.

As he neared the cabin, he stopped to ask a soldier-nurse, "Where's your commanding officer, soldier?"

The soldier-nurse looked up in surprise and sputtered a bit. "Officer? I guess Mrs. Bickerdyke is in charge of the hospital, sir. She's right over there," he said, pointing.

The rider raised his eyebrows at the oddity of this, moved his mule toward her, and dismounted.

"Excuse me, ma'am. Would you be Mrs. Bickerdyke?"

She straightened from her task and looked at the rider. She saw a weary, cold man in his late twenties with several days' growth of beard. His uniform had seen better days, but then they all had.

"I am," said Mary Ann. "You seem to have traveled a long way, Captain."

"I have, ma'am. Captain Bellings, ma'am," he said, straightening his shoulders and standing tall. He put his gloved right hand to his hat in a gesture of respect, even though the hat was jammed down on his head to prevent it from flying away in the wind. "I'm with the Pioneer Corps, ma'am. My men are stopped at the edge of this camp. They're pretty hungry and cold, and our mules are about all in. We have been riding all day and it's been rough going. Would you happen to have any spare rations, ma'am?

We haven't eaten in a day or so. My men would be most appreciative."

"Captain, we're almost out of wood and our fires are dying, but I expect we can fix up a little something for you and your men, if you don't mind watered-down soup. Have them come up here. They can tether their mules behind that cabin."

"Thank you kindly, ma'am." Captain Bellings turned his mule and headed back the way he came.

As his men rode up to the cabin and dismounted, a soldier took the reins and tied each mule to a rope strung along the side of the cabin. The captain and his men walked over to huddle by a dying fire, where Mary Ann gave each a tin cup of soup, steaming in the cold. They molded their hands around the cups, grateful for the warmth.

When each of the pioneers had a cup of soup, Mary Ann wiped her hands on her dress front and used a stick and her shawl to take warm rocks from the fire. She laid these tenderly around the wounded, taking the cold stones back to the coals. Captain Bellings watched her. As she brought the cold stones back to the fire, he said, "I hear there was a big battle here about a month or so ago, ma'am."

"Yes, Captain," she said, as she returned a stone to the edge of the coals. "These boys were in the battle for Lookout Mountain. They need to be inside, somewhere warm, but they've been too ill to move. And as you can see, we have no hospital building to speak of, only a few tents."

"You look sorely pressed here, ma'am. My men are about done in, but maybe a few of us could help you, after they've gotten this soup in their bellies...begging your pardon, ma'am."

She stood and turned toward him. "What could you do, Captain? I need to keep these men warm all night or they'll freeze to death. My main concern is how to obtain more wood."

"I don't think I can help you there, ma'am. The last ten miles or so, all we seen were low-cut stumps. Not a tree around. Somebody sure was busy cutting wood."

Mary Ann frowned, "There's nothing we could use to feed the fires?"

"No, ma'am," Captain Bellings said, shaking his head. He looked around and then nodded in the direction of the cabin. "We could tear down that old cabin there. Use the logs on the fire."

"No, Captain, I'm afraid not. I've put my sickest men inside. They need the shelter from this wretched weather."

The captain shook his head, "Sorry, ma'am. I wish we could have helped. You've been so kind to us."

He had turned away to rejoin his men, when Mary Ann stopped him by saying, "Wait, Captain. What about the breastworks at Chattanooga?"

Captain Bellings turned back to her, asking quizzically, "Breastworks, ma'am?"

"Well, no one really needs them for protection," said Mary Ann, more to herself than him. "The battle is long over. There should be plenty of dry wood in there. That would do nicely!"

"Ah...ma'am. You can't tear down breastworks—not without an order. That'd take someone with a higher rank than me."

Mary Ann smiled and said, "How would you and your men like a little coffee? We have a tiny bit left, but just enough, I think. Why don't you come with me?" Mary Ann put her right hand in the crook of his left elbow and escorted him over to another kettle on a mound of rapidly cooling coals. She filled his tin with coffee and then said, "This way, Captain."

Together they walked to the cabin. As the captain entered his face showed surprise. Wounded men were shoulder to shoulder over most of the floor. A weak flame flickering in the coals was all that was left of the once hearty fire.

"Captain," Mary Ann said, turning toward him, "my men are dying in this cold. They will surely freeze to death by morning. There is no officer in this hospital. Won't you please help me? Chattanooga is safely in Union hands, and the Rebels are far from here. Those breastworks could save lives tonight. If you get us wood, I'll find something to feed you, your men, and your mules. And in the morning I'll take full responsibility for the breastworks."

"I don't know, ma'am. This could cause a lot of trouble," said the captain warily.

"Here, you'll need lanterns. You can take this one, and there's another by the cooking area," said Mary Ann excitedly.

∞

Dawn lightened a cold and clear day. The storm had passed, leaving high drifts of snow against the leeward sides of buildings. Most of the residents of Chattanooga were still asleep, but reveille had roused the occupying army. Sentries on guard duty paced outside the Chattanooga Hotel, which Union forces had liberated and now used as a headquarters.

The sentries watched as a horse and rider came galloping at full speed up the main road. The rider pulled his horse to a jolting stop in front of the hotel and dismounted. Breathlessly, the rider said to the sentries, "Urgent message for the colonel from Captain Johnson, picket duty." The sentries nodded and then let the man pass into the hotel.

Moments later, the sentries heard the colonel inside bellow, "What? By whose orders? I'm going to court-martial the bastard! Get me my horse!"

A few minutes later, the colonel walked out of the hotel, followed by two of his staff. He muttered angrily to himself, "Who did this? This is…is…men…let's go!"

The colonel and his staff mounted their horses and galloped down the road. They quickly arrived at the edge of Chattanooga. They pulled up their horses stop and stood in their stirrups to look at what was once a five-foot-thick, seven-foot-high, formidable wall of sharpened logs that protected the city. The Rebels had originally built the breast-works to keep the Federals out of Chattanooga. After routing the Rebels from the city, the Union forces reinforced the wall to keep the Rebels out. Now a half mile of breastworks was missing—completely missing. Tracks of boots and mules were visible in the snow around the area, and long grooves testified to the dragging away of logs. In spite of the cold, the colonel's face turned bright red.

"Cyrus," he said to one of his men, "find out who did this and bring him to me—and bring the provost marshal. Whoever was involved in this will pay with his rank and imprisonment. Who in their right mind would tear down breastworks without a direct order? This is outrageous! And unprecedented in wartime!" said the colonel. As his men saluted him, the colonel pulled his horse around and galloped back toward the center of Chattanooga. His staff moved closer together to plan their course of action.

The colonel, angry as a swatted bee, rode back to the hotel. He dismounted and threw the reins of his lathered horse to a private. He entered the dining room and joined a group of officers at breakfast. In a loud voice, the colonel demanded breakfast be served and then angrily started telling those he had joined about the disappearance of the breastworks.

The doctor, looking rumpled, was just walking up the steps to the hotel seeking breakfast himself, when he paused on the porch to listen to the colonel's voice projecting angrily from the dining room. A look of concern washed over the doctor's face as he entered the hotel. He sat at an empty table in the dining room and ordered coffee. Then he focused his full attention on the colonel's story, being repeated for every newcomer in the room. He quickly gulped his coffee and hastened out of the hotel in search of his horse. He had a nagging feeling he knew who was involved in this crime, although he couldn't imagine how it could have been accomplished. He needed to get to the field hospital right away.

The doctor and his aide rode hard toward the field hospital. In the distance he saw huge bonfires situated in the midst of the hospital, billowing gray smoke into the cold air. As they neared, the doctor saw normal activity going on. Soldier-nurses were helping others to eat. Most of the wounded and ill had been placed around the bonfires, and for some it was so warm they had discarded their woolen blankets. The doctor and his aide rode up to the cabin and dismounted. Before going inside, he saw Mary Ann and walked over to her. She was handing a bucket of something steaming to a soldier.

"Here, young man, take this warm cornmeal to the mules. They've earned it."

"Mrs. Bickerdyke, I see you made it through the night," said the doctor.

"Why, good morning, Major. Yes, it was a difficult night, but most of the boys made it. It's good to see sunshine again, isn't it?" said Mary Ann, smiling as she wiped her hands on the front of her dress, long ago given double duty as an apron. She turned from the doctor to attend to other chores.

The doctor turned and entered his cabin. Almost immediately he shouted, "Sergeant! Get in here!"

The sergeant, who was leading the horses to the tether line, grimaced at the sound; then he handed the reins to another soldier and rushed into the cabin.

"Where's my desk? What are all these men doing in here? Find out what happened here last night, Sergeant!" yelled the doctor, as he stomped out.

A few minutes later, the doctor and his sergeant stood yelling at the sleeping Pioneer Corps. Rudely awakened, tired men were shaking off sleep to stand at attention. Captain Bellings groaned, rubbed his face roughly, and then stood at attention in front of the doctor.

"Sir!" said Captain Bellings.

"Captain, I understand you can tell me what happened here last night, as well as what happened to the Chattanooga breastworks."

"Sir? Yes…sir! I…ah…we…that is…ah…sir…it was very cold last night, sir!"

Disgust came over the doctor's face and he said, "Sergeant, arrest this man." The doctor turned and said to any who could hear, "Now, where is that bothersome woman? I'll lose my rank because of her!" He saw her spooning out warm cornmeal panado to the wounded. He strode over to her.

"Mrs. Bickerdyke! Are these the logs from the breastworks at Chattanooga?" he said, pointing to the closest bonfire.

"Yes, indeed, Doctor. And they saved many a life last night, to be sure."

"Madam, consider yourself arrested! You had no authority—"

At the very end of her patience, Mary Ann interrupted with a voice of steel, "All right, Doctor. I'm arrested. Now leave me be until the weather is warmer or my men will die." She returned to her task while the doctor, astounded, stood still for a moment; then he turned with a "Hrrrumpfff!" and walked back to his sergeant.

"Sergeant, ride into town and tell the colonel I have caught and arrested the culprits responsible for dismantling the breastworks."

❦

One week later, twelve high-ranking officers in dress uniform sat behind two tables lined up against a wall in one of the military offices in Chattanooga. A tribunal was under way. A lone chair in the middle of the room faced them, and in the chair sat Mrs. Bickerdyke, back straight and shoulders squared. Two armed guards were stationed on either side of the closed door inside the room. The officer in charge read the list of allegations against her and then asked if she had anything to say on her behalf.

Mrs. Bickerdyke smiled and said in the voice of a stern disciplinarian, "Why, yes, I do. Shame on you, gentlemen!

Shame! These men fought valiantly for the cause. They didn't hold back. If it took an arm or an eye or even both legs, why, that's what they gave, so you could win this war. They have sacrificed much more than you have. Now, be reasonable, gentlemen," said Mary Ann, standing and moving closer to them to emphasize her point. "What would you have me do? Let them freeze to death because no one took their needs into account? How would you explain that to your generals in Washington, that you let eight or nine hundred men freeze to death while that huge pile of wood sat there, utterly useless, defending no one? How would you explain that to the mothers of the North, who will surely hear about this?"

One of the officers interrupted, incredulity in his voice, "Are you threatening us, Mrs. Bickerdyke?"

Mary Ann glared at the officer who spoke as if he were an irksome child who had misbehaved. "No, gentlemen, I am not threatening any of you. But you should be thanking me! And you should be honoring the brave men from the Pioneer Corps who, though tired and hungry, went out into a bitterly cold night so your men could be warm. Think about it, gentlemen. Captain Bellings and I saved your heads!" She stretched out her arms, palms up, as if she was a scale weighing something. "Thousands of men alive, many of whom will fight another day, or a useless pile of wood. Which do you think the people of the North will hold more dear? Now, you release Captain Bellings. He's a hero, as surely as if he'd taken a Rebel force in hand. The mothers of your soldiers will hold him in high regard when they hear how he saved their sons' lives."

Mary Ann put her arms down and fished in her dress pocket for a piece of paper. Then she looked back at the tribunal. "Now, this has been a pleasant chat, but I can't stand here talking to you all day. I have a hospital to run and wounded to tend. Here's a list of supplies my hospital needs," she said, walking to the table and giving the paper to the chief officer. "You'll see to them, won't you? Now, if you gentlemen don't mind, I'll bid you good day and pick up Captain Bellings from the guardhouse on my way back to the hospital." Mary Ann smiled brightly at the officers, turned, and walked to the door. The two guards hesitated and looked to the officers and then back at her. Mary Ann's face hardened, and she lifted one eyebrow at the guards, who hastily opened the door for her. The officers were silent until she left. Once the door was shut behind her, she heard angry voices emanating from the room, all speaking at once.

The weather abated in the Chattanooga area, and the rail lines were reopened to Nashville. Supplies and men poured into the camp, relieving the desperate circumstances so many men had endured. When the army Corps of Engineers finished repairing the railway line to the North, the wounded were finally evacuated.

CHAPTER 34

Nervous Breakdown

The wounded and ill at Chattanooga were being placed on railway cars for transport to Northern hospitals. Mary Ann, tattered carpetbag on the platform by her foot, watched Andy direct the loading of the wounded. Another woman, in traveling cape and bonnet, stood next to Mary Ann. This woman appeared nervous and worried, and was wringing her hands.

Mary Ann turned to her and held her by the shoulders. In a reassuring voice, she said, "You'll be fine. Everything has been set up to run smoothly. Trust your instincts and Andy. He's been my right hand, and he'll help you settle in and obtain what you need. Now, your bags are off the train?" The other woman nodded. "Good. Show Andy where they are and he'll put them in the carriage. If you need me, reach me at the Sanitary Commission offices in Chicago. I cannot thank you enough for assuming the matron duties at the hospital."

The train whistle blew, interrupting them.

"I'd best hurry," said Mary Ann. She gave the other woman a quick hug and bent to pick up her carpetbag. "Andy," yelled Mary Ann over the sound of the train whistle, "take good care of Mrs. Barstow here. And don't forget little Jimmy's dressing change—twice a day. And the laundry soap!" Mary Ann boarded the train just as it was starting to pull away from the station. She stood in the doorway of the car and waved. Both Andy and Mrs. Barstow waved back. For the first time, Mary Ann was aware of a feeling of relief that she was heading north—to warm houses, good food, and the understanding of her friends.

One week later, several well-dressed ladies sat in Mrs. Livermore's parlor, sipping tea from a silver service and chatting. Mary Livermore looked toward the parlor door. "I can't imagine what is keeping Mrs. Bickerdyke. If you ladies will excuse me for a moment, I'll go investigate the delay. She was so eager to meet you."

Mrs. Livermore put down her teacup and left the room, shutting the parlor door quietly behind her. She walked upstairs and knocked gently on the door to Mary Ann's room. There was no response. *That's odd*, she thought. She knocked again, louder this time, and said through the door, "Mary Ann? Are you all right?" There was still no response, so Mrs. Livermore turned the doorknob and entered. The room appeared empty, and then Mrs. Livermore heard a quiet sobbing coming from the corner by the bed. She rushed over to find Mary Ann sitting on the floor, hugging her knees and crying. Mrs. Livermore knelt beside Mary Ann and took her in her arms, rocking her slowly. "Oh, Mary Ann, my dear, dear, Mary Ann. I can only imagine what you've been through. You have cared for so many others, but now it's time we took care of you."

The two women stayed that way for several minutes; sobs and sniffling were the only sounds that broke the silence. Then Mrs. Livermore stroked Mary Ann's hair and said softly, "My dear, I will send the ladies away. You have the sorrow of the world in your heart, and you, too, need time to heal. I shall return directly and help you to bed." Mrs. Livermore held Mary Ann close to her; then released her and stood. She left the room and quietly closed the door.

As Mrs. Livermore entered the parlor, one of the women said, "Ah, here you are, Mary. I was just telling Mrs. Perkins about the fair in Milwaukee to benefit the sick and wounded soldiers. Do you think Mrs. Bickerdyke would be willing to make a presentation there? I could easily arrange it. My sister is on the organizing committee. It would be a powerfully stirring event for those attending."

Mrs. Livermore responded, "I don't know, Celeste. I will consult with her and find out if she'd be willing. But now, ladies, I'm afraid I must reschedule today's meeting for another time. Mrs. Bickerdyke is indisposed and needs to rest. I must tend to her."

"Of course, how thoughtless of us," said Mrs. Perkins. "She must be exhausted from her travels. Come along, ladies. We'll meet the great woman another time, after she's had a chance to rest."

Mrs. Livermore saw the ladies out and then returned to Mary Ann's bedroom. She entered quietly. Mary Ann was still on the floor, sobs wracking her body. Gently, she helped Mary Ann to stand and undress, wrapping her in a warm nightgown and shoulder cape. Mary Ann was like doll, passive and pliable, with a faraway look in her eyes.

Mrs. Livermore said, "Lie down, my dear Mary Ann. I will bring you some tea and biscuits in a bit. But sleep now, if you can. I'll have the staff check on the fire every so often. You need rest, Mary Ann. You look so tired and thin. I will take care of you, my dear." Mrs. Livermore helped Mary Ann into bed, tucked the blankets around her, and gently caressed her cheek. Then she left the room.

Mary Ann's dreams were filled with soldiers' faces and scenes of hospitals. It was always snowing. The dead were covered with snow. Here and there a stiff blue face peered out with unseeing eyes. Sometimes, it was the face of one of her sons. Once she noticed a hand, fingers curled and covered with ice crystals, and this reminded her that snow contained death. All around—death. Frozen in place. All these boys, her boys, wounded, starved, dehydrated, and frozen to death. No matter how hard she tried. Hundreds of dead. She was helpless. Nothing made a difference. She looked down at her high-button shoes and they were frozen.

Her apron was stiff with ice. Her hands were blue. Her frozen sleeves had a delicate lace of hoarfrost. She felt her face, and it was also frozen. And then she awoke with a start, confused to find herself in a warm bedroom with cotton sheets and heavy wool blankets. For a moment she didn't know where she was or even who she was. Then she felt a great pain in her head, which focused her. Yes. She was in Chicago. At Mrs. Livermore's home. And she was ill. She had a terrible headache and a feeling of emptiness. Suddenly, she was crying, pulling up the covers for comfort and sobbing without making a sound.

The next few days, Mary Ann could not rid her mind of these terrible scenes. They came unbidden and left her horrified and numb. She went about her days accompanying Mrs. Livermore, helping the Sanitary Commission to make money, and visiting soldiers' families, but she felt strangely calm, as if a part of her were lost and nothing mattered.

CHAPTER 35

The Chamber of Commerce Speech

Two weeks later, a somewhat recovered but emotionally guarded Mary Ann sat next to Mrs. Livermore while several other ladies engaged in animated conversation in the organizing office of the fair that was being held in Milwaukee's opera house. The sounds of hundreds of people in the main auditorium could be heard through the office walls. Mary Ann was pale and had huge dark circles under her eyes. She still looked very tired, but had been eager to attend.

"Oh, Mrs. Bickerdyke, you were a triumph! What a moving speech!" said one of the ladies.

Another concurred, "Yes, it has been quite a success, thanks to you. We have been—"

Suddenly the office door opened, and a breathless woman rushed in and interrupted their conversation. "Oh! Oh my! Ladies, you will not believe this! This is simply wonderful! The Chamber of Commerce representatives gathered in the hall after your presentation, Mrs. Bickerdyke, and they have offered twelve hundred dollars for hospital relief! And they're asking if you won't attend their next meeting, to tell them how their donation will be used." There were gasps of surprise and then applause from those in the office.

The Milwaukee Chamber of Commerce met the following week. Esteemed gentlemen sat at tables arranged in a semicircle, somewhat similar to a military tribunal, thought Mary Ann. She stood before them at a podium and held a money pouch. Because of the importance of today's meeting, a large crowd had gathered. Several hundred citizens sat in the audience section of the room or leaned against the back walls. The room was filled to capacity.

The chairman was speaking. "It is with honor and pride that we present this money to you, Mrs. Bickerdyke, to be used for the men of the Union who need medical care for their war wounds. And now, madam, we would be pleased if you would inform us about how you plan to use this most generous offer."

The chairman nodded his head at Mary Ann, to indicate that he was finished. The audience and other members of the chamber applauded. Mary Ann continued to stand quietly before them. She looked at the pouch in her hand and then put it on the podium, which she gripped with both hands. The crowd stopped applauding, and a quiet hush of expectancy filled the room.

Mary Ann looked up at the chamber. "I....," she began. She paused, cleared her throat, gripped the podium tighter, and then continued. "I am much obliged to you, gentlemen, for the kind things you have said. But I haven't done much—and by the way, neither have you."

The audience gasped. The men in the semicircle looked insulted and stunned. One Chamber of Commerce member rose out of his seat as another restrained him. With anger on his face, he sat back down.

Over the murmur of the crowd, Mary Ann said, "I am glad you are giving twelve hundred dollars for the poor boys in the hospitals, but it's no more than you ought to do." At this the semicircle of men looked at each other with surprise and irritation. Mary Ann continued, "And it isn't half as much as the soldiers in the hospitals have given for you. Suppose, gentlemen," she said, leaning over the podium toward the semicircle, feeling something between exhaustion and rage, "you have to give, right now, either one thousand dollars or your right leg. Would it take you long to decide? Two thousand dollars or your right arm? Five thousand dollars or both of your eyes? All that you are worth or your life? I have eighteen hundred boys in my hospital in Chattanooga who have given an arm or a leg or both, and yet they don't seem to think they've done a great deal for their country. And the graveyard behind the hospital and the battlefield beyond contain the bodies of thousands, many of them mere children, who freely gave their lives to save you and your homes and this country from ruin. Oh, gentlemen of the chamber and citizens of Milwaukee, speak not about what we have given or done! We have done nothing—we have given nothing compared to them. It is our duty—it is *your* duty—to keep giving, and doing so just as long as there's a soldier fighting or suffering for us!"

Mary Ann stopped speaking and the room was absolutely silent. Then slowly, one person in the audience began to clap. More joined in, until the whole audience was standing, shouting, and clapping. The men of the chamber looked at each other, and then they also stood and clapped enthusiastically.

The next day, the *Milwaukee Daily* headline read: "Milwaukee Leads the Nation in War Donations!"

CHAPTER 36

Rotting Supplies

It was spring in the third year of the war. Inside a house, in what was once an elegant sitting room, General Sherman paced, hands clasped behind his back, as he dictated a letter to an aide. Sherman spoke quickly and the aide, sitting at a desk, wrote furiously.

> At Lafayette all our armies will be together, and if Johnston stands, we must attack him in position. Supplies are the great question. I have increased the number of railcars daily from sixty-five to eighty. My estimate is one hundred and forty-five cars will give us a day's supply and a day's accumulation. McPherson is ordered to carry twenty days' rations and to rely on Ringgold for renewal of his bread. Colonel Comstock will explain to you, personally, much I cannot commit to paper. We march on Atlanta on the day planned. I am, with great respect,
> W. T. Sherman, Major General
> Commander, Mississippi Division
> April 25, 1864, Chattanooga

Sherman continued speaking to his aide. "After you copy it, I want Colonel Comstock to proceed immediately to Washington and place it personally in the hands of General Grant. Comstock will need to be quick. Grant is about to take the Army of the Potomac after Lee. Now, take an order."

> All use of rail transport between Nashville and Chattanooga is forbidden for civil personnel from this time forward. Rail transportation will be strictly limited for military use only. No exceptions. Anyone found disobeying this order shall be imprisoned. By order of W. T. Sherman, Major-General

On the last day of April, Mary Ann stood on the rail station platform in Nashville, Tennessee, arguing with a very harried stationmaster. While they argued a line of hundreds of troops moved forward and began boarding the train. Down the line, soldiers loaded military supplies onto flatcars.

"But what do you mean, I can't get on? I have come all the way from Milwaukee, young man, and I mean to make it to Chattanooga! I have urgent business that needs attention there! And, I have supplies that require transport!"

The stationmaster sighed, reminiscent of a parent who had explained something many times to a child who just didn't understand. "Ma'am, I'm sorry. No civilians past this point. All railcars are for military use only. If I let you on this train, I'll go to jail. I have a family depending on me to earn their daily bread, ma'am. Now you can either stay here or go back where you came from, but you are not going to Chattanooga on this train!"

"Well," said Mary Ann, "where can I find a horse and wagon?"

"I don't think you'd make it, ma'am," replied the stationmaster. "The roads are clogged with military. Old Enrico over there"—the stationmaster pointed to a man who leaned against a platform post several cars down, oddly still amid all the hustle—"he tried it the other day. Never made it. Had to turn back. No room on the road for anything that's not military, and going overland—well, it's just not possible. The Rebels set up ambushes now and then that the military has to fight off. If you'll excuse me, ma'am, I have duties to attend to."

Mary Ann turned away and began to pace on the platform, unaware of the soldiers who made way for her. Then she noticed a large pile of crates about fifty yards from the platform. Because her vision was blocked by the lines of soldiers, she could only make out *U.S. S* and *sion* stamped on the crates. She walked across the platform, down the steps, and over to the crates. As she neared them, she saw *U.S. Sanitary Commission* stamped on their sides and she smelled a foul odor. It increased in strength as she came closer to the crates. Several businessmen, oblivious to the smell, stood arguing nearby.

"Well, I don't know!" said one of the men in an exasperated tone, using his hands for emphasis. "If I knew, I'd have done something about it long ago!"

A second man said, "All this effort—what a waste."

Mary Ann approached them. "Excuse me, gentlemen. Are you by any chance with the Sanitary Commission?"

The men all tipped their hats to her. The second man replied, "Yes! We are! Allow me to introduce myself and my colleagues, madam. I am Henry Leggett, and this is Christopher Upton, John Meyer, and Frank Marple. And you are...?"

"Mrs. Bickerdyke. I also work with the commission. Can you gentlemen tell me what these crates are doing here, and why they emit such a foul smell?"

Mr. Marple said in a hopeless voice, "They're food and medical supplies bound for Chattanooga. But we can't get them to Chattanooga. Seems the rails have been prohibited for civilian use. These crates have been here three days and will be completely useless, unless we find a way of transporting them there quickly."

"Ah, I see," responded Mary Ann. "And do you know who it is who prohibits commission supplies on the rails?"

Mr. Upton said, "General Sherman. No one dares go against him. He said he'd imprison any civilian riding the train between here and Chattanooga—and he'd do it, too. Civilian supplies are forbidden, too."

"Thank you, gentlemen. You've been most helpful. I wish you the best of luck." With that, Mary Ann turned back toward the train. The men watched as she stood directly in front of the stationmaster and rummaged in her dress pocket. She pulled out a piece of paper and handed it to him. The stationmaster read it, looked up at Mary Ann, and then reread it. They exchanged words, and Mary Ann pointed to the two piles of crates, those she had brought and those by the four businessmen. She took the piece of paper from the stationmaster and replaced it in her pocket. The stationmaster said something to several soldiers nearby, who ran to load both stacks of Sanitary Commission crates on the flatcars. The stationmaster then helped Mary Ann board the train. On the second step of the train, she turned and smiled at the commission men and gave them a little wave. They stood there gaping, wonder and surprise on their faces. And the train pulled out of the station headed for Chattanooga.

The next morning Mary Ann entered the military head-quarters in Chattanooga. The aide sitting at a desk in the outer office looked up; then, with surprise, he stood at attention.

"Why, hello! Why...how did you get down here?" he asked.

"Hello. I came down on the train, of course," she replied, smiling. "There's no other way of getting down here that I know of." Giving a nod of her head to the closed office door, she said, "I want to see him. Is he in?"

"Yes, ma'am. But he's very busy and won't see any-body," said the aide, his voice getting louder as Mary Ann headed for the closed door.

"Indeed, he will!" she said with a smile in her voice. With an impish look, she turned the knob and entered the room, closing the door behind her.

General Sherman sat at his desk, writing. He did not look up. Mary Ann walked in and stood before his desk.

"Good morning, General! I want to speak with you a moment. May I come in?"

"Aren't you already in, Mrs. Bickerdyke?" said Sherman in an annoyed voice. "What is it now?" With a resigned sigh, he put down his pen and looked up at her.

Mary Ann sat in a chair opposite him. "Why, General, it's that order of yours about the trains. You'll have to change it. We can get along without any more nurses or commission agents, but we must have supplies! The sick and wounded need them, and you'll just have to give permission to bring them down. After a man is unable to carry a gun and drops out of the lines, you expect the hospital doctors and nurses to get him well and put him back into service as soon as possible. But how are we going to make bricks without straw? Tell me that, if you can!"

Sherman looked back down at his papers, picked up his pen, and resumed writing. He did not look at her, but a hint of a smile formed at the corners of his mouth and his blue eyes twinkled with mischief.

"Well, Mrs. Bickerdyke, I'm busy today and cannot attend you. I will see you some other time." He waved her away with his hand.

Mary Ann stood and put her palms down on his desk, leaning over him. "No, General! Don't send me away until you've fixed this thing as it ought to be fixed. You had me assigned to your corps, and told me you expect me to look after the nursing of your sick and wounded. But I should like to know, how I can do this if I don't have any of the materials I need for this work? General, have some common sense!" said Mary Ann, in the voice of an angry mother correcting a child.

General Sherman looked up and laughed. He threw his pen down on the desk and said, "Well, I'll be damned!" Mary Ann looked at him in surprise. "Everyone else in this army is too damn scared of me. But not you, Mrs. Bickerdyke!" he said.

"Now, General," said Mary Ann in a stern voice, "I can't be fooling here all day! Write me an order for two cars a day to be sent down from the Sanitary Commission at Nashville, and I'll get out of your way and leave you to your business."

Sherman, still chuckling, wrote out the order and handed it to Mary Ann. She took it and turned to leave.

"It's good to have you back, Mrs. Bickerdyke," said Sherman.

She turned to look at him, a smile on her face. "Thank you, General. It's good to be back."

CHAPTER 37

Ringgold and Resaca

Dusk had fallen on the last day of April 1864. General Sherman stood behind his desk, packing his saddlebags. Lanterns lit the office. His aides in the outer area were busy packing as well. The army was about to move.

There was a knock on Sherman's door. "Enter," he said.

The door opened and Mary Ann stepped in. "You wanted to see me, General?"

"Ah. Yes. Excellent. Please be seated and rest yourself for a moment, Mrs. Bickerdyke. We'll be pulling out of Chattanooga tomorrow afternoon, heading for Ringgold, twenty miles south of here. I was hoping you could accompany my corps there. I understand you have shipped most of the wounded north and that your hospital is fairly empty now."

"Only a few wounded are left. They can easily be cared for by a local matron. Of course I will accompany you to Ringgold."

"Good. But I will let you do so under one condition—a condition that is not negotiable, Mrs. Bickerdyke."

"Sir?" asked Mary Ann.

"We're expecting to engage the enemy somewhere south of Ringgold. You are not to accompany the corps beyond Ringgold. Sanitary Commission goods are also forbidden beyond that point. The rail line stops there, and I don't want the roads tied up with civilian baggage. We will need every horse and wagon for military maneuvers. When

I can, I'll send the wounded back to you. Have I made myself clear, Mrs. Bickerdyke?"

"Of course, General—you always do. Now, if I'm to leave tomorrow, I must pack supplies. Is there anything else, sir?" she asked.

"No, Mrs. Bickerdyke. I know you have much to do. Good evening, ma'am."

After the Union took the city of Chattanooga, the Rebels retreated to Dalton, Georgia. Because the Confederate supply and artillery wagons lagged behind the army, their rear guard created a delaying tactic at Ringgold Gap. There, four thousand Rebels on the high ground fought a short but successful battle against twelve thousand Union soldiers; it was long enough to give the Confederate wagons time to escape capture.

One night a month later, Mary Ann sat at a camp table inside her tent, writing a letter by candlelight.

> May, 1864
> My dear Mrs. Porter,
>
> General Sherman readies his corps to leave Ringgold for battle somewhere south of here. He has, of course, forbidden me to follow.
>
> Several boys I tended in earlier battles are here, and they have been most helpful in packing hospital supplies on the mules that will follow Sherman's corps. With these supplies, and those I can fit into my ambulance and bread wagon, I will follow and tend the wounded.

I could certainly use your assistance, if you would be so kind as to take the rails to Ringgold immediately. I shall wait for you until Thursday of next week. If you have not arrived by then, I will assume you are otherwise occupied and will leave without you.

Your most loving friend,

M. A. Bickerdyke

Post Script: I believe your son is in one of the brigades preparing for battle. You might feel more comfortable if you were closer to him.

Mary Ann blew on the ink of the last page to dry it, folded the letter, and addressed it to Mrs. Porter. She stepped to the tent flap, pulled it aside, and asked a nearby private to take it to the post mail.

A few days later, Mary Ann and Mrs. Porter finished tucking hospital supplies into as many nooks and crannies of the ambulance as they could.

"I don't think we can fit even one more bandage, Mary Ann. This ambulance is stuffed tighter than a goose at Christmas," said Mrs. Porter.

"I believe you're right. Well then, shall we go? Andy? Are you ready?"

Andy was tying Old Whitey to the back of the bread wagon, which was also stuffed with supplies, barrels, and crates. "Yes, Mother. Are you sure you two ladies can handle that team?"

"Andrew, we'll be fine. You come along when you can."

Mary Ann and Mrs. Porter climbed up and settled themselves on the seat. Mary Ann picked up the reins, slapped them against the mules' rumps and they moved off, following the large path the army had made when it left Ringgold.

A few hours later, the two wagons traveled at a mule's walking pace miles behind the army. The sun was just dipping below the horizon and Mary Ann pulled the wagon to a stop. The sound of a cannonade in the distance made the women look at each other with worry. Mary Ann gave Mrs. Porter a reassuring pat and then flicked the reins to urge the mules forward. After a half hour, Andy pulled the bread wagon alongside the ladies, and the two wagons stopped.

"Mother, Mrs. Porter, it will be too dark soon to continue. We don't know where the troops are up ahead, and we don't want to blunder into a Rebel camp. I suggest we stop here for the night and continue on in the morning. Pull your wagon over there, by those trees. I'll build us a small fire for supper."

Resaca was a railroad town not far from Dalton, Georgia. General McPherson, under Sherman's command, was ordered to take Resaca and prevent the Rebels from retreating from Dalton. The Confederates were well entrenched in earthworks around Resaca and engaged the Union forces there for days.

After a restless night, Mary Ann, Mrs. Porter, and Andy packed up early in the morning and headed toward Resaca. They reached the edge of yesterday's battlefield by midmorning. Union and Rebel wounded of every description and severity lay in the weeds and dirt. There were so many soldiers writhing in pain that the ground looked like it was undulating. Off to the right, under a lone tree, Dr. Woodward was amputating a soldier's leg, assisted by a soldier with a bandaged head. The patient was strapped to a wide board that was balanced on top of a barrel and a large rock. Sounds of cannon rolled down from a nearby hill, and the earth shook with each thunderous explosion. Black smoke drifted down from the hill, and wisps of smoke started to cover the wounded at the far edge of the field.

Mary Ann and Mrs. Porter got down from the wagon and immediately rushed to the sides of the closest wounded. One soldier looked at them and then wiped his eyes. He looked again, as if he was seeing ghosts. "Mother? Is that you? Are you really here?"

Another soldier nearby said, "Hey, boys. Mother's here!" This caused soldiers all over the field to call out for her help.

"Stay here, dear," she told Mrs. Porter. "I'm going to speak with Dr. Woodward and will be right back." She moved over to where a soldier was attempting to stand and helped him up. "Young man, I know you are wounded, but we desperately need help. Rouse whoever you can, and see if some of the boys with less severe wounds can unload the wagon. Are you steady? Good. I'll be back." Mary Ann then picked her way over and around wounded soldiers to Dr. Woodward, the operating table, and the nearby pile of severed limbs.

Dr. Woodward, splattered with blood, was sharpening his knife on a whetstone. He had just helped carry the soldier whose leg he had amputated to a clear spot on the ground, and asked a nearby soldier to keep an eye on the already saturated dressing on the stump. "If he starts to pump blood through that, call me."

He saw Mary Ann approaching. She noticed that he looked exhausted.

"Thank God you've come, Mrs. Bickerdyke. Help me, please. I have only one assistant, and we've both been working since the battle began. I don't know how much longer we can continue."

Mary Ann looked over her shoulder and cried out loudly to Andy. "Andrew! Come here, please. Dr. Woodward needs you to lift these boys up and down from his table. Now, Doctor, who's next?"

Dr. Woodward nodded toward hundreds of men lying on the field. "I've stopped trying to care for the worst," he said, wiping his bloody sleeve across his already blood-smeared forehead. "They probably won't make it no matter what I do. Choose the closest with shattered arms or legs. If they have more wounds than that, leave them. They are already lost."

Mary Ann walked over to the closest young man and knelt by his side. He was terrified and in great pain. A cannonball had shattered his lower left leg, just below the knee. Andy had pulled a stretcher from the wagon and was now standing by the young man. Dr. Woodward's assistant was there as well. They lifted him up carefully, gently, but the pain was excruciating and he screamed at the movement. "No! No! Don't let him cut off my leg! I'm a farmer. I need both legs. No! How will I support my family?" he cried.

Mary Ann walked alongside the stretcher, holding his hand. "Hold on, son. Think of your mother and your family. You'll die if this leg doesn't come off. Your family needs you to stay alive for them," she said. Andy and the assistant put the stretcher down on the ground, lifted him onto the makeshift table, and strapped him down. She continued to hold his hand, murmuring soothing words to him.

The assistant brought over a whiskey bottle and raised the young man's head so he could swallow. "There ya go, my lad. Take a good long one. It will help ya."

The wounded man took several large gulps. Then the assistant put the bottle down and looked to Andy, who was holding the good leg, and to Dr. Woodward, who held the saw. The assistant moved to the young man's shoulders and rested all his weight on the patient. The patient squeezed Mary Ann's hand so hard, she thought he might break her bones.

Dr. Woodward made the first cut, slashing through muscles and tendons just above the knee. The patient screamed and then fainted. Dr. Woodward said, "A blessing for him. Let's be quick about it." In less than five minutes, Dr. Woodward completed the amputation, and with a large needle and twine sewed a flap of skin over the wound. He applied a tight pressure dressing to slow down the arterial flow. Without even looking up, he motioned with his hand that Andy and the assistant should move him back to his spot on the ground and bring another. "Watch him, Mother," said Dr. Woodward. "Sometimes these cases bleed out before I can get back to them." He wiped his knife on his blood-encrusted apron as the next screaming patient was placed on the makeshift operating table.

Later that afternoon, with the wagons mostly unpacked, Mrs. Porter and Mary Ann tended to the wounded, occasionally leaving their patients to stir the stew heating in great kettles over several fires. Three soldiers had replaced Andy as surgical assistants. Others walked among the wounded, doing what they could for them. When the type of wound allowed it, one soldier held the patient down on the ground while the other used a pocket knife to dig out minié balls or canister fragments. Andy followed them, stuffing the gouged-out hole with lint and wrapping cotton cloth tightly around the wound.

The battle was drawing nearer to the field hospital. Huge fingers of black smoke drifted over the wounded, making the scene appear otherworldly. The cries of fighting men and horses, shouted commands, and bugle calls were now distinct and close. The sounds of artillery drowned out the screams of wounded men, and the ground shook with the ferocity of an earthquake. The hissing sounds of stray Minié balls passing close to the hospital could be heard.

Dr. Woodward yelled, "Mrs. Bickerdyke, Mrs. Porter, there is no way we can move these men! If the fighting comes through here, drop to the ground and stay down!"

Both women nodded, understanding that the battle would overtake the hospital. Fear filled them, but they continued caring for the men in their charge.

Just then, out of a cloud of black smoke a young soldier with sword drawn appeared at the edge of the field hospital, leaping over the wounded and running with the grace of a startled deer. He called out, "Mother! I'm all right!" before he disappeared into the smoke. Mrs. Porter looked up just in time to see the back of her son as the smoke enveloped him. Tears ran down her face; she squeezed her eyes shut briefly in a grateful prayer, and then resumed her task with the soldier she was tending.

Three days later, thousands of wounded covered the ground in a now greatly expanded field hospital. The battle was over. Mary Ann and Mrs. Porter moved through long rows of their patients, checking and changing bandages, feeding those who could not feed themselves, and cleaning those who could not make it to the edge of the field hospital where there was an area designated as a latrine. The women enlisted the assistance of several healthy soldiers, including Mrs. Porter's son, who saw to it that those wounded who could work did something useful. Men with wounds in their lower limbs carved crutches and canes from sticks of wood. Men with shoulder or arm wounds walked among their comrades, helping others when they could. Men who were blind were asked to tell stories to the soldiers lying around them. A small group sang a folk song, which cheered some and brought others to tears.

At the edge of the field, opposite the latrines, sat the bread wagon with a huge mound of rising dough. Large kettles of redolent soup bubbled over well-fed fires. The hospital had a sense of permanence, as if it had always been there, waiting for the wounded to come. It just lacked contrabands.

A group of officers rode to the edge of the camp and dismounted. They had come to see for themselves the miraculous hospital that had sprouted up from nowhere. General Sherman walked through the wounded to Mary Ann, who had her back to him while she changed a dressing on a soldier with a stomach wound. Sherman greeted his men as he passed them, offering a word of solace here and there, his face hardening when he saw grievously wounded boys he knew would not make it for another fight.

"Mrs. Bickerdyke, I shall not ask how you got here. I have heard much of your wonderful deeds and know the men are glad you are here. How many wounded have you?" asked General Sherman.

Mary Ann looked over her shoulder, smiled, and then stood to face Sherman. "Many thousands, General. And since supplies were not allowed, I'm running out of everything. Would you lend me twenty or so of your men, to forage for food and bandages? Just for today, of course," she said, smiling.

"Certainly, madam, if you can guarantee that the men I lend you will return to their military duties by sunrise tomorrow. I shall have my staff arrange it. You have done well, Mrs. Bickerdyke. I'm glad you're here."

"That's good of you to say, General. I thought you might box my ears," said Mary Ann with a chuckle.

"Not likely, madam," he said, with a smile in his voice. General Sherman tipped his hat to her and returned to his men.

The Confederates finally withdrew from Resaca in the middle of the night, burning the bridges behind them. Sherman's army pursued General Joseph E. Johnston and his men southward from Resaca, past Cassville and Allatoona to Kingston. Sherman was on his way to Atlanta, followed by Mary Ann and Eliza Chappell Porter in their ambulance.

CHAPTER 38

General James B. McPherson

Atlanta was a huge manufacturing and communication hub for the Confederate army, and three major rail lines converged there. In June 1864, Sherman had dedicated troops led by Generals McPherson, Logan, and Thomas to capture the city and surrounding areas. The siege of Atlanta was long and costly in terms of men and supplies for both sides. The fighting between the federals and the Rebels led by Generals Johnston and Hood seesawed across the Georgia countryside, inflicting terrible damage. There were thousands of wounded men. Farms were looted and burned, and towns were left in utter desolation.

In June, while the Confederate forces seemed to overpower the Union forces, word came that Grant had crossed the Rapidan River and pushed Lee back to Richmond. This served to raise the spirits of the Union men, who fought with renewed vigor. In early July, Sherman marched on to Marietta, Georgia. There, Mary Ann and Mrs. Porter organized an eighteen-hundred-bed hospital.

On July 20, the battle of Peachtree Creek took place in the hills just north of Atlanta. The Rebels fought ferociously, but were eventually pushed back by Union troops to the fortifications surrounding Atlanta, and the Union siege for the great city began.

A large brick home sat on the south side of the battle's perimeter just outside Atlanta. The Howard family had left this house the previous day, when they saw Union pickets creeping in the woods around their farm. Mr. Howard could not abide having his wife or daughters caught in the middle of a battle, and worse yet, he had heard the rumors of maltreatment of Southern ladies by Union soldiers. So the family had fled, taking only what they could throw in the two wagons they had remaining. Similar to other families in the area, the Howards had made sacrifices of goods and materials for the Southern cause. Their slaves had run off weeks ago, leaving them to make do as best they could. Their livestock, even their laying hens, had been taken by Confederate patrols in their retreat to Atlanta. The family was lucky they still had two sickly mules to hitch to the wagons.

By July 22, the Howard house sat behind Union lines. Four soldiers, carrying a wide rough plank on which lay the bloody body of General McPherson, walked quickly toward the house. Five other officers followed them. They were distraught. Tears ran through the black powder smudged on their faces. Occasionally, when they heard the sound of a minié ball whizzing past, the men ducked simultaneously. Sounds from the woods nearby told of a fierce skirmish.

They entered the house and one of the soldiers said, "In here." They followed him into the parlor. One sweep of his arm cleared the table in the center of the room, and they gently laid the plank and body on it. Together they lifted the body, and one soldier removed the blood-soaked plank and leaned it against the wall. The four soldiers paused for a moment, with their hats pressed to their chests, and then left the room to return to the battle. The remaining officers were part of the general's staff. They spoke in low, sorrowful tones to each other. Through the walls of the house they could hear the sounds of fighting, punctuated by an artillery cannonade on a nearby hill.

General Sherman and an aide rode up to the house. Sherman dismounted, giving his reins to the aide who remained on his horse. Sherman entered the house and stopped abruptly in the parlor door. "Gentlemen, if you please. I'd like a moment," he said. The five officers left the room and stood politely inside by the front door of the house.

General Sherman walked over and stood close to the body of his friend. He bent his head to listen for the heartbeat of the young general. He felt he had to check for himself that the wounds were as mortal as they looked. Tears came to Sherman's eyes, and he gently took the dead man's wrists and crossed them on the bloody chest in the classic pose of peace.

The sounds of shot and canister flew closer overhead, and nearby impacts of cannonballs made the parlor's chandelier swing and the ceiling sprinkle dust and plaster down onto Sherman and the body.

"Soldier!" yelled Sherman.

One of the officers by the door came to the parlor entry and said, "Yes, sir."

Sherman spoke without turning to face the officer. He still looked upon the body. "Take General McPherson over to the hospital. Give Mrs. Bickerdyke my compliments and ask her to see to him."

"Yes, sir."

At the hospital, Mary Ann instructed several soldier-nurses to empty all the crates out of a supply tent. They then brought in a long makeshift table and placed it in the middle of the tent. Slowly the five officers, all members of General McPherson's staff, carried the body of their beloved commander and laid it gently on the table. They said their last good-byes as Mary Ann, holding a folded blanket, waited by the tent flap. Then they turned, nodded to her, and solemnly left. Mary Ann stepped in and looked the body over slowly from head to foot, counting on her fingers the number of items she'd need. She then covered the general with the blanket and stepped out. A sentry stood guard outside the tent.

271

"Young man, when the stream of wounded slows down tonight, I shall need the following items from the storeroom: a basin of water, soap, a sponge, scissors, and a bag for soiled clothes. Find the general's trunk and bring me a clean uniform. You don't need to bring boots. Meanwhile, no one is to gain entry to this tent, except me. That is an order from General Sherman. Do you understand?"

"Yes, ma'am," said the sentry, saluting her.

❦

As the sun set, the intensity of the fighting lessened. By the time the moon rose both armies had pulled back. Campfires crackled and the smell of beans and bacon drifted in the breeze. Men who survived the battle sat and talked, cleaned their weapons, sharpened their swords and knives, or just fell asleep in exhaustion. Occasionally a picket fired his rifle at a moving shadow. Contrabands had been following Sherman's encampment. They warmed themselves by their own campfires, not far from the tent where Mary Ann tended to the body of General McPherson.

Inside, the tent was lit by two candles, one on the little camp table, one by the general's head. The candle on the camp table flickered and its light was reflected by a nearby bowl full of bloody water. Bloody and torn clothing lay in a heap on the ground. On top of the heap was the general's bloodstained coat.

Carefully, Mary Ann sponged away the blood from his body and washed it out of his hair. She grimaced at the sight of his ragged wounds, now pale and waxy-looking in death. One of the contrabands outside started to hum, and soon the soft sounds of a song filled the tent, "Steal Away, Steal Away to Jesus."

She remembered doing this very same task for her husband, Robert. It seemed so long ago now—a memory from a far different world. It was a heartbreaking act of love and intimacy. For Mary Ann it had been time alone to say good-bye, to say all the things she couldn't say while Robert was alive—time to tuck away all those hurtful little things that fill the corners of a marriage. Time to whisper those last words of love, just in case a tiny bit of him could still hear sounds from this earth. But no matter what her eyes or mind told her, her hands always knew the truth. The dead might look peaceful, as if they were sleeping, but their pale coldness betrayed them. One touch and the overwhelming finality forced its way into the soul. This was forever. A piece ripped from one's very being, leaving a fragment, stranded and alone. A scar forever painful.

Considered by the people of Galesburg as a woman who could nurse the ill with gentleness and respect, Mary Ann was often called on to help prepare the dead: Melissa and Faith, both mothers who died in childbirth; little Edward and Mary Jane, and all those other sweet children who succumbed to measles or diphtheria or some other childhood ailment; grizzled old man Foxer, who died in his sleep; the Bakers' handsome Virgil, thrown from a horse when he was just beginning to feel his wings and leave the nest to build his own family; and her own sweet little daughter, Martha, who was taken by scarlet fever in 1860. It never became any easier.

And now, the war. There had been no time to bathe or dress the dead. They were simply stacked in rows until the burying detail could attend to them. No special care was given. There was no time for such a luxury. The clothes they wore when they woke up in the morning were the clothes they wore to their graves. No gentle hand cleaned the grime from their soiled faces that were so young and child-like. No one clipped a lock of hair as a last keepsake for a mother, wife, or sister, waiting anxiously at home. Sometimes the dead weren't even given their own grave and had to share a shallow hole with their comrades.

Caring for the general felt somehow normal, as if she had stepped out of a tenacious nightmare into this moment of tranquil clarity. Sometimes, she thought, it was so hard to know what was real. The whole world was askew; death was a more frequent occurrence for her than life. And with that thought, she remembered the philosopher and his reproach, and how his eyes had looked through her.

She began to dress the general, asking for assistance from the sentry to help her lift him. When finished, Mary Ann stood back to look at the young general, lying peacefully on the table. His wounds were no longer visible, and except for his pallor, he looked as if he were sleeping. She took the bowl and threw the bloody water on the ground outside the tent. She then blew out one candle and took up the bag of soiled clothes and the general's bloodstained coat, which she folded over her arm. She blew out the other candle and stepped out of the tent.

She faced the sentry and said, "Please tell General Sherman that I have done as he asked. Tomorrow morning, I want you to come by my tent. I will have a parcel that I want delivered to General McPherson's mother in Clyde, Ohio. Just a strand of hair, his watch, and his coat, but perhaps these will comfort her in her sorrow. And thank you, son, for your help. This has been hard duty tonight." As she walked toward her own tent, the strains of "Steal Away" softly filled the darkness in which she now lived.

That night, like many other nights, Mary Ann had trouble sleeping. She awoke often to sounds outside, intermingled with dreams of soldiers dying and impossibly large field hospitals. Sometimes, her husband Robert or her two boys were soldiers in her dreams. Those images she found almost unbearable. But with the early morning light, Mary Ann found herself already at work, before she could even recall the edge of what she had dreamt.

CHAPTER 39

Leaving Atlanta

Throughout July and most of August, the Union and the Confederacy struggled for control of Atlanta. General Hood aggressively attacked the federal troops on three different occasions, pushing them back from the city's gates. There were several punishing blows exchanged by each army. On September 2, General Sherman's men finally broke through a weakened Rebel line and overran the Confederates' first defensive barrier. Continued Rebel resistance lasted only a few hours before the Confederates fled Atlanta, burning the armory and destroying what parts of the city they could in their wake. For Sherman, it was a bitter victory. The death of his close friend General McPherson was an unexpected personal and strategic loss.

General Sherman situated his headquarters in the main hotel in Atlanta. His private office was a luxurious sitting room, decorated in now war-tattered red velvet and finely carved furniture. He had spent two days sitting at the large mahogany desk in the corner of the room, finishing the seemingly endless paperwork that accompanied the title of general. A cut-crystal lamp, one of the few to survive intact through the battle, lit his desk, and a large chandelier brightened the room.

Mary Ann, in an elegant ruby red satin chair, sat across from Sherman with a worried look on her face. Her rough homespun dress contrasted starkly with the beauty of the room. They had been meeting for a half hour, but the many interruptions from Sherman's aides and messengers made talking difficult.

"I have considered it, Mrs. Bickerdyke," General Sherman said, as he signed a dispatch and sent the messenger away with a flick of his hand. "I've given it a great deal of thought and have decided you cannot accompany us. In fact, I forbid it. I want every hand to carry a weapon. I'm taking no supplies and no civilians. When we leave Atlanta, the ground we're going to move on will be foraged until barren and then burned. I want horses pulling artillery, not ambulances. I will destroy whatever is in my path. The only way to end this war is to bring it into the homes and hearths of the people of the South. I need fighting men to do that, Mrs. Bickerdyke, not nurses."

"But General," Mary Ann implored, "consider what will become of the wounded. You'll need hospitals and nurses to care for them."

"No," he replied. "I will leave behind whoever cannot fight."

A knock at the door signaled the entry of another messenger. "Just a moment, please, madam," he said, as he accepted and read the paper from the messenger. He wrote a brief note and handed the paper back to the messenger, who saluted and left the room.

General Sherman continued, "This is a mission of devastation, not repair. I am going to push this mighty army from Atlanta to the sea in double time. You will only slow us down. Go north, as I have asked, Mrs. Bickerdyke. Give me no more argument about this. Tomorrow, I will set fire to strategic buildings around the city and destroy the last of the existing rail lines. You must pack your things and leave before that occurs. When I reach the coast, I will send you a telegram. That's when I'll need you. By then the men will be sorely tired and hungry, and in need of much restoration. I'll send a boat for you. If you could be prepared to fill it with supplies and accompany it, that would be most welcome."

"Of course, General. All right. I concede to you this one. As always, you can reach me through the Chicago Sanitary Commission." She paused and sighed. "I wish you would change your mind. Mrs. Porter and I had no trouble following you here. Many of your men lived because of our little ambulance."

"And I am beholden to you both for that, madam. But this may be an opportunity to finally bring this war to an end. I will do this thing without humanity. I want no attachment to the rear—nothing to hold me back. This will be total war, as we have not seen it before—savage, relentless, indomitable, and without relief or rest."

Another messenger knocked and entered the room. General Sherman put up his hand in a gesture that indicated the messenger should wait. "Now, Mrs. Bickerdyke, you must leave. Have a safe journey, so that I may call on your kind services again." He stood as she rose from her chair.

"Very well, General. The Lord God be with you."

By late morning, the last of the wounded soldiers had been transported to the rail station and loaded into railroad cars refitted to carry the ill and wounded. All but two of the seats had been removed from each car, and along each side a series of eight wooden shelves had been built. Each shelf held eight men, packed tightly, side by side—most men had only two or three inches of clearance between their noses and the bottom of the shelf above them. For the men placed in the deepest parts of the shelves, it was an agonizing way to travel because there was little air circulation and if one soldier moved, the seven on that shelf also had to move. The wood was hard and had long splinters, disturbed by the sliding and pushing of wounded into the farthest corners. Claustrophobia held many in its strangling grip.

Andy and a few other soldiers had spent the night help-ing Mary Ann pack up hospital supplies and pile them into wagons. After a quick walk-through to ensure that no one had been left behind, Andy helped Mary Ann into one wagon and they headed for the railway station. There, they said good-bye and Mary Ann boarded the train. Andy was to follow, leading a caravan of wagons and dispensing sup-plies at Union encampments where they were most needed.

Just as Mary Ann settled herself in her seat, the sound of explosions around the city could be heard—the devas-tation had begun. Very quickly curls of black smoke, with brief flashes of bright red flame, could be seen in the sky over Atlanta. Mary Ann said to herself, "God be with you, General Sherman. May he help you and may he forgive you for what you're about to do."

The train whistle blew and the wheels began to turn. Over the loud clatter of wheels on tracks, Mary Ann called out, "We are heading home, boys—to mother and family, and to rest and recovery! It won't be long before you'll be seeing all the dear faces of your friends again. Settle back and let this big train do the work. For now, we can do noth-ing but rest. We'll be in Cairo in no time, and the hospitals there are good. We are just a whisker's length from home!"

Mary Ann spent most of the journey checking on the wounded in her car, but she gave herself the luxury of a small nap for about an hour. Late that night, the train pulled into Cairo, and over the din of the station noises Mary Ann's voice could be heard directing the unloading of the wounded. "Sergeant! Add some more hay to that wagon before you put my men in it. You'll be taking some of the severely wounded, and they'll need a proper cushion if they're to survive the ride." Wounded covered the platform, more were being unloaded from the train, and a long line of wag-ons waited to be loaded with them. Mary Ann turned her attention from the wagon back to the train. "Steady, boys, steady—take care not to drop them," she called, as soldiers carried the wounded on stretchers down the steps to the platform. A soldier with a bandage around his head and over his left eye walked up to her. She turned to him, looked him over from head to toe, and then said, "Yes, you're ready to go. Get in that wagon over there, son." After indicating a still half-empty flatbed wagon, she turned back to the others. "Can you fit another one in there? Private!" she yelled sharply. "Help that man before he falls!" She pointed to a staggering soldier with a bandaged leg.

In the midst of all this, Mary Ann felt a few slight tugs on her skirt. At first she ignored it, thinking her skirt had caught on a sliver of wood from the rough-hewn station platform. But the tug became slightly stronger, and she looked down and saw a pale boy lying on a stretcher by her side, bandages around his middle soaked through with blood from a gut shot. He was trying to speak to her, but his voice was too weak to be heard over the noise. She knelt by his side and leaned over him, cocking her head so her ear was close to his mouth.

"Mother! Mother!" he said softly.

"Yes, son? I know you are in terrible pain, but it won't be long before you're in a clean hospital bed with someone to care for you," she said, cupping his cheek with her right hand and feeling how hot his face was from fever.

"Mother, you...you...you brought us home. I...thank you, Mother. I didn't think I'd make it out of the war. I didn't think..." He stopped talking to grimace through the pain and then continued, "I'd be...here...now."

"Well, you are, son," she said gently. "And your job now is to get better, so you can get home to your family. I'm sure they have missed you very much."

In spite of his weakness, he grabbed her hand. "You'll... you'll stay with us? Take care of us here, won't you?"

"Ah, my child," she said, with sorrow in her voice. "I wish I could, but I must continue my journey to Chicago. Once you are situated here, the hospital will notify your family of your whereabouts, and I suspect they'll be along very soon to take care of you. You will be well cared for, soldier. I'll see to it."

A day later, the train arrived at the Chicago station. It was a cold November, and an icy wind blew off the lake. The station was crowded with people—men in uniform, businessmen carrying official-looking briefcases, and towns-folk waiting to greet their relatives. Mary Ann, a small hat perched precariously on her ever-messy hair, poked her head out the train's door and looked around. Two fashion-ably dressed women in fur coats and hats stood to the side and waved to her.

"Mrs. Bickerdyke! Over here!" said Mrs. Livermore in a loud voice, waving one elegantly gloved hand and holding on to her hat with the other.

Mary Ann smiled, and with her carpetbag in hand stepped off the train into the full force of the wind. The women hurried toward each other and embraced.

"Hello, Mrs. Livermore! Mrs. Hoge! What a pleasure it is to see you ladies again. But you didn't have to come out to meet me in this weather," said Mary Ann.

"Dear, dear Mrs. Bickerdyke, you are a sight for my eyes. How are you? You look tired, my dear," said Mary Livermore.

"We have been so worried about you," said Mrs. Hoge. "Such horrifying stories were coming from Atlanta, and a huge influx of wounded has been arriving for days now. But, you must be exhausted from your travels, dear. How thoughtless of me to chatter on."

"Ladies," said Mrs. Livermore, "we shouldn't talk here. It's much too cold and noisy. My driver will look after your trunk, Mary Ann. Let's go home to a toasty fire and a hot cup of tea. Come."

The three women talked for hours in the parlor of Mrs. Livermore's fashionable home. They were on their third pot of tea when Mary Ann noticed that Mrs. Livermore and Mrs. Hoge were dressed in their finest, while she wore a threadbare, much-mended, and ragged wool dress she had put on several days ago and hadn't been out of since. Putting a hand to her chest in a meager effort to hide her bedraggled state, she said, "I am so grateful to you, Mary, for keeping an eye on my boys. I'm very anxious to see them. I know they've had a mixed experience with the Reverend and Mrs. Nichols. Your last letter informing me of the closing of the home after its first year has worried me greatly. I want the best for them...but...well...it's just impossible to plan for anything up here when I'm down there."

"Well," said Mrs. Livermore, "I have some potentially good news on that front, dear. Mrs. Porter has been enjoying a much-needed rest at home, in Wisconsin, since you sent her north a few months ago. I believe she is in contact with someone who may prove useful in providing a home for your sons. She has invited us to visit, but regrettably, Mrs. Hoge and I have duties all week at the commission that cannot be delayed, so we are unable to accompany you. But after you've had a day or two of rest, perhaps you'd like to visit with her and investigate this further."

Mrs. Hoge smiled and placed a warm hand on Mary Ann's shoulder. "In any case, my dear, we've discussed it, and we can look after the boys until something more suitable turns up."

"Yes," said Mrs. Livermore. "They can stay here with me. I am used to children in my home and two more won't matter. They'd have their own rooms, and Nanny can look after them."

"Thank you both for your generosity and kindness. It is more than I could have hoped for. But ladies, I believe the warmth from the fire and the tea have collided with the weariness of travel. I am very tired now and feel a great need to rest. Could we continue this discussion at a later time?"

"Of course, dear," said Mrs. Livermore. "I'll see you to your room."

A week later, Mary Ann and her fourteen-year-old son, James, sat in chairs in Mrs. Livermore's library. James had his arms crossed over his chest and an angry, stubborn look on his face. Hiram, the youngest, walked about the room, his hand out touching books in their shelves, acting as if he weren't listening but playing a game in his head.

"Hiram, please sit down," said Mary Ann, with more sternness in her tone than she wanted. "This must be talked about. I have only a little while before I must go back. We need to find you a place to stay."

Hiram walked over to the window alcove and threw himself down on the cushions of the window seat. Without looking at her, he said angrily, "Well, don't go! We want to stay with you—not some stranger! Don't we, Jamie?" With that, he turned to face his mother and brother. He swung his legs, too short for the height of the alcove, and his heels hit the paneling.

"Hiram, come over here now and sit in a proper chair," said Mary Ann. "Good. Now, Hiram, you know I can't stay with you. I have a promise to keep, and I must return."

A chastised Hiram, sitting closer, looked at his shoes and said, "Well then, we can go with you!"

"No, you cannot. It would not be safe for you there, and I would have no time to care for you."

James pleaded, "Well, take us back to Galesburg then and stay with us. I want us to be like we were before you left."

"My dear, dear boys, I must go. You two will just have to get along. Mrs. Porter has located a farmer whose sons are both off at the war. He and his wife could use a little

282

help, and it would probably cheer them to have two boys there. I plan to meet this man in a few days to talk with him. If he's a good, God-fearing, and righteous man, a Unionist of some quality and mild of temper, with a good wife, well…it might just be a place where you could stay for a while."

Still looking at his shoes, Hiram yelled in a voice full of hurt, "I don't want to go live with some farmer! I want you!"

"We are all making sacrifices, Hiram. You are too young to understand now, but later you will be able to see this is something I must do. This war has made most of us give up the ones we love the best. Don't you know how much I miss you?" said Mary Ann.

Both boys looked down; neither looked up at her.

After a long painful pause, she continued, "You'll have a roof over your heads and boots in winter, food to eat, someone to look after you, and you will be safe. There are boys, thousands of them, and many just your ages, who fight for us, for you, to have those things. And when they fight, they have little to nothing—no roof, no bed, no family, no food, no rest, and no care. They die cold and alone, far from home—*for you*, Hiram and James." In a sterner voice, she said, "Now, I won't argue anymore about it, Hi. You'll do this for me. I need you to do this."

Hiram turned his body rebelliously in the chair, so once again he was looking in the direction of the window. He was crying.

"Ah, Hiram, my little one. Someday, you'll make a good general with that streak of stubbornness," said Mary Ann. Then she looked at Jamie. "You're very quiet, Jamie."

"Yes, ma'am. I just think," he sighed, and then shrugged his shoulders, "I…I don't know. It's so hard without you. It's not the same. It's never the same."

After another long pause, Mary Ann asked, "Jamie?"

With great sadness and resignation in his voice, he looked at his mother and said, "Whoever you find will be fine with us. I'll take care of Hiram—won't I, Hi?"

"Good boy," said Mary Ann, with relief. "You remind me so much of your dear father. Now, you two boys give me a kiss and then run along and play. I have business with Mrs. Livermore at the commission headquarters."

When they had left the room Mary Ann covered her face with her hands and sighed. She was exhausted from this talk with her sons. She had no emotional energy in reserve to deal with their pain. It was a terrible struggle for her to try to make them understand how she felt. There was also a large part of her locked deep inside that demanded she, their mother, be dedicated to understanding their feelings. But she knew that if she allowed herself to consider her sons' needs, she would never be able to leave them. This placed her in a position of irreconcilable tensions. The best she could do under the circumstances was to overpower their needs with hers and find them a place she knew would be safe. But overpowering them left Mary Ann feeling guilty and ashamed. She was leaving her sons behind as she had been left so many times.

☯

A few days later, Mary Ann and her boys traveled to Beloit, Wisconsin, to meet Mrs. Porter and the prospective family who would care for her boys. They had taken a carriage to the outskirts of town to meet the farmer and his wife. After an hour's discussion, Mrs. Porter and Mary Ann rose from the kitchen table and started to put on their capes and bonnets, getting ready to leave. Through the walls of the kitchen came the sound of small children playing in another room. The smell of corn bread filled the room. The farmer stood behind the chair in which his wife sat.

Mary Ann nodded to him. "I am indebted to you, sir, for taking my boys. I don't know when I will be able to get back. I will send you my entire commission salary of fifteen dollars every month for your trouble and for the needs of my sons. Raise them to be God-fearing Christian men who love our Union."

"Mrs. Bickerdyke, I'm glad to have the help around here," said the farmer. "Since my boys left, I haven't been able to keep up with the chores. I sure do miss my own boys. I hope they're back before planting season."

Mary Ann said, "I'll take care of your boys, and you take care of mine. Hiram is full of ideas and energy. He has a will as strong as an ox. James is quiet and a scholar. Sometimes, I think he's too old for his years. He takes the weight of the world on his shoulders. They're so different. But both can read and write, and they can help you out in that way, too."

The farmer's wife stood and reached out for Mary Ann's hand. "We'll take good care of 'em, Mrs. Bickerdyke. I'll treat 'em like they was my own, and see they do their learning and keep to the Bible. Don't you worry none. They're in good hands."

Mrs. Porter sighed, "Well, we must go or we'll be late for the train to Philadelphia."

The farmer put on his coat and his wife wrapped herself in her shawl, and they stepped out of the kitchen door onto cold November snow.

"Boys!" called Mary Ann. "Come say good-bye! We need to leave!"

Hiram and James came running around the side of the house, leading a colt on a rope. They were laughing but became somber when they saw their mother standing by the carriage. They both stopped running and walked slowly toward her.

The farmer said, "Well, I see you two have discovered the barn!"

James looked at him. "Yes, sir. I hope it's all right," he said, looking from the farmer to the colt. "He was just wandering."

The farmer smiled. "It's fine, son. Later, I'll show you two the rest of the livestock. But now, say good-bye to your mother. It may be a while before you see her again."

Mary Ann bent down and hugged her two sons. "Mother is leaving now, boys. You take good care of one another. Love each other and look after each other. No fighting, do you hear? Do your lessons and be a help to this kind man and his wife."

Hiram started to cry, but both boys nodded. She gave them another hug, and then turned and stepped up into the small carriage.

The two boys, the farmer, and his wife all stood there and watched the carriage until it disappeared out of sight.

Mary Ann was quiet for most of the trip to the train station. She was immersed in a cauldron of complicated feelings. She already missed her boys and realized that she had lost a great deal of their growing up. She had always thought that war destroyed families by taking husbands and sons to be soldiers. Now she saw that it also destroyed families by taking their wives and mothers to be nurses. And yet, she felt a strong conviction that in this terrible conflict, she was making a contribution that would otherwise be impossible for her if she stayed. What she could not forgive was the cost her sons had to pay for her to feel this sense of herself.

At one point during the trip, Mrs. Porter gently touched Mary Ann's sleeve. "I'm sorry to intrude on your thinking, Mary Ann, but you look so worried. Your boys will be fine. Mrs. Livermore and I will check on them as often as possible. While we can find good families to care for them, it is so much harder to find good women to nurse the soldiers. You have a calling, and you must not ignore it—painful though its cost may be."

By the time Mrs. Porter had finished speaking, Mary Ann was looking out at the winter fields, lost again in that limbo between thinking and dreaming.

CHAPTER 40

Soldiers from Andersonville

Several weeks later, the Sanitary Commission office in Philadelphia was busy with workers. Men and women sat side by side at huge tables, tackling the enormous amount of paperwork required to obtain and ship supplies to the army. Mary Ann was sitting in a chair by the wall, a small table with empty teacups between her and two other women. One woman was telling Mary Ann about the publication they were preparing.

"And we're expecting it to be ready for printing within the week. For the western troops, you know. It's so important that they stay in touch—"

A messenger entered the room and interrupted the woman. "Sorry to interrupt. Is there a Mrs. Bickerdyke here?"

"Excuse me, please, Julia," said Mary Ann as she stood. "I'm Mrs. Bickerdyke," she told the messenger.

"Sorry it took so long, ma'am. The telegram was routed through Chicago, and we had to track you down," said the messenger, handing her a telegram.

Mary Ann sat back down and opened it. The other two women watched her. The room became oddly silent. After a moment, Mary Ann said, "It's from General Sherman. He is sending a boat that he wishes me to stock with medicine and bandages for his army. It should be arriving at Washington any day." She put the telegram on the table and looked at the two women. "I shall have to leave immediately to arrange for supplies."

One of the men working at the desk, Pastor Sattler, stood and walked over to her. "Forgive me for intruding, Mrs. Bickerdyke, but I could not help but overhear your conversation. It would be an honor for the Christian Commission to outfit the boat with all the supplies you might need. Would you allow me to telegraph the captain and have the boat diverted to Philadelphia? It might save both time and money."

"Why, thank you, sir. That's a wonderful idea," said Mary Ann with relief.

Pastor Sattler smiled and held up one of the new tracts. "Perhaps, Mrs. Bickerdyke, there might even be room for our new publication to go to the army in the South?"

"I'm certain we could find room, Pastor. The only supplies I have accumulated so far are five trunks of petticoats donated by the Reverend Beecher's New York congregation, which will make fine bandages."

A week later, Mary Ann, Pastor Sattler, and several other members of the Sanitary and Christian Commissions stood on the Philadelphia dock, watching the boat being loaded with the last of the supply crates. Andy, who had traveled to join Mary Ann, was already on board directing the stacking of crates. The air was cold, and frosty fingers of fog rose from the river.

Two sailors walked over to the small group, and Mary Ann pointed to her case. "If you please, gentlemen, that's all I have that needs to be put on the boat." As the sailors carried her trunk on board, she turned to the people who had accompanied her and said, "Well, I'll let you know what happens. Plan on sending us another ship of supplies as soon as possible. There never seems to be enough of anything for all the wounded."

Mary Ann embraced two of the ladies and shook hands with Pastor Sattler as the boat blew its horn, indicating impending departure. "I cannot thank you enough for all that you do," she said.

Pastor Sattler said, "No, Mrs. Bickerdyke, it is we who are indebted to you. Take care of our boys out there, and may God be with you."

∾

It took a week for the boat to dock at Wilmington, North Carolina. Strong winds and occasional ice had slowed the journey. Now the boat was taking on fresh water and comestibles. Mary Ann stood on the deck wrapped in her shawl, with her new bonnet tied securely under her chin. Andy stood by her side.

"Andrew, since we'll be here for several hours, I'm going into town for a few minutes. Make sure no one steals our supplies. We must get them to Savannah. General Sherman is depending on us."

"Yes, ma'am," said Andy. He watched as she crossed the gangplank and walked down the main street to a nearby hotel.

She disappeared inside the building, but moments later came striding purposefully back to the boat. She walked up the gangplank and said to the closest sailor, "Young man, where's the captain?"

"Ma'am, I think he's in his quarters."

"Please tell him I need to speak with him urgently."

"Yes, ma'am," replied the sailor, who walked quickly toward the captain's cabin.

Mary Ann walked up to Andy, who by now knew something unplanned was happening.

"Andy, get wagons and unload all the supplies here," she said.

"But, Mother, I thought Savannah—," he said, before she interrupted him.

"The whole ship. We're getting off here. We have work to do. General Sherman will just have to wait."

Andy smiled and said, "Yes, ma'am. I'll see to it."

"And find out where the telegraph office is. I need to wire General Sherman of our delay." As Andy turned away from her, she stopped him. "Oh, and Andrew, I think I shall probably need the hotel and two other large buildings close by it. See that the townspeople are informed of this, and get a message to Dr. Agnew at the hospital in Fort Fisher. We need his help immediately. Something terrible has happened here."

Andy left her as the captain walked up, putting on his uniform coat.

"Mrs. Bickerdyke, you wanted to speak with me?" he said.

"Yes, Captain. How long are we in port?"

"Only long enough to bring on fresh water and food—a few more hours, perhaps. We are already running behind schedule."

"Well, I need the ship unloaded here."

"Here? What are you talking about? General Sherman wired me very specific orders to get this boat to Savannah as quickly as possible. He's waiting, and his army is sorely in need. We can't unload our supplies here, madam!"

Mary Ann replied, "There is a greater and more immediate need here than I can imagine exists in General Sherman's army."

The captain looked at her and then said in the voice of a tolerant parent to a child, "Wilmington has been in Union hands for some time. The wounded in this place have already received care. I cannot delay the boat here, when General Sherman needs me."

"You can and will, sir," said Mary Ann forcefully. "Come with me." She grabbed his arm and led him down the gangway.

The captain jerked back from her hold. "Madam, this is most extraordinary! I can't just..." Mary Ann tightened her hold on his arm and started down the gangplank. The captain looked over his shoulder at his second mate. "Uh, Jayson, you have the helm. I'm going into town with Mrs. Bickerdyke."

Mary Ann set a quick pace as they walked to the hotel. The captain and Mary Ann appeared to be arguing, but their conversation could not be heard from the boat. They stopped outside the hotel and Mary Ann pointed to the entrance. The captain hesitated uncertainly and then slowly entered the hotel. Just seconds passed before he came out, pale and visibly shaken. He grabbed a porch post for support and closed his eyes for a moment.

"My God! What have they done? What unthinkable...," said the captain. He looked at Mary Ann. "I'm sorry, ma'am. You shall have your supplies. Whatever you need. I shall see to it." He ran back to the boat, tears streaming down his face.

ⓒⓐ

Mary Ann, reassured that supplies were forthcoming, walked quickly into the hotel. In the foyer, she stopped to take off her bonnet and place it on the coat rack. She rolled up her sleeves and carried her shawl with her as she walked quietly, slowly, almost solemnly through the hotel's common area. There was no one behind the desk, for the men working there had all melted into the back room, afraid of the specters before them and fearful of the potential for Northern revenge. Living skeletons filled the room—men reduced to bits of skin stretched tight over bones and nothing more. No muscle, no substance, no life, and no hope. The spectacle was startling; the living dead dressed in rags, in a hotel lobby that still retained a bit of its former splendor.

Some men sat and a few stood swaying, trying to lean against the walls with the little strength they had left. Some rested on the floor. Most were naked, a few wrapped in blankets. What clothes they had were just hanging, filthy rags tied on with bits of string. Old pus-filled wounds oozed a thick, yellowish green liquid and permeated the room with the unmistakable smell of gangrene. Huge open sores attested to their weakness and inability to shift their weight freely off bony prominences. Their blank eyes were black holes in skull faces. Oddly, they made little sound except for the occasional giggle of madness or strangled cry coming from the gaping, toothless mouth of one of the skeletons. Some of these apparitions were curled up on the ground, hugging their bony legs and rocking, or busy picking at imaginary things in the air. One man scooped air off the floor with shaky hands and deposited it to the side, as if he were digging.

Time seemed to stop for Mary Ann. She could not grasp what she saw. *This cannot be,* she thought. *This is a dream— a nightmare, and I only need to wake and will find this just a passing darkness. The dead are all above the ground here, in this room, looking at me.* Mary Ann walked even slower, looking at each man she passed, hoping to see a spark of life in one's eyes. Tears rolled down her face, but she had no awareness that she was crying.

She took her shawl and put it gently around a naked man. She walked toward a man crying silently without tears.

"What happened here, young man?" she said. "How... how did you all..." She could not finish, for the words turned to dust in her mouth.

The man blinked and turned his head slightly to look at her, but did not respond. His eyes were feral. She did not see sanity there.

She approached another, leaning against the wall. "Are you a soldier? Can you tell me what happened? Where do you come from?"

The man made an effort to focus his eyes and his mind on her. After a long pause, he said softly, with the slur of a dry, swollen tongue and toothless, bloody gums, "Hell. We come from hell."

"Yes, I can see that. What happened to you—to all these men?" she asked, speaking in the voice of a mother gently addressing an injured child.

He scrunched up his face, trying to concentrate, to form the words. She waited, watching how difficult it was for him to pull the strands of his mind together.

"Why...we...we was all...prisoners...down in Georgia...a place called...Andersonville. Freed by Sher...Sherman's army. We are...trying...trying to go...home." The effort to speak exhausted him, and he closed his eyes and slumped down the wall to the floor, a jumble of bones.

◑◑

When the war began, neither the North nor the South was prepared to house and provide for prisoners of war. Abandoned buildings and old fortresses served as temporary containment facilities until actual camps could be constructed for prisoners of war. Funding dedicated to the care of prisoners was minimal, and officers with no experience of prisoner or war camp administration were placed in charge. Men in camps on both sides suffered from incompetence, cruelty, and indifference. Andersonville, in southwest Georgia, was home to a Confederate camp for Union prisoners of war. Initially called Camp Sumter, it was constructed in late 1863 and opened for prisoners in early 1864. It was built to hold ten thousand prisoners on twenty-six acres, but by the fall of 1864 it contained more than thirty-three thousand. One small stream provided drinking water for the whole camp and served as the camp's latrine. The combination of mounds of human waste, overcrowding, contaminated water, vermin, festering war wounds, and little access to medical care or medicine made dysentery and infection a common cause of fatality. Voracious mosquitoes carrying malaria, and relentless summer heat and winter cold also took many lives. Barracks were unavailable, so men scraped holes in the ground for shelter. Food was scarce, and the quality and quantity given to prisoners was just slightly less than that given to the guards. Near the end of the war, the Confederacy did not have enough food to feed its fighting men, civilian population, or captured prisoners. Thirteen thousand men died at Andersonville. Fifty-six thousand men—or one in seven of the war's non-battle fatalities—occurred in prisoner of war camps.

ဆ

In three weeks' time Mary Ann and Andy had turned the hotel and two nearby buildings, an empty mercantile and a saloon, into hospitals. Many of the men from Andersonville had died, but those who lived had been bathed, and their wounds cleaned and dressed. Old mattresses or piles of hay cushioned their sore bones. They had been given clothes to wear, blankets to warm them, and introduced to food slowly. First a few spoonfuls of plain broth, then small portions of soup, and finally bits of stewed chicken, tiny slices of pickled potatoes, and biscuits made with ground buckwheat. Keeping them from eating too much at once was a struggle, and several died when they stole food from a comrade and overate, in spite of the watchful eyes of their attendants. Mary Ann had to lock the food supplies in the vault at the local bank to keep several of her helpers from acting on their own good intentions.

The need for caretakers was so great that Mary Ann enlisted—and forced, in some cases—the townsfolk to help with the feeding, bathing, and dressing. They did these chores sheepishly, with sadness and guilt. The women cried, thinking of their own sons or husbands or brothers who might be in similar circumstances in the North. Mary Ann oversaw local contrabands, who established a productive laundry and bakery.

One morning, Mary Ann sat on the floor in the common area of the hotel. Very slowly she fed a weak Andersonville survivor some soup, spoonful by spoonful. She blew on it to cool it before lifting the spoon to his lips. Since he did not have the strength to hold his head up, it was raised on a cushion from a chair. She coaxed him gently. "Just a little more, Peter, dear. And I haven't forgotten. I'll be back this afternoon to write that letter for you. We'll try a little more soup then, too." A bit of the soup ran down his chin, and she carefully wiped it away with a soft cloth.

Outside, a white-haired, poorly dressed man in patched dungarees and a crumpled hat walked down the road. He looked old and weathered, and he walked as if his joints ached. He stopped in the road to slowly read the hotel sign. Then he took off his hat, holding it between two gnarled, arthritic hands, and walked up to the porch of the hotel. He stopped at the entrance, looking down.

Andy and a comrade walked toward the hotel, holding a fresh supply of recently stolen chickens. Andy saw the man stopped at the entrance and walked up to him. "How may I help you, sir?" he asked.

The old man looked startled and then started fumbling in the pocket of his dungarees. "I got this here letter," he said, as he pulled a tattered piece of paper out of his pocket. "My missus can read some, and she says this here letter tells a Doctor Agnew or somebody is keeping care of our son. Maybe you know him?" asked the old man, a sudden spark of excited expectation showing in his eyes. "Sean? Sean Pitcher? He's with Colonel Howe in the Thirty-second Wisconsin. This letter here says he's sick, so I done come as quick as I could. First I gone to Fort Fisher, but they done sent me here. They told me he might be over here."

Andy smiled gently at the old man and handed his protesting chickens over to his companion. "Here, Ely, you take these round back to the cook building. I'll see to this gentleman here," said Andy. He opened the door to the hotel and said, "Let me show you in to the parlor, where you can sit down and rest. You look like you've had a long journey. I'll go get the doctor and find someone who will know if your son is here." Andy pulled a chair away from the table in the center of the room. "Please sit and rest yourself."

"Why, I can't sit on that! That's way too fine, and I'm dirty from weeks of travel. My missus, she would never let me," said the old man, looking at the velvet parlor chair.

"You just sit yourself right down and rest," said Andy. "I'll go see what I can find out about your son."

Mary Ann was kneeling in the hotel hallway unwrapping a bandage from around a soldier's elbow. Her back was to the parlor, but she turned her head and looked at Andy as he left in his quest for information. She turned her attention back to the soldier's elbow, which had a huge pus-filled cavity where his joint should have been. The arm and hand from the elbow down were swollen and black. *This will soon need to come off if this boy is to live*, she thought. "Let me just clean this a little, before wrapping a new bandage. It'll hurt, but you'll feel better in the long run. Can you take it, son?" she asked.

"I...I think so," he replied.

She stood up and headed toward the back of the hotel. A few moments later, she reappeared with a bowl of warm water and a sponge, a wad of lint, and strips torn from a cotton petticoat. She knelt back down and said to her patient, "Now, you take some deep breaths and try to be still. I'll do my best to be quick." Using the sponge, she squeezed warm water into the remnants of the joint and then carefully wiped away foul-smelling material that had accumulated there. She repeated this process several times and then packed a wad of lint to dry the wound. She used the strips of petticoat to dress it and hold the packing in place.

Bandaging wounds had become rote for her. Her mind did not even need to be in the same room as she wrapped the cloth around his arm. As she cared for this boy, she noticed her hands. They were rough, like an old man's who had spent his life splitting rails. The nails were cracked, torn, and dry. Her skin was reddened, and her fingers were swollen and aching. *Why*, she thought, *what happened to my hands? It looks like blood poisoning. They don't look like my hands at all. They are diseased. They weren't this way when I began at the Stables. Has the war taken my hands, too?* She remembered when her hands were young. Then, she didn't wrap wounds. Then, she had covered her two-year-old daughter Martha's body in a winding sheet for burial. Mary Ann was alarmed to see how much she had been changed. She wondered what else the war had taken from her, besides her family and her hands.

Her reverie was broken by an angry voice and sobbing coming from the parlor. "I want ta see my son!" said the old man.

The doctor's voice responded, "I'm sorry, Mr. Pitcher. You're too late. He died two days ago."

"I want ta see him. I gotta see him," the old man said, as he pulled out a filthy rag from his pocket and blew his nose into it. "I have to tell his ma that I seen him one last time. I *have* ta see him."

"That's just not possible. He has already been buried in the soldier's plot nearby. He is at rest, Mr. Pitcher."

"Please, sir, please," said the old man, his tone changing from anger to pleading. From the sound of his voice, Mary Ann thought he was crying.

The doctor sighed and then said, "All right, Mr. Pitcher. But it will take some time. Make yourself comfortable. I will see that your son's body is brought here."

Evening brought shadows to the room, and Mary Ann carried in a lantern to light the parlor. She also lit the candles that lined the walls in sconces. Earlier she had brought the old man some tea and biscuits. "Here," she said to Mr. Pitcher, "I'll get these dishes out of your way. It shouldn't be long now."

A short while later, soldiers carried in a dirty, crude pine coffin. Mr. Pitcher stood and backed away as they entered. His back was against the wall. The soldiers set the box on the parlor table and pried the lid off with crowbars. They then stood the lid up against the wall, nodded respectfully at Mr. Pitcher, and left. The doctor came to stand in the parlor doorway.

"Your son was a hero, Mr. Pitcher. He died for the Union. You will always have the satisfaction of knowing that," said the doctor.

Mr. Pitcher walked very slowly and carefully up to the table and peered into the coffin. A look of shock flooded his face, and he uttered a cry of anguish, disbelief, and anger. He moaned and started to sob, and then leaned down and raised the skeletal body of his son by the shoulders. He held his son's body close to him and buried his face in his son's neck.

"Oh, my boy, my boy. What did they do ta ya? You shouldn't a-died this way. Not this way. He starved to death? My boy starved to death?" he asked, as he looked up at the doctor. "Oh, Sean, my little Sean. You was such a good boy. There was no cause for this. No cause..."

The doctor took a step toward Mr. Pitcher. "Your son was a prisoner of war. He was treated severely. By the time he came here, he was already weak with the ague and typhoid. We did all we could. I'm...I'm sorry, Mr. Pitcher."

The old man was holding his son and rocking back and forth, crying loudly.

"Soldier, get Mrs. Bickerdyke. Now," said the doctor, as he stepped back to the doorway of the parlor.

Mrs. Bickerdyke came quickly to the parlor and looked quizzically at the doctor.

"Can you help with this, Mrs. Bickerdyke?" he asked.

"Of course." She walked into the room and gently put an arm around Mr. Pitcher's shoulders. Softly she crooned, "There, there now, sir. Let me see to your son, so you can take him home to your wife."

She helped him lay his son's body back in the crude casket. Then she put her arm around Mr. Pitcher and led him to a parlor chair. He sat, and she knelt by his side, taking him in her arms and holding him, stroking his hair as he cried on her shoulder. She looked over her shoulder at the doctor.

"Have some men take this poor young man to the dead house for embalming, so he can make the trip back home with his father."

The doctor nodded, relieved he had a reason to exit the room.

After a few minutes the old man collected himself and blew his nose loudly. He said to Mary Ann, "I'll...I'll be all right now, ma'am."

Mary Ann pulled up another chair and sat beside him. She held his hand and patted it. "We'll get your boy fixed up so you can take him home. I'm sure his mother would want that."

Between dry sobs Mr. Pitcher said, "But...but that'll cost somethin'. My boy there, he was all I had. I got nothin' to pay with."

Mary Ann put her arm around his shoulders again. "Don't you worry about that, sir. We'll manage. You have given the Union all you have. Let the Union give you this. Now, you rest here a bit, while I go make you a proper supper. It will take some time to ready your son, so you'll be spending the night here. You'll need to rest to make the journey home. I'll make up a bed for you. My boys will take good care of your son, and see that things are done proper."

Early the next morning, Andy took Mr. Pitcher to the train station. They both stood and watched as four soldiers lifted his son's coffin off the wagon and loaded it into a railcar. Mr. Pitcher blew his nose and roughly wiped his tears away. They stood together for a few moments, silent. Then Mr. Pitcher said, "Well. I guess that's it, then."

Andy said, "Just a moment. There's one more thing." He walked to the wagon and pulled out a basket of food, covered with a clean cloth. "Mother Bickerdyke wanted you to have this for your trip. She also wrote a note for your wife. It's in the basket."

Mr. Pitcher stood for a moment, looking at the basket. Tears ran down his craggy wind-worn face. "Thank you, Andy. An' thank Mrs. Bickerdyke. I feel better a-knowin' Sean's last days was spent here, with you kind folk. I'm obliged to ya." He nodded at Andy, swung himself up into the railcar with his son's casket, and took the basket from Andy just as the train whistle blew.

CHAPTER 41

The Review of Cows

It was in the spring of April 1865, and the Union soldiers in Beaufort, South Carolina, were shouting, laughing, dancing, and hugging each other. From some secret place a number of whiskey bottles appeared and were passed round for all to swig. Some men played harmonicas, while another sawed a rapid jig on his fiddle. All of Beaufort's church bells were ringing. News of the Confederate surrender at Appomattox had reached the city. Even the wounded and ill in the hospitals were celebrating. Mary Ann, who had been tending a bedridden soldier, was grabbed and hugged by her patients several times, and a few even did a brief do-si-do with her, twirling her around and making her tightly coiled hair come undone. She blushed, embarrassed, and disentangled herself from her partners.

"Now, boys," she said, trying to give some order to her hair, "this is blessed news, but there's still much work to be done. Let me get to it," she said breathlessly. She walked over to a one-legged soldier who was standing supported by a crudely fashioned crutch. "Walter! Now, look what you've done. You've pulled your stitches out and you are bleeding again. The doctor's not going to be pleased to see this, young man. Sit yourself down, right now. Let's get some pressure on this. Samuel, stop that bouncing around and help this boy. That's right. As tight as you can. Micah, go fetch the doctor."

Mary Ann looked around the room at the smiling and laughing men, the pillow fights, and the dancing. She shook her head and said loudly, "Boys, that's enough. Let's calm down. You all need to rest and gain what strength you can. You'll probably be seeing your families soon, and you need to be healed up and well for that. It's not going to look good on your tombstones that you survived the war and died of merriment afterward. Now sit down."

A few of the men went back to their beds or chairs.

"That's right. Get yourself back in that bed, Lawrence. Matthew, put your arm back in that sling. Christopher, help Barlow there. He's not looking too good," she said, directing them with both voice and hand motions.

Men moved slowly back to their beds, but their grins remained wide and their eyes sparkled. The doctor entered the ward and started unwinding Walter's stump dressing.

Once everyone was settled, Mary Ann said, "Now, boys, I can't do much for you, but I will do what I can. Are there any requests for a special celebration dinner? You've earned it!"

Suddenly men were yelling out the names of their favorite foods. "Raisin cobbler!" "Pork greens with grits!" "Bread puddin' with brandy!" One man yelled out, "Hardtack and water!" and the man in the next bed boxed his ears. After about twenty different foods had been named, Mary Ann left the ward, laughing.

Two days later, most of the men were awake before dawn. A general sense of excitement and lots of whispering filled the ward. A soldier in dress uniform was visiting each man, whispering something that ended with the warning, "Shh." Anticipation was thick in the air.

Mary Ann was humming as she entered; she rolled up her sleeves in preparation for another day of routine hospital chores. Everyone stopped talking as she came in and they all watched her. The soldier in dress uniform nodded to her and quickly left the ward, tipping his hat as he passed her, saying, "Morning, ma'am."

Mary Ann looked around the ward and realized something was very different, but she couldn't quite make out what it was. She turned around to look at the back of the uniformed soldier as he left, and then turned back to the men in her ward.

"Good morning, gentlemen. What's going on in here? You all look guilty as foxes in the chicken yard," she said. Her eyes scanned each bed; then a worried look showed on her face, and she asked quickly, "Is something wrong? Where's Reggie? Did something happen to Reggie?"

"Ah...no...ma'am. Reggie...he...ah...just decided he needed to take a little walk. Needed to take a little bit of air. He's fine, ma'am. Truly."

Mary Ann paused, still trying to figure out what was so different about her patients today. Then she shrugged her shoulders, chastising herself for being silly, and said, "Well then, let's start the day, gentlemen. Who would like to help me with—"

A soldier's scream interrupted her. He was in a bed at the very end of the ward, holding his stomach as if in great pain. "Mother! Oh my goodness! Mother! I got me one bad pain in my belly! Help me, Mother!"

Mary Ann quickly moved to his bedside, where he was groaning and curled up in the fetal position. As she leaned over him, her back was to the other men in the ward, who smiled and winked at each other, watching her tend to this sudden onset of illness. The sounds of lowing cattle and some kind of disturbance filtered into the ward from outside. Then came the sound of marching on the hospital porch and directly into the ward. Mary Ann turned toward the noise. A company of men in dress uniforms, bright with burnished buttons, marched into the center aisle. With great fanfare, the private who was leading the company called it to halt. He then turned to face Mary Ann and pulled from his uniform pocket a piece of paper that he proceeded to read out loud.

"We, Union soldiers from several assorted regiments, have gathered this day for a grand review of troops and request the honor of Mother Bickerdyke's presence."

Mary Ann was surprised and started to say to the company, "But this man here—" and was interrupted by her patient's laughter. She looked down at him sharply and then realized it had been a ruse to get her to the back of the ward. She looked with confusion at the company of uniformed soldiers and her hospital patients. For once, she didn't know what to do.

The two soldiers at the end of each column nearest her marched forward and stood before her. One took his hat and made a grand sweeping gesture in the direction of the column and said, "Ma'am, if you please."

Mary Ann, looking bewildered, allowed them to lead her to the center of the column. The column leader called out, "About face! Forward!" The men in the column turned around, and with Mary Ann in their midst they marched out of the ward. Every patient who could walk followed. Others rushed to look out the windows.

The column stopped on the porch of the hospital where chairs had been lined up. The column leader gestured toward a chair, and said, "Madam, your chair." Mary Ann sat, noticing for the first time soldiers and cows in the street a block away. She settled herself and then looked at the column leader. "My bonnet, please, Carl."

"Of course, madam. Private Dearborn! Fetch the lady's bonnet!"

Private Dearborn rushed back into the hospital to retrieve her bonnet. The column leader leaned off the porch and waved to the soldiers at the end of the street. Suddenly, hidden in the mass of men and animals down the road, a military band started to play a lively march. Men and animals parted and let the band members march in formation up the street and past the hospital porch. These musicians then positioned themselves beside it and played as columns of soldiers passed in review, saluting Mary Ann as they did so.

Then came the cows—several hundred cows. They were some of the cows Mary Ann had brought from Chicago. The cows that had walked the long distance with the army, and kept the wounded and ill supplied with milk and cheese. The cows whose lives she had protected against many commanders who wanted beef for their ranks. These cows now filed past the hospital porch. Each animal was sparkling clean and curried, and their coats glistened in the sunshine. Their horns were polished, and their hooves blackened with bootblack. Some cows were adorned with little flags, wreaths, or garlands of flowers. Some had strips of cloth fluttering about their horns, and a few wore ladies' hats. One particularly charming cow wore a lady's lace collar and had white gloves over her horns. Several wore Union jack caps and others wore bells. This silly parade made Mary Ann and the men laugh, as they pointed out their favorite cows and decorations.

"Oh, you boys, I'll remember this day with fondness until I die! You pranksters!" said Mary Ann.

After the cows passed, the men re-formed in front of the hospital and stood at attention. They stood with pride. The band finished its tune. After a moment of silence, the soldiers' leader took a step forward and read a declaration.

> By order of the thousands of men you have helped to survive this war; by order of all their loved ones; who have you to thank for their husbands, sons, brothers, and fathers returning from this war; by order of all of us here; and by order of those brave and loyal men who fell in the line of duty; we proclaim this Mother's Day and we honor you, Mother Bickerdyke, and we thank you. We hope you will accept this token of our esteem, simple though it is.

This speech brought Mary Ann to tears. A soldier stepped out from behind the band with a large bouquet of wildflowers, which passed from hand to hand until it reached Mary Ann.

Mary Ann stood to accept the flowers, and the men cried in unison, "Huzzah! Huzzah! Huzzah!" Then all broke rank, and they clapped and cheered and laughed. Mary Ann wiped the tears from her eyes.

Later that night, Mary Ann was recollecting her strange and wonderful day. She found herself thinking about what would happen now that the war was over. She knew the soldiers would return home, and the wounded would stay in army hospitals until they were strong enough for discharge and travel. She suddenly realized she did not know what she would do. Return home to her boys now, or wait to care for the last of the wounded? Complete Sanitary Commission reports and return unused supplies? She felt oddly off center, as if whatever had given her meaning and purpose up to this point was gone, and she no longer knew who she was, where she belonged, or what would become of her.

CHAPTER 42

The Grand Review

Late on the evening of May 5, 1865, General Sherman paced in his tent headquarters in Raleigh, North Carolina. As he did so, he dictated a letter to his clerk, who sat at the camp desk.

> And as the nation grieves the loss of President Lincoln, repair of this war-torn country must begin. The War Department and President Johnson have scheduled a grand review of Major General Meade's and my armies, to be held in Washington this May 23rd and 24th. Viewing stands are being erected along Pennsylvania Avenue for dignitaries. General Grant and I expect you to stand with us in the president's tent.

> Now, Mrs. Bickerdyke, I am fully aware your wounded boys need you, but could you not leave them for just a few days to honor General Grant and me with your presence? The Union can offer you little in return for all you have done and given. Let us at least thank you in this small way.

> I have reserved a suite at the Metropolitan Hotel for you beginning May 20th. Mrs. Sherman and I expect you to join us for supper that evening.

> Kindest regards,

General W. T. Sherman
Major General, Commanding United
States Forces in North Carolina

The evening of May 20 found a large party celebrating in the dining room of the Metropolitan Hotel in Washington. Mary Ann, in a simple calico dress sat at the table with General and Mrs. Sherman, General and Mrs. Grant, General and Mrs. Logan, and several other generals and their wives. The men wore dress uniforms and the women were adorned in elegant ball gowns. The table was cluttered with remnants of a fine meal, served on bone china, with the best crystal and gold service. The whole room glittered with opulence.

Sherman stood to make another round of toasts and raised his glass of champagne. "To the nation!" All at the table repeated the toast in unison and touched glasses to those nearest them.

"With liberty and justice for all!" Again, all repeated the toast with glasses raised.

Just as Sherman was about to give another toast, General Grant said, "Sit down, Cump! You've been toasting so long, this fine champagne is about to turn to vinegar! We'll be old men before you finish. Now, ladies, I believe we generals would like to enjoy a good cigar. If you will excuse us."

The ladies looked at each other, nodded, and rose from their chairs. The men stood, and as the women left the room they heard, "I understand you chewed the same one from Chattanooga to Savannah. Been saving this cigar for you. Cuban."

"Much appreciated, Sam," said Sherman.

The ladies relaxed in the tea room of the hotel, where couches, chairs, and tables were arranged for casual conversation. There were already several small groups of women there, so the generals' wives and Mary Ann clustered together at one end of the room to talk.

"What a relief to have this horrid rebellion over, and our husbands home without injury," said Mrs. Sherman.

"Well, I just hope that now the country can move on to other business. This war has consumed every aspect of our society," said Mrs. Grant.

Mrs. Logan leaned forward to join in the conversation. "But I hear there's still plenty of harsh sentiment toward our rebellious Southern brothers. I think we shall miss our dear Mr. Lincoln during our country's recovery. His compassion and wisdom would surely have led us safely through the changes to come. When the news of Appomattox reached Washington, Lincoln had the band play 'Dixie,' saying it was a fine tune that he had always liked."

"Recovery?" asked Mrs. Sherman. "I think that's weeks or even months away. My husband tells me there is still hard fighting in Texas and all the other states in the Deep South. They haven't yet heard the news. Or if they've heard it, they don't believe it."

"Yes," said Mrs. Grant. "A war such as this doesn't stop with the efficiency of a train engine. It has to play itself out. And men have their pride, which, I suppose, will keep a few men fighting for a long while. Ulysses tells me he expects fighting to continue in the backwaters of the South for some time to come. A shame, all those wasted lives."

Mrs. Logan asked, "What about you, Mrs. Bickerdyke? Will you be going home soon? To hear our husbands tell it, you and your work are the only reasons any Union soldier survived this war."

Mary Ann shook her head, slowly. "That's very kind of you to say, Mrs. Logan. I don't think I will be returning home—not yet. There are still thousands of Union soldiers in hospitals throughout the country. And if the fighting continues, there'll be even more. I was hoping to make a quick visit to see my sons in Wisconsin, but your husband has already asked me to accompany his troops to Louisville."

"My husband says it may be months, or maybe even a year or two, before all the wounded return home. That's such a long time to wait, after all the nation has suffered. You must be so eager to see your children, Mrs. Bickerdyke," said Mrs. Grant. "I do not have the courage to have left them as you did, and I know I couldn't bear waiting any longer."

"Well, Mrs. Grant, my two boys are being well cared for," said Mary Ann. She paused, and then gave a long sigh. "Besides, these Union boys are all my children, and I even came to be fond of some of the wounded Rebels— fine young men, they are." Mary Ann paused again. Her eyes saw something far from this colonnade, and her face was etched with pain. The ladies looked at each other but remained silent. Mrs. Logan leaned closer to hear.

Mary Ann continued, "All of them, North and South, will live this war every day of their lives. It's never going to stop for them. They came as young men to fight for what they thought was right, with visions in their heads of gallantry and of what they thought war was all about. But it was very different. The horror of it is inconceivable, really. And now the war is inside them, and it will shape the rest of their lives." Mary Ann stopped, and with an embarrassed look she said, "Forgive me, please, ladies. I did not mean to become morose. Sometimes…memories become trapped in one's head. Every time I close my eyes, every time I try to sleep, I see it all again. No. This war will never come to an end for some of us."

❦

May 23 dawned hot and sultry in Washington. The Grand Review was already in progress. General Sherman's XV Army Corps marched up Pennsylvania Avenue to the cheers of a huge crowd lining the street. Men held their little children up high, women cried, and children waved flags and threw strips of bright paper. The atmosphere vibrated with relief, thankfulness, and sheer joy.

Mary Ann, in a simple calico dress and sunbonnet, rode on a horse in front of the marching soldiers. As she approached I Street, she pulled her horse over to the side. An officer riding in the color guard in front of the XV Army Corps noticed and rode up to her. He tipped his hat.

"Excuse me, Mrs. Bickerdyke, but I believe the president's viewing stand is just a few blocks up ahead. We're to escort you there, ma'am," said the officer.

"Son," she replied, "I've never been one to show off. Not when there's work to be done. Now, you go back to your men. I don't think the president will miss me much."

The officer smiled, tipped his hat again, and said, "Ma'am, as you wish," and returned to the color guard.

Mary Ann rode up to one of the soldiers who stood in the front of the crowd. "Son, help me off this horse." As her feet touched the ground, she said, "Oh, that's better. Thank you, young man. Now, I'm going to need several things. See what you can do about setting up two tents right here. These boys are hot and thirsty, and need someplace to rest. Parading them for two days in the sun in full dress uniform, after they've fought a war and marched this way and that across the nation! Don't generals have any sense? I'll wait for you here. Oh, and would you have someone take this horse back to General Sherman? He's a fine-looking animal, but I much prefer my Old Whitey."

"But...but, ma'am, I can't leave. I've been ordered to keep this crowd behind the lines," said the bewildered soldier.

"Nonsense. Of course you can, son. Leave the crowd to me. I'll watch 'em. You go do as I say."

CHAPTER 43

The Antiscorbutics

It was a sweltering day in Louisville. August was always one of the hotter months, with high humidity and a stillness to the air that stifled even those born and raised there. Two men sat in barber chairs inside the barber shop on Main Street. One was reclining in the chair with his face wrapped in a steaming white towel while the barber clipped the other man's hair. White sheets covered both men's clothing to protect them from falling hair clippings. The man whose hair was being cut was reading the *Louisville Tribune*. Bold headlines read: "Woman Orders Government Steamer Back to Dock." Next to the headline was a drawing of an older woman in a shaker bonnet.

The man reading was laughing. From under the steaming towel the other man asked, "What's so funny?"

"Listen to this, Blackie. It says here that a woman turned a steamer back round yesterday, so it could pick up…what the devil—this can't be…barrels of pickled potatoes? Here's what happened."

During yesterday's fierce rain storm, two women driving a covered wagon urged their tired horses forward in deep mud, trying to get to the dock. They made it to the small rise just before the dock, when they stood up in the wagon to see where the boat was. One of them, the older one, saw it midriver, just beginning to make steam. She started yelling in a very unladylike manner and waving her arms. "Come back, captain," she yelled. When she saw no response from the boat, she stamped her foot in anger, splattering mud everywhere. Then in an even stronger voice with arms waving, she yelled, "Come back, captain! You come back here this very instant!"

Much to everyone's surprise, the steamer turned around and headed back to the dock. Witnesses who were there said the two women finally drove the wagon through the mud to the dock, where the steamer's captain awaited them. Witnesses believe they heard, "It's a good thing you turned that steamer of yours around, Captain Jackson!" They also reported the captain laughing.

And so, forty barrels of much-needed antiscorbutics left for Texas to treat the outbreak of scurvy among the soldiers there.

The barber, who had finished cutting the man's hair, was brushing clippings off his shoulders. The man rapped the newspaper on his knee and said to his companion under the towel, "Can you imagine? The gall of those women! First they get uppity with the army in the war. Now they are controlling the navy! What's next? Give 'em the vote?"

The barber removed the towel from the other man's face to reveal General Logan. He was laughing heartily.

General Logan said, "Well, if the two ladies were Mrs. Bickerdyke and her friend Mrs. Porter, and they asked for the vote, I wouldn't cross them! I've tangled with them before and know enough to stay out of their way!"

CHAPTER 44

Resigning Her Commission

On March 21, 1866, Mary Ann was serving at Camp Butler Army Hospital. She sat at the desk in her office. Morning light slanted in through the window. A tiny vase of early wildflowers sat on the desk next to a burlap bag. She was writing discharge papers. She heard footsteps on the well-scrubbed wooden floor approaching her office door. Mary Ann looked up to see a nurse in a plain dress and a white starched apron standing in the doorway.

"Mother, he's ready," she said.

Mary Ann nodded and said, "I'll be there in a moment, child." The nurse walked back through the ward as Mary Ann finished her writing. She collected her paperwork, picked up the burlap sack, and walked out into the ward.

Mary Ann stopped in the doorway to the huge ward. It had fifty beds on each side. The wood floor had been scrubbed and oiled to a shine. All the beds but one had been stripped. The mattresses were rolled and tied, the mosquito netting tied back, and clean chamber pots had been placed underneath. Sunshine through the windows caught little dust motes in the air, so the light seemed filled with specks of gold. One bed remained to be cleaned. On it sat a soldier in a tattered Union uniform. Using crutches, he rose and moved with difficulty toward Mary Ann. He was missing his right leg thanks to canister shot. The sound of crutches and one foot scraping across the floor echoed through the ward.

"Sorry to have been so much trouble, ma'am," said the soldier. "I sure am glad to have had you looking after me." He stopped and then awkwardly said, "Mother, it has been an honor to know you. Thank you for all you done for me. I thought for sure I was a gonner with that gangrene." Tears filled his eyes, and he rubbed his sleeve across his face.

"Private Blackwell, I shall miss you, too. Now, do you have everything you need to get home?"

"Yes, Mother."

"Well, take this along with you," said Mary Ann, handing him the burlap bag. "There's some fresh bread and a clean shirt for when you see your family. You can't go see your mother the first time in two years in a dirty shirt!" Tears formed in her eyes, too. "Oh, goodness," she said. "It is so hard to say good-bye. Come. I'll walk you outside. They're waiting on you."

Private Blackwell tied the burlap bag to his small parcel of belongings and then slung the lot across his shoulder. Together they walked to the ward door. The soldier turned and said, "Mother, I...," but tears prevented him from saying more.

"I know, son," she said, tears streaming down her own face.

He turned and, leaning heavily on his crutches, slowly walked to the ambulance, and the driver helped him in.

In a stronger voice, Mary Ann said, "You take good care of yourself, Private Blackwell," but her voice caught midway through these words. She stood leaning against the doorway watching the ambulance pull away and travel down the road, until it was just a spec on the horizon. She sighed, took a handkerchief from her pocket, wiped her eyes, and blew her nose. Then she turned and walked back to her office.

Mary Ann sat at her desk and took a piece of paper from the drawer. She dipped her pen in the inkwell and began to write. The pen made a steady, deliberate scratching sound across the paper.

> March 21, 1866
> Camp Butler Post Hospital – Springfield, Illinois
> I resign my appointment as field agent for the U.S. Sanitary Commission.
> M. A. Bickerdyke

Mary Ann put the pen down and her hand rested on the paper. Her hands were old and rough-looking—a casualty of the war. For a moment she was lost in thought. Then she stood up and walked back to the now empty ward. Its silence was suddenly overwhelming and its gleaming floors stunningly bright. She blinked, and it was full of injured men, dirty dressings, and bloody clothes. She looked around the room and recognized some faces. There, sitting in the back and staring at her, was the philosopher. The wounded were moaning and crying out in pain. There was disorder and need everywhere. She blinked again, and it was all gone. Only a faint memory of a war now ended.

Epilogue

After the last wounded soldier was discharged from her care, Mary Ann continued to provide for Civil War veterans and their families, establishing homes for destitute and aged soldiers across the nation. She led a wagon train of old soldiers seeking homesteads in Kansas. After the Kansas-Indian wars, when the farmers had been burned out, she reached back to her friends in the East and asked them to send railroad cars full of supplies and seeds, so that the Kansas farmers could begin again.

Mary Ann became a pension attorney in San Francisco and made many trips to Washington, D.C. There, she represented soldiers for whom she had cared during the War to the Pension Committee, often calling on her friends in Congress to assist her in obtaining adequate payment for wounded veterans.

After more than twenty years of service, Congress finally awarded Mrs. Bickerdyke a monthly pension of twenty-five dollars.

Her son, James, never married and spent his adulthood as a college professor in Kansas. Her stepdaughter, Mary Elizabeth, died of breast cancer in Kentucky after the war. Mary Ann nursed her through her illness and death. Hiram never quite forgave his mother for abandoning him as a child. He moved west, where he delivered the mail up and down the Rocky Mountains.

Mary Livermore returned to her large family and wrote her memoirs of the war. Eliza Chappell Porter lived into her eighties and also wrote her story. General Grant went on to become the president of the United States; General Sherman became a businessman, and Andy Somerville lived into his seventies. Andy attended as many reunions of the Grand Army of the Republic as he could and visited Mary Ann as frequently as possible. Illness kept him from attending what would have been his last reunion with Mother Bickerdyke.

Mary Ann died on November 8, 1901, in James's home in Bunker Hill, Kansas, with her son in attendance. She was eighty-four years old.

Bibliography

Baker, Nina Brown. *Cyclone in Calico: The Story of Mary Ann Bickerdyke*. Boston: Little, Brown and Company, 1952.

Bickerdyke, Mary Ann. "Bickerdyke Family Correspondence, 1864." Library of Congress, Manuscript Division.

Brockett, L. P. *The Camp, the Battlefield and the Hospital, or Lights and Shadows of the Great Rebellion*. Philadelphia: National Publishing Company, 1866.

Brocket, L. P. *Woman's Work in the Civil War: A Record of Heroism, Patriotism, and Patience*. Philadelphia: Zeigler, McCurdy and Company, 1867.

Chase, Julia A. *Mary A. Bickerdyke, "Mother."* Lawrence, Kansas: Journal Publishing House, 1896.

Davis, Margaret B. *The Woman Who Battled for the Boys in Blue: Mother Bickerdyke, Her Life and Labors for the Relief of Our Soldiers, Sketches of Battle Scenes, and Incidents of the Sanitary Service*. San Francisco: A. T. Dewey, 1886.

Davis, W. C., and Bell Wiley. *The Civil War*. New York: Black Dog & Leventhal, 1998.

DeLeeuw, Adele. *Civil War Nurse Mary Ann Bickerdyke*. New York: Julian Messner, 1973.

Denney, Robert E. *Civil War Medicine, Care, and Comfort of the Wounded*. New York: Sterling Publishing Company, Inc., 1995.

Grant, Ulysses S. *Personal Memoirs*. 2 vols. New York: J. J. Little & Company, 1885.

Holland, Mary A. G. *Our Army Nurses: Interesting Sketches, Addresses and Photographs of Nearly One Hundred of the Noble Women Who Served in Hospitals and on Battlefields During Our Civil War*. Boston: B. Wilkins & Company, 1895.

Kellogg, Florence Shaw. *Mother Bickerdyke as I Knew Her*. Chicago: Unity Publishing Company, 1907.

Kennedy, Frances H., ed. *The Civil War Battlefield Guild*. Boston: Houghton-Mifflin Company, 1990.

Leisat, Juanita. *An Introduction to Civil War Civilians*. Gettysburg, Pennsylvania: Thomas Publications, 1994.

Litvin, Martin. *The Young Mary, 1817–1861*. Galesburg, Illinois: Log City Books, 1976.

Livermore, Mary. *My Story of the War: A Woman's Narrative of Four Years Personal Experience as a Nurse in the Union Army and in Relief Work at Home, in Hospitals, Camps, and at the Front During the War of the Rebellion*. Hartford, Connecticut: A. D. Worthington & Company, 1891.

Long, E. B., and Barbara Long. *The Civil War Day by Day: An Almanac 1861–1865*. Garden City, New York: De Capo Press, 1971.

Lowenfels, Walter, ed. *Walt Whitman's Civil War*. Garden City, New York: De Capo Press, 1960.

Massey, Mary E. *Bonnet Brigades: The Impact of the Civil War*. New York: Alfred A. Knopf, 1966.

322

Moore, Frank. *Women of the War: Their Heroism and Self-Sacrifice*. Hartford, Connecticut: S. S. Scranton & Company, 1866.

Mureen, Beverly. "Mother Mary A. Bickerdyke." Paper, Knox College, Galesburg, Illinois, 1939.

Porter, Mary H. *Eliza Chappell Porter: A Memoir*. Chicago: Fleming H. Revell Company, 1892.

Rutkow, Ira M. *An Alphabetical List of the Battles of the War of the Rebellion, Compiled from the Official Records of the Office of the Adjutant-General and the Surgeon General, U.S.A. and a Roster of All the Regimental Surgeons and Assistant Surgeons in the Late War and Hospital Service*. San Francisco: Norman Publishing, 1990.

Sherman, William Tecumseh. *Memoirs of General W. T. Sherman*. New York: Library of America, 1990.

Stille, Charles J. *History of the United States Sanitary Commission, Being the General Report of Its Work During the War of the Rebellion*. New York: Hurd & Houghton, 1869.

Straubing, Harold E., ed. *In Hospital and Camp: The Civil War through the Eyes of Its Doctors and Nurses*. Harrisburg, Pennsylvania: Stackpole Books, 1993.

Ward, G., K. Burns, and R. Burns. *The Civil War: An Illustrated History*. New York: Alfred A. Knopf, Inc., 1990.

Wertz, J., and E. Bearss. *National Museum of American History, Smithsonian's Great Battles and Battlefields of the Civil War*. New York: William Morrow and Company, Inc., 1997.

Wittenmyer, Annie. *Under the Guns: A Woman's Reminiscences of the Civil War*. Boston: E. B. Stillings & Company, 1895.

Made in the USA
Charleston, SC
18 June 2012